"IT'S NEW YEAR'S EVE and I'm at a party. We're all having a great time. Before 12 a.m. I tell my friends that I must leave. 'Why?' they ask. 'I have to work in the morning,' I say. 'What do you do?' they ask. 'I take care of 70 Greyhounds,' I reply. Four hundred questions later, I say, '365 days a year, 24 hours a day, no vacations, no sick days.' They look at me like I'm totally crazy. 'But,' I say, 'I have the best job in the world.' They will never understand a man's love for his dogs. Next time I'll just hand them a copy of *High Stakes*."

—**Joe Trudden**
  Tru-Paws Racing Kennel, Hollywood Greyhound Track, Miami

"*HIGH STAKES* stands up for animal lovers like me. Colorful characters showing us the truth about human rights and animal welfare."

—**Maxine Bochnia**
  Photographer; Member, National Greyhound Association

"*HIGH STAKES* leaves me wanting more—more of Hevener's keen and experienced insight, and more of his outspoken truth!"

—**Tim O'Brien**
  Great-grandson of O. P. Smith, inventor and founder of
  modern Greyhound racing

"*HIGH STAKES* is a real page-turner . . . compelling, insightful . . . captures your attention."

—**Tom McQueen, Ph.D.**
  Radio personality; Greyhound kennel owner

"IT MADE ME feel like I was there."

—**Donna Moore**
  Bahama Mama Greyhounds, Inc., home of All-American winners
  Cayman Went and *Talentedmrripley*

"BEAUTIFUL!"

—**Larry Birnbaum**
  Owner of top Greyhound sire *Craigie Whistler;*
  contributor, the RaceForAdoption program

HIGH STAKES

Best Regards,
Ron Hevener

Ron
Hevener

PENNYWOOD PRESS
1338 Mountain Road
Manheim, Pennsylvania 17545
USA

P: 717.664.5089
F: 717.665.4651
E: pennywood@dejazzd.com

OTHER BOOKS BY RON HEVENER

Fate of the Stallion (Illustrated)
A classy Arabian racehorse down on his luck gets a
second chance and transforms the life of a broken family.

The Blue Ribbon
Two young women rival for the affection of a handsome
dog show judge. Forty years later, one of them disappears
into her romantic past and returns to seek revenge at New
York City's most famous dog show.

HIGH STAKES
A novel by Ron Hevener

Copyright © 2005 Ron Hevener
Cover illustrations by Ron Hevener
Edited by Gregg C. Dubbs
Formatted by Burgard Design
Cover graphics by Joan Johnson
Photography by Maxine Bochnia
Printed by Central Plains Book Manufacturing

Published in the United States of America by
Pennywood Press, 1338 Mountain Road, Manheim, Pennsylvania 17545.

ISBN 978-0-9679514-4-7

Ladies and Gentlemen . . .

In this no-holds-barred work, the author takes us behind the scenes of a sport which has fascinated the public for generations. If you think you know all about Greyhound racing and the magnificent dogs that are its heroes, think again. You are about to enter one of the most controversial novels ever written for animal lovers.

While certain incidents and characters in the story are based on fact, the rest of this novel is based on imagination, speculation, rumor, gossip and *possibility*.

For my father, John, who taught me how to keep my head when those around me are losing theirs . . .

For my mother, Jeanene, who chases rainbows . . .

For my sister, Sandy, who is brave . . .

For my brother, Duane, who believes in the power of the individual . . .

For my children—the real ones and the ones I've imagined . . .

For friends, relatives and lovers, fewer and farther between with each passing year . . .

And for a special Greyhound named Bingo for opening up the world of Greyhound racing to me, along with many new friends and adventures.

Nothing I have ever done—nothing I ever hoped for—was possible without you.

All my life, I have taken care of animals. That doesn't mean I've always been kind or perfect in what I've done. It just means I've done my best.

Animal lovers are among the most sentimental and romantic people in the world. We give our hearts and everything we have to what we believe in. Today, as society is rapidly changing around us, many animal lovers are noticing new laws and pressures from the media that, when the dust has cleared, seem to be hurting the very people who take care of animals and love them the most. And, they are wondering how this has happened.

It has happened gradually. At the root of these changes is a social movement that is gaining momentum. The difference between "animal rights" and "animal welfare" might surprise you. Taking care of your animals (feeding them, loving them, caring for their health) is animal "welfare." This is what teaches us how to respect all living things, including ourselves. It is a time-honored way of keeping our sense of love alive.

The animal "rights" movement, on the other hand, is quite different from that. In many ways, you can think of it as a military campaign without the uniforms. Animal rights is about laws and rules and taking away "our" rights to raise our animals as we have always done, or to have as many animals as we can provide for. There is violence in the animal rights movement—and an odd lack of conscience. At the same time they are taking away our love, they are asking us for the money and volunteer help to do so.

These are strong statements for me to make. And I realize that. But, as the founder of an anti-cruelty organization at the age of fourteen (Humans Against Cruelty to Animals), I am probably one of the grandfathers of the animal protection movement in this country. Over the years, I have seen many changes in our society's view toward animals and in its broadening acceptance of their emotional importance to us. But what began as a highly enlightened spiritual effort to raise our consciousness toward all life, teaching us to respect and value ourselves as well, has not reached the potential so many of us saw for it. Somewhere along the line, the very fragile animal protection movement was hijacked by mean-spirited bullies and militants who stop at nothing to force their values on society.

I, for one, am ashamed of what it has become.

Ron Hevener
www.ronhevener.com

Prologue

It was his color that got him in trouble. Or, maybe it was his color that saved him. Either way, the warm tones of his body were beautiful and his eyes—dark, glistening with a force of their own—missed nothing.

His belly, hard now from running through the woods and scrambling up deer trails in the mountains, ruled him. If he could make it to the grass field before dawn, he would find a cottontail or maybe a pheasant for which these Lebanon County game lands were known. It had been too long since his last meal. It had been days, and the relentless November chill stiffened his heart. He pressed on.

It hadn't always been this way. Growing up, he had never lacked for attention, never felt a hunger screaming loud enough to echo off the clouds or loneliness clinging to his soul. Back then, it never occurred to him that all of his instincts might sharpen like the claws of a falcon and he could survive without knowing what might happen next. How could he know his life was about to shift in a way even the most seasoned visionary couldn't predict?

Reaching the clearing, one of many small meadows on the mountain, he hesitated. It looked the same, bordered on one side with stumps and branches left to rot by savage loggers in their butchery. It looked the same as much of the mountain now: bleak and wounded.

A red fox, oblivious to him in the gray dawn, was searching a carpet of moss for fallen acorns, a delicacy of the chipmunks that she knew would soon awake. Forgiving his presence in the way of kindred spirits living by their wits, the fox understood that he meant her no harm. Not now; not today.

At the piercing scream of a hawk, the fox looked up, considered her prospects and scampered away. Squirrels, high in the trees, held their breath, praying their frosty colors would make them invisible. A rabbit had broken from the tall grass and was sprinting for safety. The hawk lifted into the air, circled and dropped. From the edge of the field a mass of muscle and power lunged from its hiding place, cleared a fallen branch with the grace of a deer and raced forward.

Mark Whittier parked his truck in the lot off Speedwell Forge Road, grabbed his lunch bag, the latest issue of *SportsAnimated* and set out for a hike.

It was a flannel shirt, jeans and LL Bean kind of day. Striding easily, a man comfortable in his skin, he was going to enjoy his hike in the woods. Bright sun, playing through the remaining leaves on almost-naked branches of towering oak and lower sycamore, dappled his hair with light, changing it from brown to russet to gold and back to brown with every step. His five-eleven frame, trim from an outdoor lifestyle, allowed him to ascend the rugged path with little trouble.

Time to himself on the Snowmobile Trail was a pleasure he looked forward to, especially in the early morning hours. The rustle of leaves as a squirrel chittered away, the burst of a startled deer, the eerie call of a wild turkey were like the intimacies of a woman getting out of bed, making coffee and gathering her clothes for the new day. She moved freely, as if no one were watching; and he let every sound wash over him, savoring the natural conversation of the mountain whispering, *"Sweet lover. You make my day begin."*

At times like this, he often thought about an Indian yogi master he had known, a great teacher promising the secret of all eternity.

"Tell me," the swami once asked: "What is it you seek?"

"The truth," Mark answered. "Just the truth."

"Truth is like a beautiful stone," the teacher in his white linen robes explained, holding an emerald up to a nearby window and pointing to its many facets. "*Truth* is different things to different people." He turned the gem in his hand until they found themselves standing within an aura of refracted prism light.

It had been a long time since Mark had thought of the swami and his guidance in the endless search for answers to life's mysteries.

Why today?

Avoiding deep, ugly scars inflicted on the ground by heavy-duty logging equipment and bulldozers, Mark wondered where the cheerful horse riders he used to see on the trail had gone. Leather saddles polished to a deep luster and their faces bright, he could still hear jokes and laughter as they trotted their horses up and down the slopes, training for races at Delaware Park or Penn National. Powerful Thoroughbreds, Arabians, Standardbreds and Quarterhorses. These trails had made many a champion for the small stables nearby. But the good-natured laughter of riders filled the air no more.

Where had they gone? They had gone away; vanished. They had disappeared like clouds evaporating in the morning sun.

This was the time to be here, he thought: when you could see and smell and hear what others almost never could. He wondered if loggers could notice the way a leaf fell more slowly through air thickened by humidity, or if they knew that by touching a rock, they could almost tell the time of day. But people rarely noticed such things.

Not looking right, not looking left, the dog ran. He ran like there never was, never had been, never could be anything more important than what he saw right then, right there, in front of him. The bird had found its prey. If he could beat the hawk to the prize . . . the power of his ancestors welling up inside him taking over as they had so often before during this exile from all that he once knew, this exile he never wanted, soon he would feast.

It was the savage law of the mountain. It was the dance of survival. Life was born only to be taken away, and he would risk anything, even the swords of a hawk whetted on flesh and bone—slashing his chest, ripping his neck, his face—as the crazed bird struggled to escape. Shredding the air with war cries, they battled. Smashing into rocks, grinding into the dirt, bursting the grass in a tangle of flapping wings and hatred, the hawk punished his attacker. How dare this intruder challenge him! How dare he!

Blinded by his own blood, desperate, insulted by the unearthly pitch of vile, avian curses, he found the crazed bird's sinewy wing. Gripping it like he would never let go, shaking the bird as if to rattle the senses out of him, he fought on as the hawk slapped and stabbed this new enemy with weapons that had never failed him before.

Their cries of agony echoed through the mountain. They fought like this until the creatures of the trees and the shadows cringed. Had the mountain finally had enough? Was she screaming out to some force greater than they knew, a force sensed on some deep, almost forgotten level?

The mountain wailed. The mountain shuddered. As the claws of a dying hawk relinquished its prey, a rabbit would live to tell its grandchildren and ran for cover.

Mark froze. How did he know; how could he be so sure it was *the* hawk, the one keeping watch? The one protecting its domain, staring at the world from its shaggy throne high in an oak tree that had defied all comers for a hundred years. He stepped up his pace.

What was happening? What dreadful fate had the hawk suddenly encountered? What do any of us know about what's ahead? he wondered. What does a wild creature know of its destiny from one day, one minute, to the next? We are all wild creatures, he decided, running now—running like a man who doesn't know if he's running away from life or running towards it. Why was he so shaken? Why was his skin prickling? Why was the hawk so important to him?

He didn't know. He couldn't explain it. How could anyone explain to citified friends or a crew of loggers that a hawk was something more than what it appeared to be? This wasn't a mass of cells with no meaning. It was wisdom; it was keen eyes through which the spirits of all who had gone before and those yet to enter these realms could see. It was confidence so strong that tree after tree crashing to the ground could not ruffle even one feather.

"Look at us!" the loggers seemed to holler. "We're big! We're strong! We can tear the world apart!"

But, the great hawk, seasoned by many winters, had not been frightened. Studying them as if aware of each man's soul, looking through them to what lay beyond, the winged keeper of the forest remained aloof. Dreadful as it was, he seemed to say, this would pass. But, not all things could be overcome, as the hawk's primal shriek of disbelief—stabbing the hearts of all who could think, imagine or feel—now testified.

Rushing to where he had so often seen the hawk circling on early mornings such as this, Mark sensed an eerie, slow-motion stickiness in the air. It was a dream, he hoped. Please say it's a dream, a frustrating nightmare. You can't run. You can't breathe. You can't scream. Where were the chickadees and cardinals, always dashing from branch to branch, scolding all who pass by for offenses only they could imagine? Where were the squirrels, missing nothing in their daily gossip? Where were they? Where were they when the king was battling for his life? Running to save their own, came the answer he already knew as a glimpse of tawny red-brown caught his eye. A startled deer?

Crouching down, Mark studied clues of the drama to which no one had been invited, clues illuminating the truth for those who searched or wanted to understand.

Touching a delicate, bloodied feather clinging desperately to a blade of tall, brittle grass, he asked himself, What had gone wrong for this hunter, so sure, so brilliant? Surely the monarch of the skies could select his prey more carefully than this. Going after a deer? Not likely that the hawk would be so crazed.

Slippery blood on his fingers, Mark considered the eternal struggle between one ruler and the next, so deeply buried in us that no living thing on this earth or in its heavens could escape its grip on the psyche. *Have or have not*, he thought, knowing he had long ago decided to be one of the Haves. *Rule or be ruled*, he thought, bracing himself.

Yet, no matter what Mark decided, no matter what he wanted to learn, to have, to discover, part of him, part of his life—his world—was being ripped away now.

Stop, murderer!

Catch him, somebody!

Let flittering chickadees and cardinals hide if they must. Let squirrels chatter mindlessly until there was nothing left for them to chatter about. The hawk . . . his hawk . . . was gone, and with it the spirit of the mountain. What desperation would drive an animal to attack a fierce bird like this? Cougars, bears and wolves hadn't been seen in this part of Pennsylvania for many years. Game had been plentiful, and no animal he could think of would hunt a bird of prey. No animal in its right mind, he thought suddenly, remembering interviews with biology experts and wildlife officials in *SportsAnimated,* the only magazine that covered it. "College Experiment Goes Jurassic" was the headline.

Even now, it jumped out at him. The genetic experiment at a noted school of veterinary medicine sabotaged by militant animal rights activists. An entire breeding colony of crossbred coyotes and domesticated dogs released into the wild—excited not only by the scent of blood, the scent of fear and weakness, but by the very thrill and challenge of killing.

Within days, their howls could be heard fifty miles away from the laboratory where they had been created. Stunned and anguished families found pet dogs lying in pools of their own blood, their last cries of warning slashed from their throats; flocks of sheep slaughtered and left to die; ducks, geese, chickens and peacocks mangled and scattered like so many feathers in a pillow fight. From a veterinary school hundreds of miles to the north, "coy-dogs" had been spotted in Perry County and Hazleton. He must turn back.

He must—but how could he?

Like an arrow bearing a golden chord, the shivering, hollow cry of the dying hawk pierced his heart. Away from coy-dogs it pulled him, away from sterile laboratories and god-like scientists taking the fragile balance of nature into their own hands, twisting it into what they wanted it to be. Nature *wasn't* always what we wanted it to be. Nature was the king of the mountain being yanked from its throne and crushed to the dirt. Nature was the mystery of the killer and the raging insanity of the unpredictable.

Had he been seen?

Trembling with each stride, running from the forces the bird had conjured in its last tremors of consciousness, he ran like he couldn't get away from the scene of their battle fast enough . . . could never find what he was looking for . . . no longer knew what he was looking for. And hadn't for a long time.

At first, he had been afraid. The sounds at night pulsing around him, through him, saying we are here we are here we are here . . . darkness so thick he could fall into it . . . when will it go away? I can't see; I'm so alone.

Fitful sleep . . . waking to the glow of light over the tree tops . . . I am back, the light assured him; *I will warm you. I will stay long enough for you to find water, long enough for you to know they will not catch you. I will stay for a while. For a while.*

It had been this way for so long that he expected nothing else. He learned to hunt and to hide until he knew every stream, every path, every rock. As only the hunter can know. He knew the chant of the locusts and tree frogs would swell to deafening pitch in the darkness and be quieted by the light if he waited . . . *if only he waited long enough.* He knew these things. He knew them from an understanding born in him, waiting for him to call. He called on it now.

What's wrong? What's wrong with me?

His legs—legs that had, until now, transported him like the wings of an angel—were rubbery cables pulling him to the ground, refusing to obey his command. The hawk's cry had filled the air and penetrated the earth . . . *calling upon the gods of the wind and sky,* Surely they would come; *surely they would find the taker of the king and destroy him.* He would face them. He would defy them to take back the flesh that would sustain him for another day. *He was king now. He was king,* even as he fell to the ground not knowing if he would ever raise himself up again.

Cool dirt. . . .

Cool dirt against his face, his chest, his belly.

Lying there . . . holding on . . . holding on to the smell of the earth, the leaves . . . the world spinning—

spinning round and round and round. . . .

What's happening?

What's happening to me?

Where did they go? How did I get here? I don't belong here—I don't belong!

Darkness . . . go away! I can't see. . . .

Alone . . . too alone to hear the unnatural snap of a twig crushed into the dried leaves as a man approached and the new king of the mountain was alone no more.

Skin prickling, gut twisting, Mark pushed aside low-hanging tree branches and made his way into the dense thicket. Not a sound reached him now; not a flicker of ebbing life or the crunch of bones. Trying to shake off the feeling of eyes watching him—his face? his back?—he followed the evidence of a crime scene beyond the jurisdiction of any court of human law. To the hush of bright crimson blood dripping from the shriveled leaves of tiny saplings and poison ivy, he read familiar footprints pressed into the sandy soil. Distinctive in their shape, and missing a toe, he had first seen such prints on the mountain in early spring, before the tough grass and low foliage grew thick enough to cover them. Curiosity aroused, he searched for signs of life. A lone killer could be very shadowy. Was there more than one? Tightening his grip on the walking stick he always used, Mark stepped forward—*and quickly pulled back!*

Less than three feet away—directly in his path and dripping with blood—there appeared to be a large, tawny animal staring directly, quietly, intently at him. Cougar? Coyote? Not a sound came from its throat as it lay there, jaws gripping the dead hawk, inhaling the bird's departing spirit in the innate and desperate struggle for survival.

Slowly, calling upon every muscle, Mark held the killer's gaze and crouched to the ground, balancing himself on his walking stick. "Easy there," he managed to say, on guard for any sign of mistrust from what he recognized now as a wild dog. "Whatcha got there, fella?"

At the sound of Mark's voice, the dog seemed to quiver, chattering its teeth together almost as if to emulate human speech. Lowering its head, the dog closed its eyes; though whether it was bowing to human attention or overcome with weakness from the gaping slashes on its throat, chest and side, Mark couldn't tell.

"I'm not a vet," Mark told the dog, moving closer. "And it sure looks like you need one," he said, knowing without his help the unusual dog would die right there, right now, in front of him.

And then he heard it: thump, thump, thump.

In the way of its kind before, since and forever, with a flicker of movement in the grass, the dog was accepting him. Trusting him.

In what could have been his last gesture on this earth, the dog was wagging his long, skinny tail. This was no coy-dog, no experiment gone haywire at the hands of people claiming to love animals while interfering with nature just as much as scientists, themselves, had done. This was a dog. A dog down on his luck. A dog asking for help in the only way it could.

Stripping off his shirt, revealing a well-defined chest and strong arms still tan from a summer at the shore, Mark eased forward and covered the shaking animal. How could he stop the bleeding? He couldn't —but he knew of a stream halfway down the hill. If he could reach it in time, the cold water of the stream would be enough to slow down the bleeding—if he could get there . . . if he could lift the dog . . . if the dog would allow itself to be touched. Could he carry what he guessed was about seventy sprawling pounds all the way down the mountain to his truck?

Hold on, boy! he thought to the dog, mentally commanding him not to quit, not to give up, offering his own energy to the fading life force of the gallant animal. He was gallant, this dog. In his presence, even now, clinging to the most fragile vestige of life, Mark sensed the power within. Pushing his arms under the dog's side, he was surprised at the animal's sharp yelp. Instinctively, as if pricked by a needle, he pulled back.

"Don't do that again," Mark whispered hoarsely, fighting to regain his balance. "I almost dropped you."

Rolling the dog on its back now and cradling him like a newborn baby, Mark stood. The dog wasn't as heavy as he had imagined, but already Mark's skin was itching just from the sight of wart-like ticks and the grainy black dirt of fleas.

Forget about it, he told himself as he began running and the fading dog's head drooped and flopped against his waist.

A dog with fleas is still alive.

I Want You.
I Want You Right . . . There!

"It doesn't look good," the vet said, shaking her head. A woman of few words, educated abroad, she examined the dog carefully, making comments to her assistant as Mark stood by.

Do anything, he thought. *Say anything. Just don't say he's going to die.*

"Hold this," she said to him, pressing a gauze pad against a slash on the dog's leg. *"We can stitch him up and stop the bleeding, but I still have to run some tests."*

"Before you even know if he's going to make it?" he asked.

She looked at him as if she didn't understand his reticence.

"I mean, if he's not going to live—if he's going to die—why put him through any more?"

"Mark, if I didn't know you from all the broken animals you bring into this place—all the birds and squirrels and God knows what else you find on that mountain of yours and everywhere else you seem to go—I'd throw you right out of here for that. Don't let him hear you. Don't ever let an animal hear you

decide for them what the outcome is going to be, unless it's on the positive side. Now, tell him he's going to make it. Even if you don't believe it. Even if I don't believe it, Mark. Tell him. And say it like you mean it," she said, in her busy-vet way.

A few years later, there were a lot of things Mark would say as he spoke with the reporter from SportsAnimated TV. He'd tell them about the dog. He'd tell them about the sport and what it takes to make a champion. He'd tell them how to roll up your shirt-sleeves, jump in and make yourself a champion, too.

And he'd say it like he meant it.

In the age of political correctness and sloppy journalism, Claude Emerson was an anomaly. Vague about where he was born, he had graduated from a prestigious northeastern college and quickly found work in New York City covering the entertainment scene. There, hobnobbing with the elite, he had sipped champagne in the Hamptons and thrown New Year's Eve confetti off penthouse rooftops with Broadway's finest.

Along the way, he had interviewed his share of music moguls and partied with singers of the moment. Not a bad life, he told himself, even if jobs don't last forever and you have to start all over again.

He had been with *SportsAnimated* for a while now. During that time, he had seen the magazine give birth to its own TV show, gaining respect from audiences around the country. He liked to think his in-depth interviews had something to do with that, but his boss, a self-proclaimed protégé of Helen Gurley-Brown, said, "Don't flatter yourself."

She knew what flattery was and did her best to avoid handing it out. Flattery was a waste of time she didn't have. Seventy-something Esmeralda von Havenburg, of dog show fame, had bought a broken-down newsletter for pet lovers and in a few short years had made it into the most widely circulated magazine for animal lovers on the newsstands. While she was at it, she morphed the publication into a magazine with its own television show specializing in animal sports and entertainment. It was a lifestyle she knew well, and which she espoused to all who would listen.

"Darlings," she said, batting her eyes at media seminars, "life is for the living. If I can do all this in my seventies from a wheelchair, just imagine how much *you* can do!"

As for Claude, what she wanted from him was something he *didn't* want to imagine.

And she wanted it right now. . . .

"You know the old saying, *Behind every success-ful man there's a woman*? Well, I've got one in back of me twisting a knife," he said, buying a round of beers for his co-workers at their favorite bar.

"You guys don't believe me, I can tell," he said, lighting up and leaning back in his chair. "OK, Madison Square Garden. Look for the blonde with the big hair skidding across the ring like she's going for a touchdown. Remember that? It's the biggest dog show on TV—we're broadcasting all over the world—and the poor woman trips on camera. *She's mortified!* But she plays it up like a real *grande dame*.

"Don't get me wrong. I'm not saying the lady was *shoved* for any special *effects* or anything. There's a difference between pushing and shoving, and we all know it. But Esmeralda, bless that seventy-year-old wicked heart of hers, sits there with a cool smile pushing buttons, saying, 'Trust me on this.'"

To a round of self-conscious laughter at the "Esmeralda line" familiar to them all, he continued.

"You're trusting her when you're falling backwards like a rock off a skyscraper and she's waving goodbye/send me a postcard/have a safe trip! *'Don't worry,'* she purrs. *'It's for your own good.'"*

"Another one we've heard before!" somebody cracked.

"Don't worry?" Claude said, mocking his boss. "This *can't be* for my own good, I think to myself. I've got a *Telly Award* sitting on the bookshelf at home where I want a mantle to be. *I've got an Emmy!"*

"Here! Here!" a buddy said, raising a beer.

"I can't get mixed up with *Greyhound* racing!" Claude said, with a knowing grin to all.

"But, '*nobody* wants to be mixed up with Greyhound racing, darling,' she says to me, sharpening her blade, or was it her claws? *'We've just heard from our mole in the State Department,'* she fills me in. 'This is major, Claude. *Big-time serious.* The decision's coming down any minute! Do you realize what this means? What it means to our *society*?'"

For a brief instant, his cronies went quiet.

Claude ordered another beer. "I think fast," he said. "Decision or axe coming down is a matter of opinion among murderers, thieves and little Alfs* running around PETA-land.† Personally, I happen to

---

*ALF. Animal Liberation Front.

†PETA. People for the Ethical Treatment of Animals. A crude and militant "animal rights" organization.

know it's jail time, court dates and NAFTA* arbitration she's talking about. I know, because she's been on the same channel for weeks. Hasn't she?"

"Yeah, she's been on it for awhile," somebody from the purchasing department agreed.

Claude nodded. " 'How the hell did the Greyhound racing industry get the *balls*?' she wants to know. 'When this story breaks, it's gonna be *everywhere*!' she rolls on. 'CNN, MSNBC, Fox, the BBC, the Networks. And we've got an *exclusive*!' Did she say *exclusive*? Now, there's a magic word for you. 'We could sway a *nation* with this thing, Claude!' she told me. 'Do it right, and you've got yourself a *Pulitzer*!' "

"No lie?" a scruffy fellow said, in a sweat-stained white shirt and loosened tie.

"Hey," Claude said, his beer glass raised in one hand and his other hand pretending to operate an automatic wheelchair. "Like we all know, the woman knows how to push buttons." As for cutting-edge, she didn't get to be their boss by letting *herself* get pushed around by *anybody*. Horse shows, racing, the Iditirod in Alaska—you name it and *SportsAnimated* was there.

"Remember that dog show at The Garden I just told you about?" Claude reminded them. "Get this: It's her best friend, Blanche, out there flopping around like a fish out of water, mopping up the floor with her tits—which, I know from firsthand inspection later, were bountifully worth every second the camera was on them. What does Esmeralda, sitting there in that

---

*North American Free Trade Agreement. Implemented on January 1, 1994, the NAFTA is an unprecedented social experiment superceding any city, county, state or federal laws affecting the income of investors doing business in the United States, Canada or Mexico.

custom-made, hand-driven, gold-plated, designer wheelchair of hers, say?"

"Zoom in for a close-up, boys," a cameraman said, remembering it well.

"Spare . . . me . . . Lord!" Claude exclaimed to the ceiling. "*That,* my friends, is an *executive producer.*"

"You turned down the assignment?" the cameraman asked, meaning *You turned down the assignment —didn't you?*

"Certainly not!" Emerson laughed. "Principles be damned! I know a hot story when I see one. And, when a woman knows every shameful secret, every fragile hope, every nasty thing *about* you," he grinned and winked, "well, fellas, *that's* a knife."

Sophisticated, dapper and a ladies' man, Claude considered his new assignment. What he knew about Greyhounds wasn't enough to make a paragraph, let alone fill a whole story. It would take a damn good researcher to put this one across, and good researchers were hard to find.

Picking up a razor and trimming the beard that showed the angles of his jaw to perfection, he decided on casual clothes that morning, in order to put the country dogman he was about to meet at ease. Even so, he couldn't resist wearing sharply pleated, brushed-wool grey trousers and matching tweed jacket. Not for today: the trademark silk tie, his concession to casual attire. Gold cufflinks, however, adorned his shirtsleeves, and his fine Italian leather shoes were spit-shined to perfection.

Emerging from the Lancaster train station to find it had started raining, he ran hastily toward a waiting cab. "Shit!" he exclaimed, as his right foot splashed into a puddle when he opened the door. He tossed a leather suitcase onto the back seat and followed it in. "Let's get out of here!" he said to the driver, brushing dirty water off his shoes.

"Where to, buddy?" the man asked.

"Ever heard of a town called Havenburg?"

"Sure. Over the river and through the woods, make a left at the end of the rainbow. That where you're headed?"

"Yeah," Claude said. "Let's fly." On second thought, let's not.

"No problem," said the driver. "What's the address?"

"Hillboro Road," Claude replied in a distracted manner. "I've got a room at a bed and breakfast. Can you take me to a place called, uh . . . ," searching his pocket he found a note scrawled on a scrap of paper, "The Mountain Inn?"

"Mountin' Inn? Yeah," the cabbie grinned in a way understood by both men. "I know exactly where you mean."

Welcome to the Pennsylvania Dutch Country, Claude thought to himself. Land of Plain Folks and fancy; land of shoo-fly pie, peanut butter cookies, Peach Bottoms, Blue Balls and Lick-dale. The place for good Fertility and plenty of Intercourse. "You from around here?" he asked, opening a gold cigarette case and lighting up.

"Nah," the driver scoffed, tapping his cigar in the ashtray with a sharp cough that was more out of habit than necessity. "New York."

"Yeah? Me too," Claude said. "Where?"

"Queens. Where else?"

"Which part?"

"Forest Hills. 215th Street, right off of Queens Boulevard."

"Small world," Claude said, rolling down the window. "Mind if I smoke?"

"Be my guest," the other man laughed, turning north on Route 72.

Claude leaned back in his seat as city bustle melted into open fields with scattered trees and isolated houses. "What do people do around here?" he asked, glad to see the rain had stopped.

"Around here? Eat mostly," the driver laughed. "Used to be more jobs than now," he said. "Now, a lot of people commute to the city. I'm talking about your really big paying jobs," he added. "Other than that, there's still a lot of small business and the farms."

"What about factory jobs?" Claude asked.

"Not as many as there used to be," the cabbie said. "Used to be, when I first came here, all kinds of factory work—RCA, Schick, Armstrong—really big employers. I look at some of these big, fancy-shmancy houses like you see right out there," he pointed to a gated community with expensive homes, "and I see 'em, but I wonder where the hell those people get the money? You know?"

"Yeah, I know what you mean," Claude said, wondering the same thing. "So?"

"So, like me, these people are coming in from out of state. They like it here because everything—even if it looks expensive to the ones who grew up here—it's cheaper than anywhere else. Hey, compared to New York, just about anything is cheaper, right?"

Claude laughed.

"These guys can make their money, then sell out and come here. They can afford to build a big house and still have money left over. It's worth the commute. Man, this state has more retirees than just about any place else you're gonna find!"

"What about Florida?" Claude said.

"Forget Florida! I figured the same thing 'til I started drivin' here. So what brings *you* all the way from New York?" the driver asked.

"I'm a reporter," Claude said. "I'm doing a story."

"Yeah? Who ya workin' for?"

"*SportsAnimated.*"

"The TV show?" the driver asked, making a right. "I watch that show. Hey, doesn't that belong to some lady from around here? I think I read something about it in the Lancaster paper, though why I think I can believe anything they say is beyond me! What's that lady's name?"

"Esmeralda von Havenburg," Claude said.

"Yeah! That's the one! Hey, don'tcha wonder what it's like having a whole town named after ya? Now, that's *real* money," he said, slowing down after about half a mile. "Here's the place," he said, coming to a stop. "Want me to wait?"

"I should be OK from here," Claude said. Telling the cabbie Esmeralda had lost her fortune and re-invented herself not once, but several times, would have meant very little to a man waiting for his fare. "Yeah," he said, handing over a bill and telling the driver to keep the change. "Some people are just lucky."

More charming than he had expected with its decorative latticework, wraparound porch and freshly painted exterior, the Mountain Inn revealed itself to be a picture-postcard come to life.

"You're holding a room for me?" Claude asked the lady in tasteful country attire who greeted him in the lobby.

"Mr. Emerson?" she asked, sniffing at the scent of smoke on his clothes.

"Yes," he said, setting down his suitcase. "With *SportsAnimated*."

"I have you right here." She smiled, opening her ledger and finding his name. "Room four. Upstairs and to the left. Will that be cash or card?" she asked.

"Card, please," he said, handing over the plastic. One thing about the show, they always paid his expenses.

"I'm sorry, Mr. Emerson," the lady said a few moments later. "It doesn't want to go through."

"You've got to be kidding," Claude said. "It's a company account."

"I'm sorry," she said again, sensing his embarrassment. "Is there another card you can use?"

Fishing around in his wallet, Claude went for his cash, but thought better of it. Handing her a personal bank card, he said, "Try this."

"Thank you. . . . Yes, this one is fine," she said.

The company credit card not going through, Claude thought to himself, as he went upstairs. Making a mental note to call the office, he found his room, set his suitcase in the closet and pulled back the curtains. It was just a mistake; he'd deal with it tomorrow, he told himself, dialing Hidden Farms. Right now, it was Mark Whittier he wanted to talk with, not the home office.

"Mr. Whittier?" he asked. "Claude Emerson, with *SportsAnimated*."

"Hello," Mark answered. "When did you get in town?"

"Just now," Claude said. "I've got a room at the Mountain Inn."

"You're just down the road from us," Mark said. "Have you had lunch?"

"I picked up a sandwich at the station," Claude said. "I'd like to get together as soon as we can. Soak up the atmosphere, get a feel for the business, you know. That kind of thing."

"You want to see the dogs," Mark said, understanding. "You picked a good day for it. We're short-handed."

"Well, I don't . . . "

"Don't worry. We won't ask you to do anything too tough," Mark laughed. "But this'll give you an inside look. Fair enough?"

"Fair enough."

"Very good, then. I'll have somebody pick you up."

A few minutes later, a black pick-up pulled up to the inn. A gentleman dressed in natty work shirt and casual pants stepped out and greeted the lady innkeeper. Dialing upstairs, she rang Claude, who grabbed a jacket and made his way down to the lobby.

"Claude?" the man asked.

"Mark?"

"No, I'm the office manager, Michael," the man said. "I take care of the books. Mark's back at the kennel with a litter of new pups. He asked me to come and get you."

Shaking hands, they headed outside, seated themselves in the truck and drove speedily along a curving, hilly road.

"Are there many Greyhound kennels around here?" Claude asked, holding firmly to the armrest, anticipating the next curve.

"We're the only one," Michael said, a sense of accomplishment in his manner. "There are dog kennels around, sure. But we're the only Greyhound farm."

"Farm? Somehow I think pigs and cows when I hear that."

"No, it's considered a farm," Michael said, smiling. "In Greyhound lingo, this is a farm and a kennel is what you have at the track."

"Noted," Claude said, cursing himself for not having a pen. "How many dogs does it take to make a Greyhound kennel?"

"Seventy or so is a nice number," Michael said. "Sometimes more, sometimes less. But not often. You need enough dogs for the active list."

"Active list?"

"The list of runners for the racing secretary," Michael explained.

Claude nodded. "So, how many must you keep on the active list?"

"As many as you can," Michael said. "All of them if you're lucky."

"Luck seems to play a pretty big part in this thing," Claude noted.

"Oh, yeah." Michael smiled, pulled in a macadam lane and passed through a gate flanked by two stone Greyhounds à la 1930.

"Looks like Hidden Farms North is pretty lucky," Claude whistled, taking in the private lake, stone house and spacious kennel buildings where they were greeted by Greyhounds of many colors.

"We've had our share every now and then," Michael said, parking near the office. "Let's see if we can find Mark."

"Looks a lot like a horse farm," Claude said, as they walked toward a long, low building.

"Racehorses and Greyhounds are born to run," Michael said. "But they really show what they can do on perfect roads with no ditches or groundhog holes to worry about. And nothing pulling out in front of them. Some racetracks are even heated."

This last statement surprised Claude. "Heated?"

"Oh, yeah," Michael said, jumping over a puddle. "I know a track that's heated so the snow melts in winter and the dogs don't get their feet cold. See over there?" he said, pointing to his left. "That grass field's big enough to play football, but it's fenced in just for the dogs."

"Lucky dogs," Claude said.

"Over there?" Michael said, indicating one of several matching buildings standing in a row. "Five separate runs for the dogs, each run ten by twenty."

"I'm impressed," Claude said, genuinely surprised. "I thought Greyhounds lived in crates."

"Only at the track," Michael said. "Not here."

"Remind me to make a note of that," Claude said.

"Here they've got plenty of room and heated nest boxes."

"No crates," Claude repeated.

"Except in the infirmary," Michael explained, "or when we're training pups ready to leave for the track."

"What do they sleep on?" Claude asked. "Silk sheets?"

"Only for special visitors," Michael quipped. "Most days, just shredded paper."

"Top Secret, CIA?"

"Cheap newsprint from every house in the county." Michael smiled, enjoying the game. "Down at the south end, we have a five-hundred-foot-long sprint field for the dogs to run in, rain or shine. The boys are running some now. Want to take a look?"

"Let's go," Claude said, glad he wore boots.

"Give me a minute," Michael said, picking up the receiver of a phone outside the building. "I'm taking your guest down to the sprint field to see some action, Mark. We'll meet you in about twenty minutes."

To Claude, he said, "Follow me," as they walked around the back of the building and climbed into a cream-colored golf cart with a green and white awning. As Claude hopped in, Michael turned the key and, with a quiet purr, the cart pulled away.

"Over there's our whirligig," Michael called out, as they drove past a large circular track enclosed by fence. "That's where the dogs learn to hug the turns. Dog that knows what he's doing, can cut off fractions."

"Fractions," Claude repeated. "Like, a tenth of a second?"

To which, Michael replied, dead serious, "No.

Hundredths of a second," and Claude whistled low.

Gliding the cart to a stop on a grassy hill overlooking a straightaway, Michael smiled. "There they go!"

Hand-slipping two pups on one side of the fence and three on the other side, several farmhands cheered the young dogs on. Whooping and hollering, they called from one end of the sprint track to the other as the dogs ran back and forth, up and down the fence line.

"And there ain't a damn thing making them do it," Michael said, still spellbound after the many Greyhounds Hidden Farms had trained, and enjoying Claude's amazement. "Gotta roll," he said, turning the key again.

The cart came to life. Claude got in and Michael headed back toward the office.

Innocently, Claude almost laughed. "That was fun."

"Yeah, we all get caught up in it here," Michael said, parking the cart once more. "Let's see if Mark's free yet!" he called out, raising his voice to be heard above the bleating of an eighteen-wheeler applying his jake-brake.

"What the hell!" Claude hollered, looking up a steep, thickly wooded embankment.

"That's the turnpike up there," Michael laughed.

"Turnpike?"

"Yeah," Michael said. "It runs the whole way along this side of the property. We couldn't build a wall like that for a million bucks."

"Why would you want to?"

"You kiddin'? The noise from that traffic is why our dogs aren't spooks. This whole place is designed as a training center for competitive sport animals. Any idea what's on the other side of that wall?"

"Couldn't guess," Claude said.

"Thousands of acres of woods and trails. All for us."

"But how do you get across a turnpike?"

"It a secret," Michael said with a wink.

Secrets, Claude thought, as they entered the unassuming building which held the offices of the farm. Unknown mysteries that made the world go round.

Taking in the array of exotic plants, expansive windows and skylights, floor to ceiling shelves lined with leather-bound books, interspersed with porcelain and bronze statuary, paintings in watercolor, oil and chalk crawling up the walls, Claude came to a stop.

"You OK?" Michael asked him, crossing over to a secretary seated at a small mahogany desk.

"Surprised," Claude said, following.

"Yeah, I know," Michael said, as the secretary finished her call. "We get that reaction a lot. Jean?" he said to the woman in a way revealing their special connection. "This is Claude Emerson, with *SportsAnimated*. Would you tell Mark we're here?"

"You can go right in. He's waiting for you."

"Before we do," Claude said, "I just have to ask . . . all these files?" He indicated several five-drawer cabinets near the entrance door.

"Our breeding and racing records," she said.

"The plants?"

"I used to work in a greenhouse," Michael said.

"These paintings and the bronzes," Claude said, "it's like walking into a gallery." Horses, dogs, wildlife, full-scale sculptures, figurines, photographs, and shelves and shelves of books and magazines filled the room. "I've never seen such a collection before."

"Mr. Whittier started out in antiques."

When Claude asked if they read *SportsAnimated,* Jean directed his attention to several rows of magazines. "Mr. Whittier reads them from cover to cover," she said, as Michael knocked softly on the frosted glass of a door marked "Private."

"Mr. Emerson?" a deep and resonant voice addressed them as they entered the inner sanctum of the master of Hidden Farms. Facing a confident-looking man, casually dressed in jeans and a black turtleneck, Claude smiled and extended his hand. "Mark? Nice to meet you."

"Michael's been showing you around?"

"Yes, I've been getting the grand tour," Claude said, taking in the mural of racing dogs on one whole side of the office and settling into a leather chair.

"Coffee?" Mark asked.

"No, thanks," Claude said, taking out his notepad and a small tape recorder. "You mind?" he asked, clearing the air before turning on the device.

"Must we?" Mark asked, glancing over at Michael for his reaction.

"Not if you don't want me to," Claude said, hesitating.

"No," Mark said. "I just, well, if you want to talk to somebody, do you have to have a tape recorder playing?"

"Hey," Claude said, putting the tape recorder away. "Don't worry about it."

Introductions made, explaining that he had to get back to work, Michael prepared to leave. "Catch up with you guys later," he said, closing the door behind him.

"Michael's shy about the press," Mark explained.

"No problem," Claude said, a look of expectation on his face.

"You can bring that recorder out now, if you want to," Mark said.

Obliging, Claude relaxed. Clearly, Mark Whittier was a man comfortable with himself and secure about anything he might have to say. But here, at a place like this? *Who wouldn't be?* Claude thought, comparing Hidden Farms North to his apartment on 98th & Broadway.

"Ready?" he asked.

"Fire away," Mark smiled.

"First, my editor—and I—want to thank you for agreeing to the interview and allowing me to come here for a story."

"You're very welcome," Mark smiled.

"I'm looking forward to going along with you on the trip to Vegas, for the conference. I appreciate anything you want to share with me about the lawsuits your Association is involved with. And Miss von Havenburg wants you to know how much she appreciates the exclusive you're giving us. I know you guys have been burned by the media."

"Burned? How about dissected, pulverized and burned all over again."

"Duly noted," Claude said. "I'm asking you to trust me."

"Give you the inside scoop," Mark said, amused.

"Yeah," Claude said, reaching for a cigarette, looking to Mark for permission, but not lighting up. "Exactly."

"Well, that contribution she made to our favorite

charity went a long way," Mark said, nodding to Claude that, yes, he could go ahead and light up.

Shaking his head no, Claude grinned. "Security blanket, that's all."

Indicating that he understood, Mark closed the open folder of pedigrees he'd been studying and pushed it aside. He would give Claude his full attention. "Have you ever studied the natural way of healing?"

"I'm not sure what you mean."

"Well, some people believe our bodies are affected by everything we touch or see or hear or feel or smell. And we don't even have to take something out of the wrapper for it to get into our systems."

It was an interesting theory, Claude thought, saying, "Like getting a caffeine fix just by smelling the coffee?"

"Something like that," Mark smiled. "Though I've never figured out how to get by just living on air."

"I get the feeling you take this kind of stuff seriously," Claude said.

"Let's just say there's a lot of mystery in life, and it more than fascinates me."

"Like how you found a wild dog and it led to all this?" Claude asked.

"Yeah," Mark said. "Things like that." Clicking his tongue, he rolled back his chair and a large, blue-fawn Greyhound appeared from under his desk and stood looking at Claude. "Hey, fella," he said to the dog, as he placed loving hands on both sides of the dog's shoulders, "This here's Claude Emerson."

"That's him?" Claude asked, surprised. "The great champion?"

"Best foot-warmer in the world," Mark laughed, as Clue went over to inspect their guest.

"I've never seen a Greyhound up close," Claude said, running his hands over Clue's sides. "Is it safe to pet him?"

"Go right ahead."

"He looks in great shape," Claude said. "How old is he now?"

"About eight."

"How do you keep him in such condition?" Claude asked. "He looks like he just stepped out of a gym."

Mark laughed. "Well, he does have his own treadmill," he said. "But, if you ask me, the thing he really gets a kick out of is running with his pups. By the way," he said, swiveling his chair around to face the windows behind him and checking his watch, "it's feeding time and I've got to head out to that building over there." Pointing to a small frame building with window shutters, he said, "That's our kennel kitchen. And quasi-whelping room. Clue's got a new litter of pups there. Want to come along? I'll put you to work."

At Claude's expression of surprise, he added, "We can find a pair of coveralls for you."

A few minutes later, Claude found himself inside the kennel kitchen/infirmary. He could hear the gentle squeal of newborn puppies under the red glow of a heat lamp.

"That's Memory and her new babies," Mark said. "Usually, the broods are in the whelping building, but Memory's kind of special," he said. "I got her at the Nationals for a song and didn't realize she was a sister of one of the Greats. She's a real sweetheart."

"Sure is," Claude said, petting the uplifted head of the gentle, brown-eyed dog. "She doesn't seem to mind me being here," he said.

"She's a pretty good judge of character," Mark said, picking up a puppy and placing it in Claude's hands.

Overwhelmed by the newborn puppy's fragile vulnerability, Claude spoke quietly. "It's eyes are closed," he said, as the puppy began snuggling against his palm in the eternal search for warmth and mother's nipple.

"They can't see or hear for about two weeks," Mark said. "But they can smell."

"This is neat," Claude said, wondering when he might ever get so close to brand-new life again.

"One of those mysteries we were talking about," Mark said, taking the puppy and returning it to its mother. Heading to the refrigerator, he found a gallon jar of goat milk. Filling up two small baby bottles, with bright red nipples, he heated them in a pan of water on the stove and tested the temperature of the milk by squirting a few drops on the inside of his wrist. Satisfied, he handed one of the bottles to Claude. "Make yourself useful," he grinned.

"Why do you let her with the puppies if she doesn't have any milk?" Claude asked, reaching for the puppy closest to him.

"Give her time," Mark said. "They were only born yesterday."

Born yesterday is something this guy certainly wasn't, Claude thought.

Feeling the puppy nuzzle his hand, searching, searching, searching, Claude couldn't help but ask, "Do you think he has any idea about your Greyhound Coalition and something like NAFTA?"

Mark paused a moment. "The only thing he cares about is where his next meal's coming from," he said. "Which you're about to give him."

"How do you work this thing?" Claude asked, struggling to keep the nipple from going flat.

"Think of a woman," Mark smiled, picking up a puppy for himself. "A little at a time."

Perfect, Claude thought, as the puppy took hold and nursed quietly.

"So," he said. "NAFTA."

Mark nodded, gently eased the puppy's mouth off the nipple and held the bottle up to the light. "An ounce is just about enough," he said. "How's your little fella doing?"

"He's got the idea, but he still wants to know how you got the guts to go up against the Animal Rights Militia."

"ARM? Let's just say I love animals as much as they do. But I love people, too," Mark said. "Somewhere along the line, I figured out an animal doesn't get very far in this world without somebody taking care of it."

"That's what they believe *they're* here for," Claude said, putting his puppy back in the nesting box and reaching for another. "Isn't it?"

Mark sighed. "Yeah," he said. "I know. But do you think very many of them have ever touched a Greyhound puppy like this and fed it from a bottle? Do you think they ever raised a puppy and cheered for it at the track like some guy rooting for his kids at baseball practice? How about sitting up all night with a brood who won't have her puppies unless you're there, and every one of her puppies falling into your hands and you holding them for her while she licks them clean?"

It was doubtful, Claude knew.

"Animal welfare means taking the best care of an animal that you can," Mark explained. "Well fed, well groomed, well cared for. Animal *rights*, hey, it sounds good. But it's political. And politics is between people. Somewhere along the line, and I'm pretty sure I know how, organizations like the ARM hijacked the welfare movement, made animal lovers their soldiers and started a war."

The stomping of footsteps and clanking of meal feed bowls signaled the time of day. "Talk about animal lovers!" Mark said. "There's someone I want you to meet."

Walking through a doorway from the whelping area to the kitchen, they met up with a short, heavy-set woman washing bowls in a deep sink, her grey hair frizzed from the steam of the soapy water. "Hey, Karen!" Mark said. "How's it going?"

"Fine, Boss. Almost ready to dish it out."

"Karen, you're always dishin' it out to somebody," Mark teased.

Laughing, she expertly placed the last shiny bowl onto a precariously balanced stack of sixty that had gone before it. "Ta-dah!" she said, placing her hands on both hips. As if the expelled breath of her uttered word was just a bit too much—pushing the leaning tower just beyond its balancing point—three sets of eyes watched in disbelief, expectation and awe. Mesmerized, arms outstretched, Mark and Claude dove to catch the pans clattering to the floor about them. Karen, hands still on her hips and a glint of mis-chief in her eye, stood above the fray. "You guys ever play Jenga," she laughed, as nine newborn puppies and their dam slept on.

"Karen, I love ya," Mark said, gathering up feed

bowls and setting them on the table, then grabbing a pair of coveralls from a nearby hook. "Try these, Claude."

"You firin' me again? An' all I did was have a little fun!" Karen moaned good-naturedly.

"Don't worry," Claude winked, trying to fit his gold cuff links through a sleeve. "I'm just temp help."

"OK, Tempie," she said, handing him a scoop as Mark said goodbye. "Dish it out."

The mindless task well under control, Claude gazed around the room. Dogs with their own kitchen, he thought. It doesn't get much better than that. Hot and cold water, a sink to wash their feed dishes, a stove, a refrigerator, fresh meat from the butcher in town, vitamins and minerals. What a life.

"What's all that for?" he asked, looking at a whole wall of the kitchen lined with leather collars, leashes and muzzles.

"You never saw a dog collar before?" Karen asked. "Leather's for the adults and plastic for the pups."

"Why the difference?"

"Pups are always chewing the collars off each other, and leather's too expensive to keep replacing all the time."

Logical, Claude thought. "What about the muzzles?" he asked.

"Part of their training. Around six months, maybe seven, we take 'em to the sprint field and they have to know how to run with a muzzle on. That's when we start getting serious with 'em. These guys get pretty excited," she said. "You don't want anybody hurting each other."

"Excited about what?"

"The chase, man! God forbid, they see something—a piece of paper blowing around, a pheasant jumping up, a 'coon runnin' along the fence! Baby, look out!"

He hadn't thought about that. You didn't see much of that kind of thing in the city.

"Some of the dogs, they don't feel right unless they've got their muzzle on. Like they're not dressed up," she laughed. "So they have their own special muzzles and we pad the nose bands with sheepskin and they're as happy as a pig in shit."

"I saw the treadmill," he said.

"I use it myself when nobody's lookin'," she admitted with a chuckle. "I use the scale, too," she said, pointing out a digital. "But it's set wrong. I always take off ten pounds."

Digital scales weren't usually wrong, he thought.

"Hey!" she said, as if reading his mind. "You think I'm lyin'?"

About the ten pounds? he asked himself. "Not at all," is what he said.

"Staying for supper?" Mark asked, stopping by later.

"Just finishing up," Claude said, wiping off the table. "Where do the empty feed bags go?"

"Behind you," Mark gestured toward a large wastebasket. "Do you want to have dinner with us?"

"Starved," Claude said.

"If you like Pennsylvania Dutch cooking, we can go to the Riding Club."

"Never tried it." Claude smiled, gladly accepting the invitation.

"Then you're in for a treat. I just have to go over some race results first. We can leave in about twenty minutes."

"We" turned out to be Mark, Michael and his wife, whom Claude recognized as the office secretary, Jean. The "Riding Club" turned out to be an old estate famed for its horse shows, boarding stables and mansion house restaurant.

"When I was a kid," Mark said, pulling in the tree-lined entrance, coasting past riders walking their horses among towering red barns, "we used to come here to the horse shows. You should have seen the crowds! Like a carnival. We weren't members. You had to be a member to go inside the clubhouse. But we had lots of fun here."

"I assume we'll be dining in the clubhouse tonight?" Claude asked.

"Yes," Mark answered, pushing a card into a slot beside the front door. "Get ready to step back in time."

Big Band music from the 1940s, laughter, chatter, the clink of silverware, dishes and the aroma of good food surrounded them.

"Good evening, Mr. Whittier," a pleasant woman dressed in black skirt and white blouse with a bow tie said. "You're table's ready."

"How are you tonight, Arlene?" he asked.

"Just fine," she smiled. "Will you be having drinks with your meal?"

Gesturing around the table, she took their orders. "You can order from the menu," she explained, "or, we have a nice buffet tonight. Would you like a few minutes to decide?"

"I think we'll go for the buffet," Mark said, to everyone's approval.

"OK, then I'll get your drinks and you can get started," she said with a smile.

Dining to music of Count Basie, Louie Armstrong, Peggy Lee, Rosemary Clooney, Tommy Dorsey, Glenn Miller and Benny Goodman, they eased into relaxed conversation.

"This place is great," Claude said, over roast shoulder of beef, cooked carrots and mashed potatoes slathered in gravy. "How long has it been here?" he asked, taking in the knotty-pine walls, fieldstone fireplace, glass cases of silver trophies lined on red velvet and paintings of English Pleasure horses and hunt scenes.

"Since the 1940s," Mark said. "It was a hackney horse farm, and it was bequeathed to the Riding Club provided they always have stables. It belongs completely to the members," he explained. "We have meetings here, films, speakers—all kinds of things."

"Wonderful!" Claude exclaimed, noticing each table with its tasteful bouquet of live spring flowers and the crowded dining rooms.

"Glad you like it," Mark said. "What did you think of your first visit to a Greyhound farm?"

"Not what I expected," Claude said.

"If you ever need a job . . ." Mark grinned.

"Thanks," Claude said, smiling. "But I'm not sure I could keep up with you guys. You're on the move every second."

"Seconds count in this business," Michael said. "What do you want, honey?" he asked the petite brunette he had neglected to introduce at the office.

"I'm OK," Jean said. "Unless there's any of that pecan pie I saw on the dessert table . . . and a scoop of vanilla ice cream."

Pushing aside his empty plate, sliding back his chair and looking toward the buffet tables, Michael glanced at Claude.

"Why not?" Claude said, ignoring the feel of his tight belt. "What did you call that apple stuff?"

"*Schnitz and knepp* . . . dried apple slices cooked with dough balls and raisins."

"Who thinks up these recipes?" Claude wanted to know.

"No idea," Mark said, smiling as they walked to a spread of hot sweet potatoes, ham, stuffed flounder, corn, green beans, peaches, pears, slices of watermelon, pies, cherry cobbler, breads, cakes, cookies and puddings.

"What's that?" Claude asked, at the dessert table.

"Cracker pudding topped with coconut shavings," Mark said. "Try it."

"When in Rome . . . " Claude said, eager to taste something new as Mark selected a piece of chocolate shoo-fly pie.

"What did you just call that pie?"

"Shoo-fly."

"What a name," Claude said, puzzled.

"It's a wet-bottom pie, molasses topped with cake and sweet crumbs. When ladies took their pies from the oven and set them on the windowsill to cool, they swished the flies away—shoo fly! Shoo!" Mark explained as Claude laughed.

"Looks good," he said.

"It all looks good," Mark said, patting his belly. "That's the trouble!"

Returning to the table, Claude tasted the cracker

pudding. "Interesting flavor," he said, to everyone's general approval.

Taking the chance to ask a few more questions, he turned to Mark.

"Thanks for letting me pitch in today."

"I didn't have a choice. We needed the help."

"It's not anything like I expected," Claude said. "Are all Greyhound kennels like that?"

"First, you have to realize that in the Greyhound business, there's a difference between a kennel and a farm. They're both kennels, but the farm is the one where the dogs are born and raised. The other is the kennel at the track where the dogs run."

"Yeah, Michael was telling me about that earlier today." Get the lingo down, Claude directed himself. "OK, what started it all for you? How do you go from being an antique dealer to all this?"

Mark smiled and shook his head. "I'm not so sure myself," he said, "if you really want to know."

"Yeah, I do. What happened? Is it something you always wanted?"

"Well, I grew up loving dogs, if that's what you mean."

"More than that," Claude said. "Everybody loves dogs. But not everybody makes dogs their life. How many do you have out there?"

"Out there?"

"At the farm? The kennel?"

"You mean, counting all the tracks we run at?"

Claude nodded.

"Well," Mark thought, "if you want an exact number, you have to ask Michael or Jean. They take care of the books and all the paperwork."

"What kind of paperwork exactly?"

"Registrations, breeding reports, whelping reports, inspection records, vet records, licenses to run in different states . . ."

"You need a license for that?"

"Absolutely."

"What's that all about?"

"Well," Mark said, reaching for water, "everything in the business is regulated. Your kennel is inspected by the state and also by the NGA . . ."

"Who's that?"

"The National Greyhound Association," Mark explained. "Our breed registry. Every purebred animal has an organization keeping pedigree records. Some limit their responsibilities to paperwork and others branch out further. In our case, the NGA can impose sanctions on members if they don't live up to certain standards."

"Like what?" Claude wanted to know, taking out his notepad.

"No tape recorder?" Mark asked.

"Too much background noise here," Claude said.

"I'll remember that," Mark said, laughing. "You want to know what kind of standards we're supposed to live up to? Well, cruelty to the dogs, for example, is something the industry won't tolerate."

"Touchy subject," Claude said, as Michael returned with his plate in one hand and Jean's in the other.

"What'd I miss?" Michael said.

"We're talking about the industry," Jean said, picking up a fork.

"I'm asking what kind of sanctions the NGA can impose on members."

"The bad ones, you mean?" Michael asked. "We're not supposed to do business with them."

"A lot of people don't know it," Mark explained, "but if a member is suspended, he surrenders ownership of his dogs, and other members aren't supposed to do business with him any more."

"You're kidding. Can they get away with that?"

"Absolutely. And I'll bet you never heard of any other animal registry with such a policy."

Assuring Mark that he hadn't, Claude pressed on. "Back to those licenses. Who regulates that?" he asked.

"The government," Mark said. "We actually have to be fingerprinted to run dogs at the tracks. You can't have a criminal record to be an owner or a trainer or even a kennel helper in this sport."

"You're kidding," Claude said again.

"No, he isn't," Jean said.

"Fingerprinted," Claude wrote in his notes.

"That's right," Mark assured him. "I wonder how many people in the ARM could pass a fingerprint check." he said, finishing his dessert, but saying nothing more.

Silence falling over them like a thin blanket of truth, they considered matters at hand.

"You didn't really answer how many dogs you have," Claude said.

"A lot," Michael chimed in.

"Fifty? A hundred?"

"A hundred, easily," Michael answered.

"That's a big feed bill," Claude said. "I can see why your dogs have to win."

"Yes, we can only grow the business as big as the dogs can support it," Mark added.

"But it isn't all just business . . ." Claude said, drawing him out.

"If you like your business as much as I do, it is," Mark told him.

"Well, what I mean is, it's not just a job."

"No," Mark said. "It's not just a job."

"I mean, a job is, well, something you *have* to do, a place you have to go. You don't have much choice about it. You've got a boss," he thought about Esmeralda back in New York, "riding your ass, telling you what to do."

"All that, yes," Mark agreed.

"So, what happened? What got you started in Greyhound racing?" Claude finally asked.

"Not being alone any more, I guess," Mark said. "Clue was almost dead when I found him. Even the vet didn't think he'd live. But she made me talk to him like he would. Man, you're taking me back a few years," he said, remembering how it was. Remembering the smell of fresh coffee filling the cottage that day. Wondering how the dog had survived in the wild and for how long he had roamed the mountain without anyone knowing. . . .

Running a finger across rows of stiff, black stitches surrounded by freshly shaved hair, Mark could still hear the cry of the hawk. He could still hear the vet saying *"Greyhound,"* as she searched for tattoo numbers in the dog's soft ears and wrote them down.

"This'll tell us who he belongs to," she explained. "Wonder how he ended up on the mountain?" she asked, saying Mark could pick him up later that day.

Wonder what he was running *away* from, is what Mark asked himself, thinking of the frail, skinny dogs standing outside big pet stores with plastic fish bowls tied around their necks as they begged for change. Pathetic dogs staring out from newspaper stories so often now that he just flipped the pages.

Why did it bother him that the vet had so quickly written down the identification numbers? After all, he reminded himself, they'd have to find the dog's owner. A dog important enough to rate a tattoo is valuable to somebody, right? A dog like this, unafraid to be touched, seeking comfort in the face of a stranger, allowing himself to be carried down the mountain like a child, had known kindness.

The dog twitched a leg and flitted his closed eyes, as if dreaming. What was he seeing in the darkness of his mind? How many savage battles had been fought to the death and won on the mountain?

Mark reached for the edge of the blanket, an old patchwork quilt made by his grandmother, and covered the dog's shoulder. Leaning back, he took in his surroundings. Wooden beams, braided rug, tweed couch . . . chipped walnut table he got from a neighbor in trade for some Erté prints. Paneled walls displayed a penchant for C. W. Anderson and Wesley Dennis horse prints, all nicely framed. There were pine bookcases on either side of the stone fireplace, glowing now with orange and yellow embers. There were first-edition hardcovers of Margueritte Henry, Jack London and Albert Payson Terhune.

Leading upstairs, a collection of family portraits and photos reminded him of graduation from a local college, early marriage and relatives he hoped would always be looking out for him.

Nestling into his favorite armchair, Mark picked a magazine off the worn coffee table. Like the table that had seen so much and belonged to so many people along the way, he wondered who the dog had belonged to, as he casually scanned classified ads offering Lladro, Roseville and collectible baseball cards for sale.

Why did he suddenly not want to know?

The loud ring of his phone cut through the cottage and broke his flow of thought. At the familiar voice of the vet's secretary, he reached for a pen.

"Here's the number for the National Greyhound Association," she said. "They keep records on all the racing dogs." Stomach cold, he wrote down the number.

"Yes, I have it," he said, wishing they hadn't been quite so efficient, but sensing their curiosity as well as his own. "What happens now?"

"Well, they notify the owner, I guess," she said.

"And then?"

"Well, that depends on what the owner wants to do. I guess whoever it is will just come and get their dog."

Come and get their dog, he thought, silently repeating her words to himself and hanging up. "Their" dog.

Funny, how good a place can feel when you're sharing it. Even when your roomie is an animal.

"National Greyhound Association," the warm voice traveling all the way from Abilene, Kansas, said. "How may I direct your call?"

"Uh, hello," Mark said, fidgeting with a notepad and pen. "Can you tell me who I talk with about finding out the rightful owners of a dog?"

"That would be Sarah, but she's on another line. Maybe I can help you. Do you know the dog's tattoo number?"

"Yes, I have it right here," he said, reading aloud.

"OK," the woman answered after checking her records. "That would be *HF Hidden Clue*. Blue fawn male, bred by Hidden Farms. His breeder and owner is Felicia McCrory."

"How can I get in touch with her?" he asked, clearing his throat. "If, maybe, I wanted to buy the dog, I mean?"

"She's listed in our directory. Do you have a copy?"

"No, I don't," he said. Could she detect the growing disappointment in his heart?

"Well, I can check for you and see if there's a number you can call."

"Thank you. I appreciate that." *But not really.*

"You're welcome. Here it is," she said, reading off the phone number while he scrawled it down. "Felicia lives in West Virginia," she said, asking if there was anything else she could do for him. It was good, helping people this way, she thought, saying goodbye with a smile in her voice.

Hanging up, he went outside to where the big Greyhound was staring up at his favorite silver maple tree. Resigned to the fact that he couldn't jump high enough to catch the squirrels living there, he didn't tire from watching them dart from branch to bird feeder to branch and back again. Had Mark ever seen a dog more beautiful? In all the pictures he had studied, in all the animal documentaries, had he ever seen a dog more exotic? A crazy scientist in some far dis-

tant lab could have said he mixed a cheetah and a
gazelle to get this unusual dog, and people would have
believed it. Surely, a Greyhound was a "cat-dog."

"Clue?" he called out. "Clue!"

Hearing his name, instantly recognizing the sound
meant only for him, the dog turned . . . and limped to
him. So, it was true, Mark thought. The heart of the
wild dog belonged to a woman named Felicia McCrory.

From the manner of the lady at the NGA, it
seemed as if Felicia McCrory and Hidden Farms were
familiar names around their office. That meant she
probably registered a fair amount of dogs.

But how could a lone dog find its way here—all
the way from West Virginia? And, more important, he
thought, remembering the emerald light of his swami
so long ago, what did it all mean?

Claude settled into his room that night and made a
few notes. These people didn't fit his impression of
Greyhound racing at all. Where were the dumpsters
filled with dog bodies like he had seen on Bryant
Gumble's HBO sports show? If Greyhounds were
killed after their racing careers were over, as he had
always been led to believe, why did he see so many
retired dogs living at Hidden Farms? It was to be the
first of many such questions. Curious about the
dichotomy of the Greyhound business—what he
thought he knew and what he was seeing firsthand—
he dialed the private number he dreaded.

"Esmeralda von Havenburg," came the all-too-
familiar voice.

"It's Claude."

"Darling!" she said, a touch too sweetly. "How are you." It was a greeting more than a question.

"What are you getting me into?" he asked, wasting no time.

"Whatever do you mean, Claude? I'm surprised at your tone."

"Maybe you should try taking me off the speaker," he said, being smart.

"Now, now," she said, as if she cared. "You know I don't hear well."

Wanting to apologize, but unable to resist pushing the limits, he asked if she had heard anything more from the State Department—and was promptly cut off. Left alone to contemplate the dismal sound of a dial tone, he thought back to when he had checked in that morning and wondered if he should have asked about the company credit card. Instead, he got out his laptop.

From: Emerson@dejazzd.com
To: Researchdept@SATV.com
Subject: High Stakes

How do I get mixed up in this stuff? I hope she really has something or I'm going to end up being a joke. Don't tell me. She'll say it's for my own good. But she's got to know something. (Why else would she hire the best researcher in town?) BTW, I thought you worked for the *Times*.

This whole thing doesn't make any sense. The Commonwealth of Pennsylvania is a powerful operation. Why did they take a stand against a national sport and why didn't it even cause a ripple in the media? I mean, look at what they've got: two baseball teams, two hockey teams, two football teams, trotting tracks, flat racing, a lottery. What's the big deal? Is Pennsylvania made up of a bunch of children who need protecting from their own selves? What's the government doing trying to control what we can or can't play?

And will somebody see what's up with my expense card?

From: Researchdept@SATV.com
To: Emerson@dejazzd.com
Subject: High Stakes

Good question. And you're not the only one asking it. As for being the best researcher in town, thank you for the compliment, but I don't know about that. Either way, right now I'm all you've got—and, yes, I'm still with the *Times*. What I've been able to find out for you is this: There's nothing inherently wrong with a sport in which dogs chase after a toy on the end of a stick. What's wrong, according to just about every press report I can find, is the industry that stands behind that sport. I'll work on digging up some balanced reporting, but at the moment my chances of finding anything are pretty bleak. I spoke with the business office and they're issuing you a new card. They're sending it to your hotel in Vegas.

P.S. Esmeralda says hello.

From: Emerson@dejazzd.com
To: Researchdept@SATV.com
Subject: High Stakes

You mean I have to cover my own expenses until then? Great. How many times have I done that lately. In the meantime, you can throw out the notion that

Greyhounds trained for racing are fed garbage and have rotten teeth. I didn't see any evidence of that at Whittier's farm today, and, thanks to some newspaper stuff I read somewhere, believe me, when nobody was around, I looked. The clock's ticking on this thing. I can feel it heating up. As soon as the NAFTA makes its ruling, we'd better roll. What can you find for me on how the sport got started? I need names, dates, statistics.

P.S. And, while you're moonlighting on the *Times*, how much is she paying you to keep tabs on me?

CHAPTER TWO

Blondes and Redheads

How many lives does a dog have? Only the gods know that. The gods who made animals of every different kind: animals to live in the air, in the water and on the land . . . animals for the greatest garden in the universe.

Clue lay on the couch as the stereo washed over him and chickadees fluttered around the bird feeder outside the window. It had taken awhile to figure out what a floor-to-ceiling window was—that he couldn't walk through it. But the man had taken care of that by installing venetian blinds. Still . . . those chickadees and squirrels flicking their tails as they scrapped for cast-off sunflower seeds were tempting.

The man brought him water. The man brought him crunchy, dry pieces of food that stuck to the roof of his mouth and clung to his throat. Was he expected to eat this? At first, he refused—waiting for, longing for, the iron smell of blood and the taste of wild flesh. Waiting. Looking to the window. Waiting . . . until the man knew, and fresh red meat appeared among the kibble, moistened with warm water. Devouring the meal, he licked the bowl clean and the man was pleased.

Is that all the man wanted? It was easy enough. Walking to a potted plant on the floor near the win-

*dow, Clue lifted his leg. "NO!" the man bellowed,
rushing toward him and grabbing a leash, opening the
door and taking him outside. The man led him to the
bird feeder, empty now.*

*Let me run. Let me free. Let me go. A few minutes
later, he followed the man obediently back inside the
house, turning his back on the woods that was once
his domain. He would stay here. He would stay with
this good man who talked to him and liked him. He
would follow him from the house to the barn and lay
on a blanket at his feet while the man worked at a
table surrounded by broken, beautiful things. And try
not to long for all that was missing.*

Brunettes are better than blondes/blondes are better than redheads/redheads are better than brunettes/
brunettes are better than?

"Make up your mind, honey. Anyhow, with your
cheekbones, what's it matter? You know you're beautiful."

"Stephan, if I ever doubted you were gay, I apologize. All you see when you look at me are *cheekbones*?"

The mirror reflected back a woman of thirty-two,
looking more like twenty-five, auburn waves surrounding an oval-shaped face and flashing green eyes
accented with eye shadow. Her small, nicely rounded
breasts were balanced by smooth hips slightly too
wide to please herself, but about which no man had
ever complained. Seated there, in tweed jacket, slacks
and a crisp white blouse, knowing she could turn
heads merely by wanting to, her bearing, her heart,
her vibrant electricity knew no bounds, and only
enhanced her mystery.

"But you always know what to say," she said, smiling, even though, today, he couldn't be further from the bull's-eye.

"Honey, I know what to say 'cause *I been* there. What's got you down? Decompressing from the holidays? Oh, what am I saying? It's gotta be a man. You always change your color when it's a man."

"*Blonde* works for *me*, Sweetie," said a recently puff-lipped, large-breasted stranger dressed in a turquoise smock from the next seat.

Felicia shook her head playfully and her curls bounced with life. "Not a man this time," she said, feeling every set of eyes upon her. "Wish it *was*!"

"Don't we all, honey," Stephan said wistfully in the baritone that made a comedy of his feminine side. "Don't . . . we . . . all."

Smiling at the colorful parade of lovers passing through their lives, Felicia managed a wistful smile. "I like parades," she said. "Make it *redder*."

"With blonde highlights," Stephan added.

"With blonde highlights," she almost whispered, though, what for, she didn't know. "The dogs'll love it."

"They don't deserve us, *those dogs*!" Stephan said, pulling on a pair of rubber gloves as tight as his plastic pants.

"Not that it's even remotely possible you and I are talking about the *same thing*," Felicia teased. Gathering her hair in both hands, she gently leaned back in the chair and lowered her head into the sink.

"Oh, I hear ya, baby," Stephan said, flipping his blonde pony tail and laughing with a satisfied frenzy that meant *I gotcha*! "But what other subject than men can there possibly be?"

Felicia McCrory: Always thinking of herself as the chubby girl from Florida with dancing eyes and frizzy brown hair her mother tied with rubber bands.

Felicia McCrory: Self-made dog trainer with her own booking at Wheeling Downs, the richest game in town.

The call from Mark Whittier a few days before had caught her off guard.

"Clue? Of course I know him. Blue fawn with a white chest. I raised him," Felicia said cheerfully, from her office. "How's he doing?"

This doesn't sound like somebody looking for a lost dog, he thought. But "The National Greyhound Association told me you're his owner," is what he said.

No longer able to concentrate on the whelping report she was filling out, Felicia put down her pen. "Well, I used to be," she said. "But they've made a mistake," she continued, removing an earring and switching the phone to her other ear. Not that removing an earring made understanding him any easier, she realized. But in the movies it was something that seemed right for a woman to do, and she liked the move. "That's better," she said, "now I can talk. *Carl, turn down the radio!*" she suddenly hollered. "Sorry about that," she said, returning her attention to Mark. "My brother likes loud opera."

That her brother's opera sounded a lot like Top 40 made no difference, Mark decided.

"Thanks for taking my call," he said, starting over. "I'm trying to find the dog's owner."

"Is anything wrong?" she asked, her forehead creasing with concern.

"I found him running loose on the mountain. Or, I should say, dying on the mountain."

"Dying?" she asked, her voice, her manner radiating an edge, the cuticle of her thumb beginning to throb from the pinch of the nail of her forefinger. No matter what, any dog she raised would always be hers.

"I was hiking a couple of months back . . . I thought I saw a deer—or maybe a mountain lion, I couldn't tell, and I wanted to find out," Mark explained, to the deepening silence between them as he filled in the details. ". . . killed and ate the feathers," Mark finished.

"He must have been *starved*! When was this?"

"Back in November," Mark said.

"*November*! But Clue left here last *spring*!" she said, anxiety flooding her now. "How bad is he hurt?" she asked, knowing a hawk would fight to the death and a Greyhound wouldn't give up.

"A paper shredder would have been kinder," Mark said, reliving the awful scene. "He was practically gutted. Skin hanging off his chest, down his ribs. I never saw anything like it—and he didn't let out a whimper. You'd never believe how many stitches it took to sew him up."

"Why didn't anybody tell me?" she asked, not caring if it took a thousand stitches, a ton of medicine, all the money in the world.

"We didn't *know* about you," Mark said, trying to calm the anxious woman. We had to save his life! He lost so much blood, the vet didn't think he was going to *live.* Then, with the holidays—I guess I just wanted to make sure he was OK first. I was going to put an ad in the paper, but the vet told me I could probably find out by starting with his tattoo number."

"I want to see him," Felicia said, her voice strained. "How do I get there?"

"He's OK," Mark said. "Almost all patched up. Stretched out on my couch, legs twisted in the air like a pretzel. I never knew a dog like this before. He's really different."

"Well, untwist that pretzel and wake him up. Are you on a portable phone? Let me talk to him. *Then* tell me how to get there."

Amused by her demand, but feeling perfectly natural about it, Mark walked over to the sleeping dog. "It's not a portable," he told her, "I *think* the chord'll reach." But she was already assuring Clue, to the dog's instant joy, that everything would be all right. Momma was coming to get him.

"It's a long drive," Mark said, interrupting the long-lost souls. "I'm not sure you could find us." But telling Felicia anything and expecting her to listen were two things not likely to happen. Of course she could find him, she said. Besides, if he wanted to locate Clue's rightful owner, he needed her help. Why he would need that, he wasn't sure. But realizing nothing he could say was going to change her mind, he conceded. "OK. But if you get lost and hungry, stay away from hawks on the mountain."

Mark hung up and settled back into his favorite chair. Did he really want to give the dog away or was it because he couldn't resist the temptation of meeting this woman who raised him? Had he learned nothing from countless newspaper reports documenting the evils of Greyhound racing? he asked himself. Or was the very danger of it all attracting him?

The phone was a great equalizer. A man could tell a lot by the inflection of a woman's voice: the natural flow of her responses and conversation. Felicia McCrory was a dog trainer of considerable success. She would be tall, he imagined. Heavy-set and commanding. A modern-day woman consumed by self-interest, permitting nothing to dissuade her from what she wanted.

Jitters hit his belly when he thought of her instant reaction, her questions and the tone of surprise melting into unabashed concern.

"Tell that boy Felicia's comin' to get him!" Like a woman used to giving orders and having them followed. He went to his desk and his computer.

Researching her name, *googling* her, as they say, he discovered that Felicia McCrory was somewhat of a legend in Greyhound racing. Starting in partnership with a few friends, she had raised a litter of pups and managed to get them all on the track. A year later, all six made it to Grade A, proving the lady knew something about raising dogs and putting her on the Greyhound industry map.

Yet, nothing prepared him for the woman he was about to meet just a few days later.

She was ravishing. But it was ravishing in a hard-to-explain, I-don't-care kind of way.

Felicia "I Don't Care" McCrory turned out to be physically opposite to everything he had imagined. A slim woman, she was almost a tomboy. But more than that, she was a vibrant redhead: a woman whose every thought, every expression, every manner radiated awareness of her surroundings and a strong love of life.

Sporting a neatly ironed blue and white striped shirt and pressed blue jeans that she filled out to perfection, Felicia got out of her car.

"You poor baby!"

Rushing straight ahead, she ignored everything but the Greyhound wagging his tail and folding his ears softly at the sight of her.

"Come HERE, boy! Come here. Oh, look at you. LOOK at you!" she said, worrying over him, running eager hands over every nick in his skin, every missing patch of fur while the dog adored her.

"I can't believe it!" she said. "I can't believe I'm seeing him again! I mean, I *believe* it. But . . . holy— excuse my French—I mean, wow, he looks great!"

"If you like stitches," Mark said.

"Oh, we can see past that," she said, reminding him that dog trainers could forgive temporary setbacks. "You're taking fantastic care of him. His *condition*! Look at his muscling, the definition across his back, his shoulders and legs—where'd *that* come from!" she stopped suddenly, touching Clue's scarred rump.

"That?" Mark joked. "That's his butt. A gift from God."

"Many a butt can make that claim," she laughed. "But I'm talking about this," she said, pointing to several oddly shaped bald patches of skin where hair refused to grow.

"From the track," he said.

"Where on the track?" she asked, cautiously. "The first turn? The backstretch?"

"I don't know," he said, sensing her sarcasm. "Don't you?"

"I've never seen any scar like that before," she said.

"But the vet . . ."

"Does your vet really know, Mark?" she asked in a weary tone of voice. "The track is my *life* and I've never seen scars like that before."

"But he's got cuts and scrapes all over him."

"Yes, and he just about got eaten by a hawk," she said, standing tall.

"It was the other way around," he reminded her.

"Maybe so," she agreed. "Greyhounds are always getting into trouble, scraping their legs, cutting themselves on one thing or the other. Their skin is so thin. It heals up just about as fast as they can run and, most times, you can't even tell. But something like this," she said, gingerly touching it again, "must have been a pretty big sore."

"But I've always heard—"

"I can guess what you've heard," she said with a sigh. "I've got it memorized. You probably heard they get bedsores and bare asses from us keeping them in cages twenty hours straight. Yes, I know. Well, I grew up around the track and I've never kept a dog penned up in a crate for twenty hours. They would pee their crates and, I can tell you, I don't like that idea much. Anyhow," she said, smiling playfully, "it would ruin the nice, thick carpet I bought to line our crates with and pad their little behinds and elbows so stuff like this doesn't happen. Not to mention the damage being crated so long can do to their muscles and kidneys. That doesn't make a winner on the track," she said. "Exercise does. So now you can put that widely circulated rumor right out of your," she sized up his profile and patted the back of his hair, "cute head."

His head, he thought, standing his ground but slightly embarrassed.

"Oh, don't pretend you never had a compliment," she said, turning their attention away from him. "Look at this butt!"

Whose butt, Mark mused to himself, admiring her tush and quickly returning to matters at hand when she caught him.

"Eczema?" Mark tried again, taking a wild guess.

"Your vet would have known that," she said. "Did he give you any salve?"

Mark shook his head. "No. And my vet's a lady. She prescribed pain medication and antibiotics."

"And, she just blamed it on the track," Felicia concluded. "Well, why not? It's easy enough, and you'd never know any different. Thanks for letting me see him," she said, turning to leave while she still could.

"So soon?"

"I have to get back," she said, petting Clue thoughtfully. "It's a four-hour drive. Did you try any of the adoption groups around here?" she finally asked. "That's where I'd start."

"I don't understand," Mark said.

"That's funny," she said. "I thought everybody knew about them. Well, every breed has a network of angels," she explained. "Great Danes, Collies, you name it, they've got people looking out just for them. We used to have a guy working for us, and on weekends he'd haul pets for some of the kennels. I know he delivered dogs someplace around here."

"Which explains how Clue got this far," Mark said. "But not how he ended up a stray."

She was miles ahead of him.

"I'd better be going," she said, turning to leave. "Thanks for letting me see him again. I'll see what I can do."

"Aren't you taking him with you?"

Was she hearing things? With a look of near disbelief, she said, "I'd *love* to."

"Well?" Mark said, offering her Clue's leash. Clearly, Felicia loved her dog and the feeling was mutual. Had a dog ever wagged its tail more?

"You missed me, boy?" she asked in a way that made the dog—her dog, no matter where he lived or with whom—tingle all over.

Did dog owners go to school for that sing-songy tone of voice, Mark wondered, or were they born knowing its cadence?

"Well, I guess that's it then," he said, handing over the vet bill and refusing to look at the fickle dog so easily forgetting him now. "Mother and child happily reunited."

Standing up to face him, pushing her hair back with a hand more manicured than he expected of a woman raising dogs, Felicia appeared to be surprised.

"But what about you?" she wondered.

Were her eyes really the color of the Atlantic ocean?

"He's not mine," Mark said, relinquishing his claim to a dog who obviously knew where his heart belonged.

Tilting her head as if he were speaking Swahili in the North Pole, she asked, "You want me to tear him away from *all this*?" She smiled. "He wants to *stay*."

Maybe he hadn't heard her correctly.

"He wants to *stay* with you." She smiled again. "He told me so."

"Told you so?"

"Just now," she said. "Couldn't you hear it?"

"I didn't hear any such thing," Mark said, unsure if she was serious or teasing.

"You didn't? Well, I could have sworn on a stack of Bibles he said it right in front of you. He said, Let me stay with this guy. Let me stay with Mark."

"Wait a minute—"

"Gotta run!" she said, glancing at her watch.

"But I thought—"

"I've got a dog running tonight."

"You're not going to take him with you?" he asked in disbelief

"Old Chinese proverb," she said, handing Clue's leash back to him. "Save a life and it's yours. Which is why some people don't get involved, I figure."

"According to the National Greyhound Association, he's still yours," Mark said. "You came all this way—"

"To *see* him," she finished. "Just to see him and know he's all right. That's all I needed. Just to know he's OK."

"But he's your dog."

"We'll work on that," she reassured him. "I'm not sure how it works, once a dog's given up for adoption. This never happened to me before." Why did she feel like she didn't really want to leave?

"Let me know when you figure it out," Mark said, looking at her, wishing she would stay. Why did his mind always go blank at times like this?

"In the meantime," she said, "why don't you come

to Wheeling? And bring Clue along. It's only a few hours away and you can see how he lived."

"Sounds interesting," he said, tucking the vet bill back in his pocket.

"Maybe it'll give you something to tell your friends when they stop you on the street and ask if you rescued that handsome dog of yours." Men, she thought to herself. You have to bring them along slowly. Right now, Clue was safe. But how did he slip through the cracks? And, speaking of cracks, where did those wicked-looking scars come from?

It certainly wasn't that Mark hadn't been attracted to her instantly. But he was a busy man, he told himself. He was building a business right now, and nothing could stand in his way. There was no time in his life for distraction or fantasy. Not for the self-employed.

Give it up, he told himself.

Felicia . . . Felicia with the naughty green eyes . . . eyes that had seen more than they wanted him to know, eyes still hoping for magic and easing right under his clothes.

No time, he reminded himself.

No time for an exciting woman?

Not now. Not yet. Not until the business . . . until what?

Until he was an old man? An old man with a business and nothing but a *dog* to keep him warm?

It had always been like this: survival first, then pleasure. Making his way in a world with no mercy wasn't easy. It was a world ready to run over you and not look back.

"Trade all my baseball cards for your bike!" offered the boy he used to be.

"Nah," another kid said, standing there.

"Come on, you can sell 'em for more than your bike's worth."

"I don't think so," the kid squirmed, unable to take his eyes off the shoebox of baseball cards wrapped in rubber bands.

"Tell you what. I'll let you take a pack of cards home with you. There's twenty-five cards in a pack. You look through those cards and see if you couldn't trade off half of them and keep the rest. I'll trade for the bike. You'll trade off half the cards for whatever you want and still have more than any of the rest of the guys."

And so it began. Cards for a bike, a bike for tickets to a game, tickets for more cash than the bike was worth, cash for trinkets at a public sale of household goods. By ninth grade, he was a regular at flea markets, stashing treasures in his grandfather's art studio.

"Mark, you know that crock you picked up at the sale? The brown one with the dark blue designs? Ask your grandmother to pick some flowers and bring it to me," his grandfather would say from behind his easel. "And ask her to put on an apron and bring along her broom."

Their doors shutting out the world . . . silence louder than any words . . . their laughter of the kind only known by lovers.

Sneaking into the studio later that night, hands sweaty, knees soft as the cloth under which it was draped, Mark faced the painting: *Swept Off My Feet.*

Could he ever love like they had loved?

Could anybody love like that today?

Lips, skin, hair, scents of passion from one body to the other. Life had a way of taking things into its own hands, he was discovering. Just when you give up on romance, it comes knocking on your door.

Why does the phone always ring just when you're in that deep *deep* sleep? Fighting off dragons that turned out to be bedcovers, Mark dropped the phone, picked it up again and mumbled something not even remotely sociable.

"Well, good morning to you, too," Felicia said.

"Oh!" he stammered. "It's *you*! You sound different . . . is everything OK?"

"*Ah-hem!* . . . Sure . . ." she said, clearing her throat like one who stayed up all night. "I didn't get to sleep, talking with my mother, solving the problems of the world." She paused. "Am I calling too early?"

"It's late . . . early," he said, correcting himself as he glanced at the alarm clock glowing in the dark.

"Oh," she said, embarrassed. "I'm sorry. I shouldn't have called."

"No, it's all right."

"Sometimes I forget people actually sleep at night."

I try to, he almost said. "Do you always torture men this way?" he asked.

Stillness fell between them. "If it's too early . . ."

"No," he said, knowing sleep was out of the question. "Five-thirty in the morning is just fine."

"Come on," she laughed. "We've already fed and

watered the dogs and turned them out to play. I'm on a break. Want some coffee?"

"Spike it with hot chocolate and rum if you want to get my attention."

"A mucho-mocha man," she cooed playfully. "Twice the *umph!*"

"*Twice* can be good," he teased.

"Twice *can* be good," she cooed, smiling. "Want to know why I called?"

"Tell me it's because you care," he said, sliding out of bed and making his way to the kitchen. "Not now," she heard him say, but not to her.

"Uhmmm . . ." she said, suddenly not sure of herself.

"I'm here," he said, giving her his full attention, clicking on the coffeepot and going back to bed.

"You're not alone," she realized. "I didn't know."

"No?" he said, seizing his chance to play, suspecting her call was premeditated. "Well, 5:30 in the morning is a good way for a woman to find out. Do you want to say hello?"

"No!" she said, just a bit too quickly. "I mean," she said, trying to regain her composure, "what would I *say?*"

"You'd *say,*" Mark smiled warmly, savoring his turn at the controls, "whatever you *like*, because my guest doesn't understand a word of English."

"Oh," she said, a certain electricity ebbing from her voice now. "You're into foreigners."

"It does make things, *s'il vous plait*, interesting," he said, smiling.

"French style," she said, disappointed. "I see."

"Last night—"

"I don't want to *hear* about last night!" she said, abruptly.

"But don't you want to know what we *did*?"

"No, I don't want to know what you did! What kind of woman do you think I am? Look, this was a mistake," she said, catching her breath. "I shouldn't have called. Enjoy your mocha. Say goodbye to your *paramour* for me."

"What if I don't *want* to say goodbye?"

"To me or your friend?" she wanted to know.

"Neither," he said, and she could feel his grin.

"In bed with one and on the phone with the other. You're *sick*!" But she didn't hang up. "I thought . . . last night. Oh, *forget* what I thought! I'm sorry! This was a mistake. I shouldn't have called!"

"Ooooo, that feels good," she heard him whisper.

"I'm hanging up!" But she didn't.

"You should feel this tongue," he said, deviling her. *"Stop it!"*

"Put it *there*!" he laughed playfully.

"Disgusting!" she said, threatening again to hang up. He knew she wouldn't.

"Oh, come on, Felicia. Be nice."

"I'm letting that up to your *friend* there," she said, asking herself how she could be so wrong about someone.

"Suit yourself," he said nonchalantly. "But a man can get awful lonesome playing with his dog."

Very awkward silence now.

"So . . . *that's* what you were doing?" she asked.

Not sure what she meant at first, but suddenly getting the picture, he burst out laughing. "Is *that* what they call it where you come from?"

"Well, what are you *laughing* about?" she scolded. "This is too *good*!"

"Oh, I'm *sure it is*!" she said, like one being left out of a joke. "Don't let me interrupt your pleasure— I'd never want to do *that*!"

"*You* think—" he started.

"Don't *worry* about what I think!" she fired back. "I'm a big girl. When you're done laughing, say good-bye to your *friend* for me. Next time, I won't call when you're in bed."

"Clue," he called, turning to the dog tangled in his bedcovers. "Felicia says goodbye."

Like a pebble sliding into the Grand Canyon, Felicia's heart dropped.

"Uh-oh." She took a long breath. "I'm in trouble." Not knowing what else to say, she took a deep breath and counted silently to ten. "You must think I'm a goddam idiot."

"No, I don't," he said.

"No. I'm an idiot."

"Suit yourself," he said, amused.

"I shouldn't have said what I did."

"Why not?" he asked, drawing her out.

"I shouldn't have just assumed you were—"

"*Playing* with myself?"

She couldn't answer.

"Come on, Felicia, *you're* what I was playing with," he said. "Can't you tell? But if it makes you feel any better, there's a 34-D redhead in the shower, a juicy blonde dripping for me in front of the fireplace and a pair of Barbie twins knocking on my front door with their tits."

"I deserve that," she said, genuinely meaning it.

"What are you going to do with me now?"

"Well, at the moment, I'm thinking about all kinds of possibilities. Mostly X-rated."

She paused. "Umh," she said, trying again, "the reason I *called*—"

"At this ungodly hour, interrupting my wild party."

"Yes, at this *ungodly hour*, is because I was thinking."

"I've had a sample of your thinking, thanks."

"Ouch. But it just so happens, it was Clue I was thinking about."

"Clue. The one licking my feet."

"Right," she said, gathering her courage.

"What I was thinking about . . . I mean, it's up to you, since he's your dog now. What I was thinking was . . ."

"I'm waiting," he said.

"Well, what if we, you and me, us. What if we went together and—"

"And what?" he asked, enjoying those X-rated ideas.

"Well, Clue's in such good shape and all now, I thought maybe you'd like to try running him."

"In a race, you mean?"

"Not just one race, Mark. I couldn't know for sure until we'd try. But I think he might be pretty good."

"So *that's* why you're calling," he said. "And all this time I thought it was because you liked me."

"*Like* you!" she scoffed. "I'm through with men! And if I wasn't before, after this I should be. I'm calling about your dog."

"The one between my—"

"Don't!"

"You don't want to know what he's licking *now*?"

"All I want is for you to think about my offer," she said, knowing he would pick on her to his heart's content. "Mark, if you turn him over to me, I could train him for you and he could run right here, at Wheeling, like he was supposed to."

"Mmmmmm . . ." Mark moaned, pretending to be distracted. "A little more to the left . . . yeah . . . *that's* it."

"Mark!"

Bursting with laughter again, having her *exactly* where he wanted, he said, "I don't know. I'm getting to like this."

"*Now* who's into torture," she said. "All right. Fair enough. But you're missing out on a thousand a week."

Was that a thousand a week she just said?

"Your share," she said. "Plus fifty percent of any stakes," she added, just to sweeten the pie.

"You'd pay *a thousand a week*?"

"The track would," she said. "If he's fast enough. He's bred for it, Mark. His sire set track records and his dam was a powerhouse."

"You're serious," he realized.

"Of course," she said. "And he's almost all patched up. As fit as he is now? Another couple of months and he'll be good as new. Maybe better! He's just not the same dog he was. He's different. Keener, somehow. More alert. It's not just his physical condition. I can tell there's something more . . . *alive* about him now. I can't put my finger on it, but I believe in him, Mark. With my help—*our help*, I mean—he could be a champion."

So, champions looked like Clue, he thought, saying he'd call her back.

"Promise?"

"Promise."

Hanging up, Mark swung his feet to the floor and Clue jumped off the bed, following him through the living room to the sliding glass doors that opened to the wooden deck.

He liked this time of morning. Opening the door and letting the dog trot outside, he liked the smell of fallen leaves still wet from the night and the feel of dry coal heat on his naked skin.

Fir pines and boxwood he had planted gave a peaceful touch to the solitude of his home amid the open meadows that once pastured his grandparents' horses. My house now, he thought. *My house, my shop, my life.*

"You," he said affectionately, knowing that the Greyhound, tensing and shaking with excitement at a squirrel too savvy to catch, couldn't hear him as he watched through the window. "Don't bother going after that one," he said aloud to the dog that was changing his life. "Unless you can climb trees." A small matter which nobody bothered telling Clue he couldn't do, Mark noticed, as the dog leaped against the tree trunk.

But could he run again?

Did he *want* to?

A dog couldn't talk. No, he couldn't do that. But if he could, if Mark could get inside the dog's mind, what would Clue say?

If only Mark knew more about the sport he was flirting with, not just the woman.

Clicking on his computer, he searched for Grey-hound racing—only to meet site after site knocking the "cruel" sport of "forcing" dogs to run. Scrolling past gruesome pictures that would make any dog lover cringe, he found himself asking why anyone who loved dogs would allow the world to see such tormented images of them. Weren't you supposed to respect what you love? Enhance it? Make it beautiful and show it in the best possible light?

No web sites from the industry? he asked himself as he continued his search. Nothing to contradict the dominance of rescue, rescue, rescue? From what were the dogs being "rescued"? How could a sport prosper under such a flood of bitterness? he wondered. How could any business thrive under such public disapproval? If the critics were right, the sport of dog racing would have disappeared long ago. Was it possible the experts were wrong? Even *remotely*?

Felicia McCrory believed Clue could be a champion. Would a dog lover mutilate or starve her own champions? Could someone like Felicia be so cruel and horrible?

His mind swirling, Mark considered the graceful dog romping outside his window. Clue was so different from any other kind of dog he had ever known: a dog that could twist himself like a cat and run like a deer; a dog that could look at him with dark eyes possessing a life of their own; a dog making him remember things he had never done and places he had never been.

His grandfather had often said *the outside of a horse is good for the inside of a man*. What was it about this Greyhound that struck a chord in him?

Searching further, he could find very little information about the sport that had started nearly a hundred years ago in this country, but so long before that in the sands of time. A hundred years of American tradition being held accountable by restless protesters caught up in the frenzy of bringing down their prey.

Like attracts like, he realized. People resemble the nature of their pets. The old and ancient code of attracting what we, ourselves, are inside.

Was the Greyhound industry defending itself? Or, like the sight hounds it honored, was it staying focused only on the game?

Which side was more true to the nature of the dogs it loved?

In a race for the ultimate prize, which side would win?

He dialed her number.

"Well, that didn't take long," she said, a note of victory in her voice. "I guess we know what motivates Mr. Whittier."

"What motivates Mr. Whittier," he said, knowing she didn't, "is truth and curiosity."

"Hidden Farms?" he asked the security guard at the gatehouse of the racetrack kennel compound.

"Who did you want to see there?" the man asked, noticing Clue in the passenger seat of Mark's truck.

"Felicia McCrory."

"And who's calling?" he asked as he picked up a phone and dialed.

"Mark Whittier."

"Pull over there," the man said, indicating a parking space. The westerly sun made elongated shadows near the building where he parked. A few minutes later, a smiling Felicia pulled up in a bright red van. "Mark! Clue!" She smiled, not getting out. "I have to make a run back to the farm. Hop in!"

Felicia, the dog-raiser . . . Felicia taking him to her farm and a dog race. Farms, he had seen before. But he hadn't exactly grown up wanting to see a dog race. He was busy, remember? Watching a dog race wasn't like trying to make every day go faster, every year, until you hit sixteen and could get a car. Or like cutting your driver's teeth on the steep and narrow roads she was sailing over and he was trying not to watch.

"Nice view," he gulped, swooping down the mountain. "No guardrail."

"I grew up on these roads," she said. "Well, not really. I grew up in Florida mostly," she explained. "But I know these roads like the back of my hand."

Good, he thought, gripping the door handle tightly. If these were the kind of chances she took, this was a whole lot bigger than a dog race they were on.

He had seen kennels before, but not great kennels. Like others from Lancaster County's farm country, Mark had grown up around dogs of all kinds. But he had never seen a facility quite like this.

A matching house and barn, red with white trim and cedar-shingle roofs, appeared among a grove of evergreen trees and flagstone walkways lined with neatly trimmed boxwood bushes and flower beds blanketed in last night's early snow.

"Must be beautiful in the summer," he said.

"It's beautiful now," she responded, explaining that the place had once been a goat dairy. "I love it here," she said, pulling up to a small building that appeared to be a milking parlor next to the barn. "Sometimes, I pretend I'm living in Switzerland."

"Easy to imagine," Mark said, taking in the mountains and fields between which the farm was nestled.

"I'll just be a minute," she said, leaving the car running. A moment later, she returned, setting a heavy cardboard box in the back seat.

"What do you grow out there?" he asked, noticing a field with rows of fence stretching as far as he could see.

"Champions, we hope," she said. "It builds their competitive spirit. One of them barks and they all take off, like a wave on the ocean."

"An ocean of Greyhounds," he said, picturing it. "I can see why you wouldn't want to live anywhere else."

Returning to the compound at the track, Felicia stopped at the guard's station, checked in, and they drove past the chain-link gate.

Immediately, Clue raised to attention as Greyhounds of every color announced their arrival.

"He knows," she said.

So this is how racing dogs live, Mark thought. They don't look bad off to me.

"Surprised?" Felicia asked, pulling her scarf closer around her neck as he took Clue by the leash and they made their way along an icy path.

"A little," Mark said, not admitting it was a great deal more than that.

Inside, the warmth of the building, light scent of disinfectant and freshly shredded paper wrapped themselves around him. The floor was washed, every table wiped, every window spotless.

To their left, a lanky young man in jeans and white T-shirt was grooming a large white and brindle dog.

"He's running tonight," Felicia said, waving.

The dog, or the man, Mark wanted to ask, feeling

somewhat out of place. But she was all business. This was her turf. These were her dogs and her employees.

Heading for the kitchen, Felicia gave a busy woman a hug. Obviously, that one was more than an employee, Mark realized.

"Look who's here!" Felicia exclaimed, turning the woman around to face Clue.

"I must be seeing things!" the woman said, having fun. "Take me now, Lord!" she pretended, raising an arm, pressing the back of her wrist to her forehead.

"Doesn't he look good?" Felicia asked.

"Well, I think he looks *great*!" the lady said, startling Mark with her striking resemblance to Felicia.

"Twins?" he asked, but knowing otherwise.

Appreciating his compliment, the woman smiled, but said, "No," as she held up her hands like an old dish-washing liquid commercial, "*I'm* the *mother*."

Turning to Mark with a wink, Felicia said, "Hard to look old when you have your first child at eight. Right, Mom?"

"Right," the brown-haired woman replied, pinching her daughter hard.

"Ow!" Felicia rubbed her arm and made the introduction. "Mark here, is the one who found Clue."

"Kenita," the lady nodded, pronouncing her name distinctly. "Nice to meet you."

"My pleasure," Mark said.

"I just love this dog!" Kenita said, giving Clue a hug. "Carl, get over here and see Clue!" she hollered to the young man.

"Almost done here!" he called back.

"You should have seen Clue when he was a puppy," she said, not even noticing his stitches. "How's my boy?" she sang to him. "How's Clue?" she asked, as the dog brightened to the familiar sound of her voice. "Skinny as hell, he was!" she said to Mark. "Couldn't get him to eat no matter what. But he always had that personality, you know? You couldn't keep this boy penned up in anything! He could jump over a fence six-feet high!" she said, admiring how much he had grown.

"Perfect for Europe," Felicia added, as Clue basked in their attention. "What do you think? Should we set up a branch there?" she asked. "In Europe," she explained to Mark, "some of the dog races have jumps like steeplechase horses."

To Kenita, she added, "Are you making sure everybody gets those new vitamins?" Then, reaching for a bottle of fish oil capsules, she looked to Mark, and explained, "For shiny coats," as she popped one in her mouth, too.

"How often do you feed the dogs?" Mark asked.

"Twice a day," Kenita said, counting out the aluminum feed bowls. "Mornin' and night," came the steady reply as she adjusted her glasses and mixed fresh green beans and hard-boiled eggs in a blender. "Carl," she said to her son, who was joining them now, "this here's Mark, by the way. He's the one Felicia told us about."

"Hey, Mark," the dark-haired young man said as they shook hands. Were those eyes really the same color as Felicia's, Mark wondered? "How ya doin' fella?" Carl said to Clue, patting the Greyhound strongly and scratching his back. "They love this," he said, all smiles, as Clue arched his back and swayed side to side. "So I hear you're a bird dog now, huh?"

he said to the dog.

"After what he did, I don't think any bird is safe," Mark replied.

"Well, he's got a good home now," Carl said. "That means a lot."

"Ready for the main dish," Kenita announced.

Carl removed a large cardboard box from the refrigerator, slid it onto the table and cut open the plastic bag inside to reveal fifty pounds of fresh, raw chicken backs and necks. Turning to Felicia, he asked, "Did you bring the extra box?"

"In the car," she said.

To Mark's look of mild surprise, Kenita said, "Didn't your mother ever make chicken soup or pot pie?"

"Yes," Mark said. "She did."

"I thought so," Kenita said. "Felicia told me you come from the Pennyslvania Dutch country."

"We just don't happen to eat our chicken raw," he said.

"And you're not a dog."

"What about . . . " he struggled for the right word, "salmonella?"

"Getting sick, you mean?" Kenita said. "No. We've never had any problem with that. I'll tell you what we do have though," she said. "Good clean teeth. Show 'em, Carl. Show him The Blue Queen," she said proudly.

Walking over to a pair of crates, stacked like bunk beds, Carl opened the upper crate and helped a sleek blue-colored Greyhound to the floor.

"Here, girl," he said, taking hold of her head and opening the dog's mouth.

"Go ahead," Kenita said. "Smile for the nice man. Have you ever seen pearly whites on a dog?"

"Who's her dentist?" Mark asked, amused.

"Dr. Chicken Bones," Kenita said. "And his assistants, The Green Beans," she added. "Something about 'em helps."

"The only thing we want on a dog's mind is winning the race," Felicia explained. "Anything bothering them has to be eliminated. Would you run your best if you had a bad tooth?"

Secrets of success, Mark thought.

Carl pulled on a pair of rubber gloves and pitched in, grabbing handfuls of raw chicken.

"Straight from the butcher," Kenita said. "Two hundred pounds a day. Breakfast, it's kibble, goat milk and special supplements. For supper, they get chicken, ground up greens from the blender, hard-boiled eggs and more goat milk."

"Goat milk?" he asked.

"Nothing better," Kenita-the-kennel-chef added grandly. "We raise our own goats at the farm, just so it's fresh."

"And vitamins!" Carl added.

"Chicken, goat milk, greens, eggs and vitamins," Mark said, making sure he understood. "They eat better than I do."

Make yourself useful." Felicia smiled, tossing another pair of rubber gloves at him and pointing to the box. "Carl, can you help me get the rest of the dogs ready?"

"Is dinner part of this arrangement?" Mark asked, holding up a chicken leg good-naturedly.

"I like a sense of humor in a man." Kenita

laughed. "This guy's OK, Felicia! No," she said, to him, "around here, we like our chicken bar-be-qued!"

As for the dogs, she explained, "You don't want 'em running on a full stomach; so, no, the one Carl was working on, and the others running tonight, they get their meal after the race, when they come back. But you mustn't forget their special massage, and always be sure to check their nails, teeth and all the rest."

"Can't have nothin' bothering 'em if you wanna win! That's your *paycheck* you're messin' with!" Carl said, showing good common sense. "Besides," he added, "they can get awful cranky when they don't win. Some of them can't even stand it."

He liked these people. They were easy-going and down to earth, the kind of people you could talk to.

"It's Mom's fault," Felicia explained. "She worked as a waitress at a restaurant near Hollywood, outside of Miami. On her days off, she'd take us—me, Carl and our sister—to the track so she could play the horses with her tips."

"I was *lucky*, too!" Kenita added.

"You sure were," Felicia told her, with another hug. "Mom's luck bought our farm when we moved here."

"Thanks, honey," Kenita said. "We gotta stick together."

"Hey," Mark nodded in Carl's direction, having some fun. "Sure you don't want a piece?"

Carl lightly stroked his fledgling goatee and just smiled. Clearly, he knew where to get a *piece* of whatever he wanted, whenever he wanted it.

Allowing them their diversion, Felicia briefly filled in the rest of the details about her married sister,

Jeanie-Beth, who left and moved back to Florida. She paused. . . . "Ever married?"

"A few close calls," Mark said, hiding any note of regret.

"More than one?"

"Yeah."

"Well, trust me," she smiled, knowingly. "It ain't all it's cracked up to be."

Everybody laughed, knowing maybe it wasn't always the greatest, but marriage was still worth a try now and then.

"I'll remember that," he said in a way that left her wondering just how often he had tried.

Marriage wasn't a game to be taken lightly. But it was never far from Felicia's mind. Hang in there, little Johnny and Mary, she thought to her imaginary kids.

"How's he look?" she asked, and, by this time, Mark knew she was talking about a dog.

"Like a champion," he said, not knowing what champion race dogs looked like, but pretty sure he knew quality.

"Bet on him," Kenita said with a firm nod of her head. "You'll make money."

"Think so?"

"We're almost top kennel this year so far," she said proudly.

"Cross your fingers!" Carl yelled from where he was leading another dog to the waiting trailer. "Felicia knows how to train 'em."

"Well, it helps to have a good team," Felicia said with a modesty not easy for her to come by, Mark guessed.

"Well, now that you know where your dog comes

from," Felicia said, "would you like to go to the races tonight and see what he did for a living?"

"Love to," Mark said.

"Good," she said, explaining where they could meet. "I've got a lot to do before then," she said, "but Carl can stand in for me later."

"I got a date!"

"That one from the bar?" Kenita asked loudly.

"Maybe," Carl said.

"*After work*, buddy-boy!" Kenita said in tones offering no compromise.

Felicia turned back to Mark. "We can meet at the back of the casino . . . downstairs, at the betting windows. I'll be free around seven."

Recalling a few antique places he had seen in town, Mark said he would be there. "I look forward to it," he said. "What about our friend?" he asked.

"You can leave him here," she said. "I'll fix up a crate for him, with his favorite shredded paper—did you know he only likes 20 lb. stock? A printer in town saves it just for us. This'll be good for him. He can get the feel of things again. Would you like that, fella?" she said, as Clue wagged his tail.

Making their way between rows of sleeping dogs in spacious crates, some on plush carpet, others snuggled in fluffy nests of paper like candy in an Easter basket, she found Clue's spot.

"Nice touch," Mark said, about the brass nameplate designating his special place.

"First class." Felicia smiled, tapping the crate to get Clue's attention. "Go to your room," she said to him. Surging into the crate, playing with his bedding as if finding a long-lost toy, Clue nuzzled deep into the fresh paper, turned around several times and settled comfortably.

Felicia pushed aside the curtain and stood by the window, watching Mark as he walked to his car.

Felicia and Mark, she thought . . . it was nothing serious, nothing new. She always did that with a man she liked. *Felicia, Mark and little Johnny.* Felicia, Mark and little Johnny in a perfect house with blue shutters, and salmon, purple, lavender and white impatiens. Felicia, Mark, little Johnny, little Mary and Clue.

"He's beautiful," she said out loud.

"Uh-oh," Carl moaned.

"Felicia . . . Felicia," her mother said, shaking her head with a knowing smile.

"I'm talking about *Clue*!" Felicia protested, to Carl's sarcastic, *"Right!"*

"I'm serious," she went on.

"We know," Kenita said. "Every time a good looking man drops—"

"Oh, my virgin *ears*!" Carl shouted, covering his ears and rolling his eyes playfully.

"Carl, I wasn't gonna say his *pants* and you know it!" Kenita said, throwing a dog brush at his head and missing him by a mile. "What I *meant* was, every time Felicia falls in love, the kennel takes a dive."

"Not this time, guys," Felicia shook her head. "I'm just talking about Clue."

"Don't hurt the guy, F'leesh," Carl said, talking about Mark again, but thinking of his sister, too.

"Oh, he's safe," she said, letting the curtain fall back into place and walking to the sink to wash her hands. "For now," she winked. "How many dogs are we running tonight, gang?"

"Five, all together," Carl said.

"Ready to load up the rest?" she asked.

"Who the hell are you talkin' to?" Kenita fired back, picking up the pace and raising the excitement. "Of course they're ready! *We're* not the ones spending all afternoon primping for Mr. Right. Carl! Go get Jumbo and Big Boy and put 'em in the trailer! I'll get the girls," she hollered, heading down one of the far aisles. "Hey! Who moved Blue Queen? If it wasn't for me, this whole damn place would fall apart! Where's Dee Dee?"

"I switched 'em around cause they were messin' with each other and Dee Dee couldn't get any sleep," Carl hollered.

"You let your hands off The Blue Queen!" Kenita scolded. "That's her crate so she can look at me in the kitchen! I got her toy in that crate. . . . Where's her toy? She can't win without her toy!"

"I gave it to Dee Dee!" he snarled, pressing as many of his mother's buttons as he could.

"Whooooooo did you give it to?" Kenita asked, narrowing her eyes and putting her hands on her hips. "Did I just hear somebody say somethin' *stooo-pid*?"

"You know damn well *who*," Carl said, of the little bitch he co-owned. That she was four years old now, had never made a dime for him, and cost him a fortune besides, wouldn't compromise his hope that o*ne day* . . .

"Carl-boy, the day you win a $2 bet on that mutt is the day she can have any crate in this whole damn place!" Kenita griped, turning her back so he couldn't see her gleeful smile. Picking on her kids could be so much fun. "Get a move on!" she shouted as gruffly as she could. "We're gonna be late! We were never late when *Barry* was here!" Carl wasn't the only one who knew how to press buttons.

"This what you're looking for?" Felicia asked, holding out a stuffed green koala bear.

"*That's* it!" Kenita snapped, swiping the toy from Felicia's hands and tossing it to an eager Blue Queen.

"Baar-ry, Baar-ry, Baar-ry!" Carl whined as Felicia put her hands to her ears and moaned "Oh, Ghod!"

"Baar-ry was never late!" Carl screamed. "Baar-ry grew up in the *business*! Baar-ry's *father* grew up in the business! Baar-ry's *GRAND*father grew up in the business. Where the hell's *BAAR*-RY now?"

Hard work, minimum wage, no questions asked.

Barry Dunmoyer was a drifter with track experience and a craggy smile. All Kenita wanted was the kennel to survive Felicia's divorce.

"Does it pay enough for me to take the boss out to dinner?" he had asked.

"I'll let you decide about dinner. My *daughter's* the boss," she said, her face suddenly feeling warm.

"Is that so?" he smiled, broad face, wide teeth. And real. "Clever, putting your daughter in charge like that. Is she as pretty as you?" he asked boldly.

"Flattery can get you just about everywhere," she said, "but it don't give you a raise."

"*I'll* be the judge of what gives me a *raise*," he said

with a devilish grin. "When do I start?"

From the sound of it, he was starting right now. Here was a man she could pick on and get away with it. "Why don't you turn out the boys in that bottom row?" she told him.

Did she really say *turn out the boys*? "Do you have a place to stay?" she said quickly, hoping to cover up her Freudian slip.

"Not yet," he said, not getting it. "I thought I'd ask for a week's advance so I can find myself a room."

"Who'd you say recommended you?" she asked cautiously.

"Jimmy," he said, as if there were only one Jimmy in the world. "Jimmy Miller from Airstream Kennels. You know him, right?"

Asking Kenita if she knew anyone at the track was like asking a commander if he knew his troops. "My son Carl's his caddy sometimes," she said. "What did you do for him?" she wanted to know, as in what kind of favors were owed.

Looking her in the eye like one accustomed to stretching the truth if he had to, Barry said, "Nothin'." She could handle that, she decided. Knowing you had a liar to start with made it easy when you had to fire him.

"We've got a bunkhouse for the help back at the farm. Nothin' to brag about. Bed, bath and a hot plate. But it's clean. And you're gonna keep it that way," she said, pointing at him. "Cross me once, and you're out," she said, in the manner of one who had seen her share of help come and go.

"No problem," he said, slipping muzzles on the dogs with one smooth motion. This one wasn't going to be easy, he decided. "I'll make it work 'til I get my own place."

Returning to the kitchen area after the last of the dogs had trotted to the turn-out pen, Barry paused in front of an upper crate. "Hey, there, girlie. You look like you could win a race or two."

"That's The Blue Queen," Kenita said with pride. "Keep your hands off her."

"Yours?" he asked.

"Lock, stock and barrel."

"Graded?"

"Stakes," Kenita said. "I'm waiting for her to come in season."

"Who you breeding her to?" he asked, like a connoisseur of pedigrees and bloodlines.

"Molotov," Kenita said. "But Statesman or Fortress could do the trick."

"Top of the line." He smiled, understanding why. Stakes meant Kenita's bitch had won big money.

"Only the best for The Blue Queen," she replied.

"Yeah," he grinned, glancing at the table. "I got that feeling after watching you slip her that oatmeal cookie."

"Nothin' wrong with a treat for being good. When did you see that?"

"Through the window when I was getting up the nerve to knock on the door."

"Peeping Tom!" she said, laughing. Earthy. Full. Like one starved for laughter.

"Yeah, but my name ain't Tom," he said. "Any more of those cookies?" he asked, taking a chance, and, in a way, unable to help himself.

"Why don't you turn out the other bitches first.

Then I'll put on some coffee and we can find out," she said, smiling.

Had she really said that?

"Oh shut up and get in the truck!" Kenita screamed now, fluffing her coat and pulling on a warm wooly hat.

If only dogs could talk, thought Felicia.

"She's in rare form tonight," Carl said.

"You shouldn't pick on her," Felicia retorted.

"Keeps her going," he said.

"Maybe. But you know she misses him."

"I know. But she's got us, right?"

"Right," Felicia whispered, almost to herself.

"You coming?" he asked.

"I'll be along," she said. "Take care of her."

He knew he would, knew he always would.

Felicia waved goodbye to her brother and mom as they drove off, and she returned to the kennel alone. Inside, she switched on her office light and studied the rows of photographs framed and neatly lined on each wall. Each picture a win, each picture a story, she thought to herself, going to her files.

She had imported the Irish pups with such hope: two gangly pups from a prize litter, frightened, shivering and fussed over by dock workers after arriving at Kennedy Airport.

"What kind of puppies are *they*?"

"Greyhounds," she said, pushing her fingers through the slats of their sturdy, wooden crate fitted with brass hinges and latches.

"Pretty," somebody said, of the male pup nuzzling her hand.

"*Powerful* is what I'm hoping for," she said, transfixed by the puppy's wide chest and strong-looking legs.

Taking the folder from its drawer now, she sat at her desk shuffling through notes, copies of vet bills, and clippings from British and Irish sporting magazines . . .

"New Racing Dynasty in the Making . . . "

"Greatest Greyhound . . . "

"Derby Winner *Some Picture* Found Dead . . ."

Everything but a registration certificate for the blue-fawn Greyhound. Thinking back, trying to remember the names of the dogs who had gone to Pennsylvania with Barry that day, Felicia pulled their files as well.

Except for one important detail, all appeared to be in order. Missing from Clue's file was not only his registration certificate, but also the receipt she always asked for from the adoption center.

Classy touch, the home office sending Esmeralda's personal driver for him. Maybe he should complain to the boss more often, he thought, on his way to the airport as he tried putting things into perspective.

If all this was about racehorses instead of Greyhounds, he would be flying to a convention packed with officials from Churchill Downs, Philadelphia Park, Santa Anita and every other track in the *Daily Racing Form*. That's power.

"Thanks," Claude said, as the driver pulled up to the entrance of Harrisburg International's terminal building. "Say hello to Esmeralda and all the Collies for me," he said, taking hold of his suitcase and getting out.

"Will do," the man nodded. The von Havenburg kennels were famous for their Collies, going all the way back to 1945. That was power of a different kind.

Making his way to the ticket counter, cursing the airline's demand that he be there two hours early, Claude checked in, found the departing gate and stood in line.

"What's with this shit!" a heavy-set woman in sneakers and yellow sweats in front of him blasted as they stood in line taking off their shoes. Inspectors numb to insults of every color, variety and creed, accustomed to such insults, ignored her.

What must they be thinking of us, Claude wondered. Were they the enemy? Could weary inspectors spending all day watching gray plastic trays of valuables gliding through x-ray machines on a conveyer belt have the stamina to organize international government take-overs by night? Inspectors weren't the enemy, he reminded himself, wiggling his toes and rocking back and forth in his stockinged feet as the woman in yellow was told to step aside.

"What! What the hell are you doing with that thing!" she squawked to the inspector wielding a long metal detector. "Get your hands off me!" she croaked to the uniformed woman taking her by the arm and leading her away as the rest of the passengers, like cattle in a slaughter chute, pretended not to notice. "Don't you touch me!"

Walking calmly through the metal detector, breathing a sigh of relief, Claude collected his belongings on the other side. Stooping to tie his shoelaces, he couldn't help but shudder. No matter how easily his gold watch and other valuables had passed through, something far more important hadn't made it. Back there, along with an astounded yellow woman spread-eagled by airport security guards running a hand-held metal detector up and down her butt, was his dignity.

Waiting now to board, he found a seat and took out his laptop. . . .

From: Emerson@dejazzd.com
To: Researchdept@SATV.com
Subject: High Stakes

Thank the home office for early morning lift. Nothing like Tina Turner screaming on the radio to wake a guy up.

From: Researchdept@SATV.com
To: Emerson@dejazzd.com
Subject: High Stakes

Tina Turner wanting to know *What's love got to do with it?* could be more profound than you realize. From what I'm uncovering, passion rules when it comes to animal rights. The very name evokes parental feelings, yet it's somewhat misleading. There appears to be a major discrepancy in the public's understanding of the term. I haven't had a chance to do any surveys, but going by the slant of most reports in the media, it doesn't take much to see that most people don't know the difference between animal rights and animal welfare. I've been able to dig up a few books on the subject. Will ship to you in Vegas. You're booked into The Mirage. Esmeralda's compliments. BTW, I checked with the business office and the driver didn't come from them.

From: Emerson@dejazzd.com
To: Researchdept@SATV.com
Subject: High Stakes

The Mirage? That's more like it. I lost a girlfriend to Steve Wynn and maybe I'll look her up. I don't know what old Steve looks like by now, but *this* boy's been working out. <G> OK, cut the crap. I know I smoke. And, pass me a beer while you're at it. OK, pass me two beers. But I am going to the gym. One of these days—honest. I'm working on that six pack.

What have you got for me on this convention we're headed for?

P.S. About the driver. Don't wear yourself out. He was Esmeralda's. I knew she had an inside scoop. Count on it.

From: Researchdept@SATV.com
To: Emerson@dejazzd.com
Subject: High Stakes

As you know, you're flight leaves from Harrisburg International and you arrive in Vegas tonight. The convention is for the AGTOA (American Greyhound Track Operators Association). I'm finding a lot of initials in this industry: GRA, NGA, AGC, just to name a few. And that doesn't even touch the initials of the ones against them. You'll be attending seminars of all the latest developments in the Greyhound business. Have fun.

From: Emerson@dejazzd.com
To: Researchdept@SATV.com
Subject: High Stakes

I hardly think it's going to be fun hopping a flight when you don't even know if you'll get where you're supposed to go these days. The real trip is who you meet along the way. Not that the airlines, themselves, aren't entertaining. The plan against terrorism, it seems, is simple: Bankrupt the airlines and mess up everything as good as you can. That way, even the bad guys can't depend on flight schedules. What's the point of hijacking a plane if the engine's so bad it can't get off the ground? What's the point of planting a bomb if the flight's going to be late?

You can find out a lot by hanging out with somebody. I'm finding out Whittier talks to his dogs. Not out loud. No, this is a self-made man and he does things his way. Whittier talks to his dogs by *thinking*. And he believes *they understand*. He believes a lot of things, I'm discovering, and I'm not sure where belief starts and reality ends.

From: Researchdept@SATV.com
To: Emerson@dejazzd.com
Subject: High Stakes

Well said. But what you're in the middle of right now is very real. Did you know some of the most well-known animal rights groups are listed as terrorists? And states are passing laws against them?

CHAPTER THREE

Perfect Timing

Home again, Clue lay among others of his kind. To his left, a black and white dog lay curled up in his bedding, the sheen of his coat reflecting the moonlight from the kitchen window. To his right, a brindle male lay on his side, his head raised on a pile of bunched up paper, his pillow. Above them, were smaller dogs, mostly females or young males, who knew how to jump easily into their boxes. They were in their rooms, their dens, their private spaces in a world far bigger than themselves.

He was warm here, protected. Not like his nights on the mountain, when every moving shadow kept him awake, and every sound chilled him.

Mark . . . Felicia . . .

Drifting off to sleep, running across the grassy hills of Ireland, he remembered his littermates, the sound of Irish voices and the safety of being home.

"Talk about a quickie!" Mark said, as eight dogs rushed across the finish line that night. "Just blink and it's over!"

"Yeah, but *that's* the kind of quickie a lady can like!" Felicia laughed, figuring out how much she had won. "Now, pay attention to the next race and I'll tell you what to look for."

"Should I place a bet?"

"No time."

"Heeere comes Spunky!" the announcer said, drawing their attention to the row of numbered boxes to their left. The doors flew up, dogs rushed past and Felicia leaned close.

"See how Number 6 is hugging the rail?" she winked. "If you want to get something done, you gotta do it from the inside. My grandma told me that."

"Good advice," he said, as the inside dog took the lead.

"The dog that gets to the first turn in the lead, that's the one that usually wins," she explained. "You have to make sure your dog has the stamina to hold on to the very last hundredth of a second."

"I can see that," Mark said, as the lead dog, so brilliant at first, began fading at the far turn. "Guess it's back to the gym for that one."

"If he was mine, I'd give him some time off. Freshen him up, you know?" she said.

"Works for people," he agreed, thinking of vacations in the Bahamas that had done the trick for him.

Ten minutes later, she squealed, "Our race is next!" jumping up and down like a teenager.

"Must you help with anything?" he asked, hoping she didn't.

"Carl's got it covered. Look!" She pointed. "There's Jumbo wearing the green jacket!" she said, as attendants walked their athletes to the starting boxes.

"Just like the post parade at a horse race," Mark observed.

"I still get excited," she said, taking a deep breath. "Nervous?"

Standing on her tip-toes, she nodded.

"Heeeere comes Spunky!"

Bursting from the boxes, the Number 4 dog lagged slightly behind the others, and time stood still. Heat building from his chest to his neck to his head, hands forgotten, Mark leaned forward and knew—just knew—that it didn't matter. It wouldn't matter if the dog won or lost tonight. If he lived to see a thousand races or if he ended up in a wheelchair strapped to an oxygen tank like the man who owned Smarty Jones when he won the Kentucky Derby, it wouldn't matter, because this was it. This was the truth Mark was searching for. Right here. Right now.

"Come on, Jumbo!" Felicia hollered as the dogs flew down the homestretch like gazelles. *"Come on!"* she screamed as her dog took charge, grabbing the lead by three lengths and crossing the finish line first. "*Woooooh!* Did you see that? Did you see it? He came up from behind and closed like a roller coaster. I raised that pup!" she yelled to everybody within earshot. *"That's my dog!"*

A few races later, each as exciting as the one before, hazy smoke rose up through tropical palm trees as they made their way up the stairs and into the casino. Not exactly little Switzerland, Mark thought, recalling that afternoon and Felicia's farm. But this whole adventure was out of place somehow.

One minute he was at home, working in his shop with a beautiful dog at his feet, and the next, he was finding out more about the dog's life than he ever imagined. Same dog, but different worlds; each world complete, acceptable; each with its own rules, codes, characters and mystery.

Here, nobody picked a winner by looks, political party or a myriad of other class distinctions.

Here, in this bizarre oasis, winners—dogs as well as people—were those who were strong enough, smart enough, fast enough to cross the finish line first.

His faith shaken—what he had just seen didn't compute with what he had been told about the supposed evils of dog racing—Mark hesitated. Should he ask her? Would she tell the truth?

"Welcome to the Island!" Felicia said loudly, over ringing bells, tumbling coins, groans of defeat and screams of elation. It wasn't unlike the disharmony of an orchestra priming for a concert, he thought. Yet, what astounding effects the maestro could make.

"Quite a performance out there!"

"I didn't know you were in show business!" she said, over the noise.

"I'm not!" he called back.

"Well, *I am*! Welcome to my *stage*!"

"It *is* pretty entertaining," he agreed, remembering how his chest swelled when her dog rushed to the front and crossed the wire ahead of the pack.

"You mean you aren't *offended* by all the *fun* the dogs are having?" she wanted to know, her jab tapping his psyche. "Never mind," she said, as he floundered for an answer. "Just tell all your friends you saw a dog race and everybody went home happy. That is, if you have any friends *left* after you say it," she added, with a knowing tone.

"Did you have any money on him?" he asked.

Shaking her head, Felicia laughed. "Mom's the real gambler in the family," she said, finding a table in the restaurant so they could watch the races on giant closed-circuit TV screens. "Ten to one, she bet a hundred on Jumbo."

Knowing the odds, Mark figured Mother McCrory had just fluffed her nest by a few hundred feathers. "Does she bet often?"

"Every time we run," Felicia said, as the wine steward approached them.

"I never drink," she told him sweetly, as Mark ordered a glass of merlot. "It's not good for you."

"So I've heard." He smiled indulgently. "But one thing experts are consistent on is changing their minds."

"I hear *that*!" she laughed. "Fat's bad for you—oh, no, it's good for you. Puh-leese!"

"So, your mother bets on the dogs," he said, after they had a good chuckle.

"Often and well," Felicia smiled. "Dogs that we raised and ones we lease too. If she's in charge of feeding them, she's going to bet on them."

"Maybe it's *you* she's betting on." Mark grinned, knowing *he* would. He'd bet on her any chance he had.

"Don't let appearances fool you," she said. "It's Carl she's betting on. Mom and I have had our differences. Oh, we get along—now. But she wasn't always so thrilled with *this* child, let me tell *you*!"

"They say we're toughest on the ones who remind us of ourselves. Something about not wanting them to make the same mistakes."

"You're a psychologist?"

"My Dad was, and I guess it rubbed off," he said.

"Human nature is just about the most fascinating, unpredictable thing I can imagine. Don't you agree?"

"If that's your way of guiding me into saying what you want to hear, I'm sorry to disappoint you," she said.

"I'm hurt."

"No, you're not," she smiled. "You'd be hurt if I was easy."

"Easy isn't bad."

"When you're coming out of a divorce from a man your *mother* adored a lot more than *you* did, it is."

"Why would you marry a man you didn't adore?" he asked.

"Well, I did—adore him. At first. That's when he was the best trainer in the business. I couldn't get him out of my mind. Nobody could beat his dogs on the track."

"And that's why you married him?" Mark asked. "Because he was the best trainer?"

"Power is the greatest aphrodisiac," she responded. "And trainers are everything in this business."

"What happened?" he asked, breaking his rule never to mix a woman's past into the chemistry of their first meeting.

"You don't want to know," she sighed. "Another time, maybe. What about you?"

Ah! A woman of considerable dating experience, he realized, as he pretended surprise at her curiosity.

"Me?" he asked, as if nothing about him could be remotely interesting to her or anyone else.

"Married? Kids?" she pressed.

"Not at the moment to the first; and, sadly, no to the second."

"I sense a common bond here," she said, brightening.

"Tell you what," he said. "Maybe I'll take you up on that offer and we can swap stories another time."

"Fair enough," she said. "Or, maybe we should just stick to dogs. It's safer!"

His laughter said volumes.

"Well?" she went on. "A *dog* won't ever leave you, right?" Although there was something sad in her comment, he didn't ask.

"Unless his name is Clue," he said, opening the door again to how such a dog was lost.

"Only he knows the answer to that one," she said, mysteriously. "I still wish I had known he was missing."

"Can I take your order?" asked a waitress, or was it the young woman's cleavage speaking.

Raising her eyebrows without a word, Felicia peeked over the top of her menu.

"Lasagna sounds good," Mark said, not quite able to raise his eyes to her face.

"Hi, Cindy," Felicia said graciously in the diplomatic way perfectly mastered by women reminding each other of their marital status. "How are Bill and the kids?"

It had been just another run for Barry that day. Rain, gray skies and another bunch of dogs finished at the track. Petted out for any of a hundred different reasons, but mostly because their owners only wanted to keep the very best. After all, they reasoned, it took just as much to feed a champion as a loser. And they were right. He took care of the rejects, the ones nobody wanted, the ones nobody cared about any more. He did what he had to. He did it for the dogs.

Barry liked dogs. He liked them a lot better than he liked people. He knew how to raise dogs and make them into winners. Not for their owners; for the dogs.

Because the dogs liked to run.

Barry fancied himself a better trainer than just about anybody else. He ought to be, he reminded himself. After all, he was raised in the business; his father had been a trainer, too, and his grandfather was there back in the days when it all started. That was a lot of dogs and a lot of know-how to carry around on a man's shoulders.

If they had gotten the breaks, he told himself, the name Barry Dunmoyer would have been right up there with the best of them. Right in the Hall of Fame!* They would have been going to Abilene just to see the Greyhounds of Dunmoyer Kennels. Dogs like *Rooster Cogburn*, *Westy Whizzer* and *HB's Commander*? Those dogs had nothing—*nothing*— over what the Dunmoyers raised and trained on their farm in Oklahoma.

"Come on, boys," his grandfather would say whenever they heard of a new track opening up. "We got money to win! Barry!" he'd holler, asking about the dogs' grooming. "Did you make everybody shine? Did you do their nails for 'em? We don't want any of our dogs pulling a toenail on some track they don't know."

---

*Greyhound Hall of Fame: A popular tourist attraction in Abilene, Kansas, that celebrates the "Greats" of the Greyhound industry, drawing fans worldwide.

"Yes, Grandpa! I made 'em shiny!" And he did once. Once, just to make his grandpa proud, he took nail polish from his mother's room and painted every toenail on every dog they had.

Nobody noticed.

From their classified ads in sporting magazines, Dunmoyer Kennels soon had customers from all around the country asking for puppies.

"Champion Quality Racing Greyhounds From Stakes-Winning Bloodlines" is what they proudly boasted, and what people came to expect. But good things don't last forever. Only bad things do, Barry told himself.

Like that big story on *60 Minutes* everybody was so excited about. *National publicity!* National publicity all right. Grandpa having a heart attack right in front of the TV set when it turned out to be a one-sided exposé.

The dogs went first.

It was spooky, walking around empty kennels with nothing to do. But it was the strangers that bothered him most, bargaining for furniture and taking pictures off the walls, leaving a house that had never felt so haunted.

Grandma was next.

They said she went home to visit relatives in Montana. She never came back.

His father, once busy full time working the Dunmoyer Greyhounds, found work pouring cement and pounding nails in the city.

His mother, who once shopped for a hundred champions, just packed a lunch bag now from the third-floor apartment and ignored hecklers whistling at her pretty blonde hair.

Barry? It didn't feel so good working for somebody else.

Not when you knew as much as he did.

"So, what's it like being in the Greyhound business?" Mark asked, starting their dinner off.

"Wonderful," Felicia said. "I can't imagine being
in anything else."

"You seem so," he paused, "involved with it."

"Totally."

"And, you don't have any regrets," he added.

"Sure, I wish more people would understand it,"
she said. "That's a regret. But part of me wants to
keep it all to myself. My own private world, you
know?"

"But what about all the criticism in the press and
online?" he asked. "Doesn't it bother you?"

"That? Oh, we can handle that," she said in a way
that held more meaning than the words themselves
conveyed.

"Less competition, you mean?" he asked, not
entirely sure of himself.

"Now you're cookin' with grease." She winked.

"You mean the activists in the press actually . . .
serve you?"

"Some people think so. Mark, let me put it this
way. The biggest opponents to gambling—to all this you
see around you—aren't spending their time in church."

She had said it so nonchalantly.

"Then where are they?" he asked.

"Running other casinos," she said, smiling, as if anyone couldn't figure that out.

"Double lasagna," Cindy the waitress announced, placing their orders on the table in front of them.

"Looks delicious," Mark said. "Sure you don't want any wine with that?"

"No, thanks." Felicia shook her head as she buttered a dinner roll.

"OK," Mark said, "then tell me why you didn't do what I've been asking myself about?"

"What could that be?" she said, shaking her napkin and spreading it delicately on her lap.

"Clue," he explained. "Since I get the feeling you regret letting him go, why didn't you stop it? Why didn't you get him back?"

"Good question," she said. "You'd think there was a waiting period, a protection of some kind for owners who change their minds. Or, in case there was a mix-up and it's the wrong dog. But it doesn't work like that. No, once your dog is in their clutches," she said, blowing on a fork full of steaming cheese and sauce, "your rights are over. Ooooo! Hot!" she said, fluttering her hand to cool her mouth.

Careful, Mark thought. We wouldn't want anything to happen to that particular asset.

"Who's idea *is* that—your ownership rights being over? Has it ever been tested in a court of law?"

"Probably not," she said honestly. "Pretty much, the whole adoption scene is people trying to do the best they can and everybody stepping on everybody else's toes while they do it. But the idea, itself, is a brilliant one. A win-win for everybody and something the industry endorses—really wants! As long as people don't stab us in the back to make sales, so to speak, adoption's great."

"How do they get the dogs?"

"From us."

"Do they pay you for them?"

"No. They get them free."

"Free?"

"That's right. And they turn around and sell them to the public. I know it's called adoption, but it's really selling."

"I don't see how any of this helps the sport," Mark said, confused.

"Well, if it works the way it's *supposed* to, it can be great for the sport," she explained. "See, most of the dogs adopted out aren't good enough to go back into breeding programs at the farms. Not all," she said, wanting to be clear. "But I'd say, the majority."

"OK," he said, going along with her. "Finding good homes for them makes sense."

"It's a good plan—when it works," she added. "But right now, it doesn't seem like it's going on a very uplifting course," she said. "There's so much *anger* and a lot of breeders don't want their dogs going to *any* adoption group because of it."

"What's everybody mad about?" he asked.

"It's mostly people who don't like racing," she said. "They infiltrated the adoption network and they pressure the public into taking dogs out of pity."

"Any way to get a dog a home, I guess," Mark said.

"But it's dishonest, Mark. It doesn't work. When pity wears off, some people realize they never *really* wanted a dog and they end up giving it back. Pity can turn into resentment before you know it."

"So the dog loses," Mark said, realizing now why she didn't fall all over herself just because somebody might wear an adoption hat.

"After they retire," Felicia explained, "the industry tries finding homes for every dog. When you love 'em, that's what you do. And good dogs are a great advertisement for the sport. Walking billboards!"

"Clue's one," Mark said. "Every place I go, people come up to me. He's a great babe catcher," he winked.

"I wouldn't know," she said.

"So, wait a minute. Now that I'm going to be taking care of this dog . . . "

"Babe catcher?" she asked sweetly.

"Yeah," he smiled, continuing, "I want to know everything I can. Like, if he never ran," Mark reminded her, "then how could he retire?"

"Clue retired early," she explained. "Remember, I said he wasn't a chaser? Well, your dog's got to lock into the mechanical lure when he's running—really focus with all his heart—or else he's going to lose interest and slow down and all kinds of things can happen. At those speeds, a dog can trip and hurt the other runners if it slows down. That's one of the most important things a trainer has to be sure of. For safety alone at those speeds, the dogs *have* to be chasers."

"Who would have thought?" Mark said.

"Remember," she pointed out, "in a dog race, you don't have jockeys to guide them or pull them up and get them around any trouble. Everything you see in a dog race is natural. This is truth, Mark, as true a form of competition as you can get."

He could see that. "So, a dog that's chasing after something is going to be looking straight ahead."

"Correct," she said.

"And, if all the dogs are looking straight ahead—"

"It's safer, because they aren't worrying about the dogs in back of them or to the side. You're training the body as well as the mind."

"OK," he agreed. "And, so, if a dog doesn't have the natural instinct to chase after Spunky out there," he said, referring to the mechanical lure they had just seen whizzing around the track at 45 miles an hour, "he's a danger to himself and all the other dogs."

"Precisely," she said. "And if it's something the dog just doesn't have in him, a lot of old-timers say you shouldn't breed a dog like that."

"They believe it's an inherited trait?"

"Yes, they do. I don't always agree with that," she said. "Because maybe it has something to do with the pup's life growing up. I mean, there could be lots of reasons. Looking back on it now, I can think of ways I could have tried getting him to chase. But I ended up doing what I thought was best for the whole breed. You know, taking the high road. We're the stewards of a great breed of dog," she explained. "It's up to us to keep Greyhounds strong. Nobody else can do it. So, don't infuse any weaknesses into your bloodlines. That's the first rule. And if he could get a special home, which he did," she said, reaching across the table and patting Mark's hand, "I must have done something right."

Her eyes wandered to the next race featured on the giant closed-circuit TV screen. "We've got a dog in this race," she said, crossing her fingers, "Big Boy. I never know how they'll do when they're coming back."

"Back from where?" Mark asked.

"Well, his owner gave him a rest after he broke a hock about six months ago," she answered.

"Sounds nasty," Mark said, shaking his head.

"Can be," she said. "Just like a track star hurting a leg or a football player breaking a bone."

"What do they do about it?" he asked.

"Well, Big Boy got himself a steel rod holding things together; the best of everything," she said, turning for a better view. "I'm surprised his owner didn't fly in from California for the race tonight. It's the only dog he has."

"Heeeere comes Spunky! And they're off!"

As Felicia stared at the screen, lit by the soft illumination of small lamps on every table, her hair framing her face in natural waves, Mark thought he had never seen a woman more beautiful.

The alert confidence of her posture radiated good health, as if every inch of her skin, every sense of her mind and body were completely alive. She was contagious, electrical. She smiled as her dog crossed the finish line. He sat up straighter.

"You believe in old-timers," he observed, sipping his wine. He would say anything, do anything, to hold her attention. "Interesting."

"About Clue, you mean?"

He nodded.

"Of course," she said, dabbing her plush lips with the napkin. "Put 'em together and they've got a hell of a lot more experience than I ever will!"

"In . . . ?" he asked, wanting to hear her, wanting to be with her, no matter what she had to say.

"In everything!" she exclaimed. "Business . . ."

Which was her main interest in life, he noticed.
"Politics . . ."
A subject surely of little or no concern to her.
"Love!" she brightened, like one whose heart had never been broken, no matter what she said about divorce, which wasn't much.
"Interesting subject," he said, his search plane coming in for a landing.
"And one you're experienced in?" she asked, her eyes twinkling.
"That depends on who's asking," he said, shifting his feet and nodding a few times as a warm silence fell between them.
"Maybe I'll ask sometime," she said, after what seemed like a hundred miles.
"So!" he said, clearing his throat nervously and leaning forward. "Clue wasn't a chaser," you said. "Well, what's chasing got to do with anything?" he asked, knowing it had everything in the world to do with love, but would she pick up on it?
"No chase, no desire," she said sadly, with a look of mischief.
Maybe she had.
"No desire, no thrill. No thrill . . ."
Quite possibly, she had, indeed.
"What's the point if there's no thrill?" *Definitely, she had.*
"I see," is all he could manage to say, heat kissing the edges of his ears and running down the back of his neck.
Stacking their dirty dishes precariously on a tray, the waitress asked, "Dessert?"
"Coffee," both said in unison, before looking at

each other and laughing.

Curling her pinkie as if to hook into his, Felicia's expectant look threw him back to his childhood when such synchronicity meant good luck for those who made wishes.

"You know, I had such hopes," she went on, bringing them back to Clue as she stirred a sugar cube into her coffee. "Big plans. I mean, really big. Do you know how exciting it can be, having a stakes winner?"

"No," he admitted. "But I can imagine."

"Well, imagine if your dog was good enough to go from track to track, competing with the best Greyhounds in the whole country, and multiply it a hundred times."

"Heady stuff," he replied, thrilled by her passion, seeing how real it all was to her.

"That's what I want some day," she said. "And Clue was going to be the one."

"I can see how disappointed you must have been."

"I'll just have to go back to the drawing board," she said. "Clue's sister is doing just fine and she has an identical pedigree."

"Creating your big winner," Mark said, showing her that he understood.

"But the minute Barry took him," she went on, "I felt I lost something more important to me than I ever knew. Not like other times," she tried explaining, as she looked at him. "This time, I felt like I was losing something really important in my life. I knew Barry was taking dogs that day. And I always say goodbye to them and thank them for being with us. But I couldn't say goodbye to Clue."

"Goodbye can be very important," Mark said,

wanting to comfort her, not knowing exactly how just yet. "Who's Barry?" he asked, noticing the deep red lipstick on her cup as she set it down. If he was entitled to a wish, he could think of a hundred places he would like to have those lips.

Tonight.

Tomorrow morning.

Right now.

"He worked for us," she said, bringing him back to earth. "Remember, I told you?"

"Oh," Mark said, staring once more at her mouth as she spoke, relieved to find out that *Barry* wasn't a jealous boyfriend.

If Barry Dunmoyer could undo that night, it would have been unraveled a thousand times since then instead of becoming a spinning, whirling ball of yarn growing bigger instead of shrinking with each passing night.

If only the dog hadn't gotten away from him. If only things had gone the way they were supposed to.

It had been going so well. The McCrorys had liked him. The pay wasn't great, but he knew what he was doing and they respected him for it. Finally, he had a future. Why did he go and mess it up?

He had to. If he hadn't, if he hadn't gotten out of there—right then, that night—they would have found out. And once they found out, they'd have sacked him and it would have all been over anyway.

What would he take with him, he had wondered, standing there. They were at the track and they weren't expecting him back until tomorrow. There wasn't much time!

Looking everywhere, afraid to miss anything, trying to remember what to take with him and afraid of being caught, Barry had pulled open dresser drawers and thrown clothes into plastic trash bags swiped from the kennel kitchen, sensing what little he had to show for his life.

A note.

He should write a note, he thought.

If he didn't . . . if he didn't say *something* . . .

Finding a pen, praying it wouldn't be running out of ink like he was running out of time—chances, hope—he wrote. Pausing, he stared at the words, considering how they would be taken. He wanted to crumple the paper in his fist and cast it aside.

Instead, taking a deep breath, holding it and slowly letting go, he folded the letter gently, lay it on the bed beside the cowboy shirt Kenita had given him, and left.

"Don't get me started on all this stuff, Mark, or it's going to ruin a nice evening. This is your first visit to Wheeling and I want you to enjoy it," she said, reaching for a handkerchief.

He was enjoying it. He was enjoying it more than he thought he would, more than she expected. It didn't matter what she talked about. She could be talking about physics and nuclear science and the Mayan calendar and he would only hear her voice, her dreams, the certainty of her convictions.

"More coffee?" the waitress asked.

"Please," Mark said, indicating both cups.

"Oh, none for me." Felicia smiled, covering hers with a hand, revealing smooth skin, as she thanked Cindy.

Hands . . . beautiful hands . . . hands touching every muscle and sinew of a Greyhound's neck, shoulder, back . . . hands running over *his* face, he thought . . . through *his* hair, over his arms, down his back, over his belly . . . lower . . . lower . . .

"One last thing," she said, bringing him back to reality as she finished off her lasagna. "When it comes to adoption groups, I don't want you to get me wrong. They're not all bad. Especially the ones that know they're part of the overall industry and that know how important they can be to cultivating new fans. I do have my favorites. Like, GPA* for example. They have a branch right here. Project Racing Home's another one, and Seaside Greyhound Park's adoption center goes above and beyond the call of duty. But some of them, Mark—and I count some of the biggest animal protection organizations in the nation—well, let's just say my Daddy was in politics and I try my best to avoid what sticks to my shoes."

Downstairs, Carl McCrory reached for his wallet and found the wrinkled scrap of paper on which he had scrawled a phone number before leaving the kennel earlier that evening. Punching in the numbers, he

---

*Greyhound Pets of America: The largest and most respected organization for adopting retired Greyhounds. While some tracks have their own successful adoption programs, GPA chapters can be found at many racetracks around the country, and adoption can be an excellent way to enter the sport.

listened to the distant ringing in his ear. After four rings, a familiar voice answered stiffly, obviously reading a pre-written message.

"Hello. I'm not here, so leave your phone number and I'll call you back. Maybe."

Carl began to speak . . . angrily.

"Barry? Carl McCrory. Remember me?"

A few minutes later, Carl slammed down the phone and stormed back to the holding area at the track.

Mark and Felicia walked outside.

"Back where we started," he said.

"I never met a man who looks at life as a parking lot," she commented.

Seeing cars in a way he hadn't considered until just then, Mark scanned his prospects.

"Maybe they're the bodies and we're the souls," he said.

"A view with some possibilities," she said, falling into step.

"Where to from here?" he asked, looking at her, meaning where to for them.

"Back to the kennel to pick up Clue, I guess, then east on 70 . . ." she said quietly, sparing herself in case that wasn't what he meant.

Standing there in the glowing lights of the casino, he wanted to touch her, wanted to take her in his arms like he was James Bond, saying all the right things, making all the right moves.

He wanted her to put down her weapons, swoon, never let go. But they weren't standing in the aura of an emerald reflecting light from the hands of a holy man.

This wasn't a slick movie.

She wasn't oozing with desire.

He wasn't James Bond.

Later that night, Felicia hesitated outside her mother's room. "Mom?" she asked, knocking. "Still awake?"

"Saints have mercy, go away," came the weak reply from a woman neither Irish nor Catholic.

"We have to talk," Felicia said, feeling the texture of the carpet ease her bare feet as she let herself in, walked over to Kenita's bed and sat down. "It's important."

Moaning about her aching back, sore feet, and what time she had to get up in the morning, yet not considering saying no, Kenita propped herself up with a pillow. "How was dinner?"

"I let him order," Felicia said, though not sure why she had yielded, since the invitation was hers. She paused, uncertain how to continue.

"My daughter having heart trouble again?" Kenita asked. "I can recommend a *legal doctor* who'll straighten you out real fast—Smith, Jones & Miller, Esq. Remember them?"

"Don't remind me," Felicia said, wincing at the name. "Not yet, anyway . . . but I can't get him out of my mind." She paused. "I'm talking about Clue," she added quickly.

"Sure," Kenita said, messing with the covers. "Right," she cleared her throat. "I knew that."

OK with that for now, Felicia faced her mother and asked, "Did Barry lose him and that's why he quit? Clue isn't neutered, Mom."

"I noticed," Kenita said.

"Then you *know* something didn't go right," Felicia said, "and it must have happened before Barry got there. It couldn't have been any other way."

"Well, you know as well as I do, Felicia. With them it's neuter first, ask questions later."

"Thank God it didn't get that far," Felicia said. "His conformation is incredible, Mom. If he can run—if he's anything like his sister—we might have a monster on our hands in time for the Governor's Stake."

"We haven't had a monster around here in quite a while," Kenita said. "But he isn't yours any more."

"I'm not sure about that," Felicia said seriously.

"Why not?"

"It all depends on what happened with Barry and the papers, doesn't it?"

"I guess so," Kenita said thoughtfully. "You can call the NGA and find out whose name they have on his records."

"There *can't be* any other names," Felicia said. "Because he wasn't re-homed. Right? He never went through the whole process and the job was never finished."

"You're thinking, if he wasn't adopted out, then, officially, he still belongs to you?" Kenita said, fully understanding.

"That's why Mark called me," Felicia said. "I must be the only name on Clue's records."

"Makes sense," Kenita said. "What does Mark think about all this?"

"I haven't brought it up yet," Felicia said. "I suppose I could just thank him for what he did and take

Clue back. That's what he wanted. I don't know why I
didn't when he offered. There we stood. He came all
this way to give Clue back to me, and all I could think
of was, how can I get this guy to stay?"

"So you gave him Clue."

"I guess so. I don't know. It just seemed so important for him to see what our life's all about—to *understand*."

"All of us want to be understood, honey," Kenita
said, placing a hand over Felicia's.

"But I've got a feeling about all this," Felicia said.
"Clue's *good*, and I think—"

"You think you want him to have a second
chance."

Felicia nodded.

"And somebody must get in touch with Barry. And
you're thinking me."

Felicia nodded.

"Forget it," Kenita said, shrinking under the covers.

Placing a hand on her mother's foot and jiggling
her big toe until Kenita kicked her away, Felicia
smiled. "Will you think about it?"

"No!" Kenita screamed the next morning. "I don't
want anybody botherin' Barry!"

Turning away, tears stinging her eyes, she pleaded,
"Why did you *do* that, Carl?"

"I wanted him to know we have the dog!"

"No, you didn't. *You just wanted to make him look
bad!* You couldn't stand it, me likin' Barry. Well,
you're the one who's bad, Carl. I'm never going to
speak to you *again*!"

"F'leesh!" he said, looking to his sister. "Tell her!

Tell her I was just thinking of the business!"

"Mom," Felicia said gently. "We know how you feel—honest."

"No, you *don't*!" Kenita cried, inconsolably. "You don't know what it's like!"

"Sure, we do."

"You *don't*! Wait 'til you get to be my age. Just wait!"

How could Felicia—how could anybody—know how it felt looking in the mirror, wondering whose lined face that could possibly be looking back at you? How could it happen so fast? How could you be stupid enough to care about a million other things and let your own body melt away? *"You don't know!"*

"But, Mom," Carl said, "if Barry knows what happened, *he could tell us*."

"And if he doesn't," she said, "he's going to think you called *because of me*."

"No, he won't."

"How do you know?" she asked her son. "You don't know how he thinks. Neither one of you does," she said, looking at them both. "And you never liked him anyway!"

"Sure, I—" Carl started.

"Don't lie to me!" Kenita snapped. "You didn't like him and Felicia didn't either. If he did anything wrong, you'd just love to know. Well, I'm not helping you!"

Funny, how *different* things can be just a hundred fifty miles away. . . .

Barry Dunmoyer tossed his coveralls on a pile of dirty clothes in the corner of his bathroom. Another fifteen Greyhounds delivered. Another bunch saved from the clutches of greedy owners fattening their bank accounts off flabby arms pulling slot machine handles. Another fifteen delivered to greedy adoption guerillas.

Welcome to the dumbing of America, Barry, he thought to himself. You've lived to see it, and you can't get rich on either side.

Reaching for a filmy cup, he pulled out his dentures and gargled.

Instead of brightening his prospects, laughter from the used TV he had found at a local pawn shop only seemed to fill the space of his dimly lit apartment with more clutter. He'd get around to cleaning things up and doing the dishes stacked like quarters in the kitchen. Some day he'd have a housekeeper, he told himself. Yeah, right. Housekeepers were for the rich guys. Housekeepers were for big-time owners who didn't give a damn about guys like him and sure didn't give a damn about the dogs.

He'd show them, he thought to himself, rubbing his aching feet with the same liniment he used in the kennels. Damn that hard cement they made him walk on all day. Cheap bastards. A million a year and they can't afford carpet.

"Shut up!" he snapped to a popular comic as he clicked off the TV. "You make me *sick*."

Taking off his watch, he lay it on the table beside his glasses, wallet and keys, remembering his years in the service. Look at me, he thought. Sixty-two and what have I got? I should have re-enlisted, he thought, pushing the play button on his answering machine. But the damn owners won't give their help a cut. I shouldn't have to live this way! *They're using me!*

Nothing had changed since he made the switch.

"Take 'em around back," the short-haired adoption lady had said as they unloaded dogs on one of his trips.

"Know what your problem is, Barry?" she asked, smiling, handing him a few bucks.

"No. What?" he said, jamming the cash in his pocket.

"Your dogs look too good," she said, walking to a shed behind the old house she operated from. "See them dogs over there?" she asked, pointing to a row of crates. They're not gonna look that good . . . tomorrow," she said slyly, peaking his interest.

"What're you tellin' me?" he asked.

"Those suckers with their *bleeding hearts*! They gotta have a *reason* to open their wallets. *Pity* pays."

"What do you do? Go out back and break a leg or two?" He was joking, of course.

"Oh, Barry," she smiled slowly. You disappoint me. We're more subtle than that," she said, as if sharing a dirty secret. "Could be worth a few hundred to you . . . interested?"

They're using me—*all of them*!

"Barry?" the voice on the answering machine said. "Carl McCrory. Remember me? I want you to know a dog of ours—one you supposedly found a home for— just showed up, and the guy says he found him half-dead up there in the woods in Pennsylvania somewhere. And he wasn't neutered. What's goin' on?"

"Shit!" Barry hollered, swiping his arm across the table and knocking everything to the floor. *That damn*

dog, he thought, his mind rushing back to the desperate animal twisting away from him, leaping, screaming wildly, biting at his arms, then slipping his collar and running for the woods.

Rubbing his fingers, his palms, the back of his fists, he opened and spread his scarred hands wide like two prisoners begging, crying out for freedom. Again and again, he did so, remembering what he had tried so many times since that day to forget. "Damn you!" he said out loud.

Even Marlene Dietrich in *Judgment at Nuremberg* couldn't have said it better.

Damn you!

Shuffling back to his seat, exuding the patience of what Roman god he didn't know—asking himself if there even was a Roman god of patience—Claude found the window seat.

"Excuse me," he said, stepping over the legs of a couple from Ohio. Not saying much, they let him fumble over them. "Why him?" Claude could almost feel them asking. "How come he gets the window?"

Just luck, he figured this time, thanking the Roman god of good fortune and wondering if the couple from Ohio could hear his thoughts the way Mark's dogs could hear his.

"We're on our way home from the Bahamas," Vicky Bastille from Cleveland told him. That was her name. And her husband's name was Ed. Ed Bastille, also from Cleveland. Plumbing contractor, she said.

Nice people on their way home from Nassau.

"Did you have fun there?" Claude asked.

"Oh, yeah!" Vicky laughed, jabbing her husband in the side. "Lots!"

"Where did you stay?" Claude wanted to know, making polite conversation as the rest of the passengers jammed suitcases and bags into the storage compartments above their heads.

"In pink satin sheets in a great big pink palace!" Vicky smiled. "Palm trees, green-checkered carpet and all the windows open to let in the breeze. Oh, I can't wait to go back!"

"Did you like the Bahama Mamas?" Claude asked, referring to the fruit and rum drink.

"*Loved* them!"

Wondering what had taken them from Ohio to the Bahamas, he asked if this was their first trip to the islands.

"Oh no!" she laughed. "We go every few months."

"Every few months?" Obviously not a very busy plumber.

"Yeah!" Lowering her voice, she whispered, "Ed has a special bank account there."

"I see." Claude almost asked what kind, but her whisper told him more than enough.

Further curiosity was interrupted by a flight attendant demonstrating safety gear. Claude sat up. "Ladies and gentlemen, may we have your attention please . . . "

As the attendant finished speaking, the engines surged and the plane sped down the runway for liftoff. Claude felt himself being forced against the back of his seat as the plane rose up like the greatest roller coaster ever imagined, leaned sideways for a turn, and leveled out.

"Life Saver?" Vicky from Ohio asked.

"No, thanks."

"It'll keep your ears open," she coaxed. "You sure?"

"Sure," he said.

"Where are you headed?"

"Vegas," he answered, enjoying the savvy sound of it. Was he coming across like a high roller?

"First time?" she asked him, bringing him down faster than he'd ever want their plane to drop.

"It shows?"

"Just a little," she grinned, nodding toward his hands gripping the handles of his seat.

"Oh!" he grinned, relaxing his grip. "Usually, I go by train," he lied.

"Ladies and gentlemen, this is your captain. We're approaching Pittsburgh International and will be arriving fifteen minutes late. Flight information and arrangements can be made at the ticket counter. Please return to your seats, turn off all cell phones and other electronic equipment, and fasten your seatbelts. Those of you making connections to other cities, information will be available at the ticket counter when you debark. Thank you for flying with us, and be sure to check the overhead compartments for your carry-on luggage before departing the plane."

Inside the terminal, Claude found another uncomfortable, pre-molded plastic seat, this one was blue, and logged on to his laptop. . . .

From: Emerson@dejazzd.com
To: Researchdept@SATV.com
Subject: High Stakes

I don't get it. You send me this info on the sport and I just don't see what's the big deal. Do people get killed in a dog race? Do the fans get hurt? Come on. It's not like the athletes are attacking their own fans the way some sports are getting. Does the government lose money on this, like that one article you sent me says? I can't see why they're taxing sports like horse and dog racing, but not (forgive me for saying this) football or anything else. What's up?

From: Researchdept@SATV.com
To: Emerson@dejazzd.com
Subject: High Stakes

Good question. The government doesn't lose money on Greyhound races. In fact, it regulates them; and when slots go in at a racetrack, the overwhelming percentage of money goes to the government. You're right. More people get hurt from football, baseball, hockey and car racing than from Greyhound or horse racing. Maybe even tennis or golf. And that includes the fans.

From: Emerson@dejazzd.com
To: Researchdept@SATV.com
Subject: High Stakes

But none of those other sports are controversial. Something about live animals racing for the finish line stirs the blood. I know that feeling. I've been there. I'm a jogger. But why is somebody out there trying to sterilize us? Don't you find political correctness just a little boring?

From: Researchdept@SATV.com
To: Emerson@dejazzd.com
Subject: High Stakes

Boring compared to what? In a few generations, we'll be gone and nobody's going to know any different. People with passionate souls will just be called sick, and they'll be put on medication. Do you want me to look anything up on adult Attention Deficit Disorder?

From: Emerson@dejazzd.com
To: Researchdept@SATV.com
Subject: High Stakes

Only if you want to drive home what I already suspect. You can dress up a bully in college degrees. You can spin them in fancy clothes and wash them in sudsy, politically correct soap. But they still stink like bullies to me. Esmeralda knows that. She knows a lot I'd like her to forgive and forget. And now she's got me right where she wants me. On the road to Vegas with a real-life, bona fide crusader. How often does that chance come along? She knows the answer to that: Not often. Keep digging. That Pulitzer's going to look great on my résumé.

CHAPTER FOUR

Casting Call . . .

Howling winds of March awakened the Shenandoah Valley, kissing the Blue Ridge Mountains and ushering in the songs of early spring.

Trumpeter swans, Canada geese and mallards decorated the skies in victorious glory, announcing their survival of yet another winter.

We are home again, their oboe-like cries seemed to say to Mark, as he hiked with Clue on weekend excursions in the secluded grounds of Swananoa, not far from Waynesboro; camped on Chete Mountain, outside of Durbin; and walked beside the winding creek in cattle fields near Bartow.

Hesitant at first, the dog had pressed himself tight against Mark's side, as if the very air between them could whisk his master away, spinning him; spinning him into a whirling vortex from which there might be no return.

Slowly, the dog's confidence returned and flourished, until the slipping off of a delicate leash was no longer felt; and freedom was given so gracefully that it seemed as if it had always been his—rushing through the grasses, leaping over logs, digging into the soft, natural mulch of a rotting tree stump in pursuit of what mysteries were hiding there.

At first, the Greyhound merely trotted, sniffing the scents that took him back to his own mountain, back to before.

Slowly, his legs returned to their former brilliance; his coat glistened and his eyes regained their haunting certainty that he was what he was born to be, wanted only to be.

Seeing Felicia on weekends lifted Mark higher, like the song on the radio said it would. Trips to West Virginia were his thinking time, his time for figuring out where he was really going and how to deal with what might lay ahead. Life was uncertain. These days, life was as unpredictable as the outcome of any race. Like he, himself, was running in the dog races that were becoming ever more important to him, Mark focused on the changes Clue was making in his life.

"Clue!" Mark called out.

The elegant Greyhound, now fully eighty pounds of chiseled muscle, moved effortlessly to his side. It was time: time to fulfill the promise he had made to Felicia.

"Is he a rescue?" strangers would ask, as if there could be no other reason for him to have such an animal by his side.

Laughing it off, Mark would say things like, "Full circle," to their looks of blank dismay.

"Couldn't make it in adoption," he'd say, "so I'm sending him back to the track. Right, fella?" he'd ask, playing with Clue's ears.

To the sound of his master's voice, the Greyhound would invariably arch his back and sway side to side, leaning his powerful neck and shoulders against Mark's leg. "See you at the races!" Mark would say, moving on. But close friends weren't so easy to brush off.

"What the hell are you messin' with dog races for?" they wanted to know, bashing what Mark knew they had never seen for themselves.

How could they, when a sport was all but banned from mainstream TV and the papers. How could anyone follow it?

"It isn't on ESPN," his friends would say. "If it ain't on ESPN, it ain't a real sport. ESPN covers *everything*!"*

Yeah, Mark thought: *Lawn mower races*. "Maybe I like to make up my own mind," he'd tell them.

"Well, don't get us messed up with it."

"And share a sport that's just about the cleanest thing in America?" he asked. "Since when did I share anything?" he kidded.

"Get outta here, man!"

"What do you want from me?" he'd fire back. "You want me to lay around watching football, where they plan the whole game ahead? Come on. What's the fun in that."

"Shit! I don't believe what I'm hearing!"

"Maybe you want me to watch fake wrestling," he said. "There's an honest sport for you."

"Lay off!"

"No problem! But dog racing is the only sport where the dog is king. Hey, I know. Maybe you just can't stand *testosterone*."

"*Fuck* you!"

---

*ESPN: A television network that claims to cover all sports, but refused to broadcast Greyhound racing even if the sport paid for its own air time.

"Only if it's on my terms," Mark countered, shutting him up. "Nobody's out there coaching, telling the dogs what to do, or *making* them run. Nobody's hollering at them, nobody's on their backs *whipping them with a stick* and nobody's putting the pedal to the metal on a machine with no mind."

"So what?"

"*Think* about it," Mark said. "A whole sport purely depending *on the athlete's physical desire alone! Nothing else! That's like the Olympics. That's exciting! It makes my blood rush!"*

"But it's gambling."

"So is the lottery. But here's something you can gamble on and your chances of winning are one in eight."

"How do you figure?"

"Eight dogs, one of them wins."

"Eight?"

"Yeah. It pays down to third place, plus there's a trifecta and a quinella besides. All kinds of ways you can win."

"What's all that shit."

"Quinella is betting on two dogs and it doesn't matter which comes in first or which comes in second, you win!"

"Yeah."

"Trifecta is picking the winners in the order of one, two and three, and that's how they have to come in. Win for first, place for second and show for third. OK?"

"OK."

"Now, a trifecta box means you get paid no matter what order those three dogs come in. But you're also paying three times the amount of money."

"Uh-huh."

"Now there's one more bet you have to know."

"This is too hard."

"The exacta is betting on the first two finishers in the race. But, unlike the quinella, you can only win if they finish in the order you pick. Now, just like the trifecta *box*, you can bet an exacta box. Which means, the two dogs you pick in any order will pay you. It's more expensive, but the payoff is better."

"So, I'm gonna go out and make a fortune on this dog you got?"

"I don't know," Mark said. "I hope so."

"It's the woman. That's all it is. Pussy."

"Maybe," Mark said. "What of it?"

"Hey," his friend said, reminding them both how well they knew each other. "Give me back my bike."

"Give me back my baseball cards."

The hotel was one of those places you sometimes find along old country roads, forgotten by time. Forgotten by the people living there, too.

"What are you getting me into?" Mark asked, knowing if the dog answered back in some way, it wasn't nearly as important as having someone to talk to.

"Is this what Greyhounds are for?" he asked, stroking the dog's noble head.

If Clue could speak, just then he might have said, *"But of course! Why else are we born except to lead our masters where they would otherwise never go?"*

That's funny, Mark would counter. I thought it was people leading you. Dogs were lucky, he decided. All they had to do was find somebody to love.

"Welcome back," said the hotel manager as Mark checked in that night.

"Same room?" Mark asked.

"Near the pet area," the manager said, "Like always."

Mark thanked him, signed the register and took the familiar key.

Once inside the beige-on-beige-on-beige room, Mark took in the matching prints on the wall, the TV and air conditioner. Deciding where to put Clue's feed and water bowls, he took off his shoes, lay down on the bed and found the phone.

"Hidden Farms," came the answer.

"Hey, there," he said.

"Mark! When did you get in!" her voice electric.

"Just now. Come over."

"I'd love to," she purred. "But I can't. Why don't you come over here and we'll get Clue ready?"

"Hey, bud!" Carl waved, as he looked up from mopping the floor. "F'leesh is waitin'."

Leading Clue to the grooming area, Mark stood him in front of a wooden stand resembling a step. "Hup!" he said, and Clue put both front feet up, his back on a slant like a canine sliding board.

"Hand me that sander, will you?" Felicia asked, kissing him on the cheek.

"The Dremmel?"

Reaching out her hand, she nodded yes and plugged in the tool.

So much to learn, he thought. "What are you doing with that?"

"His nails," she explained, picking up a front foot

and examining Clue's nails. "You haven't been taking care of them," she reminded him gently. "Don't you know how important a dog's nails are? It all starts with the feet. A little soreness—like sand between the toes, or a clump of dirt or maybe a tick—can give you trouble. Maybe it's OK for a while, but, next thing you know, a shoulder is bothering the dog. And then a back leg, and before you know it, a broken hock! I've seen more broken hocks from something like that, than from just about anything else. Hocks are very serious business," she explained.

"I'll remember that," Mark said, moving closer for a better view as she squeezed the toenail forward and started the drill. "Ouch!" he joked.

"Don't be silly!" she laughed. "I didn't touch you!"

"My tooth hurts," he teased.

"Scared of dentists, are we?" she said, eyes wild as she held the drill high above his head. "Open up and let me take a look!"

Right into his arms she came, and he was holding her before he could even think. But he had thought about it so often that no amount of thinking would have stopped him. He kissed her above the eyes, on the cheek, on the mouth—and stayed there.

"Mmmm . . . it feels like I hoped it would," she said, finally. "Do you always wait so long to kiss a lady?"

"Only when I'm playing for high stakes," Mark said honestly. Taking the drill from her hands, turning it off and laying it down on the table, he wrapped his arm around her again, hugged her close to his chest and ran his other hand through her hair. "You're beautiful," he whispered.

"I am?" she asked, leading him on. "Tell me more."

"You make everything around you—the whole room, the air, the sky—brighter. More electric."

"You mean, I make static, like in a sweater?" She smiled, swaying with him in a dance to which he could almost hear music.

"You *are* the static," he said.

"But static means standing still, doesn't it?"

"Not the kind I'm taking about," he said, kissing her ear, running his lips up and down the side of her neck, cupping her breast in his hand.

"Whoops!" Kenita, standing in the doorway, yelped. *"Sorry!"*

"Oh!" Felicia exclaimed, pulling back and arranging her blouse as Mark caught his breath. "We were just—"

"Grooming the dog," Kenita finished. "Yeah, Barry was a good groomer, too. Don't let me interrupt you. I just have to wash the feed bowls and I'll be out of your way." Turning to him, she added with a wink, "You know, the more time you spend grooming a dog, *the better it runs for you.*"

Sly Kenita. I'll bet she could tell a story or two, Mark thought. "Thanks for the advice." He smiled, picking up the sander and resuming the work at hand. Nice of Clue to hold his position.

"Well, I like a man who takes charge," Felicia cooed, in a way that said *don't take what I just said to heart.*

"Now what are you doing?" he asked, as Felicia picked up a pair of scissors.

"Hold his head steady and you'll see," she answered, trimming whiskers around his muzzle, on the sides of each cheek and above each eye. "Wind resistance," she explained. "Some people think I'm superstitious and it doesn't make any difference. But I think it does."

"And if Felicia thinks it does, and it makes her happy, then it's one less thing for us to worry about around here," Kenita said, removing chunks of freshly thawed meat from the refrigerator.

Felicia smiled. "Now, we brush him," she said, slipping her hand into a soft plastic glove covered with hundreds of small nubs. Working in a circular motion, she loosened dead hair and Clue wagged his tail.

"He likes that," Mark said.

"Sure, he does. They all do. Every dog here gets groomed once a day."

"How do you have time for anything else?" he asked, beginning to sense the commitment it took to correctly run a racing kennel.

"What else is there?" she teased, as he looked in her eyes and drank in her stare, washing, dripping over him.

"Maybe I'll show you sometime," he said.

"Maybe you will," she said, still holding him with her gaze. And he knew he would. He knew he would a thousand times in a thousand nights for as long as he could possibly know her.

"Aren't you finished with that dog yet?" Kenita asked, leaving them alone.

"We're working on it," Felicia said, still holding Mark's attention. "Hand me that bottle of oil," she said softly.

Finding a small bottle in the grooming box beside the table, he picked it up. "For me?" he whispered.

"You never know," she whispered back to him.

"Well, I've seen you do some amazing things to this dog so far," Mark said. "Just what are you going to do with that stuff?" he asked, as she poured some into one palm and rubbed her hands together.

"Come here," she said to him, running her hands through his hair.

"Mmmmmm," he sighed, breathing in the light scent of emu oil. "Will this make me run better?"

"I have a feeling you run just fine without it," she said.

"You don't have to stop," he smiled, as she turned her attention back to Clue and ran her hands over the dog's face, along both sides, up and down each leg and along the length of his tail.

"I can feel that," Mark said.

"Why don't I do it again?" She smiled, repeating the massage.

"No wonder your dogs win," Mark moaned playfully.

"Shhhh . . ." she whispered, putting a finger to her lips. "My secret."

"I'll bet they feel like a million bucks," Mark said softly.

"I hope so. Wouldn't want to think I've lost my touch."

"Let me be the judge of that," he said, standing closer, pulling her against him, pressing his crotch against hers.

"Getting bolder, I see." She smiled, rubbing her hands over his butt, cupping both cheeks in her hands. "Nice," she whispered, pressing her breasts against his chest.

"Very nice," he agreed. "What are we going to do about this?"

"Well . . . from the smile on your face . . . "

"Yes?"

"I'd say you're the kind of man a girl could make pretty happy."

"Very happy," he said.

"So it's only fair that I warn you," she grinned, slipping her hand in the front of his pants. "Once I get my hands on something, I *never* let go."

"Ahem!" Kenita cleared her throat as she looked in on them again. "When you two are done groomin' each other, let me know."

"Don't move," Felicia whispered, looking in Mark's eyes as Kenita walked away.

"Wouldn't dream of it," he said, completely in her hands.

"That was . . . quite a surprise," he said, tucking in his shirt.

"A pleasant one, I hope," Felicia teased.

"I'd like to return the favor," he smiled.

"You mean you want to help me out?"

"Anytime," he said, reaching for her.

"How about right now, sport?" she said, handing him the sander.

"No problem," he said, the light in his eyes fading. "But won't Clue jump off the step?"

"He hasn't so far, has he? We train them to stand on this platform when they're puppies. Just be careful with that sander, Mark. We don't want to lose training time waiting for him to get over a sore toenail."

Assuring her that he was a big boy . . . "I can attest

to that," she grinned with a naughty look . . . wanting to prove he could fit in and handle the task . . . "Oh, I'm sure you're up to it," she smiled, "by at least seven inches" . . . he resumed manicuring Clue's nails, shortening from underneath and rounding off the edges like she showed him. Checking each nail's length by placing the dog's foot on the table and making sure the nail didn't touch, he worked, remembering their conversations, her voice. . . .

"George Curtis, the trainer from England. He wrote a book about training Greyhounds. I have a copy around here somewhere; I can loan it to you. Anyway, he talks about grooming, and I follow his advice. Hey, if I could win as many races as he has, I'd be a happy girl!"

"Aren't you happy now?" he asked.

"Sure! But my bank account would be healthier, and that would make me real happy!" she'd laughed, giving him the chance to make an observation.

"They say happiness depends on what you're doing," he said. *"Did you grow up wanting to be a dog trainer?"*

"Nope." There was that smile again with those crinkly I-like-being-outside lines around her eyes. *"I wanted to be a ballerina."*

"A dancer?" he asked, trying to hide the amazement in his voice; hoping she didn't think he meant to say as if in disbelief, *A dancer? You?*

"Yes," had come her offended, but not really, answer. *"Not just a regular, run-of-the-mill ballerina, either. I was going to be a Prima Ballerina in the Russian Ballet!"* she exclaimed, standing tall and

waving her arms as gracefully as she could with a dog brush in her hand.

"And," he chose his words carefully this time, "did the girl from Florida ever become a Prima Ballerina with the Russian Ballet?"

"Nyet," she had sighed dreamily. "Nureyev took one look at me and knew he could never match my greatness! So now? I leave the ballet to my dogs!"

Some might have laughed at her story, but graceful ballet was a fitting description of Greyhounds leaping magically as they ran.

"His loss," Mark said, playing along with her fantasy. "Had you taken to the stage, the audience would never have seen anyone but you."

"Nice job," Felicia said, inspecting Mark's work.

"Everybody OK in the recovery wing?" he asked.

"Amazing what some tender loving can do," she said, nodding. "I swear, just talking to them is the best medicine I can give. Come with me," she said, snapping a leather lead on Clue's collar and giving a quick tug. Obediently, the Greyhound dropped to the floor.

Even he would have followed Felicia if she had shined him up and snapped on a leash, Mark thought, amused.

"Where are we going?" he asked.

"On the greatest adventure of your life," she told him.

That night, at the hotel, she was different; softer somehow. She was dressed casually, wearing a tan-colored down jacket, pressed woolen slacks and high brown boots polished to a soft luster.

"You look great," he said, kissing her cheek politely, letting her in, noticing the light touches of makeup she had added just for him.

Her green eyes radiated depth through lush lashes enhanced by dark liner. Her cheeks appeared rosy from the cold weather, or was it blush? Her lips, more inviting than the week before, seemed fuller somehow, parting just enough to invite him closer.

Tongue-tied, suddenly looking for something to say, he sputtered, "Nice . . . nice hat."

"You like my . . . *hat*?" she said, of the only cap she'd had her whole life, the white fluffy one with the pom-pom starting to fall off she had worn as a kid. "Is that *all*?" she asked. "You should meet my friend Steven." What was it with men all of a sudden? Had they all sworn off women?

"No! No, I like . . . your jacket, too. Nice boots. You look . . . you look," he paused, searching for the right word, "OK," he said, pleased with himself for being so politically correct.

"OK," she said, nodding with disappointment and a trifle annoyed. "Well," she said, looking him up and down. "I like your shoes. *Nice*. Do they *pinch*?" She grinned, knowing it was a comment no brighter than his own. Afternoon delight had a way of shifting things into awkwardness, it seemed.

Not fast enough for a comeback, willing to let her have the last word of their repartee, Mark bowed his head with an air of good sportsmanship, as if to say, *"touché."* A second later, he was knocked aside.

In a move reminiscent of 1950s pro-wrestler Gorgeous George taking out the infamous "Ugly

Brothers" tag team, Clue leaped out from his hiding place in the alcove, delivering a spinning drop-kick that landed both of them—first, Mark, then, Felicia—on the king-sized bed.

"Whoa!" Felicia yelped, trying to catch her balance. But down she crashed, landing smack on Mark's chest, his arms open, their faces within a breath of each other.

"You look even more OK from here," he managed to say, with a devilish grin.

It was an ice-breaker.

"Well!" she said to Clue with a wink meant only for him. "I can see *somebody* isn't teaching his dog any *manners*!"

"I'm afraid you're right," Mark said. "See, he has this awful habit of throwing people at me. I think I need a trainer. Bad."

Pausing, she relaxed. "With a trainer, you have to do whatever she asks."

"Absolutely," he said, looking into her eyes and touching her hair. "Absolutely, I would."

"No matter what? And follow *everything* she tells you?" Felicia whispered.

"With my fullest attention to every . . . *intimate* . . . detail," he said, his eyes still holding hers, knowing it was time for them, wrapping her in his arms. Follow her? Right now, he would follow her to the ends of the earth.

"I'll do whatever you want," he said again—his face, his skin, his hands drinking her, needing her.

"Anything . . . anything," he said, as she ran her hands under his shirt. Easing off her pants, she tossed them aside and moved closer. Looking into his eyes, she slowly unbuckled his belt as he slipped his hands under her panties . . . down . . . down . . . guiding her hips to him, spreading her legs . . . raising them high over his shoulders.

Pressing against her, he began rubbing . . . rocking . . . side to side. Moving his thick cock sensuously, as if every second, every minute was forever, he moved his pelvis in adoring circles and her hungry, musty wetness sucked him into a starving love from somewhere that no man had ever touched before. She wanted him—craved him from the minute she first saw him—and she would never let him go!

She kissed him. Reaching for her bra and panties, she whispered softly, "That was beautiful."

"Stay," he said, pulling her close to him.

"We have an early morning," she said, finding her blouse among the covers, knowing if she didn't leave now she never would.

"Let's go naked," he said, rolling on his back for her to see all of him in the dim light of the city flowing through the cracks in the curtains. "Naked lovers and a Greyhound in the forest. Classic Erté."

"You'd get goose bumps. Would he paint goose bumps on you?"

Considering that Erté had been dead a while, Mark knew he wouldn't be painting much of anything.

"I'll ask him," he smiled.

"And, maybe I don't want anybody seeing . . . this," she said, taking his cock in both hands, rolling it, feeling the warmth as it grew. "Or these," she said, pinching his nipples. He didn't wince.

"I know what you want," he teased, rolling on his

side, propping his head on a pillow and spreading his legs like a male centerfold. "You want me all for yourself."

"Show-off."

"All for you," he grinned. "Every inch."

"Then save every inch for me," she said, "and I'll see you in the morning."

"I don't know if I can," he smiled, waving his full erection at her.

"Don't tempt me," she said, coming back to him, tracing it with her finger, petting his hip, down his leg and back up again.

"I won't," he said, kissing her breast.

Don't think about anything . . .

Don't think about anyone . . .

Don't think about anything . . .

Just be here . . . with me . . . right now.

"We're good together," he said later, as they lay there. He loved the sight of her, the feel of her, the smell.

But she had forgotten him, grown quiet.

"I know what it is, Mark!" she said finally, an eerie strangeness in her voice.

What was she talking about?

"Clue," she said, as if talking to herself. "*Your* skin's smooth," she said, rubbing his chest, her voice growing excited. "*You* don't have a scar like that on your whole body," she said, "because *you've* never been *burned*!"

"I take exception to that," he said, contradicting her, kissing her neck, letting her go on. He could think of lots of times he'd been burned. Things he had bought only to find they weren't worth what he had paid. People he had believed in who lied.

"No, Mark. Really!" she said, as his tongue slid down her neck. "There's no way you'd sit that beautiful ass of yours down on anything hot."

"I wouldn't say *that,* either," he said with a dirty smile, kissing her neck in a slow and easy way as her face went red.

"Don't tempt me," she warned. "This is business. I'm talking about dogs."

"I've heard they've got their own style," he grinned, reaching for her, turning her around. "Shall we try it?"

"Mark, listen to me," she said, on her knees beside the bed now. "Clue's scar is from a burn. And a Greyhound would never end up with a scar like that unless somebody held him *down*!"

"You want me to hold you down?" he said, naughtily.

"He was in a fire!" she decided.

"I'll show you a fire," he said, pulling her tight against him so she could know just how big a fire he had in mind and how hot it was burning. Clue, and all dogs, all business but the business at hand, were forgotten.

As the moon grew high and the stars began to fade, she tickled his ear with her tongue and whispered, *"I promised you an adventure."*

"Mmmmm," he moaned. "You delivered."

Pausing, she thought to herself, Not yet, I haven't, my darling, as she reminded him of their plans and turned on a soft light.

"Pain!" he said, rolling away, both hands covering his face.

"I'll show you pain! Get up!" she said, playfully slapping his naked butt.

"Ow!"

"Couldn't resist!" She laughed, smacking him again.

"Hey!" he said, suddenly awake, grabbing her arm and holding it away from him. "You're *enjoying* that!"

"Oh, come on, Mark!" she laughed. "Let a lady have some fun!"

"There's fun and there's *cruel*," he grinned, rubbing his ass.

"Aw, here," she said. "Let me kiss it for ya."

"Mmmmm," he moaned.

Smack!

"You tricked me!"

"Get dressed!"

"Nope!" he teased. If this was cruelty, he thought, warming up to her again, give me all you've got.

"You're right," she whispered, rubbing his shoulders, his arms . . . climbing on top of him. "I should lock you up and keep you all to myself."

But all he could hear was her tongue at his ear . . . all he could feel were her loving hands.

In Grandma's day, he thought later, as they started out from the hotel, West Virginia mornings before dawn smelled like wet oak leaves and moss, flavored with hickory smoke rising from fireplaces in the chill air. Grandma used to say patches of smoke and fog clinging in the hollows of the mountains were witches "stirrin' up their brew." She ought to know, Mark thought. She grew up in these mountains.

But Grandma wasn't here now, he told himself. Grandma, wife of the man who became an artist, was far away on Sylvia Brown's "Other Side" watching her grandson leaving the hotel with Felicia and finding an all-night diner midway between Bartow and Wheeling.

"Early enough for ya?" she asked, her eyes glittering with shared secrets.

"*Love* the hours you keep," he groaned, and *not* meaning it as he savored his morning brew. "Ask me after coffee." Maybe his brew wasn't witches' but it's all he had to summon his sanity at 3:00 a.m. "Why so early?"

"Because we don't want to *be seen*. Remember *The Borrowers*? The story about tiny people who live under the floors and steal thimbles and crumbs? Come on, Mark. Tell me you remember it."

"I remember being in bed!" he cranked, reaching for a piece of toast and spreading strawberry jam.

"Come on," she coaxed, pouring him a second cup. "You're not over the hill," she teased.

"You should know," he said. "Anyway, you're a busy woman with a busy life and no room for that kind of thing."

"That kind of thing?"

"You know," he said.

"Tell me," she smiled, playing with his mind, forcing him to say it out loud. Forcing him to say what they both knew was thick in the air between them, around them, all through the diner and on their minds from the moment they had first met.

Looking at her face, staring into her eyes, he held her gaze . . . and she—bold and classy in a red-headed Maureen O'Hara/Katherine Hepburn/Rita Hayworth kind of way—stared right back at him.

"Sex," he said. "Fucking."

Without raising an eyebrow, without fluttering a lash, without a corner of her mouth twitching, she sizzled through his skin. . . . "And what do you know about fucking?" she asked, tempting him, insinuating that he couldn't *possibly*, but knowing much better now.

"A man learns these things," he said, reaching for another piece of toast, playing along.

"A man who knows about fucking," she smiled, trying to trap him—always trying to trap him, outsmart him, outwit him. "A rare find."

"As rare as a woman who knows the same thing," he said with conviction.

"Should a lady thank you for the compliment," she said, fluffing her hair, "or say *ouch*?" She clutched her chest.

"I'll kiss it for you," he smiled.

Squinting her eyes and tilting her head sideways, Felicia took a deep breath and held it. Was she going to say something? What was on the tip of that tongue that he sensed could either soothe a man with kindness or slash him with a thousand knives?

"I'll tell you what to kiss, Mr. Big Shot," she said, reaching for the check.

"My pleasure," he said, reaching across the table and placing his hand on hers. "Let's go back to the hotel."

"I should slap you!" She was smiling, but not resisting.

"I've noticed you like slapping me," he said. "What do I deserve it for this time?"

"Making me feel this way!"

"How do I make you feel?"

"Slithery," she said, her voice oozing sex. "Every time I'm around you."

"Slithery," he whispered, still holding her hand, looking into her eyes. "I like that."

"Stop it!" she scolded, sitting back and straightening up. "Or I'll slide right off this seat. I wanted to be there no later than four, and it's almost a quarter of."

"But when are we going to finish this conversation?" he asked. "I'm a man who believes in finishing what he starts."

"Mister Whittier—"

"It's *Mister* now."

"Mark," she said sweetly, "if you move any faster, you'll break the track record."

"Kenita would bet on me."

"I'm sure she would! What have you done to my mother, anyway?"

"What a thing to accuse me of!"

"She hasn't liked a guy I've brought home since my date for the high school prom."

"A good judge of character," he smiled.

"Oh, she picks the *characters* all right."

"Well?" Mark questioned.

"Well, what?"

"When are we going to finish what we've started?"

"Ask me when our dog wins his first race," she said with a wink, snapping up the check as fast as she had snapped the lead on Clue the day before.

Sleepy evergreen trees stood watch at the entrance to Hidden Farms, secluding the lives of all who dwelled there. As gravel crumbled beneath the tires of his pick-up, Mark drove slowly, hoping not to waken the dogs or frighten anyone still sleeping.

"Do they know we're coming?" Mark asked that first morning, half-expecting a wild-haired Carl to rush out with a shotgun.

"Sure do," Felicia said, blowing a kiss to the house as a sleepy-eyed woman peeked out from behind fluffy curtains. "Mom'll probably have breakfast for us when we're done. You like pancakes?"

"But we just ate," he said.

"You'll be hungry again," she assured him. "I swear, she's just about the best cook anywhere around these parts. Mmmm-mmmm-mmmm! Just thinkin' about it makes my mouth water!" she said as she pointed to a rusty metal gate and they drove into an open, grassy field. "This is it!"

"It" appeared to be an abandoned airstrip surrounded and made private by poplar and oak trees whispering secrets to each other in a sudden downdraft.

"Just about everybody trains their dogs here," she said, helping Clue out of the truck and pulling the woolen scarf tighter around her neck. "The man who built the place had a plane."

"Oh?" Mark asked. "Isn't that unusual for somebody around here?"

"He was an unusual man. He was also Cecil Hutchin's daddy. You'll meet Cecil and Edna Rae tonight, at the Coalition meeting."

"Coalition meeting?"

"Yeah. Didn't I tell you? I think it's time you meet some of my friends."

He would be glad to, he said.

"Good. It's political stuff, and I have to give a report. But you might find it interesting—and, even if you don't, the people can be pretty colorful."

"Every shade of the rainbow?" he asked.

"Something like that," she said. "I'll let you decide. But I was telling you about Cecil's daddy. He was comin' in for a landing from Fourth of July celebrations over in Harrisonburg one time, and a few of those trees over there got in his way. A landing like that can make up a guy's mind pretty fast. Especially when it kills ya."

"He was killed here?"

"Yep. Nobody around here could hardly believe it at first, according to what Mom found out after we bought the place. Cecil's momma, Mrs. Joan Hutchin, no relation to the movie star . . . "

Which movie star was that? he wondered.

". . . never liked him playing around with that plane, and when it finally killed him, she just kind of closed up. You know, like people do when nothing matters any more and they won't even talk to anybody or go out or do anything."

He had heard of that, yes. "She was grieving," he said.

"Grieving, hell! She just shut up because she didn't have Cecil's daddy around to tell him, *'I told you so!'*"

"That could be hard on anybody," Mark said, trying to sound sympathetic.

"She sold off the goats, packed up those boys and moved into town. The next week, she went to work."

Interesting, how some people could make up their minds so quickly, he thought, while others agonized into the most minute emotional detail.

"Mother Hutchin and her boys were off on a job working for a roofing contractor a few miles from here when Cecil's ladder slipped out from under him. Lucky for Cecil, his brother was on the ground looking for a hammer he'd dropped. The ladder just about smashed his brother, and Cecil was up there screamin' and hanging on to the rain gutter with his bare hands!"

"What happened?" Mark asked, as if he could see the desperate young man swinging from the edge of the roof, his legs dangling.

"Well, his brother took hold of that ladder and swung it up against the barn faster than just about any of my dogs are ever gonna run!"

"What happened to Cecil?"

"I can tell you, he grabbed hold of that ladder, slapped them shingles out and came slammin' down like somebody on a pole in a three-alarm fire. And he never went up a ladder again!"

"What about the roof?" Mark asked.

"Best job anybody ever saw!" Felicia laughed. "At least, that's what the legend says. Well, after that, Mother Hutchin didn't feel like losing her boys, so she rented out an old garage in town, and that's where they started in business for themselves. Cecil ran the office, his brother handled customers and Mother Hutchin took charge of the crew. They say she worked 'til she was way up in her nineties."

"Amazing."

"Dog people are like that, Mark. Amazing. Haven't you noticed yet?" she asked, blinking those green eyes.

The truth was, he had noticed. He had noticed the

careful attention to detail everywhere he looked. The grooming, the feeding, the clean facilities—in the very routine of care itself. Felicia was fully aware of the value of her Greyhound athletes . . . more valuable to her than diamonds or Ming vases.

"Ever been married?" he asked her again. By now, they knew each other better. Maybe she would tell him more.

"I already told you that. You know I was."

"But you didn't tell me what happened," he said.

"It ran its course, that's all."

"Like a play? A show? You love everybody and it's a big family—but, in marriage, it's a real family. And all of a sudden it just runs its course? It's over?"

"Kinda like that, I guess. Yeah."

"And then, after a while," he went on, trying to figure her out, "you don't feel that way about them any more, and you bump into each other and you wonder what you ever saw in them?"

"Oh, do I ever know that feeling!" she said quickly, hoping it didn't sound as if she knew the feeling *too* much.

"What's that about?" he asked. "How can we love people—cry with them, have sex with them—and then it's over and we act like we never even knew them? Like we can hardly remember them at all?"

"Mark, if I could answer that, I'd hang up my shingle, write an advice column in every paper and I'd be living in a big mansion," she said, laughing. "Oh! Excuse me! Ann Landers already did that."

"Well, it's something I wonder about."

"But you were married, too," she said.

He hadn't told her. He was sure of it. He hadn't

told her because he hardly ever talked about it to anyone. "You know I didn't tell you that," he said.

"Yes, you did. At the track, when you first brought Clue. Remember?"

"You mean, the same way Clue told you he was mine now. But then decided he wanted to race again."

"You're catching on," she purred, pulling a duck call out of her coat pocket. "Let's see. She was the love of your life and she broke your heart. How close am I?"

"Too close," he grinned, trying to hide his embarrassment. "How could you tell?"

"I can always tell," she said. "I can just feel things sometimes. Mostly, I can feel things I've been through myself. But that's not how I knew. Maybe, it's just because some guys are nice because they're trying not to get hurt again. You know, putting on their best behavior so a woman will always treat them good."

"I never thought of it that way," he said. "Is that really how it looks? Not very strong of me."

"Oh, I wouldn't say you aren't strong." She laughed, squeezing his arm. "Why don't you take this whistle and jog down the runway—not far at first—and start calling him with it?"

"What about you?" Mark asked.

"I'll hold him until you start making a racket. And, when you get his attention, and he wants to run to you, I'll let him go. Now, we're not working on speed exactly. Not yet at least. But this'll give us an idea how he runs. Got it? It's called a hand-slip and a sprint."

"Sure," he said, taking off for a few hundred feet.

"Far enough!" she hollered. "OK, *now call him*!"

Pittsburgh . . . city of bridges, potential and pot-holes. City of some of the most attractive American women Claude had ever known. City of a former wife of his, now living in Florida and who shall never be forgotten. How could he forget? How can one forget someone who helps you, puts you on the map. No, he couldn't forget her, even though surely by now she thought he had. Pittsburgh International Airport would be home for a while.

Claude watched as people hurried by. He loved people. He loved their laughter, their accents, their styles. He would write a Broadway show someday, he decided: *The Airport Show.*

Twins smiled at him from their stroller as a middle-aged mother rolled them past on their way to Gate B. Not a litter, but getting close. Mom's college educated, he guessed. Graduated with a 4.0 average and became a successful corporate type. Rocky love life, too strung out to give it her best shot. Too little time for anything romantically serious. Too critical of men to understand love and probably afraid of it, besides. Afraid of anything bigger than her, anything she couldn't control. Welcome to *Kidsville*, he thought.

A businessman went by in a classy dark suit, carrying himself with smooth confidence the way a man of the world does. Nice touch, Claude thought, noticing the silk tie. How many corporate transactions had this man seen during his career in the boardroom? How many stock battles had he waged as he starred on the business stage? And what was *his* paycheck?

The noise of a radio playing hip-hop pulled

Claude to a rough-looking couple wearing baggy pants, shades and loose shirts, dragging their luggage through the crowd. Scary, Claude thought. But there it was: They were holding hands. Sure, they may have slapped each other around that morning. But, here in *The Airport Show,* it was family time. Tenderness was a seed blowing in the wind, landing wherever it chose. He would make them his musicians in the show.

Women in stylish coats and heels, elegant men, frumpy women and their mates . . . these could all be the chorus line.

Ah! The announcer was calling his flight. That one would be the Master of Ceremonies. *"Ladies and gentlemen! May I have your attention please?"*

They were calling for rows seventy and above. Passengers were boarding the plane from back to front. Yes, he was in this group, he said, showing his ticket.

"Have a pleasant flight," someone said, as he boarded and the show went on. . . .

From: Emerson@dejazzd.com
To: Researchdept@SATV.com
Subject: High Stakes

What's the Greyhound industry's position on bad reviews?

From Researchdept@SATV.com
To: Emerson@dejazzd.com
Subject: High Stakes

According to our research, there doesn't seem to be any "official" industry position. Each governing body from the breed registry to the welfare organization to the track operators seem to have their own policies. The Greyhound Racing Association of America (GRA/America) appears to be the most protective of the sport's national image and the most in tune with racing fans.

From: Emerson@dejazzd.com
To: Researchdept@SATV.com
Subject: High Stakes

My kind of people. See what else you can find out. We're sitting on the plane and the flight's delayed. It'll give me something to read. And, can you do me a favor? Can you ask Esmeralda if I can borrow her chauffeur next time?

CHAPTER FIVE

A Cast of Thousands . . .

Like an Irish houndsman on the shores as the salty breath of the ocean cries Now! Now! Come to me! Mark hollered, "Here, boy! Clue! Clue!"

Head up, ears tight, powerful neck arching, the eager Greyhound tensed every muscle. Leaping from Felicia's arms, he ran, head low; front legs pulling, back legs pushing, the dog flew—intense, resolute, consumed.

"Look out!" Felicia yelled, but it was too late. Mark was mesmerized, entranced by the determination of the dog running: running straight at him, running like nothing else in the world mattered to him, running as if every cell in his body, every thought, every impulse now and before he was born—all this— was driving him, forcing him, flying him forward!

He had never seen that look on a dog's face before. He had never known a dog could have such focus and concentration. What was he thinking? What was he remembering? Where was all this coming from?

The dreams—the dreams of graceful dogs chasing impala across the desert sands of long-ago ancient Egypt . . . dreams stamped into his DNA or maybe into the mass memory of all who are drawn to these dogs that aren't really dogs, but crosses with cheetahs, as if from some alien experiment—came rushing back with the force of consciousness, breaking out of amnesia, finding the clue hidden from sight until now, this moment, right now.

"He's going to run you down!" Felicia yelled, but Mark couldn't hear her, didn't want to, didn't care. He was a man overcome by the beauty of it all, struck with the splendor of a dog trusting, believing—never doubting—that someone would catch him, someone would always be there.

Suddenly, his skin whitening like a kabuki dancer in full regalia, eyes popping with horror, Mark felt a force of raw will slamming against his chest, flopping him over like a dummy in a high-speed collision test!

Feet—his feet? The dog's feet? Whose feet?

Legs! Dog! Man! Dogmandogmandog!

Claws! Teeth! Over him, around him!

Rolling, rolling!

Mouth! Eyes! Tongue!

"Mark! Mark!" he could hear her voice coming in gasps and gulps. "Are you all right? Get away, Clue! *Get away!*" she screamed, catching her breath, shoving the dog aside to no avail. *"Clue!"* she commanded sharply, slapping the dog on the shoulder.

"Mark! Let me see you!" she said, rolling him over, touching his face, the face that, in just this short time, had become so familiar, so special.

"Look at you!" she fussed. "You're muddy—you're face—*you're bleeding*!" she said, touching it with a handkerchief. "I saw him," she said. "I knew he was headed right at you . . . but I never thought . . . I never thought he'd go after you like that!"

"He didn't . . . he wasn't . . . it wasn't like that," Mark protested, his head pounding, trying to see her more clearly. "He was just happy. Really happy! He wanted me to feel it!"

"Well, he made sure of that!" she said, dabbing away at his cheek, his forehead and above his right eye. "He attacked you, Mark! I saw it. He jumped at you like a wild animal!"

"No, Felicia," Mark said, grabbing her arm. "It wasn't like that. He *didn't* attack me!"

"Mark, *I saw it*. These are hunting dogs. Fighting dogs! They get excited. Worked up! You haven't seen some of the stuff I've seen. You don't know! They get so wired. The adrenaline starts pumping and they can't stop! They start shaking. Something goes right through them and they forget where they are. They forget everything. Like they're possessed! I've seen them *tear each other apart* and not feel a thing! They can turn on a dime, Mark. The slightest thing can set them off and they forget they even know you!"

"Were you scared for me?" he asked her now, sitting up gingerly.

"Scared for you?" she asked, as if he hadn't comprehended a word she'd said. "He's *wild*—maybe too wild to come back. It's like saying to a soldier, a guy trained to kill, well you're back home now and shooting people's against the law here."

"Laws are a matter of geography," Mark said, quoting the comment of the bigamist confronted by both families in *The Remarkable Mr. Pennypacker.* Why he was thinking about bigamy just now, he didn't know.

"But they're still laws," she said, and he pleaded

with her soul that she wasn't one of those who held back because "teacher said so." He didn't believe that of her, didn't want it of her. What kind of mother would she be to those children he sensed every time he was close to her, every time he was included in her world? "Maybe we're asking too much of him," she said, and his heart sank. His heart sank not because of what she was saying about the dog. No, he had seen the very same thing, though not from the same perspective. But he wanted to believe she would know, feel, understand, what Clue had made so clear to him.

His heart fell and fell and fell as if it would never reach bottom at the thought of her abandoning their plans now, stopping their dream, their adventure—stopping *them*—because she was afraid.

"You can't," he said.

"I can't?"

"I won't let you—not now," he said. "Not after I've seen this."

"You won't *let me*?"

"If you think, Felicia McCrory, that you're going to put the brakes on all this—on making Clue the greatest champion anybody ever saw—then you aren't half the woman I want to believe you are!"

"What are you talking about? That bump on the head. What's got into you?"

"Maybe you've trained a lot of dogs, lady. But you never trained one like this. *You never had the chance!* You never had the chance to take a dog that found his natural instincts—*a real Greyhound*—a dog that can do what he was *made for*, and prove what you can do with a dog like that. Clue isn't like the others in your kennel. He's ahead of the game. He's ahead of you.

He's ahead of me. He's ahead of anybody who thinks they know how to train a racing dog and you know it, and you're scared. *You're scared!* You're scared he's *too much for you.*"

"What the hell are you talking about? You got knocked on the head and you're bleeding. I'm getting you out of here."

"No!" Mark hollered, shaking her off. "Haven't you ever wanted to feel—really *feel*—something in your life? Well, I have! I've wanted to feel something powerful enough, big enough, *important enough* to make me forget everything else just for one minute! *One stinkin' lousy minute!* I'd give anything—*anything* to say at the end of my life I LIVED! I REALLY . . . really . . . *LIVED*!"

"Mark—"

"Felicia!" he said now, trusting, hoping she wanted to understand. "You saw what he did—you saw the life in him! You can't take that away. *You can't possibly want that!"*

"But if he's too wild, Mark—if he goes after the other dogs when he's running—he'll be called a fighter. It won't work. He'll be ruled off!"

"Then we go to another track. And another and another! We keep going until we find a place that takes him."

"But we can't do that!"

"Why not? You saw him, Felicia! You talk about *heart*! He ran with more heart just now than any dog you ever saw. I haven't seen anywhere near as many as you have and *even I know it*!"

"Yes! *Yes!* He ran! He ran like he was bred to. Like I wanted—like I hoped—like *everybody* hopes," she said, putting her hands to her face.

"Then what's stopping you?"

"I don't know," she said, shaking her head. "So much could happen."

"*What*, Felicia?" he asked. "What could *happen*? . . . You could have a true Greyhound? *An honest dog?* Are you scared to stand up against forces choking us everywhere we turn, cutting us off from our natural instincts, grinding us to a halt—*castrating us*—from what, deep down in our souls, we know we could really be? *Is that what you're scared of?*" he asked, the enormity of it hitting him now.

"You're like everybody else I run into these days—afraid to stick your neck out and take a chance! *God help us* if we dare to take a chance and raise ourselves above the crowd, or stand out in any way. An assassin's bullet waiting for us, a knife in the back from people we thought were friends, an IRS hunt, a target letter, cruel rumors waiting for anyone who goes for it—*really goes for it* and breaks out of the mold the way this dog just did! *I love this dog!* The man in me *loves him*!"

He knew. He knew with all his thinking powers— all his logic, all his imagination—he was hitting the truth. Grand as she was, special in a bright and shining way that only remained in romantic movies, she was afraid. She was holding back. "Quit pretending, Felicia. Forget about pleasing anybody else and be real with me. We can break out. I feel this. *I feel it!*"

But she was far away. She didn't understand. She wasn't The One.

"Maybe you're right," he said, pulling back, but not wanting to. He was different. He knew that. Wanted it.

Make her be different, God!

Taking her hand, reassuring her that he hadn't lost his mind in the gritty dirt they were crumpled upon, he said quietly, "It's OK. . . . Maybe you're right. He's nothing special. Just a dog that likes to run."

"No, Mark," she said, steadying his gaze now. "He's not just a dog that likes to run. *He's like we are.*"

What was she saying?

"He's racing against life," she said, with a sense of conviction as she returned from that faraway place. Gathering her strength, her sense of conviction, she said, "People like us? No matter what it takes, we chase after dreams. Nobody thinks we'll make it. But once in a while," she said, holding up the stopwatch for him to see the time that stunned her, "we catch them!"

They were colorful misfits, the members of the Greyhound Racing Coalition.

They were renegades, teachers and clowns from every walk of life, every corner of the racing community, called to arms for the battle at hand.

They were trainers, haulers, people just starting in the business and those who could think of being in no other.

They were jewelry designers, muzzle and leash manufacturers, veterinarians, stock market analysts, professional gamblers, graphic designers, racetrack owners, mechanical engineers, karate experts, students, professors, representatives from the NGA, the AGTOA, the AGC and GRA; lobbyists from Washington, D.C., presidents of statewide breeders associations; racing authorities from Australia, New Zealand, and the United Kingdom—connecting, awakening, lifting the consciousness of the sleeping giant that was their industry.

Hear us! *Voice of the Greyhounds!*

We're strong! *Strong as the fighting heart!*

We're noble! *Noble as the blood coursing through our veins.*

We chase our love! *To the ends of the earth!*

Following love "to the ends of the earth" turned out to mean navigating a narrow dirt lane for the meeting of the Greyhound Racing Coalition that night. Dried and twisting boards on the barn, like dancers poised for the curtain to rise, cast eerie shadows. "It's *déjà vu*," Mark said, his car leaning sideways as it negotiated a deep rut, and the glowing eyes of a cow reflected back in his headlights. Scooting across the open field, religiously kept trimmed by a few shaggy sheep, he parked among a conglomeration of vehicles and lingered a moment before ejecting the CD of a piano concerto.

"Good music relaxes me," he said.

"After today, I'm surprised you have the strength for anything," Felicia said. "Are you sure you're OK?" she asked, touching his head.

"Ouch!" he winced, assuring her that he was "just fine." It took more than being run over by an eighty-pound dog at forty-five miles per hour to knock him out of the game.

She believed him, she said. But, if he wasn't sure, if he needed anything . . .

"I'm OK," he said, sitting quietly. "Are we late?"

"The porch light's still on," she said, fixing her makeup, running a brush through her hair and putting it back in her purse as they got out and walked. "That means they haven't started."

Struggling with the rickety gate of a picket fence that once may have been white, Mark said with a conspiratorial grin, "They're waiting for you. The star of the show."

Pleased, but modest, Felicia took him by the arm and stopped. "And you're my escort," she said, kissing him, wrapping her arms around his waist, tight. "Lead the way."

"Don't tempt me," he said, his voice husky as he searched for a way to change his mind. "What did you tell me this Mr. Hutchin of yours does?" he asked, finding the perfect subject.

"Besides raising some of the best dogs around?" she asked, breaking from their embrace, knowing there would be another time and another and another.

"Besides that, yes."

"Can't you tell?" she asked, knocking on the front door of the house now. "Cecil has a paint store."

"Well, there you are!" a sixty-ish woman in a light blue caftan said in her thick West Virginia drawl as they entered her parlor. Ivory droplets in gold earrings reaching to her shoulders matched the perfect teeth of a mouth painted to match the rose-colored wallpaper. "Where *ever* have you *been*?" she asked, loud enough that no one would miss her Cleopatra eyes swooping Mark's way.

"Edna Rae, this is my friend Mark."

"Delighted!" The exotic woman smiled, raising her chin and tossing back her head ever so slightly for a better look. "Nasty cut on your head," she remarked.

"Happened on the track this morning," Felicia interjected.

"Oh?"

"We hand-slipped a pup and he got carried away," Felicia said, not mentioning who the pup was.

Aware of her reluctance to mention Clue's name, Mark added, "Yeah, I didn't get out of the way fast enough."

"And he ran over you?" she asked calmly.

"Plowed me under," Mark said.

Satisfied, the woman turned and asked in a worldly, Olympia Dukakis way, "Beer, Felicia?"

"Not *good* for you," Mark whispered smugly, mocking Felicia's earlier comment.

"Oh, put those eyebrows back on your head!" she snapped in his direction, hissing a "No, *thanks*!" to the amused Edna Rae.

Heading into the dining room through a curtain beaded in lapis lazuli and gold, Mark noticed potted cactus plants in clay urns and a mural of the Egyptian pyramids spanning one entire wall. At the base of the pyramids, and not unlike images of the great Akhenaten and his beautiful Nefertiti, stood two figures holding hands and facing each other. Glancing from the painting to his hostess and back again, Mark noticed they were dressed exactly alike.

"You've been to Egypt?" he asked, striking up a conversation with the hostess, who was becoming more interesting with each moment.

"Oh, yes." She paused as if recalling something far away. "Many times," she said in a dreamy Southern drawl. "I died there," she whispered, as if trusting him to keep a secret.

"You know," she went on without batting an eye, "I just love anything Egyptian. The ancient Egyptians believed life energy comes from the rays of the sun." It was a comment not surprising of one whose manner, jewelry and home décor revealed such an interest. "Can you think of anything more sensible?"

"It's as good an explanation as any," Mark said, "Especially for its time."

"It became their abiding philosophy," she said, not caring about anything, anyone else in the room.

"Their religion," Mark added, though he wasn't certain if that was entirely true or if it was just the explanation of historians, "was a way of controlling the masses."

"Is that what you think?" Edna Rae said, pleasantly surprised by his knowledge. "What about setting the masses free?"

"Chaos," Mark said. "Anyone who studies political science knows the masses can't handle themselves."

"Set them free and it all falls apart," she summed it up, leveling her mysterious gaze on him.

"I'm speaking from a political perspective," he said, intrigued to discover such intellect. "But I have to agree, when the individual in us begins to show itself, and needs to spread its wings and fly, what kind of religion would hold us back and keep us from growing?"

"Not a very loving one, I guess," Felicia said, letting them know she had been listening.

"Not a very loving one," he repeated, looking at her.

"Mark's an antique dealer," Felicia explained.

"He's not an antique dealer," Edna Rae said. "This man's a philosopher."

"Thank you," Mark said modestly. "But what I actually do is restoration."

"Putting broken things back together again," Edna Rae observed. "Which gives you an appreciation of what the mind can imagine and the hands can make."

"I like to think so," he said, with a smile. "Working in my shop is like being in a time capsule."

"I can understand that." She smiled, encouraging him to go on.

"I see all these things, all these creations, and I know how great the mind can be," he said. "Then I turn on the radio or check out the news and it all disappears."

"Like the setting sun," she said.

"Not nearly as magnificent," he said, understanding how skillfully she had cast her golden thread around their conversation.

"Did you see Edna Rae's antiques?" Felica asked.

A presence seemed to vanish from Edna; her expression, posture, manner seemed to shift. "Oh!" she sparkled, the door to a deeper nature closing as easily as it had appeared. "Well, then, I'll bet you noticed some of the nice pieces here in my collection. You know, I never miss those shows on TV. You know, the ones where they go someplace and everybody brings their treasures and the appraiser tells them what it's worth and they act all surprised and everything! Do you think they're really surprised or do you think they already know?"

Regretting the disappearance of the Egyptian incarnate, Mark adjusted his level of communication. Perhaps they would talk again. Perhaps it was gone forever.

"I imagine some of them are, in fact, quite surprised," he said, "especially if they never really liked the piece in the first place."

"Well, I like everything in my collection," Edna Rae said fondly, like a little girl now. "I've been saving this stuff as long as I can remember."

"It wouldn't matter how much it's worth," Felicia said. "You could tell her that vase over there is worth a million dollars and she wouldn't part with it."

"That?" Edna Rae asked, of a rose-colored porcelain vase with a delicate painted Greyhound on it. "Oh, no. That one's special."

"You wouldn't let it go," Mark asked, "even if it went to a museum where thousands of people could see its beauty every year?"

"Not even then," Felicia answered for her.

But, Edna Rae asked, "Would they touch it every day, talk to it and keep the dust off?"

"It would have its own special curator," he said, as if to a child. "Maybe even a special glass case."

"You know," she said, her eyes growing distant again, loving. "I found that piece in a little shop not far from where I grew up. It belonged to an old woman who nobody liked very much. She didn't talk like us, and she didn't really dress like us, either. She wanted five dollars for it, she said. And I didn't have five dollars, so I asked if there was any way I could help her around the shop and earn the money to pay for it. Before long, I was cleaning for her, and that's where I met Cecil, when he showed up to paint the windowsills one day. If you look, you'll see it's broken," she said to us, pointing, as Mark picked up the lovely object, examining its exotic craftsmanship.

"There's a chip in the back."

"It's exquisite," he said, sensing the chip itself was part of the story.

"Cecil bumped the shelf it was sitting on when he tried opening one of the windows. I could never get them open myself. They mustn't have been opened in years. Anyway," she said, "it fell off and broke."

She paused, catching her breath. "I almost cried," she said, still feeling the loss of that day. "Of all the pretty things in that shop, why did it have to be the only one I loved? Well, Cecil felt terrible. He ended up paying the lady for it. And then he looked at me like he had the grandest idea, and he handed the pieces to me as a gift. But only after I agreed to talk to him the next day and the day after that," she paused and smiled at the memory.

"By the time Cecil and I were done talking," she said, "the pieces were glued together again like you see it now. That place had the prettiest windowsills, and walls and porch rails and front door of any shop in town!" She laughed. "And I had myself a ring!"

"Felicia's right," Mark said, loving the story, wanting to know if they lived happily ever after. "You couldn't part with anything like that."

"You know, Mark," she added. "That very shop is where we have our store today. But I hear what you're saying. Some day I'll part with that fancy thing you're holding. The pieces and the glue. But I'll never part with what it means to me or how it brought me and Cecil together. That's ours. Wherever we go."

Nodding politely, Mark handed the vase back to her. It belonged to her and to no other for as long as she cared. As it was, had always been, would always be.

He sensed Felicia's hand on his arm as she tugged him toward their seats at a conference table on which there were glasses of ice water, notepads and pens. He was here to unlock mysteries. He was here to sense the pulse of a waking giant.

A few minutes later, falling into their monthly ritual, a bald man with a neat goatee spoke up. The head was shaven, Mark noticed. The shirt, though it appeared white, was linen. The tie, a burnished tone of gold, radiated the importance in which he held his responsibility. The man greeted everyone with regal courtesy and an aura of wisdom.

"Welcome to the meeting of the Greyhound Racing Coalition," he said. "I think everyone's here, so I guess I can call the meeting to order." Glancing at his notes, he paused for a sip of water.

"That's Cecil," Felicia whispered, as if they were in church. Mark gave a nod of understanding.

"We have a lot going on this month," Cecil announced in a strong and determined way. "I spoke with the attorney, and I asked if he could tell us how things stand with the bill in Pennsylvania. The land to the north," he added.

"Pennsylvania's banning Greyhound racing," Felicia whispered to Mark.

She couldn't be serious, he thought. There weren't any dog tracks in Pennsylvania.

"Pre-emptive legislation," she explained.

Land to the north . . . pre-emptive legislation. "It's military talk," he said, incredulous.

"They're gathering their forces," Cecil went on.

"Their Senate is voting in a few days."

It was as if they had all been transported to another place, another time.

"Are people still writing letters?" a woman wanted to know. In another era, she could have been wearing robes, asking about the troops in the desert, asking about hieroglyphics on clay tablets.

"Yes," Cecil said proudly. "From what I under-stand, we're flooding the governor's office. They must be getting thousands of letters and e-mails in Harris-burg."

"What about our press releases?"

"Before you as we speak," he said, holding up a piece of paper. "The new press release, envelopes and stamps for each of you. We must have everything ready by the time we leave tonight."

"There's a mailbox where I'm staying," came a voice from the back.

"Then you get the job, Poppy," Cecil decided. "You can drop them off tonight."

"Done!" she said. Poppy Schwartz would do what-ever she could for Greyhounds. . . .

"Boo!" she said to the brindle Greyhound she lived with. "Out of my way!"

Pulling two pairs of panties from her drawer and two pairs of socks from another, Poppy tossed them into the open suitcase on her bed. Let's see, she thought. One pair of jeans; two T-shirts sporting her logo, "Adopt NOW!"; and one matching sweatshirt. That would be plenty.

"TIGER! GET OUT OF THE LITTER BOX!" she yelled. That damn dog was too easy to cat train. He

thought he was a cat. And an argumentative one at that!

Poppy filled a second case with dog food, a water bowl and several chew toys, dragged both suitcases outside to her car, stowed them in the trunk and returned to her bedroom. Well, that's it, she thought. A couple of days in West Virginia for the Coalition meeting and, if she was lucky, the big stakes race.

"TIGER! Leave the cats alone! Do that one thing for me and I'll take you for a walk," she bribed.

The dog perked up his ears at the familiar words . . . dropped a screaming kitten back into a box in the corner of the room . . . and trotted to the door to wait for his mother.

Cecil reached for his glass of water and addressed the group. "Jason Greathouse will take over from here."

"We're covering every paper, every TV news show and radio station in the Northeast," said a heavy-set man in a white cowboy hat and matching white mustache. "I brought along a few ideas for new ads," he said, opening a leather briefcase and passing out samples as he smiled at an attractive woman sitting nearby.

"Jason was on Wall Street before starting his kennel."

What she didn't know is how empty Wall Street can be, even when the streets are crowded. Jason knew. Growing up in Maryland, helping his Dad catch crabs in the Chesapeake Bay, running barefoot on the sand, he dreamed of bigger things. One day, he would have a fancy car. One day, he would have enough money to pay every bill his Dad worried about. One day, he'd be able to go fishing and catch crabs without worrying that he might find his Dad's boat missing, his mother crying. *"Wanted,"* his classified ad in the local newspaper said, *"My Dad."* It ran for weeks with no answer.

"See that pot-bellied guy over there with the tall brunette?" Felicia asked.

How could anyone miss her, Mark wondered, recognizing her picture from the sample ads now circulating around the room.

"That's Barbara Bastinelli and her husband, Brad Taggert. Watch out, guy," she said with a naughty chuckle. "They're on the lookout for fresh semen."

"Excuse me?" Did she just say what he thought she did?

"You heard me," she said, waiting for his reaction. "They buy straws of frozen semen from champion dogs, horses, zoo animals, and put it in storage. They have it banked all over the world. Barbara started out as a fashion model in Europe," she explained.

So, the attractive woman really was what she appeared to be, Mark thought, wanting to know more.

"The story is, Barbara had just made her first big splash in *Vogue* when her father died. She left Europe and came home to take over the kennel. That was back when frozen semen was just getting started. She knew it might be a long time before she'd get her hands on the kind of money she was making as a model, so she bought straws of *Kunta Kinte, Downing* and some of the other greats. Smart move. She's worth millions now. She tells everybody she married Brad 'cause when semen is your business she'd be in big trouble if he looked any better. He's not allowed to go to the gym, nothing. Only fancy restaurants and golf. He's allowed to do that. Which is pretty funny, because the truth is, he's so crazy about her, Brad Taggert wouldn't know another woman if she fell over him with her ass in the air and her panties rolled down to her ankles!" Felicia smiled cattily. . . .

It had been a long day for the young model, standing under the hot lights while the photographer found the right angle, the right attitude, the right look for each dress. Paris was out there. Oh, Paris! The air, the sounds, the sense of being so far away and so free. Blue lights at night? Yes, they really were blue. The food? The food was different everywhere the agency sent her. She smoothed a hand over her tummy and the photographer threw down his light meter.

"No! A thousand times, I tell these American models what to do and they cannot do it!"

"I'll call the agency," his assistant said, scrambling to pick the meter off the floor and grab the phone at the same time.

"No! No more! I ask for a model. A real model. I ask for Audrey Hepburn and they send me Sandra Bernhardt!"

He was an artist. He was a professional. His photos were seen in every major fashion magazine in Europe.

Standing there, maintaining her pose, Barbara waited. It was like this. It was always like this. The one behind the camera was the star, the one giving her work was important. Like the magazines she posed for, only to be thrown away, she was replaceable. She was nothing.

"*Mademoiselle,*" *the assistant said gently as the photographer stomped out of the room. "He wants you to go. But I . . ." he looked at the floor. "I would like you to stay.*"

Still holding her pose, straight pins scratching her skin where the dress was too big, Barbara tried to whisper. Painfully, unbearably, she tried again . . . "I'm hungry," she said.

Looking around for something, anything to offer her, the assistant said, "A glass of water?"

"Please," she said, a tear in her eye.

Passing around the last of his glossy prints, Jason's enthusiasm filled the room.

"We're focusing the campaign on special-interest publications. Clubs, that kind of thing, and it's going well," he said. "From here on, it's just a matter of freshening up our ads every month. After that, I think we're ready for mainstream. Every city has a main paper and a few smaller ones," he told them. "If you combine the small papers, sometimes you end up with a wider circulation than by advertising in the big paper that just about always has the attitude to go with it. See how it works?" he asked, to a consensus of agreement from around the room. "Let's thank Barbara for putting her name and image to our ads, by the way."

Everyone clapped spontaneously. Startled, Barbara raised her hand and diplomatically answered, "I'll let you know if my agent starts calling!" she joked. But agents, keenly aware of her love for a sport too controversial for their comfort, had stopped calling long ago.

"When the phone starts ringing again, we'll know Greyhound racing is hot!" Brad said, looking around at everyone and reassuring her life decision.

"You look great in sequins, honey!" Edna Rae pitched in, to which someone else whistled.

"I couldn't agree more," Jason nodded with a broad grin. "We got the portrait photographer M. J. Bochnia to take these. Couldn't believe our luck, she's usually so booked. But she wanted to do it. Turns out her family had Greyhounds years ago, and she wants to help set the record straight. These ads are going to start running in every paper and magazine we can buy into."

"People? Time?" Felicia asked.

"Better! Remember, I said we couldn't believe our luck? Bochnia has a contract with *SportsAnimated*."

"Is he talking about the magazine?" Mark asked Felicia.

"I think so," she said.

"She offered to show the ads to their editor."

"What happened?" Poppy asked, excited.

"They loved them!" Jason said. "Turns out, their editor is a lady named Esmeralda von Havenburg. She's an older woman, in a wheelchair."

"I've heard of her!" someone pitched in. "I saw her being interviewed on TV."

"She's quite a character," Jason said. "A real believer in country living. And I can tell you she's not scared of anything. Her Dad used to run Greyhounds back when the whole thing started. She even met Owen P. Smith when she was a kid. Totally different from any other magazine I can think of," he continued. "You could just feel the fresh air all around you when we got down to talking business."

At the sound of his enthusiasm, Felicia seemed to relax. "Maybe there's hope," she said quietly.

"Their ad department came up with a plan for positive editorials, even a feature story at some point, and they want to start publishing results from stakes races if we could arrange it."

"Any chance of that?" someone asked.

"Publishing race results, you mean?" Jason asked. "I think the *Daily Racing Form* would be the way to go on that one," he said. "I talked with Steven Crist about it on my last trip to the city. He's receptive."

"Any chance of getting him for a speaker sometime?" Cecil wondered.

"Good idea. He's a real player. Believe it or not, he got his start at the dog tracks, back when he and a college friend were writing a book," Jason said, tipping back his hat and concluding his report. "I'll ask him."

"Can we have the membership report?" Cecil asked a dark-haired bodybuilder whose biceps looked like they were bursting out of his shirt.

"That's Jack Halstead," Felicia whispered, licking a stamp and pressing it onto an envelope. "A hunk. We could make a ton of money selling his pictures on a calendar. He'd sell them himself. Years ago, he went out and got himself some investors and they turned a little pharmacy into the biggest thing since Purina. They were the first heavy hitters to support our campaign. Good man to have on our team."

"Since our debate on that Internet radio show," Jack said, "we've had a surge of interest. Almost seventy new membership packets went out since then. Forty-three new members joined since our last report.

I think we can kick that up if we expand our advertising program. . . . "

Selling. He had always been selling. Landing in Chicago, a kid out of high school, he sold himself into a job at Harry's, a room and a membership at the gym. A restaurant job to cover the rent and feed him; a gym to stay in shape. He was in business.

Finding prospects wasn't difficult. Women and men both were attracted to the handsome young bodybuilder. Extra cash was easy enough to come by, depending on what he was willing to do for it, how far he was willing to go. Jack Halstead always had extra cash. But Jack also had a plan.

Business. A guy like him, a guy trading on his charm, could write his own ticket, as they say. And, Jack was hungry. He wanted the fancy car, the fancy clothes, the fancy house. He just . . . wanted.

Power.

The first time it came to him, the idea that he could put together a business, he put it out of his mind. What he knew about health foods, vitamins, supplements could fill a book, sure. Anybody who spends very much time in the gym is a walking encyclopedia of such information. But what he knew about pets wouldn't amount to an electrolyte.

"Doesn't matter," the guy said, "all you have to do is show 'em the pictures. You go to the dog show, set up this table and put out all the vitamins."

"But I don't even like dogs."

"You like pussy, don't you?"

And so, it began. Bussing tables at Harry's during the day, the gym at night, dog shows on weekends.

Before long, Jack was setting up two tables. After a while, it was two tables and a rack of shelves offering nutritional supplements for stamina, for joint flexibility, for bone development. Then it was two shows instead of one, sometimes three, and goodbye to Harry's.

After a few questions and remarks from around the table, Cecil resumed directing the meeting. "Could we have the finance report?"

Standing to read, Felicia disclosed the figures for contributions and membership dues. "We also have commitments from Greyhound breeder associations in a few different states, and some of the tracks are talking about a percentage from some of the races to help out. So, all in all, it's looking pretty good."

"Thanks, Felicia. Any questions?" Cecil asked, glancing around the room. "If not, I'd like us to move on to Internet activities."

"Wanda Wharton," Felicia whispered, nodding in the direction of a smiling platinum blonde, "of WorldWideGreyhounds—WWG—the biggest racing community online. She's married to Clyde Wharton, but he's not here, and I can't introduce you because he never comes to the meetings. She's one of the founders of the campaign, but Clyde never gets involved. He's the private type from Europe. They race their dogs in Ireland, Scotland, England, the U.S. and Australia. Hard to believe all that and she's so young. I just love her. . . . "

Fathers and mothers are strange creatures, a young Wanda decided. They say they love you. They say they're going to love you forever. And then they go and take away the very thing you love most—them.

It wasn't that she didn't see them any more since the divorce. It wasn't that at all. It was, that, when she did see them on alternate weekends, they didn't want to talk about her. They wanted to talk about each other.

"Is your Dad seeing anyone?"

"No." Not that she would ever know, anyway.

"Well, don't tell him about Bill." Or Bob. Or Clayton. Parents.

Her father wasn't much better. "If I ever catch another man around her, I'll kill him!"

Not that he could. He wasn't exactly a crack shot.

No wonder she spent more time with her dog. No wonder she went riding on the old Arabian mare every chance she got.

Some day, she would have lots of dogs. Some day, she would have lots of horses. Some day, all her friends would have them, too.

"Hello, everybody," Wanda said. "I just want everybody to know our web site is right up there at the top of Greyhound sites being visited by surfers on the Net. If you check us out on Google or Yahoo, we're either the first or second site that comes up under *Greyhound* or Greyhound racing. Um . . . I also wanted you to take a look at some of the improvements and changes we've made to our site when you have a chance. Other than that . . . Oh! . . . a couple of the members on WWG have been posting about a new radio show they want to get going . . . so, if we're interested, that might be another place we could advertise."

"Thanks, Wanda. There's a computer in my office if anybody wants to see the changes Wanda just told us about," Cecil said. "I'd like to go over old business now and then move on to new business. Then we can take a break for refreshments and get to work."

As members of the Greyhound Coalition made their reports and planned their strategy, Mark once again considered the Egyptian mural. Edna Rae and Cecil side by side among pyramids, hot white sand and palm trees. Felicia and Mark in a shower of casinos, asphalt parking lots, dollars. And palm trees.

"What about the adoption report?" a saucy spirit demanded.

"After the adoption report," Cecil said, smiling graciously at everyone as he turned the meeting over to Poppy. "Just wanted to make sure you were awake," he said to her.

"Oh, I'm awake all right!" came the retort. "Just let me get started and you'll see how awake I am!" said the casually dressed lady in men's overalls. Dark eyes flashing and pushing back her shoulder-length brown hair, she started. "We've been dealing with a bunch of crap on the chat lines. Did any of you see it? Some farm in the Panhandle was raided and they're desperate for homes for about twenty dogs. But they can't get any haulers to take them because none of the adoption groups down there have any money. It's not like up here, where the streets are lined with slots, you know.

"Anywaaaay . . . what they want is for us to give them some money to get these dogs homes. And they're saying stuff like we don't give a damn, and they're threatening to go to the press and tell everybody. I keep tellin' 'em to give the Coalition a chance, that it takes a while for things like this to get off the ground and we're gonna do whatever we can to reach a hundred percent adoption real soon. But, hey, what do we do about any dogs down there right now?

"That's what they want to know. And if we don't give them an answer, well, it's just another black eye for the industry. So, I called a hauler I know, and I twisted a few arms and the dogs are on their way to— guess where?—Connecticut even as we speak, and we're putting them into our adoption program at the track where you all know I work. So, hopefully, that's taken care of. But the other thing we need to take a look at is this thing in Massachusetts.

"They want to pass a law giving a percentage of the races to a big adoption fund, and it's supposed to be administered by neutral groups—not pro-racing, but not anti-racing either. And I can almost guarantee you most of that money is gonna go to the anti-racing groups that don't even adopt out near as many dogs as we do. So, that being said, I think it's something for us to keep an eye on."

"How is the adoption directory coming along?" Cecil wanted to know. "Any idea when we can print it?"

"Almost finished," Poppy said. "We have over three hundred groups identified, and we've listed their stand on racing. Not a pleasant task, let me tell you! But, when we're done, it'll be the first time anybody's had the guts to show Greyhound owners who they're really giving their dogs to.

"Well, that's all I have to say. Thanks, everybody. I really believe in the Coalition, and we've got to keep fighting. I know these people we have to deal with. I know what they're like, so don't give up. Don't give up, no matter how tough you might think it is. I can tell you we're making a difference. So, stuff those envelopes and get out the word and you'll be surprised what a difference you can make. You really will."

"Poppy's our resident cheerleader," Felicia whispered.

After old business was discussed and new business explored, Cecil faced his loyal Board of Advisors.

"We're going to beat this thing in Pennsylvania," he told everybody. "We're gonna get so many press releases out there and make so many calls tonight, this industry is never going to be caught sleeping again! Fans are going to jam the governor's switchboards and fill up the post office! Let's think about that when we're stuffing these envelopes and raising donations for the legal fees tonight. If we stick together, this will never happen again!"

"Hey, girl!" Felicia called out, over refreshments. "Grab yourself a plate," she said, dishing herself some salad, cheese, finger sandwiches and cold chicken.

"Hey!" Wanda laughed, coming over and pouring herself a soda. "How are you doing?"

"Just fine," Felicia said. "Mark, I'd like you to meet Wanda Wharton."

"My pleasure," he smiled, shaking Wanda's hand, noticing her accent. "Irish?"

"How can you tell?" she laughed. "Our farm is right outside of Dublin, but this year we leased a place in Delaware, here in the States, for the horses."

"One place for the horses and one place for the dogs," Mark observed. "Nice arrangement."

"Arrangements are the story of my life," she said. "Or at least they seem to be."

He smiled. "Arrangements" seemed popular these days.

"I was just filling Mark in on this legislation," Felicia said. "He says he's gonna have to have a talk with his TV set."

"You're TV's bad?" Wanda asked, amused.

"Well, apparently, from what I'm finding out, it doesn't really know any better," Mark said, appreciating her comment. "The news has it programmed," he smiled.

"I'm finding out a lot about American news," Wanda said, appreciating his statement. "And what does your TV say about Greyhound racing?"

"Not much, really. But when it does, it's not good."

"Well, slap that thing!" Felicia interjected, smacking his arm playfully.

Blushing somewhat, Mark said, "So far, I just can't see anything wrong with this sport."

"But your TV can," Wanda said, her eyes twinkling. "Just by sitting in your house."

"Yeah," Mark said, playing along. "That damn TV."

"Propaganda," Felicia said, having fun. "We gotta be tough."

"Propaganda," Mark said, mulling around the term. "There's something I haven't heard for a while."

"You know," Felicia declared, tapping her head. "Brainwashing?"

"Wanda! Wanda! There you are! I have to talk to you! About this problem in the Panhandle!" the out-of-breath trooper said loudly.

"*Poppy!* Calm down. Let me introduce you to Mark," Felicia said. "He's thinking about joining us. Mark? Poppy Schwartz, head of adoptions at Seaside Greyhound Park."

"Nice to meet you," he said, hoping he could keep the names straight.

"Yeah, nice to meet you too—Wanda, I got thirty-two dogs I hafta place by the end of the meet and I sent four of them to Cynthia—and, oh, well, you know Cynthia, she gets on some chat line and . . ." Just before they disappeared from view, Mark noticed Wanda glancing back and smiling with a helpless shrug.

"Brainwashing went out with the Russians and the Cold War," Mark said, sorry to see Wanda go.

"*Brainwashing,*" Felicia countered, quick to yank him out of any fantasies she wasn't privy to, he was discovering, "otherwise known as *spaced repetition,* is the underlying principle of *advertising.*"

"And you know all about it," he said, in a patronizing tone.

"I know, because I've been talking to Jason. He says if we pick out a few basic issues and just keep hammering, eventually the nail sinks in."

"A proven method to just about anything, including the old saying 'the dog waiting at the door eventually gets in.' "

Not sure what that had to do with it, she narrowed her eyes. "I don't know where you come up with these things, but some of them make sense."

"It's the grandmother in me," he said. "She wanted to be a movie star, but she never knew how. Years went by, but she never got to Hollywood and the movies never came to town. After a while, she just made up her mind and started living like one."

Grandma Nadine. Working in the chocolate factory, making candy bars for "The Boys" of WWII. Grandma Nadine at the local movie house every Saturday night so she'd have something pleasant to think about in church the next morning. Grandma Nadine in her fancy dresses, her jewelry and her bright red lipstick.

"My kind of lady," Felicia said. "She figured out some of the most famous people in the world aren't really beautiful or specially talented."

Struggling with bad skin, comparing himself with other guys who were more popular . . . it hadn't been easy growing up.

"Publicity just says they are," Felicia said, bringing him back. "And they act like they are, and before you know it—*voilà*—the whole country believes it."

Maybe he should have had one of those "publicities."

"Do an experiment," she said. "Curl up in front of that lyin' TV of yours. Forget everything and wrap yourself up in a blanket and have yourself some popcorn. You know, find some old movies and get some of that *cinema therapy*," she kidded him.

The silver screen of his mind scanned a thousand studio images, he saw Crawford's manly shoulders and firm jaw in *Johnny Guitar* as she hoisted a rifle against the likes of an insanely jealous Mercedes McCambridge. He saw Harlow's too-dimpled chin and slumpy posture and Gable's big ears. Good thing Clint Eastwood ignored comments about his Adam's apple or we might never have seen *Dirty Harry,* he thought to himself. And without Arnold's body would we have paid as much attention to his films? Michael Jackson being perceived as a modern day Peter Pan? Well, Michael hadn't needed a studio for that. He made his own.

"OK," he finally said, getting her point. Publicity had a lot to do with it, and if you wanted to call publicity propaganda, then so be it. "But you can't fool reporters."

"Earth to Mars!" her eyes flashed. "Honest reporting takes *work,* Mark! It's so much easier to let activists do that for you." Shaking her head at him as if she were dealing with a two-year-old, she pointed out, "Heaven help us, any reporter drawing a paycheck should dig for the *truth* when the competition's already turning in their story! *Work*, Mark, takes *time*."

"You don't gain credibility with phony stories," he countered.

"Credibility!" she scoffed. "I can see *you're* a man who makes his own rules and lives in a bubble. This isn't about high-minded credibility or ideals. It's about *deadlines*. Sucking attention from the public. Racing critics, or, in our case, animal rights militants, can't be rock stars. But they sure figured out how to get their picture in the paper. Banish the thought they should ever go out and raise a dog right, win a race and get their picture in the paper that way. Oh no, that's too much exercise!"

But he didn't get it. He didn't *get it* at all. Since when did responsible journalism fly out the window? Since when did the press stop checking the facts and give a balanced story for people to make up their own minds? Had the world turned into a dog race? Had he missed something when he blinked?

"I don't know about you," Felicia said, "but last time I checked a dictionary, *agenda* came before the word *truth*."

Whatever it takes to get what you want. As long as they spell your name right.

Just like the old Madonna, he thought.

Maybe even the new one.

A friend of his in the music business pointed it out to him. "Grow up," he said, as they were standing outside in the cold hawking antiques at a flea market. "You ain't gettin' no place fast. You gotta think big! You gotta think big *money*! Take a tip from Madonna. She don't take no shit from nobody. And look where *she* is. *That* bitch ain't standin' around in the cold sellin' old dishes!"

If she was, they'd be the best dishes around. But along the way, she and others who emulated her had set the pace for a whole generation of followers and made it cool to be tough. Cool to have no conscience.

Qualifying his pronouncement, his musical friend said, "Don't get stuck on that grandiose philosophy stuff of yours, baby. It don't pay the rent." Clearing his throat in the sharp, all-business way typical of a man growing up on the streets and making it to the executive level, he shook his head. "What I'm sayin' is, plenty of people can *think*. It's what they think *about* that matters."

Yes, it mattered. It mattered very much.

"Your industry's under attack," Mark said, the full impact of his statement starting to take hold. "It's an attack on a—"

"*National* sport," she finished for him. "And it's

under siege by who? Didn't you ever read Claude M. Steiner's *Scripts People Live?*"*

He hadn't. But, upon asking, he discovered she was quite serious about her study of people and what makes them do the things they do. Perhaps her observations about brainwashing hadn't been unfounded. Perhaps Felicia McCrory did more than read dog magazines.

"Look at it closely, Mark. Look at the word *rescue*. That should tell you all you need to know about our critics."

Still, he wasn't following. "Steiner maintains that all of us map our lives according to how we are psychologically influenced growing up. Which means, that's how we look at relationships, how we deal with situations, how we look at everything around us."

"I'm aware of that," he said, beginning to understand why he sensed deeper waters in her nature. "And, you're saying the critics of Greyhound racing are caught up in a psychological role-play of some kind?"

"I'm sure of it," she said. "Their payoff, or reward, if you want to call it that, isn't money."

"But, you said—"

She knew what she had said. "But I wasn't talking about the volunteers who are out there on the front lines. I was talking about the ones behind the scenes. Higher-ups."

It was a lot to take in. "Let's cut through all the political correctness and be real," she said. "A lot of

---

Scripts People Live: The ground-breaking study of psychological patterns of behavior shaped to get attention in childhood that determine the roles we play in relationships and business throughout our lives.

people out there are hurting. That's life. That's just how it is. You've got your *haves* and your *have nots*."

"I didn't know you were so politically tuned in," he said.

"There's a lot you don't know about me," she grinned. "And I aim to keep it that way."

He *liked* her. "I get the drift," he said. "And I'll keep plowing."

"I would hope so," she winked.

"OK, you two. Break it up," Poppy said. "If flirting was fog I wouldn't be able to turn on my wipers fast enough to see. If I was following before we took a left turn, Felicia, here, was saying the psychological reasons why people get so wrapped up in animal rescue was . . . what? Or, did I get lost somewhere?"

She hadn't gotten lost.

"Look," Felicia said. "They act like a bunch of insecure high school girls who can't get a guy's attention any other way except by getting him mad. So, they just pick and pick and pick until he finally looks at them."

"I've never been picked on," Jack Halstead said, joining them.

"You, they didn't have to pick on," she said. "With you, they were too busy running away!"

To general laughter, Mark pitched in again. "Sounds like *you're* the one doing the picking," he said to Felicia. "Aren't most women supposed to stick together?"

"Are *you* ever an idealist!" almost came in unison from the female members of the conversation. "Obviously, you've never been the prettiest girl in town," Wanda said, catching up with them. *"RrrrrOWWWW!"* she squealed, arching her fingers and clawing the air.

Certain he had never been the prettiest anything, Mark leaned back for another appraisal of Felicia McCrory. "It doesn't sound as if you like your fellow sex very much."

"Oh, I like sex with fellows," she assured him, pleased with her own wit.

"Women, on the other hand," Poppy said, "can be an overrated but necessary component of the citizenry."

"Overrated? You surprise me," he said, feigning shock.

"Cross my heart," she smiled sadly, tucking her chin, batting her eyes and putting her right hand up to God.

"I've never looked at a woman that way in my life," Jack said. "I look at them as rare treasures."

"Sex objects, you mean?" Poppy said, laughing. "Goooooood boy. You just keep it that way!" she winked. "Especially when some of them are picking your pockets!" Oh, she was feeling good tonight.

"Overrated?" Mark said again.

"Present company excluded, of course," she said, to smiles all around.

"For a minute there, I thought you might ruin my feelings about the human race," he teased.

"Tell me," Felicia asked, smiling, playing with his mind, "what does winning the human race *pay*?"

"Friendship, feeling good about yourself, knowing you've left the world a better place when you're gone," he said, looking into her eyes. "For starters."

"And Pennsylvania hasn't outlawed it? Oh, Mark, what*ever* is the *State of Independence* waiting for?"

"The lady doesn't like what I'm saying," he noticed, glancing all around for support.

"What I don't *like* is you living in a 1930s black-and-white film. The world isn't black and white any more. It's been *colorized*, Mark. As in Ted Turner? People are different now. They're jaded. Celebrities are saying *stay away from me.* Hockey players and basketball stars are throwing things at their fans. About the only heroes left with any *decency* are dogs or horses. People just let you down."

If he had felt any more hopeless at that moment, his heart would have fallen right through the bottom of his shoes. An attractive woman, at the height of her career, believing that? Where had all the fun gone? The inspiration, the hope? Sports *were* supposed to inspire us, weren't they?"

"How do you fight back?" he asked. "I mean, I see the letters, the press releases tonight," he continued, looking around. "But how does your industry stay on top of it, really?"

It was Wanda's turn to smile. *"The Net!"* she said, in her Irish way. "We chat all the time. How else can we know what's going on and have a head start on what to do about it?"

"Don't forget *The Review.** It comes out every month from the NGA," Poppy added.

"And that's the extent of information for the whole industry?" Mark asked, incredulous.

Wanda nodded. "Word of mouth is very powerful. We talk with each other, and that's the same as having

---

*The Greyhound Review: The official publication of the National Greyhound Association, reporting race results, informative articles and breeding statistics; published monthly.

scouts everywhere. There's so much happening out there right now. The industry's taking so many hits from the press. Sometimes, I feel like we're the target of a conspiracy. Don't you?" she asked, looking around at everybody.

Until then, until that moment, nothing else had made sense. Greyhound racing was the sport of an industry appealing to fans all over the world, pouring money into state coffers for nearly a hundred years, yet boycotted off the face of the sports pages.

Absurd!

"It's bad publicity in a nation of dog lovers," Felicia said. "That TV of yours found people who were killing their dogs, and it told its friend the newspaper, and it told its friend the radio. And they blamed all the rest of us who never even hurt a dog in our life."

"Flawed logic," Jack said.

"I'm starting to see what you mean," Mark said.

"No, you don't," Felicia said firmly. "You don't know anything until you roll up your shirt sleeves and pitch in."

"Why should I do that?" he wanted to know.

"Because you're one of us now."

It had been a good meeting for the Coalition. A strong meeting. Waving good night, Edna Rae stood on the porch, arms folded against the chill. Good nights were the worst part, she thought, as they faded into a lonely darkness glittering with stars. Sadly, she closed the door, her only portal to the world into which she never ventured any more.

"Coming to bed?" Cecil asked, in his robe and standing in the hallway lined with pictures of winning dogs they had raised over the years.

"In a minute," she said, keenly aware of what kind of pictures were missing from those walls as the quiet closed in on her. There were no baby pictures, no sons or daughters in graduation gowns.

"You OK?" Cecil asked.

Nodding, she braced a hand on the back of an over-stuffed chair and slipped off her shoes. "I'll be all right," she said, in a way that conveyed volumes to the man with whom she had shared most of her life. "Thinking about the kids," she said, of the circle of Greyhound friends who had become that to her.

"They're doing fine. I was proud of them tonight," he said, coming to her side and taking her in his arms. "And you were beautiful."

Beautiful, she thought. *Tell me I'm beautiful and I'll stay with you forever.* It's what she thought, what she always thought, even though she knew it made her vulnerable to his slightest criticism, his slightest wish.

What invisible thread held them together, she wondered? How were they connected? By spiritual chords mentioned in the books scattered throughout their house? Or, were they bonded by the usual things people go through: the great and the mundane.

"It went well," she finally said.

"I thought so," he agreed. "What did you think of Felicia's friend?"

"I liked him," she said.

"Me, too. He thinks for himself."

"Yes, I listened to the conversation," Edna Rae said. "I think he can be very helpful."

"Did you notice how Jack handled the situation in Texas?" Cecil asked.

"The guy wanting us to help with their vote on slots? Yes, I thought he handled that call very well."

"I loved it when he said he'd trade for some help in Pennsylvania. Valdez wants to run more of his dogs at Wheeling. His son is enrolled at Penn State. They fly the dogs into Pittsburgh and his son drives them to the track. Do you know that boy is paying his tuition with what the dogs are winning?"

"Must be pretty good," she said, not really paying attention.

"Not easy looking out for an industry this big," he said.

"It's not easy looking out for an empire, period," she sighed.

"From the sands of ancient Egypt all the way to my arms," he said, tenderly rocking her side to side. "My queen."

"Oh, my pharaoh, what has happened to the world?"

"When I'm with you, my love, I forget the world. When I'm with you, we are back again in the city of our vision, among the petals of rare flowers, the force of the one God flowing through us."

"It is all so different now," she whispered, her eyes soft, as if seeing what only they could, what they had been born knowing.

"Yes," he said sadly. "What we thought was the new Egypt is not so. The people are strong, but they don't understand."

"I loved them," she said.

"And they loved you, my queen. Come," he said, taking her hand. "Let me wash you in oil from the finest groves, scented with the fragrance of the deepest Nile waters on the night we sailed under the moonlight. Do you remember?"

"I long for it."

"Our ship is waiting," he said in tones warmer than anyone would ever expect from the paint store owner tucked away in Durbin, West Virginia. And in the house that was a palace among the rotting sheds and barns that were the city of Tel el Amarna, peopled with cattle and sheep that were followers of whomever fed them, he lit the candles in their golden vases. Dropping her blue caftan to the floor, she stared into his eyes and he let his robe fall open.

"I adore you," he whispered, reassuring her that she was, had always been, would always be, the love of his life.

In the glow filling the room they had made their private chamber, shadows of palm tree fronds draped the ceiling in mystery. As the incense of roses surrounded them, he kissed her. He kissed her hair, her face, her mouth. "Beautiful One, Beautiful One," he chanted as if it were a mantra, and as he did so—as the rhythmic chant of his voice grew deeper, darker, more intense—she blossomed like an exotic flower in the night.

Lying on the bed, spreading her legs for him, she raised her arms and ran her fingers over his head.

"Beautiful One . . . Beautiful One . . ." he chanted as she arched her back and offered him her breasts.

Running his tongue around in circles, he wetted her nipples, kissing them, sucking them. "Beautiful One . . . Beautiful One . . ." with each kiss, she gained strength, power.

"Ahhhhh," she sighed, pushing her hands under his

robe, clawing his shoulders, his back, his buttocks with her painted nails.

Higher and higher . . . deeper and deeper . . . stronger and stronger . . . until their screams echoed through the valley of the Nile that was the valley of mountains that was a land, a place, a destination only they could feel . . . only they could know . . . only they knew how to find.

Waiting for takeoff, Claude considered the pieces of the puzzle. To him, the mystery wasn't what critics of Greyhound racing said. The real mystery would be found on the other side of the issue. The side the public never heard. At least, not until now. He was a reporter. He earned his living by finding out what animal lovers wanted to know.

Cruelty and abuse? They wanted to know about that, no matter how bad or how bloody. And Greyhound racing had its share of grizzly pictures floating around. He could hardly imagine a more effective smear campaign.

Who stood to gain?

From: Researchdept@SATV.com
To: Emerson@dejazzd.com
Subject: High Stakes

Anyone who collects donations against animal cruelty stands to gain. It's big business. To get donations, you need a target. And to keep the donations rolling in, you need a steady supply of incidents. An isolated occurrence won't do because it becomes old news real fast. An ongoing sport, with the infrastructure of a whole industry behind it, is ideal. Not to mention that the product is dogs, and most people like dogs.

From: Emerson@dejazzd.com
To: Researchdept@SATV.com
Subject: Confidential

I like dogs, too. But, emotion aside, who can prove where those grisly pictures were taken? Or when?

From: Researchdept@SATV.com
To: Emerson@dejazzd.com
Subject: High Stakes

Our information is that some of it never even happened in the U.S. In a widely broadcast TV ad campaign, an anti-racing organization tried getting a foothold in the public's favor by showing Greyhounds being hung to death from trees, tossed into ditches from pickup trucks and all manner of cruelty. To the best of our knowledge, the public was never told the footage was from Spain. And, on top of that, it was over ten years old. Nor did they acknowledge that such treatment and disrespect is not an accepted practice by the majority of people in the Greyhound racing business.

CHAPTER SIX

As Long As There Are Greyhounds . . .

In the familiar surroundings of the kennel, safe in his nest of soft, shredded paper, Clue took a deep sigh. It was good to run fast, knowing nothing was chasing you, no branches or rocks to scratch you, no thorns to pierce your toes or rip your skin as you ran through the forest.

He missed the forest, at times. He missed the sparkle of water falling over smooth moss-covered stones as the sun chased away the darkness of night. He missed the smell of wet leaves and wild animals, new and different in their sounds, the way they moved, how they lived. He didn't miss being hungry. Or cold. Or, worst of all, lonely.

A man with a familiar voice was crooning to the dog in the crate above him. He remembered Carl, but he wasn't fond of the flowery aroma drifting from Dee-Dee, beneficiary of the latest high-priced shampoo. "You're worth it," Carl reassured his favorite, as Clue buried his nose deeper in the newspaper. Would Felicia and Mark let him run again in the fresh air tomorrow?

Saying good night to each of the dogs by name, Carl turned out the lights.

Mark pulled over at a service station and took two more ibuprofen. That clunk on the head was something he hadn't counted on. Maybe it would do him good, he joked to himself. Maybe his swami was trying to tell him something.

Strange, that he should still be thinking about Edna Rae and her memories. He was leaving a few of his own in West Virginia. And walking into an empty cottage, now that Clue would be staying with Felicia, wasn't going to feel so good. He would get used to it, he told himself. He could get used to lots of things. He got used to having a dog around, didn't he?

But hiking in the woods by yourself isn't the same as having a dog rush out in front of you, as if danger lurked ahead. Or stopping suddenly, as if pulling information from the very air you breathe.

Life was easier, fuller, more fun having someone to talk with. Even if that someone had four legs.

It sounded freaky when you put it that way. *"Someone with four legs"* sounded like a headline from a supermarket tabloid: "Man Falls For Someone With Four Legs!"

Well, he thought. He could forgive a lot of shedding on his sofa, maybe even a chewed up pillow every once in a while, if it meant having company.

Even if they had four legs.

I've never felt like this before, he thought . . . yes, he knew. It was a line from an Andrew Lloyd Weber song performed by that ragingly gorgeous woman Kim Criswell. He knew, because the way she sang that song got him in trouble many years ago that he still wasn't completely over. Every time he heard it, he remembered walking through his living room at the precise moment when *"she"* was singing "Unexpected Song" on TV. Could he have helped falling hopelessly in love?

No more than a bird could keep from flying, he thought. No more than a Greyhound could keep from running as fast as its heart would allow.

Never felt like this before? No, he hadn't. And, this time, his reasons were entirely different. His life was changing. Growing, maybe? He could sense it, feel it. And, as they say, you can't go "back to before."

Felicia McCrory.

What have you done to me.

You and your entourage aren't professional singers speaking of love, yet you hold your emotions at arm's length because you're afraid to be touched. You're not afraid to risk popularity like politicians afraid to offend their public, the hands that feed them by voting them in. You and all the rest of your Greyhound Racing Coalition are like a band of gypsies, putting your names and reputations right out there for the whole world to see. And living a truth that others can only pretend they know.

Was all this just another boy-meets-girl thing? he wondered. How could he know for sure? What if he was making a mistake, walking into something that would ruin him, cost him everything he had, leave him broken and penniless on the streets? Well, maybe not on the streets, but on the trails in the woods.

The woods were filled with chances and obstacles. Filled with the eternal question of which path to take.

Maybe in the final analysis that's all his life really was. Boy meets girl meets boy meets girl meets girl meets boy meets meets meets. Maybe that's what the aliens who put us here in the first place were counting on, he thought, with sci-fi maniacally tinged laughter. Maybe, like plants transforming carbon dioxide into oxygen, our romantic encounters generated some kind of dizzy excitement far more essential to other forms of life than we realized. It was a possibility.

What was he contributing to this dog? This dog turning his life upside down was another form of life, right? Would somebody please give him a clue? *Somebody already had.*

Felicia, he smiled to himself, his thoughts drifting back to racing. But anybody could run a race, right? We're all racing against something or other from the time we're born. Racing against time. Catch me if you can—ha! ha! ha! Catch me 20s, 30s, 40s . . . . 80s, 90s and a hundred.

Greyhound racing could take your mind off what ails you, he thought, and show you how to win. It was good knowing anybody still could, he thought, asking when he had become so cynical.

Cynical, he might be. But even a cynic knew there was more to racing than met the eye. It was a sport as free of human interference as a sport could be. Easy to understand why such an activity was a threat to the powers that be. If people ever realized how free they could be, then who could ever control them? If people really understood the meaning of *heart*, why would they settle for anything less?

Questions. His life was filled with them now. Filled with more questions than ever, like pieces of a puzzle bigger than himself, bigger than all he could see or think or feel. If each question led to an answer, as he had always been told, then surely there were reasons for living that few of us could ever know—and this Greyhound adventure would reveal them.

He could still see Clue's eager face running at him. Trusting. Sure that all was as it should be in his world. Nothing mattered to that face except what it felt, what it wanted and where he was going at that instant. If only he, himself, could be like that, Mark thought. If only he could live for each day, each moment, unaffected by the latest news, the latest phone call. A moment? How about a second? A millisecond?

If only he could have a dog's faith that someone would catch him when he jumped off a cliff.

He had taken Clue into his life without thinking, without questioning, without debating what might happen if he didn't. Clue was only a dog. A simple dog. But his was a living mind made up. Without considering the consequences, Mark opened his arms to that mind!

And was centered.

From now on, he knew, his life wouldn't be ruled by subjective opinions of judges or juries or peers and teachers. It would be determined by what he, alone, could decide and accomplish. As in the ritual of eight Greyhounds rushing out of the starting boxes, each dog figuring a way to get ahead of the pack and everybody knowing the winner is the one who crosses the finish line first, it would be on his own terms. He would live by an honest sport with no jockeys to bribe, no secret game plans in sweaty locker rooms and no professional odds-makers predicting the outcome any better than anybody else. No wonder they want to get rid of Greyhound racing! *Ban the thing!* It's too honest. *Drive it into the ground!*

If what he was seeing for himself was true, he had stumbled across the cleanest sport in America! Was it possible he was the first to figure that out? He knew, sensed, dreaded, people were going to think he had lost his mind feeling this way about something all of us were supposed to know was wrong.

Wrong? *Who said so?*

He may not have seen much so far, but he had already seen more about Greyhound racing than a lot of its critics had. How could he tell? He could tell by the way they talked about it; by what they said—by how they said the same things *over and over again* as if recited, memorized, programmed.

His hands went cold on the steering wheel. Felicia was right. *Say it often enough and people will start believing it.*

Like his life up to now, the miles whizzed by, and his thoughts returned to racing. The basic, instinctive drive to give all your heart and soul to get where you're going. He had searched *his whole life* for truth so pure. If not for a wounded dog, he might never have found it until the minute he drew his last breath.

Was it luck? Or fate?

He was lucky, some people said, for making his life into pretty much what he wanted it to be. But luck, as wise men and wise-crackers say, had very little to do with it. More important than luck was the ability to see a picture, a dream. To hold an idea so clearly and so strongly that you could feel it, taste it, believe it would happen no matter how long it took. No matter what it took from you. He pulled over again to rest.

Racing was pulling him in, like this rest stop on a night when he was weary. *Come to me. You are safe with me. You understand me,* she seemed to say. When the dogs were running, he was right there with them! He was seeing through their eyes. They could hear him, sense him!

"You're one of us now," Felicia had said.

He was a Greyhound stretching every muscle in his body, trying—trying to get ahead in this rat race of a world—but not because he had to. It wasn't like that. He was going for something, trying for something, reaching for something, yes. But, like eight dogs chasing a toy on the end of a stick as the crowd cheers them on, he was going for it *because he wanted to*!

Weeks that used to be filled with so much action it almost made him believe time was moving faster than ever, were no longer evaporating as fast for him. Without Clue by his side, the conversation of customers in the shop that used to be his grandfather's wasn't as stimulating. Finding bargain-priced heirlooms of Bacardi crystal and Limoges porcelain and selling for a quick profit wasn't quite as tempting.

Instead, a yellowed book from England, a torn photograph from Australia, a deco-framed poster from the Jacksonville Greyhound Park celebrating sixty years of performances—these held his attention in a way that the most valuable art collection couldn't hope to any more.

It was still stimulating, yes. He had grown up with it and studied art, and treasures of the Third Estate would always be part of his life. He had grown up in a family of artists passionately debating the politics of the day. But training Clue with Felicia was more politically charged than anything he had ever encountered. Suddenly, it wasn't about what a simple dog could do any more. It wasn't about how far a dog could run. Suddenly, it was about how far people *themselves* could go.

He couldn't explain it. He didn't know why. But, suddenly, through a twist of fortune, he was caught up in something far bigger than himself. He was caught up in one of the greatest issues of our times.

The United States of America, a country of such power that it shattered the mind, a people so bold that they traveled the earth, bashing any boundary in their way, and the universe touching the stars. But something had drifted when no one was looking. Like many others, he could sense it: Americans sitting back watching the news, watching bombs explode on foreign cities, watching bloodied people scream and cry. Pass the chips, please. Toss me another beer. Welcome to the new America, they seemed to say. Welcome to an America desensitized to anything off its shores, raising its children not to care if people are demoralized, cheated, murdered or raped. But God forbid if a dog or a cat or a rat is hurt in any way. You're "allowed" to get upset about that. Freak out! Be my guest and have another beer.

He could understand emotions. He had spent a lifetime observing them, living them, exploring them. He could understand the value of animals keeping a sense of love and compassion alive in this world. A world ever more combative, more emotionally isolated. In that sense alone, the debate of animal care and protection had great importance. Nobody of a sensitive nature would argue that. But there were deeper issues running in the waters. People were changing, as Felicia had said. They were disconnecting, losing intellectual skills, looking the other way. Something basic, something real, was being short-circuited, and it was showing up in a public that didn't seem to understand what was right or wrong any more.

"One wouldn't have seen such demoralization of the masses when Rodin was living!" Mark could still hear his Uncle Frank say at their family dinner.

"Shut up, Frank! Don't let me hear another word about Rodin! He treated Madame Rose like shit! After all she did for him—covering his clay sculptures with damp rags so they wouldn't crack and dry out! Saving his ass with coins she scrounged together for years when the war hit France! Don't tell me about that man!"

That was Grandma Nadine talking.

"Momma, if you don't get off your high horse and pass me the potatoes right now, I'll never finish that portrait you want."

That was Grandpa.

"Fifty-three years! I'll be dead before you get it done. I'll say what I want to about that Rodin. *All she did for him!*"

Did he dare interrupt such weekly dramas over Sunday dinner to say, "But Grandmomma, the money she had, she *stole it* from him. I read it in one of my art classes at school." Or let anyone know Rodin never loved Rose and he was honest about it. He never loved their son, either.

"Well, he *married* her, didn't he?" Grandpa would holler.

"Yes, and look what *good* it did her!" Grandma yelled back, looking like a painted actor in a black-and-white silent horror film. "They were both *unconscious* from pneumonia!"

Had his grandparents actually *known* Rodin and Madame Rose? Possibly. But, in truth, no. They had never met the artist and his woman. Yet, no one ever asked for proof of the well-rehearsed and made-up intimacies they recited. Over time, it had all just become real.

"Am I sorry I brought it up, you're asking me?" Uncle Frank would laugh and slop gravy on his plate as Mark's grandparents glared at each other. "*No! I'm not sorry!* This is the greatest show on earth, and I, for one, wouldn't miss it!"

"Finish that portrait," Grandmomma would command Grandpa in a low and measured voice.

"No," he would say every time. "Not until you apologize to the greatest artist that ever lived!"

"The greatest artist that ever lived? Grandmomma would ask, leaning back in her chair and leveling him with cold eyes as everyone knew what was coming because they knew her so well. "Then I apologize to *Picasso!*"

"Ahhhh!" their grandfather bellowed, shaking off cousins, aunts and brothers as he lunged for her.

"Picasso! Picasso! Picasso!" Grandmomma said, laughing, tossing her napkin and running for the studio.

"Let me go! *Let me GO!*" Grandpa hollered, slapping them away, hurling himself after her.

And so it was, Sunday after Sunday: the meal, the fight, the disappearance into the barn that was his grandfather's studio, and the lusty laughter that followed. Late into the night, Grandfather would paint and she would pose for him naked . . . as they had done, as they had always done, as they always would. . . . How many times the portrait had been finished only to be started again was their everlasting and well-kept secret.

He longed for that kind of love.

He longed for driving power that didn't care about the kind of bland "political correctness" spreading like a fungus everywhere he turned, breeding fear in schoolboys for kissing little girls and wiping out racial references in literature affirming the differences that make us unique. He longed for what Greyhound people knew as *heart*. For the willpower and guts that kept racing fans going no matter what anybody said about it, no matter how often they were insulted, scolded and humiliated in the press. He didn't see "heart" very often these days. He couldn't find much of it in political leaders, religious leaders or celebrities. Unlikely as it seemed for one, like him, who had grown up believing anything is possible, but seeing his heroes slandered and assassinated for trying, he had found a bold and unlikely symbol untouched by scandal. He could see it—sense it, feel it—throbbing with life in a racing dog named Clue.

He looked forward to their weekends. As Felicia trained Clue, he was finding answers. He was finding the kind of answers he hadn't been able to find in school or church or by making it on his own in the workplace. Since Clue ran on the airstrip, ran for glory, Mark's life had shifted and expanded in ways he hadn't ever considered. As long as Greyhounds were being born, somebody would be taking care of them. As long as Greyhounds needed to be fed and watered and groomed and cleaned up after, somebody would have a job. As long as fans were screaming, laughing and hollering, the dogs would show them how to go after what you want in life, like there's no tomorrow.

There would be love. There would be passion. As long as there were Greyhounds.

Felicia cupped one hand beside her mouth and held on to Clue with the other.

"Ready?" she hollered to Mark as he stood again at the far side of the airstrip, feeling more confident in his role as dog catcher this time.

"As ready as I'll ever be!" he called back, waving his arm and letting her know it was OK to turn the excited Greyhound loose.

Whoom!

Frizzzzzzzzz!

The string on their battery-powered *ground lure* sizzled across homemade wooden pulleys they had staked into the ground, whipping crazy life into a bright red plastic bag as it went. Head low, bearing down like a bull chasing a matador's fluttering cape, Clue did his best to catch the elusive object dashing insanely away.

"Come on, boy!" Mark hollered. "Come on!"

Right into his arms, Clue rushed again, knocking him over, laughing at anyone for being foolish enough to think they could stop him. Hadn't Mark learned anything last time? Or all the times before that?

"You're gonna have to learn to let him go," Felicia

huffed, as she caught up. "What's he gonna do if you're not standing at the finish line?"

"I didn't think of that," Mark said. "Next time, I'll do better."

"At this rate, he might not be on the ground for you to catch!" she laughed, holding up her stopwatch. "He's ready, Mark."

"Ready?" he asked, his heart sinking. "As in, we're done?"

"As in, if we don't get him to the track now, we might as well forget it. He's never going to be better than this."

"But what about honing his skills?"

"Easiest dog I ever trained. Mother Nature took care of it," she pointed out. "He's honed and She's hired."

"So, we're done," he said, almost to himself. "Wow . . . it was so fast."

"Hey, brighten up. We can school him on the track now and make some money."

"Sure," Mark said, as if that's what it had all been about. Not that making money bothered him. But . . . well . . .

"What's the matter, Mark?"

"Nothin' " was all he could say as they made their way to the house and Kenita's morning coffee. Straightening his shoulders, he clicked his tongue and Clue snapped to attention. "Wanna go see Kenita?"

At the sound of the familiar name, the name of the one who gave him raw hamburger treats, Clue trotted to his side. "Good boy," Mark said to him, careful not to fall into that sing-songy cadence he had promised himself he'd avoid at all costs. After all, he told himself, "my" dog was an athlete. "My" dog had a real job. "My" dog wasn't just a pet.

Not that there was anything wrong with being somebody's pet, he reasoned. Not at all. As a matter of fact, every dog, cat, bird, horse, cow, goat, sheep and pig he could think of was somebody's pet in one way or another. Maybe some of us weren't the best *masters* in the universe, he thought, and who among us would go down in history just for being a great pet *owner*? But, whether doted upon and sleeping on a silk pillow or working under the hot sun pulling a plow, every animal belonged to somebody, he figured. And every domesticated animal was *somebody's* pet.

"So, Clue-Boy," he said, as Felicia silently looked from him to her stopwatch and back again, "are you a winner?"

"We won't know until the lights hit him on the track at night,' she said, hiding her excitement. "But I can tell you, Mark, he's got the power to blow them all away."

"Well, he sure looks like a million bucks to me," Mark said, about Clue's shiny coat and rippling muscles. "I know I'd bet on him."

"You and a hundred others. First, we have to school him a few times," she said, as they walked back to the house, "so he knows how the track feels. Just about every track feels different to a dog," she explained. "Be sure to bet on his first race, because his odds'll never be worse than they will right then. After that, everybody's gonna know what he can do and he'll be a favorite. Tough to make money on a favorite unless you bet big. I know a guy who bet ten grand on the favorite. And, wouldn't you know it, he didn't win. That's the funny thing about all this. You just never know."

"He blew ten grand on a dog?"

"Every dollar of it," she said. "Was his wife ever mad at me!" she hooted, dying for him to ask why.

"Mad at you? What was she mad at you for?"

"It was my dog. And she wanted the money back. I tried telling her it wasn't my money, but they were from Africa someplace and she said they didn't understand."

"What happened?" Mark asked.

"I already told you," she said, as if he hadn't been paying attention.

"But after that."

"Oooooooh. You want to know the *rest of the story*," she said playfully. "Well, it turns out this guy and his wife, they were both in their early thirties, I'd say, it turns out they weren't just from Africa, they were from Nigeria. And they weren't just from Nigeria—they were from the royal family of Nigeria!"

"The royal family," Mark said, thinking back to his political courses in school, not at all sure they had a king in Nigeria, and saying so.

"Oh, yes!" she said, serious now, her manner taking on a shadow of intrigue. "And there's always someone plotting to overthrow the government. Which is why Buckinham and Stephanie had to get away for a while."

"Had to get away," he said, with a quiet, knowing nod as he fell into her tale.

"Mark, we can only imagine what it must have been like for them, day after day in the palace—not knowing if your windows were going to be shattered by rocks or fire-bombs. Not knowing if the doors would be smashed open during the night and you and your whole family would be killed or taken away and tortured."

"Sounds like the people really loved them."

"Oh, they did," she assured me. "The people loved them! The people weren't the problem—it was the *Opposition*!"

"Oooooh!" he said now, trying to be as serious as he could. "Yep. Gotta watch out for the opposition."

"You don't know what it was like for Stephanie and her *baby*," Felicia pouted.

"That would be the crown prince," Mark said, certain he knew the outcome.

"No, smartie. *Buckinham* was the crown prince. The baby was going to be a Duke. If it was a boy, they were going to name him Duke *Ellington*. Isn't that cute?"

"Yeah," he managed to say, "cute," realizing Princess Stephanie of Nigeria, on vacation at a dog track in West Virginia, was pregnant. "And if it was a girl?"

"Doris." She smiled. "That was my idea. After Doris Duke, the famous tobacco heiress. I told them if they named her Doris, they'd never have to worry about betting on the dogs, no matter how much!"

"Which they were," he said, bringing her back home. "Betting on the dogs and worried, both."

"And rightfully so. After they blew $10,000 on my dog, they didn't have any way of getting back home!"

"No kidding," he said, dreading what came next.

"They were embarrassed to ask me, being royalty and all, but after we got to know each other it was OK."

"Don't tell me," he said. "They asked you for car fare."

"No. But they did ask me to help them get money out of the country—for the baby, so they could set up a trust fund."

"And what did you do?"

"What did I do?" she asked, slowly raising an eyebrow in amusement and leaning back her head for a better look at him. "I ordered them both dinner, asked them to stay *right there* while I checked on my dogs, and went straight to Jeri in the office. When I found out nobody could have placed a ten thousand dollar bet that night, I called security and pointed out Buckinham and Stephanie in the restaurant."

"What were they doing?" he asked.

"Munching on crab legs and corn on the cob." She smiled fondly.

"Did they see you coming?"

"As in spotting a fool a mile away?" she asked coolly. "Not as fast as I spotted them," she said sweetly. "When they took her away, Stephanie was swinging her head around looking *everywhere* for me. She wore one of those big sheets wrapped around her head, you know, like they do in Africa? I was so scared it was going to fly off and land on somebody's table!" She laughed. "And Buckinham, he looked so classy in his linen suit. He slipped an extra crab leg in his pocket when they took him away. He winked at me when I saw him do that and we waved goodbye."

"What tipped you off?" Mark asked, almost

ashamed for thinking anyone could make a fool of Felicia McCrory.

"Well, I might not ever have met the Crown Prince and Princess of Nigeria," she said, "but I certainly know the *outline of a pillow* when I see one. Let me tell you, when I say that woman Stephanie could stretch a dress so tight you could see every corner of that pillow including the price tag," she said, laughing, "I'm *not* kidding!"

His faith in her restored, they reached the house and he motioned to Felicia to wait. "Allow me." He smiled grandly, bowing low and opening the door for her. It isn't every day I can escort someone who knows *royalty*!"

"Mark Whittier, has anyone ever slapped you?"

"Slapped me?" he asked, taken aback.

"Right across that smirky face." She smiled, like the scorpion before it stung the frog that had just helped it across the stream. What did you do that for? the dying frog asks. To which, the scorpion, with no conscience, smiles broadly and says, "Because I'm a scorpion."

"Well, don't try it," he said, stepping inside and quickly pushing the door shut to her surprise. "I was raised in the era of women demanding equal treatment!" he shouted.

"Open that door!"

"No!"

"Let me in!"

"What for?" He laughed. "You want to slap me."

"Now more than ever!" She laughed back, pushing just enough to struggle, but not nearly as hard as they both knew she could. No, Felicia McCrory, if she wanted to, could floor a man and not even notice. She could floor Mark with one comment, one punch in the nose or one icy stare—which he was about to get right now if he didn't give in.

"OK," he said, taking his hands off the door handle and quickly stepping aside as she almost fell. "You win!"

"You rotten . . . !" she managed to spit out as she floundered for something, anything to hold on to. "You're mean!"

"Yeah?" he said, smiling. "Then why are you hanging onto my belt that way?"

"Oh!" She shivered with rage. "You're so arrogant!"

"Arrogant now, am I? Well, just a minute ago, I was a smart ass. Now I'm arrogant, too. Gee, if we keep this up, who knows what the lady might be calling me next!"

"Well!" she said, brushing indignation off her clothes and tossing her head so her hair bounced attractively. "I don't know where you learned your manners, but I can assure you it wasn't anyplace I've ever been—or *ever* care to go!" she added with the rest of that icy stare she hadn't quite finished.

How they managed to get into Kenita's kitchen without another word or what made Kenita say what she did, are the kind of things a good mystery is made of, but Kenita McCrory was nothing if not mysterious. Serving fried eggs and oatmeal with sliced peaches, she took her place at the table, fluffed her napkin on her lap and leaned forward. "Mah, mah," she said in her sweetest Southern drawl, "but, you sure do make a *purrrty* couple."

Lift off . . .

Level out . . .

Close your eyes.

"Excuse me."

Please don't be talking to me, Claude thought.

"Excuse me. Sir?"

"Sir, would you mind moving over?" the flight attendant asked. "I think you're in the wrong seat."

Wrong seat. OK, where's the right seat? Claude wondered, checking his ticket and the anxious couple standing in the narrow aisle.

"Oh! I guess I'm supposed to be over here," he said, shuffling to the window seat. "Sorry about that."

"No problem," the man said, moving all two hundred and fifty pounds of himself next to Claude. "My wife needs the aisle seat," he explained. "Bad leg."

Nodding, Claude returned to his laptop. . . .

From: Emerson@dejazzd.com
To: Researchdept@SATV.com
Subject: High Stakes

Remind me not to fly any more. Hurry up and wait? Body searches? I thought I was out of the military.

From Researchdept@SATV.com
To: Emerson@dejazzd.com
Subject: High Stakes

You're never out of the military.

From: Emerson@dejazzd.com
To: Researchdept@SATV.com
Subject: High Stakes

Tell me about it. So, who's behind the fight against the ARs? (Polite way of saying Animal Rights fighters.) Who are the players?

From Researchdept@SATV.com
To: Emerson@dejazzd.com
Subject: High Stakes

No need to be polite. It's an unreported, unofficial war without uniforms. Whether or not you'll meet any of the players is anybody's guess, or they could be all around you. As for the side you're reporting on, The Greyhound Coalition appears to be an independent bunch. If I was a copywriter, I might describe them as a band of brave souls fighting to save a sport brought to its knees and raise it up to its former glory.

From: Emerson@dejazzd.com
To: Researchdept@SATV.com
Subject: High Stakes

Champions. The very thing they live for. Remind me not to let you get away from me before this assignment's over and I'm holding that Pulitzer. And remind me to use that line in my report.

From Research dept@SATV.com
To: Emerson@dejazzd.com
Subject: High Stakes

That's a lot of reminding. How cozy you get with your Pulitzer is not for me to say. But I found some of the other information you asked for. Greyhounds were brought over to this country to help reduce the jack rabbit population out West, and racing was a natural outgrowth of that. It developed into a competitive sport somewhere around a hundred years ago and took hold when a man named Owen P. Smith came up with a mechanical lure for the dogs to chase around an oval track. He and Mrs. Smith transformed Greyhound racing, and she became the first woman to lord over an international sport.

From: Emerson@dejazzd.com
To: Researchdept@SATV.com
Subject: High Stakes

Quite a distinction. Are there many women in the sport today?

From Research dept@SATV.com
To: Emerson@dejazzd.com
Subject: High Stakes

Considerably. Some of the most successful owners, trainers and farmers are women. It is, after all, called "The Sport of Queens."

CHAPTER SEVEN

Just Another Damn Cult . . .

Clue raised his hackles and both dogs snarled at each other through their muzzles. Up on his toes, his chest expanded and tail raised high, Clue stood his ground. He had defeated greater opponents than the red-and-white dog challenging his rank in the turnout pen. He had defeated a winged savage, armed with razor-sharp talons and no conscience. He was the ruler now. He would always be. He was king.

"Clue!" The sound of his name brought him back from the edge of attack. Knowing there would be another day, the other dog lowered his head and trotted off. Glaring, keeping his eye on the retreating opportunist, Clue walked to the nearest fence post and began to mark his territory.

Wanda stood outside the paddock in a brown tweed jacket, a crisply ironed white blouse and knee-high leather boots, the picture of gentility. She secured her riding helmet with a snap. Mustn't ride without your helmet, she told herself. Mustn't ever do anything in life without protection. Wasn't that the way it was now? Homeland Security? Patriot Act I . . . Patriot Act II. The land of perfect victims, she thought, knowing she couldn't hope to explain her feelings, or what she knew, to anyone.

Crazy. That's what they would call her.

Leftist.

Liberal.

But isn't that what they called anyone who didn't fit the mold back in Nazi Germany? Or, for that matter, Nazi Anyplace?

She had just left her home office. Turned off her computer, dumped out the half-finished glass of orange juice, guilty of not finishing her daily dose, and walked away. Breathe, she told herself. Breathe. It'll go away. It'll all go away.

Everything will get better, and things will be the way they used to be.

But she knew they wouldn't. Monitoring the chat boards every day, her fingers on the pulse of something bigger, far bigger, than the Greyhound business alone, she knew. Right before our eyes, right under our noses, society was changing. As sure as Ireland had cracked, as real as the Civil War in *Gone With The Wind*, the free-wheeling life she had known was fracturing, pulverizing, dissolving. And in its place were rules, laws and limits rumbling at every turn.

It wasn't one society any more, where people knew if they had a dream and worked hard and stayed out of trouble everything would be OK. It was in pieces, as if an earthquake had broken apart the very foundations under you—until you were rushing down the streets through fire, jumping from one chunk of ground to another, the very land you ran upon falling apart.

What could she do? What could anyone do?

"Good morning, Mrs. Wharton," a polite stable-hand greeted her, tipping his hat as she entered the barn carrying her tack.

"Good morning, Sam," she said. "Is Briggin behaving himself today?" she asked, running her hands over the face of the big, liver chestnut Arabian she had raised since a foal.

"A little frisky, mostly because of the weather, I guess. But he'll be glad to get out some."

And so would she. If only she could. If only she could get away from it all.

"There you go," Felicia said, placing the water bowl in Clue's crate, and splashing him playfully. "Have fun."

But fun wasn't on her mind. Wanda's call was. . . .

"Did you hear?" Wanda asked, in a shaky voice.

"I hear a lot of things," Felicia said, trying to lighten her up. "Mostly dogs barking."

Wanda didn't laugh. "We lost Pennsylvania," she said, and they both went silent.

"How?" Felicia asked, after a long pause, her voice lifeless.

"We were creamed," Wanda said. "The vote was almost unanimous."

Felicia sat down on a nearby countertop. Legs weak. Heart pounding. "But we were doing so well," she said. "Our campaign. We had so many people writing letters, making calls."

"It wasn't enough," Wanda said, trying her best to remain steady. "It just wasn't . . . enough."

"All we did . . ." Felicia said, drumming her fingers in frustration. "Does anyone else know?"

"It hit the boards just now on WWG," Wanda said. "We had a pretty quiet night, and you know how you get a feeling that things are just *too* quiet? That's how I felt last night."

"You're pretty intuitive," Felicia said, remembering many times when her Irish friend seemed to know what was right around the next corner.

"Call the others," Felicia decided, remembering Mark asking, *When is the industry going to start fighting?*

She was beginning to ask the same thing.

During the emergency phone conference that night, the members listened.

"Dishonest legislation!" Cecil concluded. "*Fraud!* Tacking a ban against Greyhound racing onto a bill outlawing minors being tattooed without the consent of their parents?" His fist hit the table with a bang. *"Absurd!"*

"Absurd enough to pass," Jack said, matter-of-factly. "Like all shit does," he smirked. "Sooner or later."

Illegal to race Greyhounds for money? What about the races *they* held to raise money for vet bills or haulers' fees, they wondered? Why should those races be legal but putting food on the table of a trainer or a farmer and his family be against the law?

If they got their way by slapping dishonest riders like this onto Senate bills—knowing full well it hadn't been the kind of bill a governor could line veto—how long would it be until animal militants tried the same dishonest legislation in other places?

"*Lovers of Greyhounds?* They're phonies! Fakes!

Somebody should know about the time a bunch of anti-racing Greyhound owners turned their pets loose in a high school football field," Poppy said, "and let them chase a Jack Russell Terrier. Somebody should know what happened to that Jack when he got caught."

But *that* was legal, somebody reminded her. *That* wasn't for money.

They were going to spin like tops all night. They were going to spin and rant and rave like their industry had done for years. But it wouldn't win back Pennsylvania.

"Look, everybody," Felicia said. "We can talk about it all we want. *We lost.* Weird as it sounds, a state passes a law against something it's never had and now it's illegal to ever run our dogs for money there."

"Well, it's not like they had a track for us to run on anyway," Poppy said. "Not like what happened in Vermont when all the track folks came back for the meet and found out there *wasn't* one!"

"I never understood that," Edna Rae said, almost in a whisper.

"Neither did all the people who worked there—or the fans!" Poppy said.

"Never forget the fans," Jason reminded them. "It's all for them."

"And the dogs!" Poppy added.

"Well, I get a kick out of it, too," Jack said. "Not that I'm getting rich the way my pups are doing, but I love the sport."

Taking the opportunity to do some business, Brad asked Barbara, "Should we tell them about that hot stud from Australia?"

"I don't know if they're ready for that," she said.

"Brett Lee, you mean?" Wanda asked. "It's all over the boards."

"What?" Jack asked. "You guys have a deal on him?"

"We're in the negotiation stage," Brad said, dangling the possibility of good fortune for them all.

"Listen, guys," Felicia said, bringing them back to the matter at hand. "The militants moved in on Pennsylvania Lovers of Greyhounds. It's the only thing that makes sense."

"When did that happen?" Poppy wanted to know.

"Well, I can tell you from watching their posts on WWG, there's been a definite change in their point of view," Wanda said.

"I saw that," Jason said. "Almost like a split in the ranks."

"Yeah," Wanda agreed. "They were always pretty level-headed, I thought."

"Well, I know we always sent dogs to them," Felicia said. "Until I found out what happened to Clue. I always thought they were our friends, you know? Working *with* us."

"They were," Poppy said. "They were about as pro-racing as anybody gets. They even started a few people in the sport."

Cecil spoke up. "When's the last time anybody heard from them?"

"Well, I called about those dogs I was telling you about from the Panhandle. And the lady I always dealt with wasn't there any more. They had me talk with a doctor . . . Morgan? Merton?" She struggled to remember the name. "She said they could take some, but not right away. She made me feel like what I was talkin' about wasn't worth her time," Poppy continued. "They had somethin' *big* comin' up."

"Probably this vote," Jack suggested.

"That doesn't make sense," Poppy countered, still puzzled by her conversation with the doctor. "If they're pro-racing, why in hell would they double-cross us like this?"

"New leadership? New philosophy?" Cecil asked.

Then somebody stated the obvious: "They've been infiltrated by the A.R.M."

A chill went up Felicia's spine.

As members of the Coalition voiced their indignity and disappointment, Felicia snapped the point of a pencil, silently raging like a pacifist ordered to bear arms. But Felicia McCrory was no pacifist. Were the Pennsylvania Lovers of Greyhounds just another branch of the Animal Rights Militia? The very thought slammed Felicia backwards in a wave of whirling, frozen ice water.

It wasn't that industry critics were bad people, she thought to herself. Animal lovers were in a class by themselves. Maybe some of the classiest in the world, if good intentions counted for much. Weren't the ones from Pennsylvania trying to make the sport better, more efficient, more honorable? Why were they suddenly tearing it apart?

Easy enough to figure out. Somebody new had taken them over. Even a moron could tell it wasn't Greyhounds that mattered now. Politics were the objective. Power.

Jason Greathouse, formerly of Wall Street, found dog politicos and the whole idea of an animal militia to be entertaining in a crude sort of way. Nevertheless, those in charge had certainly studied their psychology, he decided. The whole thing, not just the anti-racing legislation, but the whole animal protection movement was a study in slick advertising and good profiling of the average pet lover's belief system.

Until the Coalition understood precisely what it was that motivated pet lovers to action, Jason figured, it couldn't gain any ground in the struggle for public acceptance. As the battle cry for animal protectionists declared, "We must be the voice of the Greyhound!" (because the dogs couldn't speak for themselves), only those who raised and cared for them could say what was born in a Greyhound's heart.

As for Poppy, the whole thing just made her sooooooo angry. You never knew what was going to happen next. Labradors? Cocker Spaniels? Let the next guy have them, she thought. Let them go to the animal shelters and pick as many as they wanted out of the millions put to sleep. Hell, there were more Labrador Retrievers born every month than all the Greyhounds registered in a whole year! And she should know. She used to be a dog groomer, not a particularly glamorous profession. But if someone like Barbara Bastinelli was a dog groomer, she thought, that would be a whole different story. Barbara Bastinelli's grooming shop would have a billboard up in lights on Times Square.

Barbara, herself, might have posed with a hundred different dogs of a hundred different varieties if it made her point. If she believed in what the billboard was all about. Jason's idea of an ad campaign showing dogs bursting from the starting box with Barbara hugging the winner superimposed in the foreground was exactly what she believed in.

"Run it in Nashville," Barbara had said. "I've heard they're trying to ban outstanding achievement in school."*

Taking away recognition for achievement meant killing the spirit of a winner. Neither Barbara, nor any fan of Greyhound racing, would stand for that. And certainly that's not what Greyhounds were about. Unable to speak for themselves? Greyhounds didn't have to talk. They *showed* how they felt. They showed it by running every day, every night of the year, because they *wanted* to.

Wanda's thoughts went in a different direction. We have to make Greyhound racing entertaining again. Like it is in Europe, where the whole family goes to the races, and the tracks have dancing late into the night. People need to have more fun!

Brad Taggart, studmaster extraordinaire, put a deeper agenda on the table.

"If what critics of Greyhound racing said was true, then it was time to carry the logic the whole way. Knowingly, or not, Greyhound breeders were protectors of the breed's gene pool. By selectively breeding for physical ability and proving their breeding stock on the track, Greyhound breeders had strengthened the breed to levels unmatched by other dogs. Yet, if everyone in the industry was as cruel and twisted as

---

*Writing for *Reader's Digest* (November 2004), author Michael Crowley revealed in *"A" is for Average* that schools in Tennessee, California, New Hampshire, Texas, Indiana and Kentucky are taking away recognition for individual achievement in favor of protecting the feelings of students who don't measure up. A plan for mass mediocrity? You decide.

the press wanted to believe, what might happen if anti-racing forces ever got their way?"

"No idea," Mark said.

"Come on now," Brad said, the voice of reason. "If racing is outlawed like they just did in Pennsylvania, and all of us in the business don't have any con-science, like the militants say, then how long does anybody really think all the dogs out on the farms would last?"

"But you're talking—" Mark started.

"Mass slaughter," Poppy finished. "We *know*."

"No, what you're talking about is mass *rescue*. Get it? The end of the NGA Greyhound," Brad said. "Which wouldn't bother the hard-liners any. I mean, use your head! Every adopted dog gets neutered or spayed. See how it works? A flawless plan of annihilation."

"We caught onto that *real* quick," Poppy ex-plained, the sound of shredding paper softening her words. "They've painted such an ugly picture of the business that most people don't believe we have a heart to our names. It's the press that hasn't caught on."

"Poppy's right," Jack Halstead said, his eye forever on the money trail. "But what I keep seeing is the millions in donations. Where the hell does all that cash go? It's an all-volunteer workforce. Find the money, find the brains. Strip away the bullshit and it's just another damn cult!" he shouted.

At that, no one could speak loud enough. The jum-ble of voices scrambled the wires.

"Take it easy!" Cecil called out. "Quiet!" he ordered, tapping his gold watch on his phone, hoping he would be heard. "We can't hear each other!"

Suddenly understanding, able to put a name to the

movement aligning itself not only against Greyhound racing, but against all they knew—all they believed in and held sacred—the group settled down. Staring them in the face. Nobody had seen it: Anti-racing mania . . . *Animal Rights Militia* . . . a cult.

A cult: *An obsessive devotion or veneration for a person, principle or ideal.*

Save a Greyhound? *Rescue* it? Bullshit!

Rescue a Golden Retriever? A Beagle? A horse? A cat? A tiger? A goldfish?

Bullshit!

What the hell were they being rescued from?

Rescue meant to save . . . to free an animal from a trap. Save an animal from a fire, or a flood or a fate worse than death. That was rescue. Rescue made you a hero.

Adoption? *Adoption, on the other hand, spells responsibility.* Not nearly the glory, drama or personal praise.

Which catch phrase—*which call to arms*—stirs the soul as it searches for meaning in life?

"Love starts right here," Felicia put a hand on her chest, "and it swirls around and it goes right to your head. That's if you're lucky. You can't stop it, you can't control it; it just happens! It's like . . . like a race! And if you *love* something enough—if you love Greyhounds *or anything*—and you want to make things better, what you *should do*—"

"—is roll up your sleeves and jump right in," Mark finished. "I've been listening." He smiled, suddenly understanding the *real* activists weren't out there picketing at all. He was surrounded by them.

"What if we could overthrow this decision?"

Felicia asked them. "What if we could blow the militants right off the map?"

"I'd want to press *that* button," Barbara Bastinelli said, surprising everyone with her candidness.

"I'd be right there with you," her husband said, in essence, speaking for them all.

"Go ahead, Mark," she said. "Tell them what you told me."

Only a few months ago, he didn't even have a dog, Mark thought. Now he was in politics. "All right," he said. "If you really want to do something about this whole thing, there's a way. But it takes a lot of guts."

"We're at a dead end," Cecil said. "We need an option."

"OK," Mark started. "But it won't be easy."

"Can't be any harder than making a Greyhound cat safe," Poppy said, thinking of Tiger.

"Well, I'm in the antique business," Mark began. "You might not think that has a whole lot to do with big business, but you meet all kinds of interesting people through it. The other day, I was on a call, and I met this professor. He teaches business law at a college and collects Staffordshire."

"Porcelain," Barbara said, recognizing the name. "I bought some of their animals when I was on a magazine shoot in London."

"There was a striking piece in his collection," Mark said. "A Greyhound. We started talking about Clue, and racing. Right away, he gets into how the industry could take charge of things." Mark leaned back in his imitation leather recliner and sipped hot mocha from a large red mug.

As he unfolded the plan, a sobering silence fell

upon the members.

Not a sound . . . not a breath.

"You mean," Jason finally said, "We could *bypass* this decision?"

"Totally," Mark said.

"If it works," Cecil said, "it'll wipe . . . them . . . out."

Take off your belt, Barry had been ordered the first time he showed up for work at the wooded kennel compound where new dogs were brought in from the track. What for? he wanted to know, hoping to make the right impression his first day on the job, even if it meant initiation by fellow employees. This was his big chance. His chance to be in charge of something again. Pennsylvania could be his territory. In time, if he played his cards right, he could be in charge of the whole Northeast corridor. Why take off the belt?

"*Because I said so,*" came the slightly nasal answer from a thin, mousey woman walking up to him. "You're new here," she said, knowing he was, but wanting to fill the air between them with it. He was new. She, clearly, wasn't.

He smiled. Best to smile when you weren't sure what else to do. "Barry Dunmoyer," he said, offering his hand, willing to go along with whatever ritual this was.

She stared at him as though he were a buffoon.

His hand dropped to his side. What had he done to offend her?

A sudden, frantic outcry from every dog in the compound rose up, washed over them and spilled into the surrounding woods.

"See that dog?" she said, pointing to her left but ignoring the animal, keeping her eyes only on Barry's face.

He nodded, recognizing the young blue-fawn-colored Greyhound.

"One of yours, right?"

"I brought him here, yeah," Barry said, noticing the others gathering nearby to watch.

"Yeah?" she sneered. "Around me, you speak *correctly.*"

"I'll remember that," he said, vowing to do better, but not saying "yes," as he was certain she wanted him to.

Clue bolted playfully from one side of the compound to another, but watchful volunteers, oddly out of place as they gathered, made no attempt to catch him. Their quiet demeaner set Barry's nerves on edge.

Unsure, feeling the woman's eyes on his pants, he waited.

Was he supposed to do something? Say something?

"Nice belt," came her nasal assessment, not giving him the chance. "Ever use it?"

"More than for holding up my trousers?" he asked, not clear on where this was heading.

"I know lots of ways to use a belt," she said, her face expressionless. "That dog? Call him."

"Here, boy," he said, feeling uneasy for the second time.

"Aw," she moaned, disappointed. "You can do better than that. Put some *balls* into it. You've got balls, don't you?"

"Here, Clue!" he called out, deeply, holding forth

his open hand. At the sound of his name, Clue stopped in his tracks, raised his head and perked his ears, looking in Barry's direction.

"Clue!" Barry called again, and the loving dog bounded to him as he had done so many times before.

"Hit him!"

What did she just say?

"Take off that belt and hit him!" she ordered again, both hands in fists, chin tucked to her flat chest.

Holding onto Clue's collar and keeping the dog at his side, Barry didn't move.

"You want him to get a good home, don't you?" she said.

"Of course."

"Then do as I say. Take off your belt and *hit that dog.*"

"I don't think so," Barry refused, standing his ground, looking to the others for help and getting none.

"Barry . . . dear, dear Barry," the woman said, shaking her head, looking down, then looking directly at him and holding his attention. "Don't you know who I am?"

His silence was her answer.

"Of course you don't," she said. "You don't know I run this place and all the others like it, because you don't read, you don't listen to the news, you don't ask. Did you finish high school, Barry? No," she said, shaking her head again and raising her hand to silence him. "Don't tell me. I don't want to embarrass you. We're here because we love animals," a faint smile crossed her tight lips. "What we care about here—

what I care about—is getting these dogs into good homes. Now, you may not agree with how we do that. No, you might not think it's right, or kind, or fair. But after you've been here a while you'll understand. Even without a high school diploma, you'll learn that God smiles on those who are brave enough to do whatever it takes to help his poor creatures."

"Not that," Barry said.

She sighed. "I didn't think so," she said. "He's not the kind of man who beats dogs, I said, when they asked me."

Breathing easier, he relaxed his grip on Clue's collar slightly. He had passed the test. Now he could get on with his chores. "Do you want me to put him back?" he asked the woman. Standing there, studying him like a scientist in a laboratory might study a rat, she reached in the pocket of her jacket.

"Not yet," she said, holding a small bottle and unscrewing the cap. "I want you to take care of his fleas," she said, handing him the bottle and a pair of rubber gloves. "I wouldn't be too hard on myself, if I were you, Barry. Not knowing everybody's name, I mean. Stick around long enough and you'll get the picture."

She walked away.

The others went back to work.

And Barry doused Clue with the contents of the bottle.

Prisoners were treated better than this, Barry thought, looking down the row of dogs in chicken-wire crates, whining and staring at him with their sad eyes. Brindle dogs, fawn dogs, white dogs, black dogs. Month in, month out, the same.

Stinkin' hellhole prison.

Stomach lurching at the smell, he considered their fate. Like the Statue of Liberty, he had gathered them. Give me your tired, your poor, your huddled masses. I'll take them. What he didn't say is, by the time I'm done you won't know them any more.

"Here ya go, pup," he said, sliding a dirty dish to a dull-coated female with a torn ear. "Eat it."

Ribs showing, spine sticking out, she sniffed and looked away.

"What'sa matter with you?" he shouted gruffly. "Not good enough for ya? You want meat? Well, there ain't no meat around here. *She's* a vegetarian. She don't believe in *meat.*"

Marion Malloy didn't believe in a lot of things. Mostly, she didn't believe in dog racing. Oh, she believed it was *there*, all right. She just didn't believe it was acceptable. People shouldn't be *allowed* to race dogs. Greyhounds shouldn't be *forced* to run.

How she came to believe all this was a matter of conjecture and innuendo. Some said she worked in an animal shelter as a young girl and was so affected by the death toll she never got over it. Others said it was the result of a hot and passionate love affair with a Greyhound man gone sour. Still others said that was bull. They said Marion Malloy could never have a love affair. She didn't have a loving bone in her body—especially not a man's.

Truth is usually somewhere in between. But truth wasn't on the agenda for Pennsylvania Lovers of Greyhounds. Not since Marion's volunteers had taken over.

"Eat up," Barry said to the frightened dog as he moved on to the next. "You'll be out of here soon."

Out of here soon. Too bad he, himself, wouldn't be. Prisons didn't always have bars.

"They want to see you," a short, stocky woman with dark brown hair said in a quirky accent. "In the office."

The office, he thought. Always in the office, like they were big shots. "Tell them I'm busy," he said. Tell them to get lost is what he was thinking.

The woman took a count. "Only twenty-three?" she asked. "We got thirty-six in ours." At our dog center, she meant, if you could call it that. A storage trailer sans wheels, holes cut in the sides and wire runs five-feet long. "Whatcha gawkin' at?" she asked when he first saw it. "Beats the hell out of what they get at the track."

He knew better.

They wanted to see him in the office. What for?

"You gotta drive a load to Philly tomorrow," the dry woman said. "They want twenty-eight. Are the dogs ready?"

Ready is what they called it.

The dogs were ready. All but one.

Barry entered the austere office, noticing three people to his left and one seated at the desk. They could have said, Come in, sit down, make yourself at home. Instead, they ignored him. Swiveling a leather desk chair around, the one in charge turned away as if his presence disturbed them, invaded their privacy.

He sat down in front of the grand inquisitor, picked up a magazine, and waited. Putting the magazine aside, he picked up another one. Low-budget newsletters . . . animal society magazines . . . a scrapbook of clippings showing Marion Malloy picketing a pond of ducks at a university . . . shaking hands with a well-dressed young man at a fund-raiser . . . hobnobbing with an old movie star nobody could recognize today . . . Marion outside a mink farm in Wisconsin . . . Marion in front of a courthouse in Oregon. Marion Malloy was "somebody" in the animal rights movement. She knew people. And they knew her. They knew Marion and her son, the smart kid who never made it through college, now her bookkeeper. What was his claim to fame? Chinese checkers. That was it. No, Barry thought, his claim to fame was that he had been able to survive with a man-hater.

It made him sick, looking at her skinny face with her baggy eyes and stringy brown hair. *Sick* of the narrow mouth that never smiled except to smirk when she made someone feel bad. Sick of her buttoned-up collars.

If those around her spoke up, challenged her, offered a different point of view, she would belittle, accuse, shame. She, after all, knew the *real* story. She had heard it all; she had seen it all. With her own baggy eyes.

But for the rare one doing as she wished, there was praise. "God will reward you. He understands. He looks after those who protect his innocent animals."

The one on the phone, behind that big desk, stacks of papers all around, a black Greyhound nearby, knew he was waiting.

No problem, he thought, lighting up.

Without skipping a beat, without turning around, the instant snap of fingers with index finger extended like a drill sergeant command caught the dog's immediate attention. How many times had the dog heard that sound of disapproval? But it wasn't for him this time.

Barry took a long drag, exhaled the blue-grey smoke slowly in their direction, and didn't budge.

"No," he heard the one on the phone saying, louder now. "*Just somebody here to see me . . .* nobody important. Did you get the deposits?"

"Put it out," someone said to Barry.

"When I'm finished," he said, blowing smoke at the stooges to his left.

"You disgust me," the voice hissed.

"Good," he said. "Then *you* can drive those dogs to Philadelphia."

"We can't," another said, reaching for a handkerchief to cover her nose. "We have a fund-raiser with Marion in Los Angeles."

"Give my regards to all the has-beens," he said, like a man who couldn't be less interested.

"You should talk," came the jab. "Aren't you the one who used to make a living in the industry?"

"A lot of people did," he said. "Before you guys came along."

"Power is a wonderful thing, Barry. You should try it."

Maybe he would, he thought. But for now, twenty-eight dogs would go to Philadelphia. Twenty-eight dogs, thin and cowering at the sound of a man's voice. That was the thing that bothered him most.

"If you ask me," Kenita said, pouring coffee in her kitchen, "*Some Picture* was the greatest racing dog that ever lived. He was a black dog from Ireland by

Slaneyside Hare, out of Spring Season. Beautiful animal! I have a tape around here of him running. That dog almost won all three of the big Derbies in England, Ireland and Scotland! Never was done before and never since. That's like the Triple Crown of the Greyhound world," she explained to Mark. "The only reason he didn't win the last one is 'cause he finished lame. But he made the finals and he tried," she said. "*That's* what makes a champion: *Heart*."

"Clue has heart," Mark said, looking at a very quiet Felicia. It would take heart for The Greyhound Coalition to win the battle ahead of them.

"As well he should," Kenita said. "If I know my pedigrees, Some Picture was his grand-daddy, wasn't he?" To which, Felicia could remain quiet no more.

"Clue's dam was a *daughter* of Some Picture. She held a track record for 810 meters."

"That's a long race," Mark said, thinking how much it would take to defeat the A.R.M. "Aren't most races in the five-hundred-yard range?"

"Over here, they are," Felicia said. "And that's exactly why I wanted him. You always have to be looking for an edge."

"Most Greyhound breeders around here think Irish blood is what they call short," Kenita said.

"Can't go the distance," Felicia explained.

"But what they don't know is, some of those races in Scotland, Ireland and England are even longer than ours," Kenita went on.

The McCrorys would have to run the distance. Did they know how far? He hoped they would remember Clue's dam in the months and years to come.

"I see it. You wanted a dog that could run longer

than the competition," Mark said, letting them know not all of those coming to the sport from the outside were dense.

"Very good!" Felicia laughed with glee. "I *knew* there was hope for you!" she teased.

"Hope is one thing I've got plenty of." He smiled. "So are you going to tell me what happened to Some Picture?"

"Nobody really knows," Felicia said. "He was retired to stud after the Irish Derby and they found him dead."

"Rough life, being a stud," Mark grinned, certain that was a great way to go.

"Foul play is how I read it," Kenita said darkly.

"A Dick Francis novel," Mark observed.

"Honey, what happened to Some Picture would leave Dick Francis in the dust, and his horse, too. That dog was the hottest thing around, and everybody knew it," Kenita said. "There's no way he didn't get the best of everything. He was set to make his owner a millionaire. Can you imagine?" she asked. "A dog making you a millionaire?" though she had imagined it many times and Mark was beginning to. He was also beginning to ask why more people weren't trying.

"A good stud dog can sire hundreds of litters," she went on. "Some Picture was found dead after how many, Felicia?"

"Something like eighty, I think," Felicia said. "Maybe a hundred, I'm not sure."

"Well, compared to that, most of your top sires end up with thousands of pups out there. But, from just a few litters, his percentage of winners was phenomenal. That one dog could have transformed the whole breed!" Kenita said, her eyebrows high in astonishment.

"And you say Clue is a grandson?" Mark asked, making sure he understood the connection.

"Grandson *and* out of a track record holder," Felicia reminded him.

"So, how's he doing?" Kenita wanted to know.

To which, Felicia said, "I've never seen anything like it. This just isn't the same dog. He's so *alive* now—so *awake*. He can twist and turn and jump in the air, and he's alert. Everything about him's alert. He's brave. He's not scared of anything. I don't know what happened to him out there, Mom, but he's *got it*."

Exactly what the Coalition needed to pull off their plan, Mark thought. "Whatever he's got, I hope there's some to go around," he said.

"I know I'll take some," Kenita said. "But six months is a long time for a dog to be on its own, run-nin' wild. He had to figure out how to get food, water. That'd toughen anybody up."

As tough as we have to be, Mark thought.

"I've never seen a dog so muscled up, Mom. When he runs, it's like he pushes himself with those hind legs of his and jumps—well, it's gotta be twenty feet at a time!"

A quantum leap. A leap of faith. Just like we're taking now, Mark realized, as Kenita hooted, "No!" her eyes imagining such a sight. "I have to see that."

"And he loves it—doesn't he, Mark?"

"Well, I'm not an expert, but you *can* feel some-thing just by watching him," he said, trying to convey what he had seen, what he had sensed on the airstrip that first time. Determination. Victory.

"Hope," Kenita said, with conviction.

"And we almost lost him," Felicia said.

"Not only him," Mark said, considering the broader scope of things from a man's point of view. With the legislative defeat in Pennsylvania, they had almost lost hope in everything.

"I just love figuring things out!" Felicia said.

"Love is a damn powerful emotion, lady." Mark smiled.

"And I guess you know all about it," she said with a knowing wink.

"I've been around."

"Around the block and all over the neighborhood is more like it," she teased.

"And you haven't?" he asked.

"Why, Mr. Whittier, you surprise me!" she said, clasping her hands to her chest and batting her eyes. "I'll have you know I'm a proper young lady!"

"Oh, I'm sure of that, Miss McCrory," he said, looking to Kenita for support. "Proper as a nun."

"You can be so insulting!" Felicia huffed, enjoying their game.

"Only when it comes to you, I'm discovering."

"Well!"

"You were saying about love?" Kenita asked, bringing them back to the subject at hand like a fried egg being flipped sunnyside in a hot pan. "This oughtta be good."

"Love," he said, taking on a serious tone. "Love for a living thing is the ability to let the object of your affection find its own fulfillment and happiness. Being able to love is a talent, a skill most of us aren't born with, but we can develop. I know, because I've seen it happen. And because I've been lucky enough to be given that gift by others. Not that I've ever been able to pass it on to anyone else, mind you. But I'm working on it."

"Oh, you'll get there," Felicia said, patting his hand indulgently. "Now, about what else you were saying?"

"I've forgotten."

"Dogs," she reminded him.

"I wasn't talking about dogs. I was talking about coffee. Any more around here?"

Pulling into the Valley Forge truck stop, Barry found a lonely spot away from the other drivers. Crossing the parking lot, he entered the building, visited the men's room and then walked to the food court. What would it be this time, he asked himself, smelling hazlenut, Colombian roast and vanilla bean. Amaretto, he decided. Good name for a dog, he thought. Forget it, he wasn't in that business any more. Not in the official sense, at least. But the way Marion's crew was feeling, maybe he wouldn't be going places in this part of it either. Pouring a steaming cup, he fumbled with a lid. Damn these places. Nothing ever fit. Oh well, he thought, tossing the lid, checking his watch. Another hour and he'd be at the usual drop-off point; the usual chain-link enclosure of freight trailers converted into kennels outside of town. The usual no thanks for anything.

Outside, he hurried back to the rig, though why he should bother hurrying he didn't know. For the dogs, he told himself. The sooner he got them to Philly, the sooner they'd be out of Marion's clutches and into safe homes. Funny, how different things turn out from what you think they will. Or hope they will.

"Whatcha haulin'?" a young guy with spikey blond hair, in jeans and a jacket, asked, stepping out of the shadows and standing near the back of the trailer.

Where did he come from? Barry wondered, looking around the parking lot.

"Who's askin'?" Barry wanted to know.

"Justa coupla animal lovers out for a stroll," came the steady reply.

The young man's eyes. What was it about those eyes? he wondered. Why did Barry sense that he could see those eyes when he shouldn't be able to in the darkness? Where was the young man's life, his heart?

"Dogs," Barry answered. "Greyhounds," he said, offering no more.

"Where are they going?" the young man asked, touching the latch to the trailer door.

"Uh, they're going to new homes," Barry said, his instincts telling him, urging him, to put a good spin on it. Tell him what he wants to hear, he thought. Say you're taking them to a land of silk pillows where they'll be fed caviar and wine and wear diamond tiaras for the rest of their lives. Tell them anything, for God's sake. But get out of here.

"Yeah? You wouldn't be shittin' me," the guy said.

"Why would I do that?" Barry asked. "I don't even know you."

What a stupid thing to say, he thought. I don't even know you. Of course he didn't know the guy. Was he saying he'd only mess with somebody he knew? Is that how it sounded? "Well," he said, pretending to look at his watch in the shadows, knowing he couldn't tell, wanting to get out of there now, right away, fast. "I'm runnin' late," he said, as the trailer door opened and out stepped a girl, shaking her head and mumbling something.

"What's going on?" Barry demanded.

"Don't worry about her," the guy said, raising his chin. "Give me the cash," he said.

Had Barry been a different man as he heard the soft click of a switch-blade, he might have been in a slow-motion nightmare, clouding his mind, paralyzing his lungs, his legs, his reason. But Barry had survived many such moments in life. Tightening his grip around his hot coffee cup, forcing the pain out of his mind, resisting the urge to rush to the cab, lock himself in and step on it, he moved closer.

Surprised, the young man backed up, bumping into the girl behind him, saying nothing. His eyes, those lifeless, empty eyes, said it all.

"You better be damn sure you can use that thing," Barry said, staring at the knife.

Tossing the knife from hand to hand, crouching like a defiant wrestler, the young man glared back.

"Let's get outta here, baby," the girl said.

But nobody was going to boss him around. Nobody was going to tell *baby* what to do. *"Shut up!"* he snapped at her. *"Shut up!* The cash," he said to Barry. "Give it to me!"

Splat!

"Shit! SHIT!" the guy screamed, bending over, both hands pressing at his face.

"No!" the girl moaned, reaching for him. *"Oh, my God!"*

As fast as a hound on the break, Barry was in the truck, revving the engine, pulling away. And two lonely thieves were shrinking in the silver of his rearview mirror, smelling like amaretto latte.

Picking up speed, making up for lost time, Barry rolled through the toll booth onto the expressway. Traffic was thin this time of night, and light reflecting from every droplet of water on his windshield only made the weeping of his life seem more real. What the hell was he mixed up with? What the hell was happening to people? Those were kids back there. Somebody's *kids*! Opening presents on birthdays and laughing at the sky. But the sky wasn't laughing now. The sky was crying. America was crying and her kids were playing with switch-blades, holding up truck drivers in parking lots.

He should have brought a hat, an umbrella, a raincoat, he thought, cursing his luck, putting the surprised faces of those kids into a compartment of his mind that nobody could touch and throwing away the key. Forget about it. They weren't the first desperate souls out there. They wouldn't be the last.

At least he had a job, a paycheck, a place to stay. At least he had the dogs.

Beeping a horn, he waited for a tall, skinny man in loose clothes and a cap to open the gate. Not a smile passed between them. Not a nod, nor the wave of a hand.

Ignoring it, Barry drove slowly into the compound and parked outside the familiar office. Gathering his

paperwork—a mix of medical records, notes and registration certificates for identification—he swung
down from the truck and went outside to check on his
charges.

Everything OK, he decided, after walking through
the trailer and shining a flashlight in on each dog.
Then he saw it. Halfway down the aisle, upper level to
his left. Peeking out from the shredded paper bedding
in one of the dog boxes. The corner of a manila envelope taped to the wall. The girl at the service station
on the turnpike. Is this what she was looking for?
Opening the empty compartment, reaching for the
envelope, pulling it loose, Barry found one, then
another and another. Pushing aside the bedding, he
found the whole floor of the dog box lined with identical envelopes. Setting down his flashlight, taking an
envelope in both hands, he began tearing it open—and
felt someone watching him.

"We'll take it from here," a middle-aged man with
thinning white hair said from the doorway as Barry
felt a flashlight on him.

"What the hell's this?" Barry wanted to know.

"None of you business," he was told, stepping
aside quickly as the man and two helpers pushed their
way past him and stuffed the envelopes into a suitcase.

"Did she send anything else?" the man asked.

"Just the dogs."

"The dogs," the man said. "Any with a coursing
collar?"

Before Barry could answer, one of the helpers
spoke up. "I'll check," she said, taking Barry's flashlight and shining it on the dogs. "This one," she said,

opening a door, pulling out a dog and slipping off its collar.

"Give that to me," said the man. Then, shining his flashlight in Barry's face, he said, "*Someone* thinks pretty *highly* of you. I hope you . . . *stay* awhile." Turning to his helpers, he said, "Unload 'em and turn 'em out." Pointing at Barry, he said, "*You!* Come with me."

Through the rain they went; cold, damp, to a building on the far side of the enclosure, under the floodlights, mist rising from the ground. Inside, fluorescent lights gave a sickly appearance to anything living, plants or people. But there were no potted office plants, no flowers, no fishbowls. And the only other person was facing him now.

"Make yourself comfortable," the man said, offering a chair.

Barry settled into an upholstered chair and made no comment as the man walked over to a well-stocked bar. "What would you like to have?" he asked.

"I don't touch the stuff," Barry said.

"Oh," the man said, slowly pouring himself a brandy and raising it to the light as if nothing could be more delicious or fascinating to him. "Too bad."

"I . . ." Barry started. "I used to—"

The man looked at him, looked through him, like one jaded with life and all it offers. "I know," he said, stopping Barry in mid-sentence. "You, I've been briefed about."

"Briefed?"

"Of *course!*" the man said, walking back to where Barry sat. He tapped Barry on the shoulder and forced an insincere smile. It was a smiling face with sad and weary eyes. "*You*, she told me about," he said, his New York accent showing. "*You,* she wanted me to meet. She has great faith in *you*, Barry," he said. "Barry *Dunmoyer* we have great faith in."

If surprise was a bowling ball scoring a strike, Barry's amazement was a turkey.

"They don't like me," Barry said. "What makes you think they like me?"

"They don't *have* to like you, Barry," the man said. "Not as long as you do your job. Sure you don't want a drink?"

Barry shook his head.

"They don't have to like you because what *they* say and what *they* think don't *matter*! What matters is if *I* like you. And I *do* like you, Barry. Yes, I like you *very much*. I like you because you're a man who says what he believes. A *man's* man! You don't care what anybody else says. You don't care if they've worked— *worked for years*—making plans, setting things up. Setting things up for the greatest act of freedom people have *ever seen*! A country, *a country*, Barry, isn't much different from an individual *person*. You *see*? And countries can get *sick*! They can be *diseased,* like . . . like our *own* country, Barry!" he ranted, eyes wide but no longer seeing Barry, no longer seeing anything but his own grand vision. *"See what I'm saying?"*

Barry thought of the two kids trying to rob him at the rest stop. Their hunched posture, lifeless expressions.

"Who are you?" Barry asked.

"Who *I* am doesn't matter," the man said. "Who *I* am changed, anyhow, a long time ago. But *you,* Barry," he said, holding Barry's gaze, "what matters is who *you* are. How long have you been bringing dogs here? Huh?" he asked, suddenly pushing. "How long?"

"A while now. Since last year," Barry said.

"And in all that time, did anyone ever bother you? Stand in your way?"

Seeing that Barry didn't get his drift, the man put it another way. "Did anyone ever criticize you, look down on you, blame you for hauling Greyhounds?"

"No," Barry said, still not seeing his point.

"Of course they didn't! They didn't—and they never would—because it's a good cause! And everybody knows it. And we keep it that way. Don't we?" he said, with a knowing look. "We keep it that way. Barry, oh, Barry, if you only knew how difficult it is to shape the opinion of the masses. To guide them and show them the right thing to do!"

Never having cared much about "the masses," Barry just raised his eyebrows and gave a close-lipped smile.

"Call me *Silverback*," the man said, patting Barry on the back.

Silverback. As in some kind of fish? Before him, Barry saw a man of about 50, a man with some degree of professional bearing, a man accustomed to better clothes than the hooded sweatshirt, jeans and sneakers he was wearing. A rounded face and thick neck on a pear-shaped torso weren't particularly complemented by the blond mustache and sideburns that didn't quite match the dark eyebrows. If Silverback was what the man wanted to be called, then Silverback it would be.

"What did you want to see me about, Mr. Silverback?"

"Silverback," the man said, correcting him. "Like your name is *Rhesus* now. OK? Is that OK with you? I mean, if it's not—if that's not OK—we can wrap it up, call it a day, and this whole conversation is over. We can do that—we can do that if you want to. Is that what you want? Is that what you want?" he said again. "Tell me now if that's what you want."

Silence filled the room as Barry stared at the man and considered his options. He could stand and walk to the door. He could drive away, if he made it to the truck without being stopped, and never turn back. But Marion would know, and all the rest would know, and if it was a mistake . . .

If it was a mistake, what?

If it was a mistake, he didn't know what would happen.

"Funny name," is what he heard himself say.

"Funny man," Silverback countered, his sallow face expressionless and deadly. "I'm waiting, Rhesus. For your answer."

"Isn't that the name for a monkey?" Barry asked.

"See? I *knew* you were a smart man! You're a *smart* man," Silverback said quickly, speaking in choppy, almost frantic bursts. "That's why I said, he should be called *Rhesus*! Rhesus is a *smart* monkey. You know, the others, Barry, they weren't so sure about you. But I was. *I was*, Barry. I told them you were the right one."

For what? Barry wanted to know. Right for what? If he was suddenly right for anything, it was news to him. His whole life, he hadn't been *right* for anything.

"What's all this about?" he asked, taking out a pack of smokes.

"Go right ahead," Silverback said. "You're my guest."

Guest or prisoner? Barry asked himself, certain that if he tried leaving, making a run for it, he wouldn't get away.

"I've got a video I want you to watch," Silverback said. "There's a VCR in the bungalow. But right now I'm tired. We'll talk in the morning. You'll be staying here tonight. Don't worry about the truck," he continued. "It's all arranged. I hope you don't mind. Others have found our hospitality quite . . . adequate."

With those closing remarks, two helpers appeared. "Bungalow Three," Silverback told them. To Barry, he said, "They told me you could be difficult. A difficult man who loves animals and can drive a truck is just the right kind."

Escorted through the rain, Barry was taken to Bungalow Three, another storage trailer. Swinging open the steel door, they guided him up the steps and into a wooden-paneled room not unlike a motel suite, but without windows. "Have a pleasant stay," one of them said. A woman, he noticed.

"Do I have a choice?" he asked her.

No one answered that. "It's important work," she said, handing him a VHS tape, locking the door as she left.

Bathroom, bed, a chair, a desk. Even a Bible. Barry looked for a phone, lifted the receiver, hung up. Just as he thought, connected to the "motel operator."

"Shouldn't us drivers have cell phones on these trips?" he had asked.

"No need to," he was told. "You never know when they're gonna ring."

Rain pattered on the metal roof of his trailer like an unending round of bullets.

Not a dog could be heard even though he knew the compound must be full of them.

He punched in the video and hit the play button.

"Oh, *fuck*!" he moaned, at the sight of the familiar, sallow face.

"My name is Marion Malloy," came the nasal drone of the whiny voice. "You are watching this tape because someone thinks you are worthy of being part of Project A.P.E., the Animal Protection Effort. Tomorrow night, you will be called on for a very specific task in your part of the country. Don't let us down. The animals of the world are waiting, pleading, for their liberation. I hear them. I feel them. Every day I walk this earth. There is no good zoo, my friends. A zoo is a fancy prison. Prisons are slavery and slavery is inherently cruel. Thank you. Thank you for being part of this great effort. Thank you for taking on the greatest mission of your life." The screen went black.

They were right about those phones, he decided a few hours later as he lay in the darkness. Ringing disturbed something important, like the sleep he didn't have. Don't answer, he told himself. Let them worry.

"Good morning, Rhesus," came a familiar voice out of nowhere. "You didn't sleep very well."

He hadn't figured on the place being wired for sound.

Sitting up, he ran both hands through his hair and answered Silverback's familiar voice. "Yeah," he said, coughing.

"You really should do something about that,"

Silverback said. "One of our members is a doctor. I'll see that she prescribes something for you."

Barry coughed again.

"You'll be joining me for breakfast," Silverback said. "I'll send someone for you in twenty minutes. You can shower and do anything you like in the bathroom," he said. "Don't worry," he added with a sneer. "I won't look."

Twenty minutes later, a knock came at the door. Hair combed, his skin soapy fresh, Barry was pleased to see the same woman from the night before.

"Good morning," she said, her voice intent, her manner serious. "I know these rooms can be cramped. How did you sleep?"

"Not good," he said, wondering how she could have expected a different answer. Of course he hadn't slept well. How could he?

"These will help you get through the day," she said, offering two small red pills. "Don't worry," she said, at his hesitation. "I'm a doctor."

Good thing to have around, he decided, helping himself to a glass of water and swallowing.

"There," she said. "You'll be bright and alert for the work ahead."

"What's going on here?" he asked.

"God's work," she said. "What the G.O.—*The Great One*—tells us to do."

The Great One, he thought, following her outside to the first trailer, up the steps and into a luxurious apartment, complete with skylights, paintings, and Persian rugs on marble floors.

"Good morning, Rhesus," Silverback greeted him.

"I see that you've met Spider. Won't you join us for breakfast?" he asked, leading the way to a private room in the back of the trailer.

"Let me help you," Silverback said, placing slices of orange, bread, nuts, vegetables and a banana on a Limoges plate and handing it to Barry.

"Rhesus has been selected as our driver," he explained to Spider.

Without moving, she accepted the information.

"Rhesus knows how to get around in a rig and he knows paperwork. He's going to help us. Aren't you, Rhesus?"

Barry hesitated.

"Of course you are!" Silverback assured him. "Of course you are," he repeated, leaning forward and patting Barry's shoulder. "You're part of the team! *One of us!* Of course you know what this is all about." Looking to the woman, clearing his throat nervously, Silverback said, "Tell him."

"Freedom," she said.

"God's work, you mean," Barry reminded her.

"Exactly. Protecting God's innocent creatures," she said, with a conviction from deep within.

"And you want me to . . ."

"Be our *driver*, that's *right*!" Silverback finished. "Told you he was *smart*," he pitched the woman like a crazed car salesman. "Didn't I tell you he was *smart*! That's a smart *man,* sitting there!"

Barry didn't feel too smart. "What do I get out of this?" he asked.

"See?" Silverback flashed a look to the woman. "Already, he's down to business." Pleased, he turned his attention to Barry.

"Let me put it this way," he said, bringing Barry into his confidence. "The G.O. wants you to be Spider's right-hand man." Noticing Barry's look of doubt, he rushed in. "You don't think so? Well, let me assure you. She does! Yes, we consider you perfect for the job!"

Flattered, Barry said, "Me?"

"Sure thing!" Silverback almost shouted. "And after tonight, after we pull off the biggest act of love for animals the world has ever seen, you're going to be in charge of a whole lot more than you ever dreamed! And richer! You'll be richer than you ever thought."

Now they were talking his language.

Rich was something he could understand. Not that he had ever *been* rich. Far from it. On the contrary, *rich* was something he had only seen in others and usually not liked. But, if *he* were rich, it would be something he could even a few scores with.

He would buy back the farm where he grew up. He would show a few people how to raise dogs. He'd get his own booking and show them all!

"When do I start?" he said, smiling at last.

"That's more like it!" Silverback said, explaining the plan. "All you have to do is drive that rig out there, that one you drove all the way here. All you have to do is drive it right where we say, and when we say it. The rest is a piece of cake. A piece of cake, Rhesus. A piece of cake!"

"Just drive the truck," Barry said, making sure.

"That's it!" Silverback said, eagerly, almost frantically, looking to Spider and back to Barry several times. "Now, enjoy yourself for the rest of the day. Go back to your room, watch TV, take it easy. I have work to do. See you tonight, Rhesus. You made a wise decision. I thank you. The animals thank you," he said, shaking Barry's hand.

Talk about appreciation! His whole life, Barry had never been treated with such respect.

"Am I . . ." he started to ask.

"Free to go?" Silverback finished. "Yes, Rhesus. You're free to go. You can walk around, anything you like. And take this with you," he said, handing Barry a booklet. "It should answer a few more of your questions. We have a meeting at lunch. You like vegetable lasagna?"

Outside, Barry could see a few of the Greyhounds stretching their legs in small enclosures. "Hey, there, fella," he said to a dog he recognized. "Come here often?" he said, walking over and touching the dog through the fence. "Only once," he expected the dog would say if it could. Hopefully, never again.

A few kennel helpers in zip-up coveralls carried buckets of water. Others carried shovels and rakes. Another pushed a wheelbarrow overflowing with dog crap. Welcome to life in the big kennel, Barry thought, checking out the Philadelphia skyline.

He had seen enough. Finding his way back to Bungalo Three, he flicked on a lamp, kicked off his shoes and settled in. *Revelations,* the booklet was titled. Curious, Barry started to read.

> *"All of us, no matter how we start out, sooner or later come to the realization that we, ourselves, are not all there is. The Animal Protection Effort, or APE, is based on the understanding that no society is better than the way it treats its animals.*

*Ghandi, Einstein, Schweitzer—all great thinkers
knew this. That's why they loved animals and tried
to show us that all living things, no matter how
insignificant, are part of a greater, grander organ-
ism. All life is connected, should be loved for what
it is, what it does in this world, and must be
respected."*

Who wrote those words? Barry wondered. But,
leafing through the pages, he found only the name of
the organization and its creed: *"All life is sacred. We
are One Entity. There is no me."*

"Interesting book," Spider said later, noticing the
manual in his hand at the lunch buffet.

Seating himself at her table, Barry said, "Yeah.
Interesting."

"How long have you been on the path?" she asked.

"How long? Oh," he said, thinking quickly. "I've
known Marion for a while. Before that, I worked
around dogs, mostly."

She nodded. "For me it was mice," she said. "I
always felt sorry for them. Some of the other students
at my college set a mouse on fire and nobody cared. I
knew, in my soul, I'd spend the rest of my life hating
them. . . . So *you know* Marion?" she asked, as women
do. "Wow."

"Great lady," he lied.

"The things that woman has seen," Spider said, her
voice filled with awe. "She was there when it all started, her and Silverback. She's angel level."

Barry nodded silently, knowing from the manual
that "Angel Level" meant highest of the high.

"What about the rest of these people?" he asked, looking around. Dedicated, faceless, dressed alike in their blue coveralls.

"They live here, mostly. Working for the Cause."

"How long have you been here?" he asked.

"Since the earthquake of my life," she said, remembering what he sensed was still raw.

"I'm sorry," he said, not knowing what he should be sorry for, but feeling so just the same.

"Don't be," she reassured him, like one who has found inner peace. "It brought me here."

Here wasn't exactly a paradise, he thought to himself. *Here* was a safe haven, but no more. A safe haven for those wanting to right the wrong; wanting to raise the collective consciousness at all costs; wanting to belong to something bigger, greater, more important than themselves. Something was missing . . . here.

"This thing tonight," he said. "It's a big deal?"

Curious, she looked at him. "Rhesus," she said, as if puzzled that he could be asking. "Project APE is the biggest thing we've ever done."

The room grew quiet. Silverback was standing up, addressing the group.

"I hope you enjoyed your meal," he said. "It may end up being your last supper!" It was a joke, politely received, Barry noted, as he studied their faces. Young faces, hopeful and idealistic; older faces, determined to make their mark some way, some how. Had he seen them anywhere else, he might have passed them on the street without knowing, without sensing anything different about them, these workers for the greater cause.

"Where does he find them?" Barry asked as quietly as he could.

"Students, people who lost their jobs, homeless," Spider replied in a confidential tone. "He found the lady who works in the kitchen living in an alley near 15th and Sansom. She used to be the cook in a downtown restaurant until they cut back her hours and she couldn't pay her rent. At night, she'd raid the dumpsters for food, and we found out she was feeding about a hundred cats."

Generosity was rewarded, Barry saw.

"People don't realize how important cats are."

"To kill the rats," Barry said.

Shocked, she put a finger to her mouth to silence him. "Rats are living things, too," she said. "We feed the cats so they won't have to kill for food."

"I see," said Barry, remembering from somewhere that a well-fed cat is a better hunter.

"Do you feed the rats, too?"

"Of course," she answered. "They deserve to live. You never know who they were in a past life."

Trying to understand, feeling as cornered as a fat man in a room full of dieters, Barry let her last statement drift and turned his attention to Silverback.

"I want to introduce all of you to our driver tonight, Rhesus," he said. "Stand up, please," he pointed to Barry. "Rhesus comes to us from the central Pennsylvania territory. A few of you have seen him before, on deliveries."

Faces turned to see him; Barry nodded.

"Tonight, we embark on a great mission. Impossible, you ask? No, not impossible. The animals can not speak for themselves, and we must do it for them. After tonight, the whole nation—the whole world— will never be the same. Parents will think twice about showing off the innately cruel practice of imprisoning animals. Children will no longer laugh as animals debase themselves for their pleasure and fall into perversion."

What did he mean? Barry wondered. What was he talking about?

"From the time I was a little boy, from the time I was first becoming a man, I knew this. But, like the animals, I couldn't speak. I had no power. But I wasn't alone. As time went on, and I practiced divorce law, I met many people suffering just as much as those animals. And, like you, they wanted to do something for these less fortunate creatures.

"We live in a society that can fly to the moon, but doesn't give a damn about the cow that jumped over it! We live in a society that laughs as animals fornicate while children watch right here—right here in Philadelphia, and in Washington, Chicago and San Diego!

"But tonight—*tonight*—we do something about that. No longer will the country humiliate our animals. It's unacceptable! After tonight, when the APE strikes back, people will *beg* us—*beg us*—to stop. But we won't stop. We won't stop until every *animal slave* and *inmate* in the *concentration camps* of this nation are free and never owned by anyone ever again! *You* are brave! You're making a difference! *History!* I commend you *all*!" he said, leading a round of applause.

As darkness set in on the compound, a sense of urgency radiated from every piece of gravel, every clump of dried grass, every puddle of water in the drizzling rain.

"This is Capuchin," Spider said, looking friendly

but chilly in her jeans, jacket and scarf, hair sticking to the side of her forehead as she handed Barry directions and introduced a big, wide-faced man. "He's a mechanic. He used to have his own garage over on Broad Street until the city tore it down. You'll need him if anything goes wrong."

"Thanks," Barry said, sensing a gentleness in the big man. "Climb in."

"He'll ride in the back, with the others," she said. "I'll ride up here. Remember, if anyone asks, you're just making a delivery and I'm your wife. Hand the guard this note and everything'll be OK. Turn up the heat—I'm freezing!"

Doing as she wished, Barry read his directions. At this time of night, in the rain, they could make it in thirty, maybe forty minutes, he figured, revving the engine and passing through the gate. Same skinny guy in baggy clothes opening it for him. Same no-smile.

What the hell was in this thing, he wondered, as the trailer dragged him down. A full load of dogs never weighed this much. Deciding not to ask, shifting into low gear, he pulled steadily on.

"Mind if I play the radio?" he asked, his hand almost on the knob.

She shook her head. "It breaks my concentration," she said, and his hand went back to the wheel.

"What did you do before this?" he asked, making conversation. It beat driving in silence.

"I was a vet," she said. "Which was OK, I guess. But on the broader scale of things, not very significant."

"I think being a vet's a great thing."

"Not really," she said. "Anyhow, it doesn't matter

because the funding for my research was cut off."

Surprised, he said, "I thought someone like you—"

"Someone like me?"

"Yeah," he said. "I thought someone like you wouldn't be caught dead near a research project."

"That was a different me," she said. "Or, I should say, that's when there *was* a me."

Recalling the APE motto, he cleared his throat. "Yeah, I saw that in what Silverback gave me to read. Nice fellow, that guy."

"Nice?" she asked, dismayed and genuinely taken aback. "He's a god!"

The way she said it . . . *He's a god!* . . . the way her whole being shook when she said it—Barry almost thought she might show claws, dive at him, strangle him.

"I didn't mean any disrespect," he said, by way of an apology, deciding to change the subject. But she didn't want to.

"What Silverback has done for the Animal Rights Militia, and the tens of thousands of people he's inspired to join, is the stuff legends are made of. We're not fit to kiss the ground he walks on," she said, and meant it. "None of us—*not even the great Marion Malloy*!"

Expressway . . . Girard Avenue . . . My God, he thought, his foot lifting off the gas for a second: Project APE.

The Zoo!

Stop at the security station, hand the man the delivery papers, do as you're told, Barry reminded himself.

"Live monkeys," the guard read. "Nobody said I should expect a load of monkeys tonight."

Barry said nothing.

"ID?" the guard asked. Reaching for his wallet, Barry produced his driver's license. After jotting down the number, the guard waived him on. "Down a ways, to your right, Veterinary building. You stop there first."

Steady, Barry thought, driving through the empty lot, looking for a sign that said "Veterinary," finding it, stopping in the shadows.

"Here," Spider said.

Sensing an opening, his chance to probe further, Barry couldn't help but say, "Go easy on Marion," as he parked the rig. "I like that dame." This time, lying about it didn't bother him so much. Not that it really had before. Surely he was going to hell for this, he thought.

"The big star!" Spider said, as if it were something to be ashamed of. "Heidi Fleiss had nothing over Marion Malloy! *The queen of porn!*"

High-buttoned, flat-chested Marian Malloy in porn? Like the butt of a gun slammed onto his head, just as it had been done to the guard he had watched falling to the ground outside, Barry couldn't have felt any more stunned.

"You're kidding," he said, almost giggling.

"That's how they met," she said. "Silverback wanted to break into the celebrity crowd and Marion knew them all. They say there isn't a door in Hollywood she can't open."

Opening doors to the veterinary building was just as easy. With a sneer for Marion, Spider slid out of the truck and walked nonchalantly to the glass doors of the entrance. Pressing a buzzer, she was met by a janitor and let inside, where, oblivious to any danger, the night staff was celebrating a birthday party. A few minutes later, Barry could hear Spider whispering in his earphone. "Coast is clear. Now, get out of the truck, like you're going to check on the animals in your trailer. Open the doors and let Capuchin and the others out. Go with them. They've got surveillance cameras, but we're working on it."

Working on it. Dismantling surveillance cameras? Breaking down the Zoo's security system? What was he getting into?

Doing as he was told, Barry got out, went around back and opened the trailer door.

Silently, one, two, half-a-dozen APE members in coveralls and masks made a run for it.

Without a word, Capuchin shoved him on. "Think of the animals," he hissed, like a battle cry.

Thinking of my own ass! is what Barry told himself.

Inside, the band of raiders gathered. "Chimp," the janitor said, joining them. "Follow me."

What about security, staff, doctors? Barry wondered, as they rushed down the hall. With a lurch, he tripped—a body! A *body*! These people had killed someone!

"LaLa Land," Capuchin said. "In the Kool-Aid."

Unlocking a supply room, Chimp led them inside. "You know how to use these things?" he asked, passing out dart guns and tranquilizers. "Damn straight," said Capuchin.

"Come on!" Chimp said, as they rushed down the hall, through a side door and into the night.

"Hurry!" Spider said, as they ran. "We only have a few minutes."

"Those people back there!" Barry said, in disbelief and shock. "They were—"

"Sleeping," she said. "Just sleeping. If my dosage was right. I couldn't be sure. Hurry!"

Cats, Reptile House, Birds . . . there it was. He should have figured it would be Primates.

Immediately—not a minute, not a second to lose—the raiders set to work.

"That's . . . those are explosives!" Barry said, incredulous. But this time Spider would not answer him.

"What are you doing?" Barry said, as an innocent baby gorilla blinked her sleepy eyes at him through the glass. *"You're going to kill them!"*

"Shut up!" Capuchin hissed at him. "You're getting paid!"

Explosives . . . gasoline . . . Molotov cocktails . . . fire . . . *RUN!!!*

Through the darkness the righteous warriors ran. Jamming inside the truck, they roared away—away from the desperate screams of monkeys burning in flames, they escaped into the night.

"They're free now!" Spider said. The glowing fire illuminated the victory in her eyes. "Free!"

"Here's your money," Silverback said, handing Barry an envelope of cash as the self-appointed hit squad stood surrounded by a bank of television sets tuned to every news program. "What did you think of your first job, Rhesus?"

"Don't call me that."

"Look!" Silverback pointed at the TV. "See the

banner going across the screen? We made the news!"

*. . . PHILADELPHIA: ANIMAL RIGHTS MILITIA
SETS FIRE TO ZOO . . .*

"Now, they'll take us seriously," he said loudly, staring at the little yellow letters moving quickly from right to left. "They'll pay attention now!" he said, running a nervous hand across his mouth, over his face, putting both hands on his belt and pulling his pants higher.

"Come now," he said, his back to Barry as he faced the TV, speaking as if it were a mere afterthought. "A name's only a name."

"You're *insane!*" Barry spat. "*Sick!* And so are the rest of you!" he said, looking at them. "You keep a Bible here. How can you read the Bible and do what you've just done? *You make me want to vomit!*"

. . . BRONX ZOO IN FLAMES! . . .

"*In . . . sane?*" Silverback asked, ignoring the question. "He thinks we're insane, out of our minds, *crazytoons*! Is that right, Barry? See, you don't want me to call you by the name of one of God's creatures, so I'm calling you *Barry.* Your *human* name. Is that what you think—we're *insane*? Do insane people get on TV, Barry? *Do they?*"

*. . . CHICAGO: HISTORIC ZOO BUILDING
BOMBED . . . ANIMAL RIGHTS MILITIA
DANCES IN STREETS . . .*

Stunned, groping, struggling for an answer—drowning, suffocating at the impact of what he knew ran deeper, far deeper than Silverback and his followers—Barry searched their faces. "You people don't love animals," he said. *"This isn't about animals. It's about power!"*

"Oh!" Silverback said, pointing at the TV set like an eager child. "Look! Another banner!"

> *. . . WASHINGTON, D.C.: ACTIVISTS TAKE ZOOKEEPER HOSTAGE IN MONKEY HOUSE . . . DEMAND $$$ . . . THREATEN TO RELEASE ANIMALS . . .*

"Love animals?" Silverback said, turning now to glare at Barry. "*LOVE* animals? Oh, my friend, have *you* ever got it wrong. We love *animals* all right. But you talk and talk 'til you're blue in the face—nobody takes you seriously. They forced us to do this. They FORCED us!" he screamed, shaking. "Look what we have to do to make them see! If a few must suffer for the greater good of all, that's the price. We have no choice. *Look!*" he said, shifting from righteous anger to wild delight, jumping for joy: *"We got MSNBC!"*

> *. . . SAN DIEGO ARSONISTS DESTROY MONKEY HOUSE . . . HUNDREDS OF ANIMALS DIE IN FLAMES . . .*

"This is Manson shit!" Barry said. "Or that guy in South America, Jim Jones!"

"Did you like the Kool-Aid idea?" Silverback asked quickly, his eyes wide. "That was mine," he said. "Nice touch, I thought. Huh? A statement, if you will."

"Look!" somebody yelled, laughing. "They're naked!" she exclaimed, as cameras showed protesters stripping and handcuffing themselves to bars of animal cages. Los Angeles . . . Atlanta . . . New York . . . Saint Louis.

. . . TERRORISTS BOMB AMERICAN ZOOS . . .
ANIMAL RIGHTS PROTESTERS DEMAND FREE-
DOM OF ANIMAL INMATES . . . ARRESTS IN
LONDON . . . PARIS . . . MUNICH . . . MOSCOW . . .

"It's working!" Silverback hollered with laughter. "It's working!"

But Barry Dunmoyer had eased out the door, made it to his rig and the spare set of keys taped under the frame, slipped a hundred to the guy at the gate and was nowhere to be found.

"Kenita!"

"Barry?" she said, answering the knock at her door. "What—"

"I can't explain," he said. "Not now. I need a place to stay. You have to let me—please let me—let me stay!"

His face, his eyes! "Of course!" she said, opening the door and letting him in.

"Thank you! Thank you!" he said, taking her in his arms, holding her tight, kissing her.

"Barry!" she said, loving it, loving him, kissing him. "It's OK. You're safe. You're safe."

"Kenita," he said. "Kenita, I was wrong to leave you. I was wrong! If I only knew . . . if I only knew what was out there. We have to stop them, Kenita. We have to stop them!"

"Stop who, Barry? *Who do we have to stop?*" she asked, holding him, rocking him, trying to make it all go away.

"*The monkey people!* We have to stop the monkey people!"

He was babbling. He wasn't making any sense. He was hurt; something had happened to him. He was delirious! She ran her hands over his forehead, through his hair.

"Mom?" It was Felicia, on the stairs. "Are you all right?" she called out.

"Yes! Yes! I'm all right!" Kenita called back to her, touching her finger to Barry's lips, glancing over her shoulder, hoping, praying her daughter wouldn't come down the stairs and find them. "I'm . . . " she thought quickly, "I'm watching a movie. Go back to bed!" she said, pushing him into the parlor.

"I thought I heard the dogs barking," Felicia said, coming down the rest of the way in her big white shirt and panties. "Brrr . . . it's chilly down here," she said, clasping both arms to herself, heading for the kitchen. Pouring herself a glass of milk, Felicia closed the fridge. "G'night," she mumbled, steadying herself as she went back upstairs, tired, but not too tired to figure Kenita must have turned off the movie.

"Good night!" Kenita said in a loud whisper. Turning her attention to Barry, she sat him down. "Tell me what happened," she said. "Tell me everything."

"Oh, my God," she said later, as they watched the news. "Oh, my God, Barry. You weren't kidding."

"I had to get out of there," he said. "And we have to stop them. If we don't, who knows? Who knows what they're going to do next!"

"It's just like—"

"Like the whole Twin Towers thing," he finished. "I know!"

"Well, what are we going to do?" she asked.

"I . . . I have to rest," he said. Though how he imagined he could sleep after all this, he didn't know.

"We should go to the police," she said.

"No! We can't!" he said, his voice in a panic.

Why couldn't they? she wondered. Why couldn't they go to the authorities? That's what good citizens did, wasn't it?

"We can't go because they'll take me in."

"Why?" she asked. "What do you have to do with it? They forced you, Barry. They forced you to drive that rig for them."

"Don't you see?" he asked, pleaded. "If I could get away like I did, the cops are going to ask why I didn't try getting away sooner. Why I didn't refuse."

"But you couldn't," she said for him. "You couldn't, Barry!"

His silence, falling between them now, was the answer she didn't want to hear.

"Barry?"

He knew—he knew with all his heart—that he hadn't left sooner because until that night he hadn't wanted to.

"Going to Vegas?" the man asked. Considering the flight was non-stop, clearly he wanted to make conversation. Claude, on the other hand, did not. Seeing little use in making an enemy of a two-hundred-and-fifty-pound tourist pressing him against an airplane window, he answered, "Yes." He might have said yes to almost anything at that point.

"Me and my wife, here, have to see a specialist."

"Oh," Claude said, glancing at the woman. "What's wrong?" the reporter in him couldn't help but ask.

Over the years, he had been considered rude at times for asking people what ails them, as if it were an invasion of privacy. He, himself, never looked at it that way. He looked at it as a certain form of art. After all, if they were open enough about it to bring up the subject first, then he felt as if they wanted to share what was affecting them. With a little finesse, he had learned a great deal about people and their problems this way. He had also gained surprising insight into their determination, courage and faith.

"It happened all of a sudden," she began, then proceeded giving him not only the information he asked for, but quite a lot that he hadn't. By the time the movie was rolling its credits, he found himself fascinated by the lengths to which his new acquaintances had gone in their search for the cure of a bad leg and bad skin, not to mention a progressive loss of memory.

"It's OK," the woman said, finally. "You can ask me anything. I won't remember it anyway."

By then, Claude was wishing that anyone who could see the vision unfolding outside his window would remember it always. "Look! Can you see?" he asked her, like a child might when seeing something great and beautiful for the first time.

She couldn't help herself. Weak as anyone could be, she still wanted to see what excited him so much. "It's like a pirate's treasure spread out on black velvet cloth," she said, her voice filled with wonder.

It was Las Vegas at night, and Claude wanted to hold on to that picture and that vision of the city in the desert for the rest of his life.

From: Emerson@dejazzd.com
To: Researchdept@SATV.com
Subject: High Stakes

If every Greyhound was a light in Vegas, would it be the 20,000 a year they say are killed?

From: Researchdept@SATV.com
To: Emerson@dejazzd.com
Subject: High Stakes

Although it's been thrown around by reporters from small town newspapers all the way to HBO, Animal Planet, National Geographic and ESPN, our research shows that there aren't even 20,000 Greyhounds born a year. That hallowed figure is bogus.

CHAPTER EIGHT

Down The Hatch . . .

Like a king among peasants, Clue waited with dignity as the race drew near. It was a slow track, still wet in places from a downpour, and he was far from the favorite. His competition that night was a seventy-five pounder from Miami, two Grade A dogs from a well-known kennel at Lincoln, one of last year's stakes finalists from The Woodlands in Kansas, a dog coming over from Tri-State and two other dogs from big-time kennels based at Wheeling. It was a schooling race. None of the dogs had raced here officially, or else they had been off the active list for awhile. It was the only time an ungraded dog like Clue would run against dogs of such a high caliber. It wouldn't be an easy race, and Felicia knew it.

"Good thing he doesn't know how tough those dogs are," Mark said, as a neatly dressed young man let Clue out. Rubbing the dog's back, playing with his ears, patting his sides, the fellow seemed pleased to have Felicia's new hopeful on the end of his leash. Hidden Clue, himself, appeared calm and stately as if there wasn't a nervous fiber in his body. Making his way majestically to the platform where his muzzle and jacket were checked to make sure they were properly *secured, he allowed the attendants to smooth their hands over his racing jacket that boldly declared the number eight. It was the outside box, not always an easy position from which to win, especially if your dog happened to like running the rail.*

After a brief walk to the starting boxes that looked like miniature versions of starting gates in a horse race, the field of entries was guided into their various boxes. Barking frantically in anticipation of the mechanical lure whizzing by, they waited for the creaking sound telling them the race was on.

"You show 'em, boy!" his lead-out whispered, gently swatting Clue on the rump for luck.

"Aw, yer dog ain't gonna win!" one of the other guys complained. "Hell, your dog was petted out already! Does he have any balls? I heard this here dog came this close to a quarter million big ones at The Woodlands," he said, pinching together his thumb and forefinger.

"Yeah? Well, here's a finger for ya!" Clue's handler said, making a gesture of his own.

"Ouch!" the other guy joked. "I felt that!"

"You loved it!" another lead-out razzed. "Come on, let's get outta here," he said, as a few of them jogged to their strategic spots along the track and the rest waited near the finish line. It was friendly banter, nothing more; it was their style, the rhythm of co-workers accustomed to animals earning more in thirty-one seconds than they could ever earn in a month.

But even jaded kennel helpers sense the difference between a champion and those he will defeat. Call it an extra spark of electricity, a "bearing of confi-

dence" or the alpha look in a dog's eye—call it what you will—it is the unmistakable signature of a ruler. And, born or made, it is power.

Inside his box, Clue waited for what seemed like an eternity. Through narrow slits in front of him, he could see the wide track, and smell its moist, sandy dirt.

It was dark. Like being in a cave. Like nighttime. It was owl time, snake time, the time of the hunter. Under the haunting moonlight, shimmering over the shiny rocks in the bubbling stream beside which he used to huddle, curled tight, on the mountain . . . afraid . . . afraid until a blast of sunlight on his face would make it all go away.

"Heeeeeere . . . comes . . . Spunky!"

A blast of light on his face—like the thousands of watts of stadium lights beaming on him right NOW!

Vrooooom! Even before the door could slide open, he was pushing his face toward the light, clawing his feet into the floor—ready to burst out of the box. Oblivious to any other dogs. He did not look left, he did not look right. He . . . just . . . ran!

He ran after the moving target scampering past him in the dark as the trapdoor flew open. I see you! I can catch you! I CAN!

Bearing into the first turn, he took the lead to the sound of his name coming from the skies. . . . "It's Hidden Clue in the front by a length, followed by . . ."

"It's the number eight dog, Hidden Clue, in the lead now by four lengths . . ."

"At the far turn, it's Hidden Clue ahead by six lengths and showing no sign of slowing down!"

"Forget about the rest, it's Hidden Clue by ten lengths!"

"DID YOU SEE THAT?" Felicia screamed, jumping up and down and throwing herself into Mark's arms. "I knew it! I knew it!" she said, her eyes bright. "Did you see him? Did you see him go?"

Had he blinked, he'd have missed it. But he hadn't blinked. He wasn't going to blink even if it meant holding his eyes open with toothpicks. "He was incredible!" Mark gasped. "He was running faster and faster!"

"He's a monster, Mark! That's what you want in this business! He's everything he was born to be. We did it! We did it!"

"Felicia McCrory?" the man in golf shirt and slacks asked at the kennel the next morning.

"She's not here," Kenita said, from behind a table lined with sixty feed dishes for the dogs.

"Can you tell me when she might be back, or how I can reach her?"

"Pretty hard to say. Can I help you?" Kenita asked, mixing beef and kibble for the dogs. "I'm her mother."

"Oh," the man replied, offering his business card. "Well, I don't think we ever met before. I'm Steven Wentworth. I'm not in town often, but you probably know my trainer, Jimmy Miller."

With a look of recognition as she measured the dogs' vitamin supplements, Kenita said, "Everybody knows Jimmy. You guys are pretty tough to beat."

"Well," Mr. Wentworth smiled, "in that one comment you've said a great deal. And, fortunately, it's a deal I've come to make."

"A deal?"

"Yes," Wentworth said, looking around at the worn-out brooms, the faded curtains on the windows. "I understand you have a dog that won the fifth race last night."

"Fifth race? You'll have to do better than that if you want me to know what dog that was," Kenita said. "See, it's not all numbers to me."

"Forgive me," the man said coolly. "The dog's name is Hidden Clue."

"Could've guessed as much," Kenita said, stacking the dishes and calling for her son. "Carl!" she hollered. "Don't keep these dogs waiting!" Turning to her visitor, she asked, "What do you want with Clue?"

"Well . . . Kenita, you say?"

She nodded.

"Kenita, I see a lot of nice dogs in my travels. And I always make it a policy to learn as much as I can about them. My continuing education."

"Oh? And how educated are you about our dog?"

"Jimmy tells me he might be for sale," he said, smiling.

"Jimmy don't know shit," Kenita smiled back, even bigger.

"But Jimmy gave me a figure that could buy an awful lot of dog food."

"Dog food is something we've got plenty of around here," Kenita said, spraying the table with soapy water and reaching for a scrub brush.

"Are you saying the dog isn't for sale?"

"I'm sayin' Jimmy don't know what he's *talkin'* about," Kenita said, reaching for a roll of paper towels.

"I see. Well, in that case," he said, the tone of his voice shifting, "I'll just leave my card for your daughter and be on my way to the racing secretary's office."

Years of serving customers in restaurants had sensitized her to various tones of voice, Kenita tossed a clump of paper towels into the waste can and considered, but not for long, what she was about to say. "You know, I've been going to that school of yours myself for a while . . . and I'm not sure I like the way you said that."

"I'm sorry. Did I upset you?"

"What are you going to the office for?"

"Well, isn't it true the dog was petted out last year?"

"Yeah. And he's here now."

"Well, I may be wrong, but, it seems to me that once a dog is given up for adoption, it isn't yours any more. How do you manage to get a dog back, once you pet him out and give up his papers? Are you sure his papers are in order?" Wentworth smiled.

"Nobody's faking any papers," Kenita said, leveling a gaze right between Wentworth's eyes. "You'll see."

"I intend to. In the meantime, my offer stands. Will you have your daughter call me?" he asked, taking his leave as Carl entered the room with an "everything OK here?" manner about him.

"Mom?"

"It's OK, Carl. That was Jimmy Miller's boss."

"Jetstream Kennels?"

"None other," Kenita said, washing her hands and

drying them on her jeans. "Where's your sister? She's late."

"Haven't seen her," Carl said, helping himself to a bag of cookies. Since the press had reported the budding star was rewarded with a cookie each time he ran, Clue's fans were always surprising the kennel with goodies for him. "Thanks, Buddy," Carl said as Clue whined for one. "Only after you run. Anyhow. *You* gotta watch your diet. Mmmm. I love peanut butter."

"Did she call?" Kenita asked.

"Umm?" Carl asked, his mouth full. "Nope. Her an' Mark took off after the races last night."

"Oh. Well, how's Clue? Did he eat his breakfast this morning?"

"Straight away. Thought I'd turn him out in the field for a while; loosen 'im up."

"Do that," Kenita said. "And keep an eye on him, Carl. I'm gettin' a funny feeling."

Did he know he snored, she wondered, not daring to wake him, not daring to disturb this gentle moment. If she did, if she nudged him and he moved, the sunlight from the window might not streak his hair so beautifully. It might not glow across his shoulder and illuminate his skin as it was doing now, just for her.

Love . . . was it possible to feel again?

All she had built, all she had worked for . . . all the promises made to herself that she would never, ever, give in to what she knew had ruined the lives of so many others. Where were they now? Felicia asked herself. Why could she hardly remember them?

"Hmmmmm," he purred, a sly smile at the corners of his mouth. He wasn't asleep. He wasn't asleep at all.

"Faker," she teased gently.

Bigger smile. Hands finding her, pulling her into his arms and across his chest as he rolled back and deeper into the pillows. "Hmmmmmm . . . ."

"Hmmmm," she breathed, liking the buzz against her nose and lips . . . pressing her naked breasts against him, rubbing her nipples into his chest hair, smelling his skin, licking his ear, kissing his brow, running her hands through his dark hair, so clean from the shampoo they had made into clouds of fluffy bubbles in slippery water the night before.

"More," she whispered, as she felt one of his hands on her hip and the other easing underneath her back . . . more, more, more.

Touch . . . she wanted to touch him everywhere . . . the back of his neck as he lay himself upon her, the ripple of his shoulders, the feel of his muscular waist, groove of his spine and musty, dark secret of his ass . . . cupping his hard cheeks, she pushed her wetness to him, felt him take hold of himself, sliding into her. . . .

Perfect, she thought . . . *perfect.*

"Sorry!" the maids blushed and giggled as they slammed the door shut.

"Oh my God!" Felicia squealed, covering her face with a pillow as Mark, completely naked, exploding in passion, could do nothing to stop himself. "They saw us!" she wailed, pulling away and grabbing for a sheet.

"Hey!" Mark laughed, grinning big and fighting her for the sheet. "What about me?"

"Oh, what about you!" she said. "You don't live around here—and anyhow, you're beautiful."

"Beautiful, am I?" he said, pulling her to him and wrapping her in his arms. "No." He smiled. "You are."

"But those girls saw us," she said.

"Those *girls*," he said with an even bigger grin now, "were fifty if they were a day. You couldn't see with that pillow over your face. But I got the full view."

"You mean *they* did, Mark. They got the *full Monty*." She smiled, leaning him back, kissing his face, neck, nipples, belly. . . .

"Oh, God, I was so embarrassed!" Felicia said, brushing her hair and checking her lipstick as they pulled up outside the kennel a while later.

"How come?" Mark asked. You don't have anything to be ashamed of.

"Did you see how they looked at us when we checked out?"

"Well . . ."

"Like they could see right through our clothes," she said, with a naughty look.

"Quite a talent," he said. "Next time, we can go to my place. That is, if there's going to be a next time," he teased. "I kind of like the idea of a few extra maids, you know? *Ow, ow, ow!*" he yelped, suddenly jumping away and rubbing his butt. "You pinched me!"

Something about having a morning routine to count on reassured her, held her world together, Felicia thought. She kissed Mark goodbye. "See you next weekend, handsome." Then she hurried home to the comfort of family, friends and the job she loved.

"It's 'bout time you showed up!" Kenita said. "You had a visitor. Steven Wentworth."

"Oh? Sorry I missed him."

"You know him?"

"We've bumped into each other a few times."

"I'll take that comment no further." Carl chuckled good-naturedly. "My lips are sealed."

"Well, I'm not a nun," Felicia said. "If you want to know, we dated after my divorce."

"And why this well-kept secret?" Kenita asked, her eyebrows arched high.

"Tell all," Carl said, as he watered dogs and changed their bedding.

"There's nothing to tell," Felicia said. "He knew I wasn't sure about a few things, with the business, and he made us an offer."

"Funny, you never told *us* about it," Kenita said loudly.

"I don't remember any offers," Carl said. "Hell, I might have said go for it!"

"And do what?" Kenita asked. "This is our life. We're building a business and it's gonna be the best racing kennel in the world."

"Only kidding, Mom," he said, reassuring her that the dog business was his life. "I know the plan."

"Which is precisely why I turned him down," Felicia said.

"Just out of curiosity, what did he have in mind?"

"Besides Felicia, you mean?" Kenita asked. "Pray tell."

"He wanted a merger," Felicia said. "Of our kennels. We'd handle the breeding at our farm, and all the training. He and his people would negotiate all the bookings."

Knowing that there were bookings and there were *bookings,* Carl's interest sharpened. "Like where?" he asked, wanting to know if they were at major tracks.

"Lincoln, Dubuque, Derby Lane . . ."

"Biggies," Carl said. "And you turned him down?"

"Flat out, Carl," she said. "His strength has always been his business savvy. I'll grant you that. If anybody can cut a deal, it's Jetstream Kennels. But they don't have the broods."

Jetstream Kennels was famous in the industry for importing foreign bloodlines, having all the right connections and still falling short of its potential. Everyone knew it was the strength of a kennel's breeding stock that made the real difference. And, the McCrorys had been building their brood force for years.

"You didn't show him the farm did you?" Kenita asked.

"No. It didn't get that far. Anyway, I wouldn't do that. I knew what he was after. We'll get there on our own," she said. "Some day. Sure would be nice to get there sooner, though."

"Hey, these bones ain't gettin' any younger," Kenita said, wanting to rub her shoulder, but not wanting to mess up her shirt with chicken grease. *Barry's* shirt, in case anyone noticed, which they didn't.

"Mom, what you need is a boyfriend," Carl teased.

"Don't you worry about your ol' mom," she teased right back, mysteriously.

"Got some prospects?" Felicia wanted to know.

"Maybe," Kenita said, smiling to herself. "But it's a secret."

"I love secrets!" Carl said. "Secrets are my life!"

"A minute ago, the dog business was your life," Felicia said.

"Yeah, but I'm a man of the moment," Carl went on, having fun. "Kennel boy by day, super-spy by night!" Taking off his shoe, holding it like a phone, he whispered: "Headquarters? It's Agent 008."

"Carl, you crack me up!" Felicia said, laughing. "Promise you won't ever find a hot babe someplace and go away. I'd miss you, hon," she said, giving him a hug and a kiss on the cheek.

Mornings. Her mornings. Mornings when she knew what she was doing, where she was going . . . where she belonged.

Belonging . . . knowing who and what you were important to. Knowing why you were here, why you were alive. Sure, she had the dogs. Sure, she had Mom and Carl and a few people she'd call friends. Maybe that's all that mattered. Maybe that's what it was all about, and nothing more.

But there was more. She could sense it. Ever since she was a child, she could sense something bigger, stronger than herself—a bigger mission, perhaps? A greater purpose?

What could it be? Did anyone know why they were here in this world, why they were doing what they were with their lives, why they were born?

A dog knew why it was born: to live. And if that wasn't enough, her Greyhounds knew they were born to run. They couldn't help it. They didn't question, didn't debate what was right or wrong, what was "acceptable" to others around them. A Greyhound just ran . . . a Greyhound just "was."

Mark was right. There was something grander than themselves in the Greyhound and the industry built for it. There was . . . there it was again . . . truth.

Mark. A man coming along when a man was farthest from her mind. Well, not really. Men were never too far from her mind. But this one. This very unusual one. He was on her mind, in her mind, inside her body and all over her skin.

What was it about him?

His eyes? Surely, she had seen eyes that color before. But did they have the same expression?

His hair? Lots of men had hair just as beautiful. But did she want to run her fingers through theirs?

His body? Not every man's body made her want to wrap her arms, her legs, her soul around him.

Mark . . . Mark Whittier . . .

Felicia . . . Whittier . . .

Hidden Farms in the antique business?

Kenita and Carl would never go for it.

She must forget about romance, put it out of her mind. Falling in love was for people with no goals, no plans; falling in love was out of the question.

"Did he say anything else?" Carl wanted to know, snapping Felicia out of her daze.

"Yeah, but he won't get very far with it," Kenita answered.

"What did he say?" Felicia asked, her mind regaining its focus now, back on business.

"He wanted to know about Clue," Kenita said.

"Clue? What for?"

"Well, unless I don't know people as well as I *think* I do, he wants to make you an offer."

"Clue's not for sale," Felicia said. Sell Clue? Sell not only a good dog, maybe the best dog she ever had? Sell her connection to Mark?

"Any dog's for sale," Kenita said. "For the right price."

"Look who's talking!" Felicia fired back. "I think The Blue Queen would have a thing or two to say about that. And don't you even open your mouth, Mr. Dee Dee," she snapped at her brother.

"Nobody's sayin' anything, F'leesh," Carl said, hands up in mock surrender.

"If you could have seen him last night. If you could have been there."

"That good, was he?" Kenita teased.

"Mother!"

"Come on, F'leesh," Carl chimed in. "It's not like we don't know where you were."

Stepping away, standing by the window, she pulled aside the curtain as she was often wont to do. He had been there only a short while ago. He had held her in his arms, showed his love in a thousand ways and kissed her goodbye.

"I'm a grown woman," she said. "And Clue's not for sale."

Clue wasn't for sale now or anytime soon. Even if she would consider it—*if* she would—Steven Wentworth was right: there was still the problem, the gnawing fear, about his original papers. He was running on a duplicate registration. "I've misplaced his certificate," she had lied. "Can you issue another one?"

"Certainly," they had said.

It wasn't entirely untrue, she reasoned. She had, in fact, lost the certificate. She just hadn't lost it in the usual way.

"If he comes around again," Felicia said, "if anybody comes around here snooping about Clue, tell them to mind their own business."

Telling people to mind their own business was easier said than done. Word about the young star in the McCrory kennels was spreading, and track regulars were taking notice: When's he running again? they wanted to know. How's the champ feeling today?

"Carl! What's the matter with you?" Kenita asked, interrupting Felicia's thoughts, as Carl pressed both hands to his stomach.

"I . . . don't know!" he said, his face a deathly white.

"Felicia! *Felicia!*" Kenita screamed.

"Mom!" Carl moaned, his eyes wide as he fell to the floor, wretching in vomit.

"Oh! Carl, Carl!" his mother said, cradling him in her arms, rocking him back and forth as Felicia scrambled for the phone, dialing security.

"Get me an ambulance—quick! *Carl!* Hold on!"

"What's the matter?" Felicia cried. "What happened?"

"He was eating those cookies," Kenita moaned.

"Don't touch them!" Felicia said, looking at her brother, touching his forehead. *"Oh God!"*

Hurry, ambulance! Hurry! Don't take my brother from me, God. Don't take my crazy, dumb brother!

Minutes . . . long minutes filled with nothing but

waiting, as Carl's breathing became shorter, more shallow.

"Carl!" Kenita shook him. *"Carl!"*

Slapping!

Shaking!

"Oh God, no!" Felicia screamed, tears washing her face, chills falling over her head, her arms. Hands numb. Her heart! The world grinding to a stop even as the siren of the approaching ambulance seemed to be wailing in slow motion.

Funerals are hollow, shocking rituals.

Tears are dry; hearts raw . . .

Carl . . . dear, dear Carl . . .

Kenita, dressed in black . . . Felicia falling into a sorrow with no bottom, Mark beside her . . . the Coalition standing true . . . Carl's friends and lovers from the local bar where he sang to the radio and wowed them on karaoke nights.

Carl . . . oh, Carl. Why did you go before me? I'm the oldest, not you. I'm the one who should go first. Unable to take another step, her hand tight on Mark's arm, Felicia stumbled and felt his arm around her waist.

"Not now," he whispered, holding her tight, speaking for the angels, for those who have gone before us and wait for us to join them. "Not now."

"When?" she moaned, her heart overflowing.

"Just," he said softly, "not now."

As Cecil spoke a eulogy, his voice resonating throughout what once was the ballroom of the grandest mansion in town, they fell silent.

Clearing his throat, Cecil rose to the occasion he dreaded, speaking words that he hoped would comfort, knowing they would always be remembered. There could be no mistakes.

"We knew him," he began, and the room swayed, or was it his own mind shifting into what minds are known to do on such occasions.

"We loved him," he said, and a young woman bent forward, covering her face.

"He was one of us . . ." he started, letting go of the notes he had prepared, slipping them into the pocket of his suit jacket, looking to Edna Rae as she projected love and support to him. There was no need for notes, not now.

"Carl McCrory was a good soul. He would do anything for you; all you had to do was ask and he would do it, or try to. And if he couldn't, he'd find somebody else who could. I guess there's a name for that kind of person somewhere. A psychological description of such people. I don't know what that name is, but I can tell you, the people who can claim it are very few."

Scanning those who had come together from as far away as New England, Cecil searched the crowd for Wanda. "He wasn't a computer whiz. I can tell you that. But he was creative. He could think of more excuses to keep his *Dee-Dee* than anybody else I know."

In spite of themselves, a smile or two crossed some faces; a veil of darkness lifted, then fell again.

"And no dogs ever shined as bright as the ones he fussed over before each race."

"Amen!" Poppy called out from the fourth row.

"Carl's heart was in the sport. He was part of it. He was one of us—on our side. Don't forget us, Carl. Don't forget us."

One by one, members of the Coalition stood to pay their last respects.

"I just want to say, to Carl, if you run into some of the bad guys up there, kick 'em in the butt. That's all I ask," Poppy said. "Am I nuts?" she whispered to Barbara as she sat down. "What made me think the bad guys get to heaven?"

Barbara was standing. "Carl didn't always get to our meetings, but he always knew what was going on. You could count on him to write letters and make calls, and I know he got his friends to sign petitions even if they didn't have Greyhounds. Thanks, Carl. You'll be missed."

"Look after your mother and sister from over there," an awkward Jack Halstead said. "I'll take care of the weights you left in my garage." There would be no need for them any more.

Edna Rae, Brad Taggart, Jason Greathouse and others.

Standing.

Weeping.

Saying goodbye.

Through it all, Kenita sat as still as the stone that would mark her son's grave. "Take me home," she finally said, when the casket was lowered into the ground.

Not a moment longer will I stay here, she thought to herself. This isn't my Carl. Carl's back at the farm, with the newborn puppies. He's playing with the dogs. Flying in front of the racers, calling to them as they cross the finish line. They were running to him, all of them. Just as she, herself, would run to him with open arms some day.

It's a tradition in some quarters to feed the weary guests who come to funerals. Such was so for the McCrory clan as Hidden Farms opened its doors to those who knew Carl. Stories, laughter and plans for the future lifted them, reminding them that life goes on.

"Any more from the cops?" Poppy asked, using paper towels to sop up punch from her paper cup.

Wanda considered her options. She could answer directly and say no, or she could explore the possibilities she, herself, had been investigating. "They're going on the assumption that Clue was the target."

"Well, the bag of cookies did have his name on it."

"Yeah, but it had to be somebody who knew how to get the cookies to him, right?"

"That's no big deal. You just send them in the mail."

"Which brings up other legal issues, but doesn't guarantee they'll get to the right dog." She had a point, they agreed. "If you don't get them to the right dog, it's just a shot in the dark."

"In which case, you'd never know where in hell they'd end up," Jack said.

"And you wasted your *cookies*," Jason added, a touch of cynicism in his remark.

"What are we saying?" Poppy asked, certain that Wanda had thought it out more thoroughly and had taken the next step in deduction.

"I'm thinking somebody gave those cookies to Carl, themselves. You know. Somebody he trusted. Like, here ya go, man. Something for your dog."

"And, don't forget," Barbara added, "they had to know peanut butter was Carl's favorite."

"Murder," Cecil pointed out. "They'd know the cookies would never reach Clue . . . "

"Because Carl," Poppy jumped in, "would finish them off first!"

"Wait a minute," Edna Rae said quickly. "What if the murderer—the one who made the cookies—*didn't* know peanut butter was Carl's favorite. What if the whole thing was a *mistake*?"

"I've been wondering the same thing," Wanda said. "Because just one cookie wouldn't have been enough to kill anybody. I mean, Clue only gets a treat, right? That's *one* cookie. Like giving your dog a biscuit. You don't give your dog a whole box of biscuits all at one time."

"If it *was* a mistake," Jason realized, "somebody out there just killed a good friend!"

"So, who makes peanut butter cookies?" Poppy asked, as if she had never heard of such a recipe.

"I know a place," Mark said, walking over to them. "A little deli back home. Peanut butter cookies are Pennsylvania Dutch."

"OK," Poppy said, adding it up. "What've we got here? A killer from the Pennsylvania Dutch Country who likes dogs. At least when he's not out there poisoning them. And a friend of Carl's, too, don't forget. So, who was it?" She paused. "*You,* Mark? My aunt's Italian. Does that mean if somebody chokes on spaghetti and dies it's *her* fault?"

Insult washing over him, sickening him as he realized how easy it is to accuse and how difficult to defend,

Mark said, "Sort of leaves us hanging, doesn't it?"

Eliminating most of the Coalition from the list of suspects was easy, Mark thought. Since Carl was usually too busy to attend the meetings, he had never really established any close or intimate relationships with any of the members. Not that he didn't believe in their cause. Everybody in racing did. And not that he didn't love the dogs. He loved every dog in the Hidden Farms kennel and would have done anything in the world for them—especially for Dee-Dee. But Carl had always left the political end of the business up to Felicia. He *trusted* Felicia. . . . No, Mark thought, putting that out of his mind. Absolutely, totally, completely out of the question. *Erase. Erase. Erase.*

Kenita? Carl's own *mother*? He wouldn't even consider it.

Barbara straightened her back and jutted out her chin. "Are you saying it was *one of us*?"

"Let's not even go there," Mark said. "Let's just think back over the past few days and see if we can come up with anything the police have overlooked."

"What about another kennel?" Brad asked.

Jack frowned. "Every kennel at the track wants to know who it was, just as bad as we do."

"Yeah, but if Clue *was* the real target, who stands to gain with him out of the way?" Brad asked.

"That's easy enough," Jason offered. "Any of the kennels running dogs in *The Wheeling $100,000*."

"Eight kennels, eight trainers, eight owners," Barbara said. "It's a start. But you can knock out two," she looked at Wanda.

"Yeah," Wanda said. "You can take Felicia out. And

Clyde and me have a dog running, and it wasn't us."

"*Love* the name of your dog!" Poppy said. "Wharton Whompum. Early speed, I presume?"

"Oh, yeah, "Wanda said. It's fierce, watching him."

"Pedigree?" Edna Rae asked, unable to resist.

"Stapler's Jo out of a Westmead brood," Barbara said, joining them. "I looked it up on *Greyhound-data*."*

"Thanks," Wanda said, pleased to have her dog noticed.

"Carl's kind of dog," Mark said, reeling them in. "So, we're down to six dogs from six kennels, trainers and owners."

"No, we're not," Cecil said, walking out of Felicia's office, where he had just checked the dogs listed on her chalkboard. "It's five. Two of the dogs belong to the same owner."

"That narrows the odds," Mark said.

"I say we let the police narrow them even further," Cecil said.

"What for, honey?" Edna Rae asked. "What makes you say that?"

"I'm thinking of you—all of us. This wasn't just about killing a dog," he said. "It's about making a statement. And who makes a statement this way?"

"Exactly," Wanda said, heating up again. "It makes more sense if the killer was out to mess up a star dog. And then hoped it would get in the news. For all we know, they might try it again."

Poppy wanted to know more. "Keep going."

---

*Greyhound-data.com: An international database of Greyhound pedigrees and racing information.

"But the *kennels*—" somebody started.

"I don't think it's them," Wanda said.

"But it hits the news either way, doesn't it?"

"Not in a big way," Wanda said. "The media doesn't care about one dog missing a race. But *now* . . . a threat on an important dog like Clue—a dog that had his picture in all the papers, had some kind of story about him and lots of people know—and a murder? *That's* news. What we have to do is ask ourselves who's always trying to get in the paper. And, if you ask me, *that's* where we should start."

Always trying to get in the paper. Hooked on publicity. Craving it, whoring for it. *Using* it.

"Well, *that's* no mystery," Poppy said, saying what was foremost on everybody's mind. "The only ones I can think of who *use animals* for their own publicity are the *militants*."

She had finally said what everybody sensed—but couldn't prove.

"Well," Wanda said. "I know they monitor WWG all the time. We don't make a move in this industry that they don't know about. They knew about the race, Clue, everything."

"Posting information on chat lines," Mark said. "A double-edged sword."

"What is it, Wanda?" he asked, at the sudden look on her face.

She shook her head. "Nothing," she said. "For a minute I . . . "

Her words were drowned by somebody calling out, "I hear Steve Wentworth wants to know if Felicia's keeping the kennel now that Carl's gone!"

"She told that guy to take a hike!" Poppy fired

back. "He's gonna get a *beatin'* tomorrow night!"

But Wanda's skin was crawling. All her life, she had been able to tell when something wasn't right. Put it out of your mind, she told herself. The police will sort things out. Don't get involved. Still, she couldn't shake the idea that something she had seen just a few days ago was a lot more important than she thought. "Is there a computer here?"

"In the den, off the living room," Edna Rae said. "You look worried."

"Come with me!" Wanda suddenly cried, as if there were no time to waste. "What's the password? Where's Felicia? Get Felicia. *Hurry!"*

A few minutes later, the computer screen blossomed into a colorful home page and Felicia stepped aside. "What's so important?" she asked as Wanda took control. "Don't you want a break from this stuff?"

"Computer junkie," Poppy teased, explaining it away as Wanda's fingers tickled the keys and she brought up the site of a Greyhound message board.

"What the hell you doin' *there!*"

"Bear with me, Poppy," Wanda said, concentrating. "I came across this about a week ago. But it didn't make any sense until just now."

"But they're anti-*racing!*" Poppy said, wondering if her friend had lost her mind.

"We can monitor, too."

Searching the topics, Wanda paged down as all eyes scanned the various messages discussing Clue's newfound celebrity.

The question in Red capital letters: "ANYONE KNOW WHO TRAINS OR OWNS HIM?"

A response in Blue lower case letters: *"friend of mine. I know him from karaoke."*

Red: ARE YOU ONE OF US?

Blue: *member six years.*

Red: NEED TO TALK. PHONE NUMBER?

"Do the police know this?" Felicia asked, her words coming slowly.

"What now?" Poppy asked, her eyes confused.

Wanda turned around with a big smile. "We follow the crumbs. Like from a plate full of cookies." Leaving the room, she returned with her purse. "Watch," she said, slipping a disk into the hard drive.

"Where did that come from?" Poppy wanted to know.

"*Experience.* Leaving my laptop in motel rooms when I need it most!" Wanda said, calling up the software she wanted. Making her way through a series of codes, she entered the database. "This whole cookie thing. It's *computer* talk! Every PC has its own serial number," she explained. "And you can trace the numbers. *That's what I thought!*" she said, pointing. "This one's from right here in Wheeling."

"So, whoever that was, the one writing in blue, comes from around here," Felicia said, her sense of privacy melting away.

"No biggie," Poppy thought out loud. "They already said they sing *karaoke* with him. Which *means*, check out the *bar* he goes—I mean went—to." She looked apologetically at Felicia as she asked, "Who do you know there? Who were his friends?"

The very idea that any friend of her brother's could do such a thing shook her faith. "I don't know," she said. "Mom would know better than I do."

"Let's ask her," Edna Rae said. "But are we any closer than before?"

"We're on the backstretch," Wanda said, her mind racing.

"But, you know, people ask this kind of stuff all the time," Edna Rae said. "Who's the trainer? Who's the owner? I know I do."

"Yeah, but *this* person is anti-racing, sang with Carl at the bar and was a *member* of something."

"Maybe it just means how long they've been a member of the chat board," Poppy guessed.

"Six years," Felicia said.

"But that's it!" Wanda said. "That's what got me."

"What did?" Poppy asked, confused now more than ever.

"This message board hasn't been *around* for six years!"

Jennifer Wilson-White sat in her kitchen, alone. Not really, she thought. Not really alone . . . she had Horris, the white cat she had found as a kitten frightened and crying by the road as cars whizzed by. Horris, crawling with lice and full of worms, as full as his belly was rolling in cat food now.

"Come here, Horris," she said, like one who can find no comfort, no rest. "Here, kitty, kitty."

She had felt like this for days. She had felt like this since . . . since the thing she couldn't ever change had happened.

For the cause, they had said. *Because the animals can't speak for themselves.*

But it'll make him sick, she had said.

Only for a little while . . . just enough to scratch him from the race. You do want to *save the dogs*, don't you? You do want to help the *cause*? If he makes the sport *popular*, we can never put an end to racing.

It was only one race, she thought.

It's not like it would kill anybody.

Staring at the dark screen of her computer, she cursed her brown hair for falling over her face, then apologized. "I didn't mean that!" she said to Horris. "I didn't." A mouse scampered across the floor and Horris leaped from the stove.

Another time, on another day, she would have screamed *"NO!"* But not now.

This time, she didn't move.

This time, she watched as the cat slapped the mouse away from the safety of its trail under the stove, under the kitchen cabinets and past the sink. Mesmerized, she watched as the mouse flipped through the air like a pizza, hit the wall and landed, stunned but running, at her feet. Not a drop of blood, not a squeak . . . only Horris, eyes wide, looking at the floor, the walls, the ceiling . . . and the twitching, naked mouse tail hanging from his mouth.

It was karaoke night at the bar. Her night to shine.

But who would take care of Horris?

Horris, the killer.

Horris, the *murderer.*

She would miss him.

Carl . . . sexy, fun Carl . . .

She missed him even more, she thought, finishing the note.

Head dropping, shoulders limp, the pen fell from her hand.

Doubling over, weaving sideways, the young woman who loved a guy who loved animals slumped to the floor.

Cecil was puzzled. Would the police do anything with the list of suspects?

"They'll move on it," he said. "But what's *happening* to everybody? Zoos being attacked? Now *this*? The world's going crazy!"

"Where have *you* been?" Jason said.

"But how does it all fit together?" Mark asked.

"Isn't it obvious?" Jack Halstead said. "They just want to shake us up."

"A moving target is hard to hit," Jason reminded them. He was right. "And, around here, they take murder seriously."

"Especially in our business, you mean," Jack said, implying the local authorities ran a tight ship.

"Not the way you make it sound," Cecil said. "This is a good town. Carl was a local boy. The cops won't just sit on it."

"On Saturday night? *Party* night?"

"*Any* night," Cecil reassured them. "We're not hicks. These boys grew up around here, too. Don't forget. All they had to hear was Felicia telling them it was somebody from the bar. They're out there right now. And they ain't drinking," he said. "I'll bet on it."

"I hate to interrupt," Felicia said, "But have any of you seen Mom?"

"Not since she gave you the list," Mark said, sensing Felicia's concern. "Isn't she upstairs?"

"That was hours ago," Felicia said. "I'll check on her."

"You OK?"

"Just tired. It'll give us a chance to talk."

She had grown up in this house, pretending each step up the stairs was a year of her life, years of the McCrorys following the dream they all shared.

"Step on it, F'leesh!" she could almost hear Carl saying. *"There's plenty of room at the top!"*

I'm on my way, she promised him. On my way.

"Hello?" Kenita answered the phone in her room.

"This is Officer Hendricks with the police department," a considerate voice said. "May I speak with Mrs. McCrory?"

"I'm Kenita McCrory," she said, her heart stopping.

A few minutes later, Felicia heard the sound of a loud dial tone as she knocked gently on her mother's door.

"Mom?" She found Kenita sitting in a chair, her solemn face to the window overlooking the puppy pens.

"Mom?" she asked again.

Kenita hung up the phone and didn't move.

It was over. Everything.

Without Carl, there was no need to try any more. No need to . . . what? No need to hope, to dream? No need to live? Is that what she felt, closing in on her, drowning her? Some chose booze, some chose drugs. Her? She chose to think about it, live it, let it swoop her up and take her along with it as far as it wanted to go, until there was nothing left to think about, nothing more to cry about, or laugh about, or feel.

Grandchildren?

Without Carl, there would be no such surprises

or diversions. Felicia never talked of kids or a family, so there was no use pretending. And Jeanie-Beth? Jeanie-Beth had made herself a boring non-entity as far as the McCrorys were concerned a long time ago.

Without Carl to tease, blame, fight with, it was over. At least this part of her life was.

Notes? Goodbyes?

They were overrated souvenirs meant for those who wallow in self-pity. She had said her goodbyes. She had said them in a thousand ways . . . but could he hear her?

My son!

My boy!

My baby! Oh, my darling, darling baby. Carl. Carl, what have they done to you? Picking up a T-shirt and a pair of old jeans, she kissed them, held them to her breast and sobbed.

"I was looking for you," Felicia said. But Kenita was far away, playing with her little boy.

"Mom . . ."

A hand moved. A hand Felicia hadn't noticed was so worn until now. A hand that didn't wear rings or fancy jewelry. The hand of a working woman.

"Mom," she tried again, taking that familiar hand, holding it in hers, caressing it.

"My purse," Kenita said finally, clearing her throat. Glancing around, Felicia noticed the familiar brown handbag on the bed and brought it to her mother.

With a shivering sigh, Kenita pulled her hand away, opened the purse and took out an envelope.

"We were going to be married," she said, her voice flat. "You and Carl didn't know that. You didn't *like* him," she said, and Felicia knew the man she was talking about. "My life," Kenita said, despair in her heart. *"My life."*

"It's OK, Mom," Felicia whispered, petting her mother's hair, touching the face that was the same as it had always been, would always be, to her. A face of wisdom, a face of love.

"No," Kenita said, looking into her eyes. "It's not. It's never going to be again."

Knowing there was more, knowing her mother had so much she wanted to say and there wasn't now, would never be, enough time to say it all, Felicia waited. She waited as every breath between them, every hope, filled the room.

"You're going to need this," Kenita said, pressing the envelope into her daughter's hand. "Take that dog and make him a champion, Felicia. For your brother. Yourself. *And me*."

No command could run deeper. No command could ring more true. From mother to child, from those before us to those to follow, the command to make a champion. Champions didn't stand alone. They were made by teams, and they carried their teams with them to glory.

Champions weren't always dogs. Sometimes, they were people.

Kissing her mother, hugging her as she had done for as long as she could remember, wanted to do as long as she ever could, Felicia stood, went to the door, and left the room.

Downstairs, she searched for Mark. Their eyes locking, she went to him and he held her, held her as if no one else mattered, as if the room faded away and spun around them and they were standing still.

"What's this?" his eyes, his face, everything about him seemed to say as she carefully unfolded Clue's registration certificate for him to see.

"All this time," Mark said, examining the priceless document.

No one—no Jetstream Kennels, no racing authority, no one—could stop them from running Clue now, or ever take him away.

"Steven Wentworth is going to be livid," she said.

"Where did you find it?" he asked.

Knowing he would wonder why Kenita had withheld something so important, she put a finger to his lips. "It doesn't matter," she whispered. "The only thing that matters is that we have it now, and Clue can run."

"How's Kenita?"

"Not good. She'll never get over this, Mark."

"Nor should she," he said. "Until the police know who did it, nobody's safe."

She had gone over it a thousand times. "It won't bring Carl back," she choked. "No matter what they find."

"Nobody's saying it can. But—" he started.

"Oh, Mark! I just can't believe all this is happening!"

"Felicia," he said, comforting her in his arms, stroking her hair, kissing her face, "I'm here. I'll stay. I won't go away until it's over." And even then he wouldn't. Carl hadn't been the target. Felicia wasn't, nor Kenita, nor anyone else. Not even Clue. *The target* was their whole way of life.

Carl's name wasn't flashing at them all over the news for attacking zoos beloved by people all over the country, all over the world. Carl hadn't destroyed priceless research projects meant to better understand the mysteries of life. He hadn't made rules and laws and zoning restrictions setting us that much farther away from what animals can teach us just by being in our care. What they can show us, how they can make us feel, simply by being ours and letting us learn what it's like—whether we're perfect or making all manner of mistakes—to provide food, shelter and health care for another living thing.

"They want to take it away," Mark said. "They want to take away everything that means anything to us, what we love," he said, looking at her closely, more closely than ever. Looking at her as if he had never seen her before and would never see her again. "They won't get away with it," he said. "We can't—we won't—I won't let them!"

"But how, Mark? We've been standing up to them for so long."

"We'll try another way," he promised. "We have to."

But where would they start? How would they start? You start by doing your homework, he decided. You start by ignoring everything you've been told, throwing out all preconceived ideas and going with your gut, your own senses, what feels right to you.

Animal *rights*? What did that mean? On the surface, if you didn't think about it, Mark decided, it didn't sound so bad. In truth, it sounded like a kind, highly evolved, and enlightened level of awareness to which we should all aspire. Didn't the fate of one life ripple through the cosmos and affect us all? Believing that, could he not understand how easy it was for sensitive people to devote themselves, their fortunes, their lives to standing up for all forms of life in any way they could?

Did he not understand how intelligent people, frustrated with an ever-encroaching, controlling society sucking the passion right out of them, cutting them off from themselves, from every natural force and desire they own, would identify with animals? Would do anything they could for something—anything—that made a difference in the broader scheme of things? That made a statement? That stood up for love?

Love drove them on, drove them to take risks, do things they would never do just for themselves. Love turned gentle caretakers of animals into angry protesters seeing that nothing they thought, nothing they did within the system, really worked. Until, faced with no choice in a world where everything else seemed more important than the needs of their beautiful, funny, innocent pets—and all animals on the planet, all *life*— they had no choice but to become as callous and cruel as the very oppressors they abhorred.

We *love animals*, they proclaimed. We love *animals*. We may not be able to free ourselves of the shackles in which we live. We may not be able to make things better for ourselves, to escape the eyes of Big Brother, the long hand of the law, the insidious spying of neighbors, tracking of our money, breaking apart of our families and invasion of our privacy at every turn. But we love *animals*. We love them so much we will do anything, *we will do whatever it takes*, no matter what it costs, to stop you from doing to them what you have done to us—to punish you for how you treat them. For what you have taken away from them; for how you butcher and bleed and manage them for their own good. Well, you don't know what's for their own good. If you knew how they felt—how they really felt—you would know. You would know without a shadow of a doubt. Without so much as a whisper against a hurricane. You would know that the deepest, most primal urge of any living thing is to live. To survive!

And you would know there comes a point beyond which no one can be pushed. A point where the office worker, monitored by the Internal Revenue Service and tattled on by his own bank, looks around and says, I can't do much about my own life any more. But I can damn well do something for my cat or my fish or my bird or my horse or my dog.

Her fingers idly playing with a string of dime-store pearls Carl had bought for her birthday, Kenita considered the officer's question. Did she know of anything called Pennsylvania Lovers of Greyhounds? Yes, she knew them, she told him. Everybody at the track knew them. But Hidden Farms hadn't sent them dogs since their position on racing had shifted. The kennel would support other adoption groups, the McCrorys had decided.

But Barry knew them. He knew them well.

"Are you sure he asked you that?" Barry wanted to know, when she called him.

"Positive."

"Why? Did he say?"

"He didn't tell me," she said. "All he told me is, they have a confession from a young woman." She grew silent.

"Kenita?" he asked, concern in his voice.

"She's . . ." Kenita almost cried, but couldn't any more, "dead."

"What?"

"Wanda and the others found a connection. They asked me for any of Carl's friends that I knew. And they gave it to the police."

"What connection?" Barry asked, trying to understand.

"To somebody from town. A friend of his from the bar."

"And they already got a confession?" he asked.

"She didn't show up to sing. They went to her apartment and found her dead on the floor. She wrote me a note, they said. She wants me to take care of her cat."

"You?"

"She wants me to set him free on the mountain, like Clue was."

"How on earth could she ask you to do *anything*!" he said.

"I'm going to do it," Kenita said.

There was no way to change her mind. He knew that. But there was something he *could* do. "Kenita, do you trust me?"

"You know I do," she said, as Felicia, who had been awakened by the phone ringing in the night, slowly hung up the receiver.

Morning sunlight was just breaking through a pink overcast as Felicia knocked on the door. "Mom?"

She sensed a cold emptiness.

"Mom, are you in there?"

There was no answer.

"Edna Rae!" she screamed, rushing downstairs.

"What is it?" Edna Rae looked up from pouring orange juice for everyone at the breakfast table.

"Mom!" Felicia said, her voice rushed, her heart pounding. "She . . . she's not in her room!"

"Oh, Felicia, darlin'!" Edna Rae went to her side, taking the frantic young woman in her arms. "It's all right. She left this morning."

"*Left?* What for? *Where?*"

"Well, she didn't say. A friend of hers came and got her, and they went for a drive."

"A friend?" Felicia asked, catching her breath.

"Not a bad looking guy. About her age."

"Did she say who he was? Did you know him?"

"Should I have asked? Really, Felicia, she's not a child. They knew each other. He didn't come in the house. He waited outside. I saw him kiss her and they were smiling. Are they dating?"

"I . . . I really don't know," Felicia said, ashamed to admit she hadn't cared enough to find out, to ask, to talk with her mother about much except her own life.

"Well, girlfriend, let me tell you, they seemed to know each other pretty well," Edna assured her. "I thought maybe they were going on a picnic. You know, just to get away an' talk for a while."

"A picnic?"

"From the size of the package she was carrying, they were gonna have a feast. Does she always wrap things in a tablecloth?"

"What do you mean?"

"Well, she wrapped their box of picnic stuff in a tablecloth. Must have been damn heavy, too, because he had to carry it for her."

"Heavy?" Felicia said out loud, her breath coming quickly as she rushed to the refrigerator and flung it

open. "No!" she screamed. *"No!"*

"What's wrong?"

"They didn't go on a *picnic!*" Felicia cried. "Don't you see? *Don't you see?"* she said, flinging aside containers of leftover scalloped potatoes, salad, chicken and cake. "She would have taken *this!*" she said, holding up a bowl of macaroni and cheese casserole. "She would have taken her *favorite!* They're *gone!*" she sobbed, desperate, inconsolable, face in her hands with grief. *"She's run off with him!"*

News of the disappearance spread as fast as news of a murder among those who had stayed the night. "Go, Kenita!" laughed Poppy, in spite of Felicia's obvious disapproval. If the lady could find love, let her grab on to it and never let go. "What's the lucky guy's name?"

"Barry *Dunmoyer!*" Felicia said.

"The hauler? I know him. Methinks you don't *like* your new possible stepfather," Poppy teased. "Do you have to say it quite so disdainfully over breakfast?"

"He used to work in our kennel," Felicia said. "He's the one who took Clue up to Pennsylvania and probably just dumped him off."

"Where was he headed?" Poppy asked.

"You'll never believe it," Edna Rae said. *"Pennsylvania Lovers."*

"You're kidding!" Poppy said in disbelief. "Why in hell would you do business with *them?*"

"We don't—now!" Felicia glared. "Back then, we didn't know any better."

"The good ol' days," Edna said, with a touch of sarcasm.

"We don't send them any dogs, either," Poppy said. "The track won't let me. You'll never believe what we've heard about them through the grapevine "

"Do tell," Edna Rae urged, with a twinkle in her eye.

"Well," Poppy started. "All I can say is, we've *heard*—we can't prove it, mind you—that ever since they became one of Marion Malloy's *franchises*, you might say—we've heard that no dog comes out of that center the same way it went in."

"You're kidding," Felicia said, remembering Clue's unusual scars. Maybe she was wrong. Maybe Clue really had reached his destination. The thought of it made her hate Barry even more. "The last time we heard, all *Barry Dunmoyer* wanted was his paycheck."

"That's what *you* thought," Poppy couldn't resist saying, her romantic heart thrilling at love's mysteries.

Felicia bristled. "Barry *Dunmoyer* wasn't going to be anyone's fucking *slave.*"

"Kenita'll fix that," Poppy laughed. "Lord, I hope I've got her guts at that age."

"*You*, Poppy?" Wanda smiled, finishing off toast and grape jelly. "You'll have 'em standing in line."

"If I do," the adoption diva said, smiling at the possibility, "the one I have *now* has to kick the bucket first!"

"Oh! Don't say that," Edna Rae scowled. "Of all times to joke about the dead!"

Changing the subject, Wanda asked Poppy if she was staying for the big race. "Can't," Poppy said. "Gotta get back. You know how it is: no rest for the weary and shit always hits the fan when you're away." Wiping her mouth with a napkin and tossing it on her

plate along with her glass, she gathered up her silverware and headed for the sink. "Actually, I'd better be
leaving right now. Thanks for breakfast!"

"Where did they go?" Mark asked, when Felicia
told him.

"I don't know, Mark! It's Barry! Last night I heard
them on the phone."

"On top of everything else, you're an eavesdrop-
per, too?" he said, amused. "I never knew you had it
in you."

"Well, it's not like I listened to their whole conversation. If I did, maybe none of this would have happened!"

"Maybe. But you've got other things to think
about now. Like how to hold on to this kennel."

He was right. No matter what happened, the dogs
had to be cared for and the farm had to be managed.
"I'll help you," he said, though how or with what, he
didn't know. "You'll teach me."

"No," she protested. "It won't work. You have your
own business to think about."

"Felicia McCrory, if you think that way—if you
even let the word *won't* enter your mind—you'll never
get back on your feet. Listen to me," he said. "And
you listen close. We've got a dog running in the stakes
race. *Tonight!*"

"I'm going to scratch him," she said, astounded
that he could even think of running Clue after all this.
"I have to."

"*Don't you dare!* Your family put all the love they
had into this kennel," he said. "And they did it for you.
Don't you dare let them down, Felicia."

From the moment she had first seen him, she
wanted this. Strange, how life can give what you wish

for. "Can you stay?" she finally managed to ask, her voice quivering please don't let him say no.

"As long as you want me."

"Is there a shuttle to The Mirage?" Claude asked the airline clerk.

"Right through those doors, and it'll stop by that limo in a few minutes." The lady smiled as he paid the fare.

A collage of impressions dissolved through him as he waited. It was warm, he thought. Like a summer night. He wouldn't need the coat he brought along. It was light here. Everywhere he looked, there was light. It was busy. Even for this time of night.

The white shuttle pulled up, and a smiling man somewhere in his sixties flung open the baggage compartment, took Claude's luggage and motioned for him to find a seat. Seating himself in the back, his spirits brightened as a laughing group of three or four young couples crowded into the front. "Did you see the sign for Celine Dion in the airport?"

"Oh, she is so elegant!"

"I want to see the Circe de Soliel!"

"Oh, I feel terrible about Sigfried and Roy. Creepy, all their signs everywhere. Do you think he's ever coming back?"

And so it went. Young friends mugging for pictures, snapping the driver, asking the stranger in the back to get a shot of them together. To which Claude said, as they handed him a camera, "How do you work this thing?" just to make conversation.

"New York, New York," the driver announced, pulling over at their hotel destination.

"That's us! Bye!" They waved, scrambling down the steps and out to the sidewalk. "Have a nice time!"

How long had they known each other? Claude wondered. Did they grow up together? Go to school together? Go to the same church? Did they work in the same town, for the same company their parents worked for? He could think of lots of people who would love to know of such a company.

"In a hurry?" the driver asked him, now that Claude was the last passenger and the night was still young.

"No," he said.

"I can take another route to The Mirage, or I can go through the city and show you the sights."

"Sounds fun," Claude said, as he began a downtown tour of the next mile or so, complete with the driver's life story about his troubled son and their daring move from Ohio. What's all this about Ohio? he wondered. "Did you happen to know a plumber named Ed and his wife, Vicky? I met them on the plane."

"Ohio's a big place," the driver said. "Or, at least it was when I left." Seems like all of us are leaving someplace behind and going somewhere else. Have you noticed? Even if we never set foot outside our own hometown, most of us wish we could."

Well, I'm here now, Claude thought to himself. Here, doing what I didn't want to do. Mark and the others were staying over at Treasure Island, and tomorrow they faced the dragons. Hard to believe it all started with one dog. Or, maybe it started with one Esmeralda.

From: Emerson@dejazzd.com
To: Researchdept@SATV.com
Subject: High Stakes

Money's in the air. Everywhere you go out here, you feel it. Slots slots slots. Ka-ching ka-ching ka-ching. Those that have it are throwing it around. Those that don't are picking it up. Are slots the answer for racing?

From: Researchdept@SATV.com
To: Emerson@dejazzd.com
Subject: High Stakes

Slots are definitely in the mix for racing. Every state around the country that has a track is considering slots. In which case, the value of racehorses and racing dogs will only go up.

From: Emerson@dejazzd.com
To: Researchdept@SATV.com
Subject: High Stakes

What about the fan base?

From: Researchdept@SATV.com
To: Emerson@dejazzd.com
Subject: High Stakes

Contrary to what the press might have us believe, fans of Greyhound racing are on the upswing. While tracks may sometimes look empty in the grandstands, the number of home computers tuned in to the races would fill the grandstand many times over.

From: Emerson@dejazzd.com
To: Researchdept@SATV.com
Subject: High Stakes

I never thought of that. Maybe I'll get myself a racing dog.

From: Researchdept@SATV.com
To: Emerson@dejazzd.com
Subject: High Stakes

Maybe you should. You're in Vegas, aren't you? Pick up some of that money you were talking about and buy one.

CHAPTER NINE

Hologram of Horror . . .

He waited . . . waited for Carl's pep talk, waited for Kenita's last-minute orders . . . and none came. What was wrong? Why was Felicia crying as she touched the grooming tools . . . who are these strangers in the kennel who don't know our names?

Mark came to him, opened the door to his crate and spoke in reassuring tones. "Hey, fella," he said, petting Clue's neck, rubbing his hands in circles over shoulders, sides and legs that would need all the strength they could call upon tonight. "You miss him? Me, too." Silence fell between them, over them. "Do it for Carl," Mark said to him. "Throw your heart out of that box," he said, his hands stronger, more forceful— as if his touch were transmitting energy to the dog that carried, personified all their hopes.

"Grab that dirt and don't you ever look back!"

It wasn't the scenery. It wasn't the trees or the farms or the streams nourishing the pastures that she saw flying past the car window . . . it was him. Something about him. Something different.

"Barry," she said, facing him now as they drove. "Did I ever tell you how I feel about you?"

"Lots of times," he said, looking straight ahead at the road, the traffic, the signs—anywhere but into his own heart.

"Well, I'm tellin' you again," she said. "I'm tellin' you now. And if you don't like it, or if you can't take it, that's too damn bad. Because I've known a lot of men in my life. A lot. More than you or anybody else is ever gonna know about. And that's how I can tell a good one when I find him."

A good one. Was she crazy? Didn't she know what he had done? How much he despised the big shots? She knew how much he had hated the Greyhound industry for letting him down, for not standing by him, for letting him waste his life.

"Steve Wentworth never deserved you," she said. "But I saw. I saw what you could be, Barry. I saw it the minute you walked into the kennel and started talkin' to the dogs."

"Kenita," he said. "You're right about Steve. And all the rest. They didn't deserve me. But not how you mean. What they didn't deserve was the loser they got. A stinkin' rotten loser."

"Barry!"

"It's true. And I know it. God knows it. I was sour. Pissed! Whining over not getting what I thought should be mine. For being fucked over."

"But none of it was ever your fault," she said. "Life isn't fair. I know that now."

"Maybe. Maybe not. Maybe life is the *fairest* thing there is. You act like a loser and that's what you get. Well, I'm different now. That's all over," he said, his hands tight on the wheel, his body leaning forward with intensity. "I don't have all the answers, but I knew when I saw those guys blowing apart the zoo, and getting off on themselves, I knew I'm not—I never could be—*I wasn't one of them!*"

"Well, I could have told you that," she said, touching his hand. "I could have told you that, Barry."

He smiled. Looked at her briefly, and relaxed. "But I didn't know it for myself," he said, wondering if she could understand, if anyone could understand, ever. "*Barry Dunmoyer*—me," he said, pounding himself on the chest. I didn't know 'til right then."

"Will this spider woman be there?" Kenita asked.

"Spider or Silverback," he said. "I know one of them had to give the orders to Jennifer."

"What if they aren't, Barry?"

"Then we'll find them, Kenita. I promise." It was a promise to her, to Carl, to himself. A promise to the man, the soul, the force he *should* have been, *could* have been *if only,* but that was the old Barry.

"The stakes race tonight," she said, as they drove. *The Wheeling $100,000.*

"I know," he said. "Are you sorry you're not there to help?"

Sorry? Of course she was. She was sorry she didn't say goodbye, but she knew she couldn't have. Sorry she wouldn't be there willing, coaxing, commanding Clue to run the best race of his life. But it was Felicia's turn now. Felicia's turn to do it all on her own.

"I don't want to think about it," she said, holding his hand, holding on like she would never let go. "Not now."

They drove on. As the sky went from blue to purple to black, they drove without stopping. They drove as if there were no yesterday, no tomorrow. Only now. Right now. The two of them.

The two of them against the devil.

Like the races they all loved—the rush for glory giving all you've got—there wasn't much time. No matter what happened, no matter why, the show must go on. Kenita had called, she was safe. Hidden Farms and its Greyhounds would go on. Feeding, grooming, exercising. Sprinting the dogs in training that Carl had brought along so well. Rolling up sleeves. Spitting in the dirt. Staring fear right in the face. Clue was ready. He was ready for the greatest challenge of his life.

Standing beside Mark now, Felicia thanked her friends.

"OK," she said, gathering her courage. "This is it. We're going out there and letting the world see they haven't smashed us. We're going to show them a race like they've never seen before." Gaining strength from them, from Mark's growing love, she went on. "Wanda," she said, smiling, "tonight, I'm rooting for two dogs. I hope you know that."

Wanda smiled. "Yeah, right! You just root for Clue. He's gonna need it!" she teased, laughing. First would be great, but coming in the money at all would be wonderful.

"Well, Carl's here and he's going to be looking out for both of us. *I feel him.* He's here tonight, just like always."

"Hell, yeah!" Jack Halstead called out, unable to squelch the drumbeat in his veins.

"*Carl!*" Jason Greathouse shouted, raising his fist in the air, calling upon the spirit of the loyal young man who wanted to be the best dog man around. "Bring home a winner!"

Almost overcome, Felicia held on to Mark's arm. "We loved him," she said. "We still do. And we're gonna go out there like nothing can stop us, nothing can knock us down. But there was more than one person involved. The police are telling us to be careful," she warned.

It was all so soon. Was it too much? Mark wondered, as he watched her taking command. Did she have the stamina to match the power of her will, her drive—now? Now, when it mattered more than ever? Now, when it mattered the most!

He couldn't bear the thought of her being in danger, of someone jumping out from the shadows in the parking lot.

A gun!

A needle!

A knife!

"Felicia," he whispered, trying to get her attention. "Felicia?"

But she went on. "They're saying we have to be on the lookout for anything different. Suspicious."

"What do they mean suspicious, exactly?" Jason asked.

Jack pitched in. "Like somebody you never saw before."

"But what's that going to prove?" Wanda asked, a note of irritation in her voice. "How do you know who's behind any of this? *Duh!*" she said, pointing to her head and making a sour face.

"Duh-*umb* is what you mean!" Jack said, "which I'm not."

"Nobody said you were, Jack," she apologized quickly. If Wanda was anything, she was fair, or tried her best to be.

"Look, guys," Felicia said, taking charge again. "Just let Security know if anything's out of place tonight. What we want is to show them—whoever they are—that nothing's gonna stop us now!"

To a round of general consensus, they gathered jackets, purses and car keys and were off to the races. She was right. Even if Clue didn't win tonight, their greatest show of strength would be the simple fact that the champion had showed up and tried. And that everybody on his side was there for him.

The blackness of night encroached outside the car windows, making conversation easier. Was this what it would be like being with him? Being with him the rest of her life? Is this how it would feel?

Kenita looked at him from the corner of her eye, a trick she had mastered so others wouldn't know she was watching. Looking off to her right, the glass of the window reflecting like a mirror, she could see him leaning slightly forward as he drove, the steering wheel clasped in his hands. His big, gnarled hands.

"What's that stuff you put on your hands?" she asked, making small talk.

"Coconut oil," he said.

"Smells nice." She smiled, facing him again, looking at his hands more closely. "Do they hurt, Barry?"

"Sometimes," he said, not wanting to get into it, but knowing if he wanted to be with her forever, sooner or later she must find out. Not now, he told himself, praying silently. Change the subject, Kenita. Talk about something else. Floundering, he looked to the side of the road and swerved. "Whoa! Did you see that?" he asked, feigning surprise.

"See what?" she asked, looking around, looking back as he pressed on the gas.

"I don't know," he said. "Whatever it was, I didn't want to hit it. The last thing we need is a flat."

No, they didn't need a flat, she thought.

Had the crowd ever been more tense than it was that night? Had people—from the restaurant, to the slot machines, to the ticket booths—ever exuded more expectation?

"Did you ever see Stapler's Jo up close?" Barbara asked aloud, making conversation as they waited for the race to start. "I always wanted to, but I couldn't get away."

"Yeah, I saw him a couple of times," Wanda said.

"Tell me about it!" Jack exclaimed.

"You mean, what did he look like or how did I feel about him?" Wanda said, knowing when Brad and Barbara bought semen, they always checked out the studs themselves.

"Both," Barbara said. "I would have loved to see that dog up close."

"Well, I liked him," Wanda said, describing the white and black sire.

"What's not to like?" Edna Rae commented. "That dog was a producer."

"A legend, is more like it," Barbara added.

"Sure was," Wanda agreed. "We bred Whompum's

dam to him and got six pups. All of them made it to the track, and we sold one of them for a ton of money."

"Good for you!" Barbara said. "Did everybody in the kennel get diamond-studded collars? I can get Poppy to make them. And half of all the proceeds go to adoption."

"Diamond-studded collars? That'll be the day," Wanda said. "We put every cent we have into the business, and the dogs are lucky to have plastic."

"You need more winners," Barbara said. "Maybe after tonight, your luck'll change. You could win a hundred-thousand dollar race!"

"I'm under no illusions," Wanda replied, smiling in her good-natured way. "Clue's going to be tough to beat. I just want my dog to do well, that's all."

"You're a good sport," Barbara said. "That's what I like about you. And I've got my eye on that dog of yours."

"Too bad you couldn't get any of Stapler's Jo when he was alive," Edna Rae said.

"Oh?" Barbara smiled, like a banker with a million in the vault. "If they were getting $5,000 a pup when he was alive, can you imagine what his pups could bring now that he's gone?" She winked. "And if Wanda's dog does well in the race?"

"Which I'm hoping," Wanda interjected.

"Wooooo-weeee!" Jack whistled, getting Barbara's drift. "Am I ever in the wrong branch of the business!"

"You're in the right branch of the business, Jack." It was Cecil, joining them. "And if we can get 'em to throw out this law in Pennsylvania and produce better and better dogs, this is going to be the right industry to be in."

"Yeah, but like Poppy's always sayin', we gotta take care of the dogs once they're done at the track." Jack reminded him, though it wasn't necessary.

"We're working on that," Cecil said. "Give us a chance."

"Media again," came the cool comment from Barbara.

"As you, of all people, should know," Cecil said. "Why not call some of your friends in New York and get them to do some photo shoots at the track?"

"Too busy posing naked for PETA," she said, with a laugh.

"Too chicken to say they like racing is more like it," Edna Rae countered.

To which, Wanda commented, "You know, I once knew a racehorse trainer who showed one of her Arabians at a horse show."

"What's that got to do with the price of tea in China?" Mark asked. "We're here for our dogs, aren't we?"

"Well, horse show people and racing people are from two different worlds, you know? Same as dog people," Wanda said.

"Not really, but go on," Mark said, scoping the crowd for anything "suspicious."

"Well, at first, everybody thought this horse was really skinny. Get him out of here. But the judges were really surprised by how fit he was, and my friend won the halter class. Do you realize how impressive that was and what it meant for Arabian racing?"

"Not especially," Jason said. "Why didn't they just let the best horse win?"

"Shows aren't judged that way," Wanda explained.

"It's not like the first horse crossing the finish line is the winner and everybody knows it. Showing animals is a lot more complicated."

"Well, count me out then." Jason laughed. "But humor me. What's the point of this conversation?"

"Just that, if the media ever knew what our dogs can really do, and how beautiful they are, I think it would make a difference, that's all."

"They will sometime," Cecil said. "But, for now, we have to focus on legislation."

"We have to focus on the race," Felicia said, though nobody heard her.

"What good will focusing on legislation do if the public doesn't know enough about us?" Wanda asked.

"Oh, they know plenty about us," Jason said. "Most of it's bad, and it damn well ain't true."

"I know! But how can they print such lies?" Wanda hissed. "That really bothers me."

"We've gone over that a thousand times," Barbara said. "This is entertainment. And if you were a celebrity or a big-time politician, you'd be saying the same thing."

"It makes your job a whole lot harder, but you learn a lot about the world," Cecil added.

"Well it's not fair," Wanda said, standing her ground.

"Wanda," he smiled in his best fatherly way, "like Joan Crawford says to her bratty daughter in *Mommie Dearest*, 'Who ever said life was fair?' "

"I liked that movie," Barbara said.

"You did?" Wanda asked. "And I thought I liked you."

"Let's just say, being in business for myself, I could understand Joan a little better than the daughter wanted me to."

"Ouch!" Edna Rae laughed. "I heard that!"

"Hey," Jack said. "We've got a race to think about and two chances for the winner. Play nice, ladies."

"Damn!" Felicia, who had been reasonably quiet up to now, said. "I can't *believe* she ran off with that *sleaze-ball*!"

Off the turnpike . . . north . . . side road . . . dirt road posted with signs saying, "Stay Out."

"Looks like they don't want visitors," Kenita said, while Barry carefully navigated potholes as if they were land mines.

"They don't get many," he said.

"Barry, are you sure the police aren't the ones we should have gone to for this?"

Surely she knew by now that he was more than fond of her, that he trusted her. But did she know how much he wanted her to be strong?

"Yep. We could have. But I can tell you they wouldn't be getting here any faster. We'll use the cell phone as soon as we have enough proof to get them arrested. Did you ever have a hunch?" he asked her. "Did you ever have a feeling in your gut that you'd better hurry because if you don't get there it's going to be too late?"

He had rushed so fast there hadn't been time to explain why it had to be now!

She thought about that. About herself, about love, about her fading chances in life. Glancing sideways into the mirror of his truck, she said, "Maybe," her voice husky with loneliness.

Poppy arrived home and lugged her stuff into the house. "Peee-ew, it stinks in here!" she said. "I ask a man to empty the cat box, and do you think he hears me? *Are you here, Frank?*"

The babble of a loud TV and a grunt of reply were her answer.

"I only left for one day!" she said, tossing Tiger in his crate, clicking on her answering machine and feeding the bird. "Do I have to do *everything* around here?" she continued, dumping the cat litter in a trash bag, slinging it out the back door and spraying too much freshener in every room. Midway between lighting candles to clear off the smell of potpourri— a tip she read from Ann Landers, maybe?—she suddenly stopped. What was that last message?

"This message is for all adoption centers from Pennsylvania Lovers of Greyhounds. *This is a warning.* We ask that you be on the lookout for a hauler by the name of Barry Dunmoyer. This man is dangerous and he may be armed. Call us *immediately* with any information you have."

Kenita!

Hitting replay, she listened again.

"Frank! *Frank!* You gotta hear this! It's from a group I used to do business with—before they went sour."

"Oh?" came a mumbled reply.

"Geez! What'll I do?"

"Hmmm?"

"Can't call Felicia—she's at the track with everybody. Her mother! She could be in a hell of a lot of trouble!"

"Uh-huh."

"She's with this guy—they said he's armed!"

"Hmph!"

"Should I call and leave a message for Felicia—I don't wanna worry her. But I *am* worried, Frank! I hope to tell ya, I'm worried."

"Uh-huh."

"Damn. Damn! I'm not good at figuring out this stuff!"

"OK."

"I'm callin' the cops! At least it won't be on my head if she's in trouble. You're my witness, Frank. I did what I could!" she said, looking around.

"Good idea."

"Where the hell's that damn phone?" she asked. "Frank! *Frank!*"

A big man in T-shirt and shorts walked through the doorway from the living room, holding a white portable phone to his ear. "Uh-huh . . . hmmm . . . OK . . . talk to you tomorrow." Clicking the *off* button, he looked up and saw Poppy. "Hey, you just get home?"

Easing Felicia away from the rest of the gang, Mark worked his way through the crowd and found a more private place for them to stand. "This is the same place we stood the first time Clue ran here," he said, reminding her of that night. "Remember?"

"Yes, I do," she said, sliding her arm around his waist and pulling close to him. "In a way, this is where it started for us."

"Not 'til then?" he teased. "I thought we started the minute I first saw you."

"Well," she grinned, brushing aside a stray hair from his forehead, looking into his eyes, "maybe you're not so wrong about that."

"He looks good tonight," Mark said.

"Yes, he does," she said, with a sigh. "So do you."

"If he wins," Mark said, blushing slightly, "they won't like it." There was no need to explain who "they" were.

"What do you mean if?" she said, focused on the parade of Greyhound athletes being led grandly to the starting box by young men in tuxedos. They were the best of the best. The finest Wheeling had to offer, and the track had gone all-out promoting the $100,000 race of its stars.

"We've had an offer to compete in the American National," Felicia said. "It's the richest race outside The Woodlands $250,000 Futurity."

"What did you tell them?" Mark asked, having no doubt she accepted.

"I said we'll think about it."

"Think about it?" he smiled, squeezing her tight and rocking her side to side. "I'll help you think about it," he teased. "That boy is going to make a big name for himself after tonight, and we're taking him all the way."

"We?" She said, grinning. "Oh, that's right. We're a team."

"Well, I figure you're going to need help now," he said. "On the farm, I mean."

"Cleaning the kennels," she smiled, amused and letting him struggle with how to say it.

"Well, I figure you can handle the business end of things and I could maybe set up my shop in one of the buildings at the farm."

"What makes you think I want to go into the antique business?" she asked.

"This?" he asked, reaching in his pocket and handing her a small, black-velvet box.

Opening it, she caught her breath at the glorious, deep green emerald surrounded by diamond baguettes.

"Mark?" she asked, suddenly not sure where to look. At the dogs? At him?

Turning her face toward the starting box, he knew nothing else for her was possible. "I'm sure," he said, as she leaned her head on his shoulder.

"Heeeeeere comes Spunky!" the announcer's brassy voice proclaimed.

And they were off. Like people off to work, like lovers craving lovers, they were rushing for what all of them wanted, all of them had to have.

There it was, in front of them—right in front of them. If only they could catch it. If only they could run faster!

Hearts had never beat faster, minds had never been more locked in to what they saw and what they knew could be theirs.

"Oh, Mark!" Felicia cried, her fingers digging into his arm, standing on her toes, catching her breath.

Smiling, he stood behind her and wrapped her in both arms as the dogs rushed past for the first turn. Cheers of encouragement, rays of hope, flashing around them like reflections from emeralds and diamonds urging the Greyhounds on.

Inch by slow-motion inch, loyal fans saw it: the blue fawn dog working his way forward.

"There goes my dog!" Wanda hollered, standing on her toes for a better view.

"Four's easing up," Cecil said to Edna Rae, standing close beside him.

"I can't tell if that dog's losing ground or if the others are picking up speed," she said to him.

"Look out Whompum!" Wanda screamed as a large brindle female crossed right in front of her dog. "Keep going!"

Looking through a pair of binoculars, both hands clenched, Barbara fired back. "He broke stride!"

"That'll cost him," Brad said.

"Get a load of Clue!" Jason said. "Go, boy!" he hollered, as if the dog could hear his command.

Wanda giggled. "People must think we're nuts!"

"We are!" somebody said, laughing. "We're all nuts to be out here watching a bunch of dogs running around after a toy on the end of a stick!"

"Yeah, when we could be home feeling sorry for ourselves!" Jack teased.

"Hell, we can feel sorry for ourselves anyplace!" Brad laughed as Barbara smacked him and the dogs rounded the far turn.

"Oh, my God!" Felicia yelled, jumping up and down. "Oh my *God*!"

Breaking away from the pack, Clue appeared to be shifting into high gear. "That's impossible!" Mark said, almost under his breath as Clue took the lead by one . . . then one-and-a-half lengths.

Two lengths . . . three!

From a mounting buzz to a collective murmur to a great roar, voices from everywhere called out to the brave dog leaping—digging into the dirt with his toes, plunging with every muscle in his body, every hope in his heart—leaping through the air with pure, blind faith. Flying as if he had wings.

What a sight! *What a feeling!*

Chills ran down Kenita's arms as Barry parked and they got out. This was it, she thought to herself. Would they find the ones responsible for murdering Carl? There was no turning back. No matter what became of this, no matter what happened, she was here to confront Carl's murderer. She was here for what the McCrorys believed in, wanted, stood for. Freedom to feel everything God gave you; freedom to go as far as you could in a society closing in all around you.

"I don't see any cars," she said.

"Around back," he answered in a hushed tone, leading the way. "Trust me."

Making their way along a sidewalk and around the building, they paused. Two cars and a pickup truck with a small dog trailer sat in the parking lot, their fresh tracks still crisp in the dirt.

"Welcome to the processing plant," he whispered. "Those kennels over there?" he asked, not wanting to alert the dogs. "Holding pens."

Mentally, Kenita counted about ten chain-link runs as he went on. "Right there, where that trailer's parked?"

She nodded, not daring to speak. "That's the finishing department," he said, with an odd timbre to his voice, his manner. "They either come out of there alive or they're finished."

She shivered. He was different again. They were trespassers, thieves. "I don't like this," she said, hoping to change his mind. But he wasn't listening. Not to her. Not to the sound of a dog's scream from inside the building and the surge of barking all around them. "Now!" he said, taking her by the hand as they rushed across the clearing and made it to the bushes outside a low window.

Did they dare look inside? There was no time to ask, no time to think. "I know these guys," he said, peering through the window.

What were they doing? she wondered. What were they doing to that dog? she asked herself, as a hauntingly beautiful Greyhound stood surrounded by several people.

Catching her attention, putting a finger to his lips, Barry pulled her into the cover of a large yew bush as they listened.

"Ear or tail?" somebody went, matter of factly.

"Boring," another commented.

"How about a toe?" a young woman said, picking up the dog's front foot and examining it. "We haven't had any missing toes for a while."

"That's who we want," Barry whispered, recognizing the doctor from the Philadelphia compound and moving closer. *"That's spider woman."*

"Done!" Spider said, hacking off a toe.

Eyes wide, the dog twisted to get away, but was held firmly in place as it screamed the high-pitched yelp known so well to owners of Greyhounds in real or imagined pain. Again, the roar of dogs barking, filling the night with their sound alarm that no one could understand.

"What's going on at that place?" "What's going on back there?" Neighbors might have asked, but didn't.

"Going on? Oh, they take in those poor Grey-hounds from the racetrack." And all would be reassured, all would be forgotten, all would go back to sleep.

None would see the blood splattering on the floor, on the dog, on Spider's clothes. None would see her make no effort to stop the bleeding. None would see her expressionless face or search for any hint of emotion as she said, "Next," as Barry waited calmly knowing there would be another and another and another. Kenita lurched to vomit.

As the barking dogs quieted, and Kenita took hold of her reeling stomach, Barry directed her attention to the scene unfolding before them. *"Jackpot!"* he said, indicating a thin, older woman with big thighs who was entering the room.

"What's going on?" Kenita asked, unable to hear, wishing she could. "What are they planning?"

Unsure, Barry considered a moment before venturing a guess. "These are new dogs," he said. "Fresh meat."

Standing just inside the doorway, making her grand entrance, the woman made her demand.

"Everything ready?" asked Marion Malloy of the doctor in charge. Dead eyes looked at no one in particular. "Well, don't all talk at once," she snapped, when the answer wasn't instant. "My time's valuable!" implying theirs wasn't. Hustling to the crates, they dragged out a delicate red brindle female and slipped on a muzzle.

People didn't understand the higher mind, Marion often thought to herself. They didn't understand sacrifice of the individual for the good of the whole.

"Looks like a broken hock to me," the doctor said, going to a toolbox and fishing out an oversized pair of pliers. "Handle it," she said to a big guy, slouching over a frightened dog trying to get away.

"I know him," Barry whispered. "He takes the east-west route. He brought these dogs in, and he's getting ready to turn around and go back. Chicago, most likely."

What's in Chicago? Kenita wondered.

"Another adoption point," he answered without being asked.

"How did you know I wanted to know that?" she whispered, taking in his alertness. One hundred percent alive, all his senses on, he said simply, "Because I know you."

Know me, she wondered? How can you know me when I don't even know myself. How could anyone "know" what makes a grown woman pushing sixty end up standing behind a clump of bushes in the middle of the night? This wasn't why she knocked herself out getting good grades in school. Was it?

Maybe it didn't matter, Kenita thought, as two helpers stretched out the dog's hind leg and the man opened the pliers wide. Maybe it didn't matter, she thought, as the pliers clenched down on the dog's leg, twisted and snapped. Maybe it didn't matter that tears were spreading down her cheeks and her sneakers were covered with mud. She had stepped in worse than that, she thought. She had stepped right into a hologram of horror. . . .

"Line 'em up," Marion ordered, as they led away the limping creature. Immediately, assistants brought out a group of Greyhounds and stood them in a row to be inspected by the one who demanded to be obeyed.

On she walked, past broken legs, torn ears and severed toes. Not once did she pause to comfort the shaken and cowering dogs. Not once did she ease their fear.

"Too much on the face," she said, of what appeared to be open sores. "Put him down."

"But we only did what you—" the doctor protested, and suddenly stopped.

"Only did what?" Marion glared.

"Nothing," the doctor said, looking away.

"Only did what?" Marion insisted.

Realizing there was no escape from ridicule or the slash of sarcasm seething beneath Marion's surface, no loyalty from others present for her humiliation, Dr. Norton backed off.

"I asked you a question," Marion said, facing her now.

"I made a mistake," the doctor mumbled.

"I can't hear you," Marion said, the faintest glint of pleasure forming in her sallow eyes.

"I," the young doctor tried again, clearing her throat, "made a mistake."

"A mistake," Marion said, looking around at every-one. "She made a mistake," she said, forming the word

as if it made a sour taste in her mouth, as if she resent-
ed everything about the attractive young woman.

"Put that dog down and bury it," she said, with a
look of satisfaction.

Without another comment, the doctor took the dog
and left the room.

"Anybody else made any mistakes?" Marion
asked. "There's plenty of shovels here if you do."
Hearing no reply, she walked on and left the building.
Crossing the clearing in the shadows and crouching
low, Barry and Kenita followed. They followed as if
everything they believed in depended on it. Don't turn
around. Don't even think about it.

Holding their breath, they ran. Thieves in a jewel
heist, art connoisseurs swapping the painting in *The
Thomas Crown Affair,* adventurers against the casino
in *Ocean's Eleven.*

Was Kenita OK with all this? Barry wondered. He
shouldn't have brought her along. Shouldn't have gotten her mixed up in any of it.

"Don't worry about me," her hand on his arm
seemed to say. And he knew he could never have
counted her out. Reaching the building, quietly opening the door, they stepped inside. Down the hall, second door to the right. How well he knew this journey.
Should they knock? Not this time. Hand on the door-
knob, he stood there.

"Come in, Barry." It was Marion. "We've been
looking for you."

Hesitating—why?—he opened the door and stood
there.

"Your friend, too," she said, aware of Kenita from
her position in the leather chair at her desk.

Kenita followed, pressing closely to him.

"Well . . ." said Marion, like the cat that has discovered a pair of mice, "what a surprise."

Stupid of him not to think they had security cameras here, he thought. "I was in town and thought I'd drop by," is what he said.

"*Thought you'd drop by* . . . and what did you expect to find, Barry?" she asked.

Dumbfounded, like a boy standing in front of the principal, unable to explain himself, unable to speak, he had no answer.

"I'd say we found it," Kenita said, with an edge. She had no history with this woman, nothing to live down.

"And what might *that* be?" Marion countered, her eyes narrowing as she leaned closer.

Sensing she faced a woman who would never allow herself to be held accountable, could always find someone else to blame, could always find a way out, Kenita stepped forward. She hadn't served tables all those years without picking up a little brass. "*Finishing* Department? What is this place? *Auschwitz?* The laboratory of *Joseph Mengele*?"

"We help dogs here," came the acidic reply.

"*You killed my son!*" Kenita screamed, lunging forward, knowing it with all her heart. "You and your guerrillas!"

"*Kenita!*" Barry yelled, trying to hold her back.

Marion slipped her hand in the desk drawer she had slowly opened and stood up. Facing them both, she raised the gun and leveled her aim. The shiny .22 revolver looked small in her hand. "Get away from me."

Quietly, Barry put himself between the gun and Kenita. He had spent a lifetime losing all that mattered to him, never believing he deserved what others more fortunate, more beautiful took for granted. No, he thought; no more, as Marion's dull eyes darted to the closed circuit surveillance screen . . . a subtle look of defeated resignation danced across her features . . . and she fired.

A flash of exploding light!

Barry saw the huge brown eyes of a sleepy baby gorilla.

Blue uniformed troopers crashed through the door.

"Drop the gun!"

"Hands up!"

"Call an ambulance!" they said, rushing into the office.

Standing in the winner's circle, photographers snapping away, Clue stood as proudly as any champion. He had pleased them. He had pleased them all. Searching for Mark's smiling face, Felicia's hands praising him, her voice light with joy, the Greyhound basked in the afterglow of a race well run.

"Over here!" a photographer called out.

"How's it feel to win a hundred thousand dollars?" called out another.

"Great!" Mark smiled, giving Clue a big hug and putting an arm around Felicia.

"What do you have to say, Felicia?" a reporter asked, his notepad in hand.

"My brother would have loved it," she said bravely, standing as tall as she could.

"Any word from the police? Do they have any clues?"

"The only clue I want to talk about is standing right here, boys."

"What's next?"

"We've been invited to *The American National*," Mark said. "A quarter million purse."

"Woooo-eee" somebody whistled.

"I'll tell you what's next!" Felicia said proudly, holding up her hand and wiggling her fingers for all to see her ring and pointing to Mark. *"This!"*

Saying their goodbyes, hugging each other and shaking hands until they'd meet again, members of the Coalition departed for home. For a moment, a moment in time, they had been one; but now they would go back to their respective lives.

Good luck, they said.

Everything'll be all right.

Let us know if you hear anything.

The usual reassurances, the usual things one says because they don't know what else to say.

Graciously, Felicia accepted their kindness.

"Well," she said to Mark. "We've got ourselves a champion."

Clue had scored, hit the charts, made the big time. "Did we expect any less?" he smiled, taking her by the hand for all to see.

Beautifully, they kissed, then made their way to Clue.

"Way to go!" smiled one of the lead-outs. "That dog's a monster!"

Back in the kennel compound, Clue was restless.

"What's the matter, boy?" Mark asked.

Sensing Mark's concern, Felicia said, "He wants his rubdown."

"A dog after my own heart," Mark smiled.

"Too late," she said. "I got there first."

"Confidence," he grinned, sliding his arm around her, kissing her neck. "I like that."

"I'll show you confidence," she said, pressing herself against him. "Tonight."

It was a deal. No thinking about yesterday or tomorrow. Only now, only tonight.

Rubbing her hands expertly over Clue's head and neck, then his shoulders, back and thighs, Felicia kneaded, soothed and massaged with expert sensitivity. If there was a wince, she would know it. If there was soreness, she would find it.

Stretching each leg, bending each joint, working her way down to each toe and all the length of Clue's tail, she worked her energy into the dog who had done so well, given his all for them.

"Come on, boy," she said finally. "Let's go home."

Handing her the leash, Mark smiled and didn't say a word.

As they entered the lane to the farm, she put a hand on his arm. "Stop here," she said, at a place where they could see the buildings in the glow of floodlights. Taking it all in, they sat quietly. "It's so empty," she said.

He didn't answer. He couldn't. Her hand slipped from his arm and he drove on. There would be times like this, he told himself. Times when, no matter how many people were around you, no matter how great the show, how bright the lights, you ended up alone. But she wasn't alone. She had him; she had the dogs.

"I hear the dogs barking," he said, reminding her it wasn't empty after all.

She nodded. "Let's go in."

Inside. Inside one's life. Allowed to know their dreams, their aspirations. Their loves, wants and fears. Never knowing what happened before you came along, never knowing what's ahead or what's around the corner. She wore his ring now. That was supposed to mean something.

"Felicia?" he said. "Carl would have been proud of you tonight."

She stopped. So lonely. So fallen. "All of us," she said, her voice thick. "He'd have been proud of us all."

They had won a stakes race. They had taken a dog cast off as if it were nothing, and polished the jewel within.

"Where to from here?" he asked.

"I guess I'll go outside and see how the dogs are," she said.

He stopped her. "I can do it. I know what to do."

The chance to rest. The chance to think.

"Oh, if you could do that, I'd be so glad," she sighed, taking off her coat, hanging it in the closet.

"I'll turn him out a while before I put him in his crate and feed him," he said, taking Clue's leash, kissing her on the cheek and leaving. He didn't have to say there would be no more cookies.

Alone now, Felicia looked around the house. Old prints of racing dogs on the walls, framed snapshots crammed on lamp tables, trophies on the fireplace

mantle nobody had used in such a long time. Dust . . .
nature's blanket . . . too much of it. Too hot to handle
the memories.

Did she love this man? If love was measured by
anything she had ever felt before, then no. Love wasn't
good enough, big enough, to describe her feelings for
Mark. Not all-encompassing enough to explain her
curiosity about him, her craving for him. Her hunger.
Maybe that was it: hunger. The hunger of one body,
one mind, one soul for another. The eternal drive to
find the other half of what once was all of us. The
search for what's missing, for what we should be. As
if we had been cut off from . . . from what? From ourselves, she decided, opening the kitchen cupboard,
reaching for a box of spaghetti noodles, going to the
refrigerator for ground beef, finding an onion in the
vegetable drawer and a cutting board.

Pots and pans. Where did Kenita keep the colander?

Outside, Mark shoved his hands in his coat pockets
and braced himself against the night breeze as he
walked to the barn. Following tight beside him, Clue
floated in the way devoted Greyhounds are known to
do. Not a sound, not a wasted move, not looking right
or left.

Funny, how things turn out just by taking a different turn, he thought. Tonight, he was trusted with one
of the richest dogs in the world. Only a breath ago, he
was hiking up a mountain.

Unlatching the gate to the paddock, Mark turned
Clue loose and relaxed in the dog's instant attention to
every blade of grass. Spreading his scent, asserting
his dominance over all other dogs in the kennel, Clue

trotted and stopped, scratched and rubbed himself against the fence, sniffed and sneezed.

"Catchin' up on the news," Mark said to him. At the sound of his master, the feel of being noticed, Clue bounded playfully toward Mark, head and forelegs down, rump in the air. Waiting. Baiting.

"Such a dog," Mark said warmly, petting Clue's head as it pressed into his hand. The most delicate silk, the smoothest glass, could be no finer. "Such a dog."

A few more playful romps around the paddock and Mark called once again. "Here boy!" he said, and Clue came to his side. Taking hold of the dog's collar this time, Mark led him inside the warm barn, to the special crate bearing his name. "There you go, fella." Mark said, giving him his food and a bowl of fresh water. Checking on the other dogs, turning them out one last time for the night, making sure everyone had water, he switched off the lights and headed back to the house.

Some people lived in houses of stone or wood or stucco, he thought, but as the aroma of tomatoes, peppers, oregano and stewed meat with onions flowed toward him, he decided this could have been a grass hut and still, a home.

Lights dim, candles lit, wine glasses full.

"You," he said, loving her with his eyes, his heart.

Saying nothing, she looked at him. Waited for him to come to her. Hold her. Rock her in his arms.

"We're good," he said.

"So's my spaghetti," she teased, taking him to the card table she had unfolded, covered in a lace cloth and set just for them.

"Mmmmm," he said, rubbing his hands together as

he looked upon the spread. "Classy."

"Hope so," she said. "It's been ages."

He looked at her, glowing. Wanting to remember. Wanting to save it always. Just . . . wanting.

"To us," she said, handing him a glass of wine.

"Us," he said, willing to go with the moment, with the impulse, with whatever happened.

Like a phone ringing.

"Don't answer," he said. Looking at him, not wanting to break their spell, knowing if she didn't their spell was ruined anyway, she pulled back. "Let me just see who it is," she said, getting up, crossing the room.

"Mom!" she said, dropping the phone, picking it up again. "Where are you?"

"I'm with Barry," came the reply, and Felicia understood that being with Barry was all Kenita wanted her to know. "We're at the hospital," Kenita added.

"Hospital!" Felicia's outburst brought Mark to her side.

"We had some trouble. There's been some arrests. It's about Carl."

"Tell me what happened!" Felicia said, raising her voice. "I'm coming to get you!"

"I told you. I'm with Barry and I'm safe. Now if you don't back off, girl, I'm hanging up! You're making me awful tight."

Reprimanded, Felicia tried again. "OK. If you say it's cool, it's cool. But why are you at the hospital?"

"I told you. There was some trouble."

"That doesn't tell me a damn *thing*! And you *know* it!"

"Damn straight I know it."

"Well, when are you coming home?"

"I'll be home when I get there. Now, my battery's goin' dead an' I can't hear you no more and I don't want to anyway. I'm hangin' up!"

The phone went dead.

"Well!" Felicia turned to Mark. "I'm calling her back!"

"Felicia, don't. Let them alone."

"But, Mark. This is my mother. And she's with that creep Barry. It doesn't feel right. It just isn't right!"

"Not right?" he asked. "Why? Because of a man we don't know as well as she does? Or, because it's your mother this is about and you can't imagine her with him."

That she couldn't imagine Kenita with Barry was an understatement.

"Mark, I want to find out what this is all about."

"Felicia," he said, pulling her into his eyes, parting his lips in a half-assed smile. "I'm starving. And then I want to fuck you."

The patient in Room 214 at the Hershey Medical Center lay still and pale. Beside his bed, Kenita prayed, as the officer waited outside. She wasn't the praying kind, and her words, her thoughts came slowly. "I know I haven't been talking to you much lately. Well. Not just lately," she started. "It's just that, you don't always seem to be there. Like you're *supposed* to be." She paused, almost amused at herself. "Like I'm supposed to think you'd be there for an old scrapper like me who swears at you more than she's ever prayed."

Was she supposed to kneel when she said these things? Kneeling stiffly, her arms folded on the bed, her head pressed against them in grief, she tried again.

"I don't know why you took my Carl from me. I guess you had your reasons." She paused. "I hope he's good for you. I was so happy when he came into my life. I was happy for all of my kids. But I loved him so much. And I think I love this guy here, too. Please. *Please,*" she said softly, her eyes stinging with salty tears, "even if he doesn't love me. Even if he blames me for getting him hurt. Don't take him away from me. Not yet. *Not yet.*"

A nurse poked her head in the door, did a quick visual of the monitors and tubes, and said gently, "They want to talk with you outside."

Nodding, coming to her senses, Kenita stood. "OK," she said, wiping her face. "How do I look?" she joked.

"You look great to me, lady" came a scratchy voice from the body on the bed.

With a jolt of surprise, Kenita looked at Barry and a smile suddenly brightened her whole being. "Don't you go anywhere, mister!" she pinched his cheek. "I'll be right back!"

The elated woman didn't feel the ground under her feet as she left the room.

"Ms. McCrory?" the officer said, introducing himself. "I have a few questions." Guiding her to a waiting room where they could sit down, he offered her coffee from a vending machine. "This is my partner," he said, introducing the other man.

"Nice to meet you," Kenita managed to say. It was unreal. It was a dream. It wasn't really happening.

"Ms. McCrory, can you tell us why you went to the dog center tonight?"

"It was Barry," she said.

"Your friend," they said. "Mr. Dunmoyer."

"Yes. My . . . friend," she said, surpressing a smile, feeling it wasn't enough. Falling inside herself. Lover? Last hope? "My best friend."

"Why did you go there?"

"It was Barry's idea," she said again.

"Did you know Miss Malloy?"

"No," Kenita said. "I didn't. Barry did. Can I go back and see him?"

"Just a few more questions," they said. "She says you broke into her office and threatened her."

"That's a lie!" Kenita hissed.

"But you *were* trespassing," they said.

"I don't know," Kenita said, shaking her head. "All I know is my son is dead and Barry's been shot!"

The warm glow of a flickering fire caressed Felicia's naked skin as she lay beside Mark on the sofa. Snuggling her butt into his lap as he slept, she pulled his arm around her shoulder and considered the events leading up to Kenita's phone call. Love, she thought. Her mother was in love.

Her mother was also in trouble.

What did Kenita mean? "Arrests connected to Carl."

Right here, right now, she was safe. Safe in Mark's arms. Tomorrow, who could tell?

Tomorrow, there would be other mysteries, other battles to be fought, other battles to be won. Tomorrow, the dogs would be watered and fed, the dogs would be cleaned, the dogs would be trained. Tomor-

row there would be other races around the oval . . .
other races in the ancient ritual . . . of starting . . .
making it to the finish line . . . falling asleep.

Edna Rae nudged Cecil and rubbed her toes across
the bottom of his foot.

"Cecil," she whispered urgently. "Cecil!"

Moaning something about ordering paint for the
pharoah's ship, he sighed and drifted off. Drifted
down the Nile . . . in the middle of the middle of the
middle of the night . . .

"Cecil! Wake up!" she hissed, zapping him back to
their bed, their house, his life.

What did she want?

"Did you hear that?" she asked.

Hear what? he wanted to know, but couldn't artic-
ulate.

"That!" she shuddered, pulling the covers up to her
neck.

"The wind," he said softly.

"No! Somebody's outside."

"Nobody's outside," he said. "The dogs would be
barking."

Of course he was right, she decided. Of course.
"Cecil," she said. "When is it going to stop? When are
they going to let us alone?"

They? Who?

"The militants. When are they going to let us . . .
be? Oh, Cecil! I don't know how long I can take this.
When is the boat leaving? When?"

To say he didn't know, to say, "How can I know?"
was beyond the edge of all the sands of all the deserts
of all the ages. "Darling . . . darling," he said, caress-

ing her hair, holding her close, covering her with his feelings, "it will leave and they will stop when all is done."

Eggs and bacon sizzled in the frying pan; fresh juice in clean glasses brightened the table; and the smell of toast beckoned. Washing his hands in the laundry room sink, Mark breezed into the kitchen and kissed Felicia. "Smells good," he said.

"Breakfast or me?" she teased.

"Breakfast first," he grinned. "Then you."

"Eat up fast," she said. "I had a call from Cecil and Edna Rae. Somebody was out at their place last night. They went out to feed the dogs and not a one of 'em was there. A bunch of us are going over and help round 'em up."

"You're kidding," he said, stunned.

"Wish I was," she said. "You're the one I volunteered. I'll miss ya, baby," she smiled.

"Who would have turned their dogs loose?"

"I don't know," Felicia said. "It must have happened in the middle of the night."

"All of them—and nobody knew?"

"Cecil said he hasn't slept that good in years."

"Well, your dogs are all present and accounted for," Mark said.

Felicia gazed off, as if a wineglass washed from the night before and drying beside the sink were the most interesting thing imaginable. Their dogs were all present and accounted for, yes. But for how long? She had offered Mark's help; she had done it willingly. But what about her own dogs? What about the farm? If people were lurking out there, spying on kennels and trespassing, how could she leave the dogs and go to the track without Carl and Kenita?

"I'm hiring some help," she said. "I'll ask around at the track today and find somebody."

"Are you sure you want me to go?" he asked.

Did she want him to go? No! Couldn't he see that? Couldn't he hear her mind, her heart, her whole body screaming?

"I'll be OK," is what she said.

But she wouldn't be.

Not even if there were twenty-four-hour machine guns protecting every inch of Hidden Farms. Machine gun patrols couldn't get inside her mind. And, right now, her mind was miles away in a hospital room she couldn't find.

"Don't go, Mark."

Standing there in his jacket, he paused.

"I need you," she said. "I need you to stay."

"What about Cecil and Edna Rae?" he asked.

"They'll understand. If anybody does, they will." Neighbors could help. Police were helping. Church members. The local 4-H club was on it. "I'll let them know."

"What do you want to do?" he asked.

What she wanted to do was stay here, locked in this house, safe in his arms forever. What she said was, "I'll call somebody to stay here, and we'll go to the track. You never realize just how much somebody does until they're gone, do you?"

"Any more word from your mother?"

Felicia shook her head and gulped her orange juice. "Nope."

"Are you going to try calling her now?" he asked.

"Don't have to," she said, setting down her glass and paying attention to the TV. "It's all over the news."

"Investigators in the arson of city zoos across the nation may be making headway. Last night, police arrested animal rights militant and former porn star Marion Malloy and several members of the A.R.M. at her dog rescue compound in central Pennsylvania. Working on an anonymous tip, state police and SPCA officials raided Malloy's Pennsylvania Lovers of Greyhounds. Among the starving and wounded dogs police found drugs, explosives and nearly a hundred thousand dollars in cash. The arrest is linked to the murder of Wheeling Greyhound trainer Carl McCrory, and investigators are looking further into the matter."

Kenita poured milk into a bowl and reached for a pack of sweetener. "How much?" she asked.

"Two," he said, quietly. "Three."

"No wonder the devil didn't want you," she teased, tearing the packets open and stirring. "Open up," she said, giving him a spoonful.

Doing as he was told, Barry finished the cereal and went on to a slice of honeydew melon. "Not bad," he managed to say.

"How do you feel?" she asked.

"OK, I guess," he answered, touching his shoulder.

"Too bad she wasn't a better shot," Kenita said with a wink. "I might have been rid of ya."

He smiled, but didn't laugh. "Where is she?"

"Out on bail is what I heard."

"I'm sure of that," he said, showing his lack of faith in the system.

"She says we were trespassing."

He made no comment.

"But that didn't help the other people the police arrested."

"Yeah?"

She nodded.

"It hit the news, Barry. The police want to ask you a few things and there was a call from a magazine."

"No kidding," he said, intrigued.

"SportsAnimated," she said, with a big smile. "They called and said their editor wants to talk with you. I wrote her name down, but I don't think I spelled it right," she said, reaching for a tablet on the table beside his bed. "Here it is." She paused. "Esmeralda. That's a different name, isn't it? Esmeralda von Havenburg. She must be foreign or something."

"Sounds hoity-toity," he said, looking for the bathroom and trying to sit up.

"Use this." She handed him a bedpan.

"Not for what I have in mind," he said, with a look of warning. "Help me off this bed."

"I'd better call the nurse," she said, taking her leave. "I'll be back when the war's over."

Looking down onto Central Park in New York City is like looking out the window of an airplane. Esmeralda liked looking out the window of the offices transformed from what used to be her apartment. She liked having two homes: the estate in the country with its kennels and horses, and her place in the city. She liked knowing everything from the Persian rug carpets to the Louis Icart prints and Hevener figurines was hers. She liked her collection of animal art. The horses, dogs and other animals she began collecting as a child made the place. Whether here, or at the farm in Havenburg where she could get away from it all, animals were her comfort.

"Pour me a drink," she said to the handsome young man going over some last-minute details for a story. "Then tell me about Claude and Blanche."

Wine for Esmeralda. Only the special holiday wine from Mt. Hope that she stocked in the winter for all year long.

"Hope springs eternal," he said, crossing the room to her. "That's what you always say."

"Yes, I suppose I do," Esmeralda said softly, almost to herself. Remembering. Always remembering. "How is she?"

"Very well," he said, of the blonde woman known so well to them both. "He didn't know she was your sister," he said for the hundredth time.

"I know," she said. "I know." Taking a sip, she paused. "Neither did she."

A stranger walking in on them might have raised an eyebrow at that last remark. Esmeralda's expression didn't change. "Make it interesting."

"This is an athlete with a story," he said. "Our readers are going to love it. Dog cast aside to die, dog found by compassionate man, dog wins big race. And the kennel's run by a woman! It's got everything."

"More than everything," she corrected him. "Passion. Murder. Intrigue. I want to know everything about that young man who died, everything about the raid on that dog place in Pennsylvania. What's the name of the woman?"

"Malloy," the assistant said.

"Remind me to stay away from her hairdresser," Esmeralda said. "And, oh!" she called out, before he could leave the room. *"Get Claude Emerson for me."*

CHAPTER TEN

Viva Las Vegas!

He liked it here, with Mark. Not that he always understood this man—his man; the man who had found him so long ago when all was lost.

Today, the man seemed restless. Clue lay beside the oak desk as Mark paced back and forth across the floor, spouting words he could not understand. After some time, the man stopped and said, "What do you think of my speech, Clue?"

Hearing his name, the dog perked his ears, and with a familiar "thump, thump" of his tail hitting the side of the desk, suggested to Mark it was good.

The intercom buzzed. "Yes?"

"Your lunch is here."

"Thank you, Jean."

Walking around to his desk, he said, "Clue. Take your place." Clue happily went to his blanket in the alcove at Mark's feet. He liked it here. He liked the large family of people and dogs and his freedom to come and go as he pleased.

He was home.

He would live here the rest of his days.

He was lonely no more.

No resort had ever been more appropriately named, Claude thought, walking into a jungle of palm trees, exotic sculpture and the incessant purr of slot machines. Following helpful signs, he entered an enormous lobby with a distinctive, floor-to-ceiling, salt-water aquarium spanning an entire wall behind the front desk.

"Welcome to The Mirage," a dark-haired young clerk said as she processed the paperwork for his stay. "Traveling alone?" she asked him.

"Yes," he said. "Not that I want to."

"Oh, I'm sure you won't be alone for long. This is Vegas," she smiled.

Hoping she was right, he thanked her, took his key-card, and asked for directions to his room.

"Follow the arrows to the escalators and the seventh floor."

Thanking her again, he left his luggage with the concierge and breezed through the casino. He had made it. What's next? he wanted to know.

Across marble floors, he passed the watch jeweler; should he ask them to replace the battery on his Accura? No. Better find his room first.

Elevators off to the right . . . going up . . . seventh floor . . . turn left . . . follow the signs to 715 . . . what a room. As a reporter, he had stayed in many rooms during his business travels. But this room was *fine.*

The bellman placed his luggage on the rack in the closet and stood waiting for his tip.

"Thanks," the bellman said, closing the door softly behind him.

Claude tossed his clothes on the bed and ran a shower. Shampoo, conditioner, skin lotion, towel dry.

Across the way at Treasure Island, Mark stretched out on his king-sized bed and dialed home. "Safe trip," he said. "Everything OK there?"

The voice of his business partner assured him it was.

"How did we do today?" Mark asked, referring to the dogs.

Miami was good, he was told. "Joe called and said we had two firsts and a third. Felicia said the dogs at Wheeling ran pretty well, and I watched the replays online: a second—what a race! You should have seen him pour it on at the far turn—and a fourth. And that Molotov daughter keeps hanging in there, too."

"Felicia says we've got a good one, there," Mark commented, missing her.

"Yeah, she believes in that one," came the steady answer, as the report continued with results from Lincoln Park, Southland, Palm Beach and Bridgeport.

"How are the new pups?" Mark asked, curious about the latest litter carrying the name of their blood-line.

"Strong," Michael said. "You should see that white one."

"Yeah?"

"Uh-huh. He's really something."

"Shall we send him over to England and train him for the Derby?" Mark asked, referring to the race the puppy's great-great-grandsire, I'm Slippy, had won.

"It's something to think about."

Saying goodbye, Mark thought about the blend of

champions that had gone into the making of the powerful athletes that had become his passion. Back then, when it all started, did he know on some level that it would turn out this way? Maybe. Their intensity, their power and their joy while running, it was very familiar in a way he couldn't fully explain—as if he understood them, as if he had been around them before in a different place, a different time.

Surely, from the time he was a child staring at pictures of Greyhounds in the encyclopedia, he knew these graceful dogs would be an important part of his life. But could anyone possibly have known just how important?

Racing was a time-honored challenge, not unlike life itself. It came with a starting point, an escalation of effort and a finish line when the job was over. Whoever crossed the line first, won the race. What could be simpler, more fair?

It wasn't like dog shows or horse shows, competitions ruled by judges deciding which entry looks best. Likewise, it was far different from horse races, in which riders urge their horses on.

No, Greyhound racing was about dogs running according to their own individual style, using their own intelligence. Maybe that was its greatest allure.

Independence of spirit had attracted him to the sport of Greyhound racing—independence of spirit that was stronger than he had ever seen.

Reviewing the results Michael had reported, intimately knowing each dog from the time it had been born—many born into his own hands in the whelping box—Mark considered the journey that had taken him from that mountain hike so long ago to this oasis in the Nevada desert. It wasn't much different from the journey of the industry, itself, he thought. Not if you looked at things in an abstract sense and compared the events of the last few years to a race. An astounding, politically charged race.

Five firsts, two seconds, four thirds and a fourth, he thought. All in all, it was a good night for Hidden Farms North.

Funny, how being away from home could make you wish for the one you loved. Lying there in the room, he thought about her laughter, her joy of life and her desperation on the West Virginia airstrip when Clue ran flying into his arms.

Reaching for the phone, he dialed.

"Hidden Farms South," she answered.

"It's me," he said.

"I knew it when I heard the phone ring," she said, snuggling deeper in the bed covers and pulling a pillow close. "How do you like Vegas?"

"Lonesome, maybe," he said. "Why don't you take the next flight out?"

"You know I'd love to," she said, holding on to the thought. But there were dogs to train, employees to take care of, the kennel booking to run. "Sometimes I think we've built ourselves a golden cage, Mark."

A golden cage, he thought. How very well she had put it.

"Your wake-up call, sir," the smooth operator said the next morning.

"Thanks," Mark answered, returning to the notes for his speech, brushing away crumbs from the toast room service had brought him along with fresh tomato juice and scrambled eggs. Would track operators want to hear what he had to say? He was taking a chance. But wasn't the sport, even the industry itself, about taking chances? he reasoned, knowing the answer before he even considered the question. He'd say what was on the minds and in the hearts of the Coalition members, he decided. He'd say what the Board of Advisors expressed so often and so eloquently at the monthly meetings that had taken them from the wobbly start of a grass-roots movement to the magnitude of a full-scale publicity campaign. He would speak the truth and brace himself for the Internet chat that always followed.

He dialed Wanda's cell number. "Wake up," he said.

"Oh! God! Where am I? What time is it?"

"Time to get yourself in gear."

"I'm awake, I'm awake" she said, clearing her senses. "Really! What's up?"

"Do you want to go over our presentations before the meeting?"

"Sure. I think that's a good idea. I guess we should meet somewhere. How was the flight out?" she asked, flooding him with questions.

"Good! The reporter and I are coming over to your hotel in about an hour."

"Reporter?"

"Claude Emerson, the guy from the TV show. He wants to talk with us before we go in."

"I only need half an hour," she said, hanging up.

Waiting for Claude outside the hotel's entrance was enough to remind Mark to pack short sleeves next time, if there would ever be a next time, and lots of them.

"Mark!" It was Claude, approaching him wearing an Armani suit, classy shades and carrying a leather briefcase. At his side were a cameraman, a young woman with a notepad and earphones dangling loosely around her neck, and a fellow in jeans and T-shirt carrying lights and extension chords.

"Up early shining your shoes, I see," Mark said, clearly wondering about the production crew.

"Oh!" Claude said, introducing everyone all around. "They flew in yesterday and got the conference room wired for sound. Did you get through to Wanda?"

"She's probably waiting for us," Mark said, uneasy with the idea of being in front of a camera, but reluctant to say so. Strange, a camera unnerving him when the thought of speaking in front of an audience had no effect whatsoever.

"Then, let's go in." Claude smiled, making things as easy as he could.

She had changed since he last saw her six months ago at the popular Greyhound Day in Dewey Beach. He remembered the art show there, and falling for a painting titled, "After The Ball," a clever and, for him, moving watercolor by Kathy Hoyne. Something about Wanda reminded him of the woman in that painting, the sad but lonely woman in her blue gown, rolling a ball across the floor to her dog.

"Saw a watercolor that belongs in my collection," is what he wrote on the WorldWide Greyhounds chat forum. A few days later, a note arrived from the artist saying it was his. Surely, the painting was the most sensual and haunting in his collection.

"I don't feel good," Wanda said, her hair still wet from the shower.

"Scared?"

"No, I'm serious. I've got some kind of cold or sinus thing going, you know?"

"Relax. You're just nervous; it's natural. Hey, I'm not so sure about this thing myself," Mark said, smiling. "But, if you dress the part," he said, jiggling his tie, "it helps."

She had dressed the part. She looked great in her jacket with the silk scarf around her neck, all business with a feminine touch. It wasn't easy believing this young woman had accomplished so much within the industry and still remained so unassuming.

"Mark's told me about you," Claude said, introducing himself and the crew. "You're an important lady."

"Thank you," Wanda said politely.

"You and your partner run the biggest Greyhound marketplace in the whole industry. I've checked it out. You're a 'net publisher with your own racing kennel and a stable of racehorses, besides. What a life!" He smiled. "How many other people you're going to meet today can say that?" he asked. "They'll like you," he said warmly.

"Well, I'd still feel better if somebody told me how this sounds," she said, indicating her speech written on two sheets of hotel stationery clasped in her hand as it pressed against her purse.

"Let's get some coffee," Claude said, inviting everyone toward the spacious downstairs restaurant. "Anybody hungry?"

"I couldn't eat a thing," Wanda said, touching her stomach as they found a table and seated themselves

"A good policy," Claude said, "before speaking i

front of people. Would you mind if I took a look at your speech?"

"Appreciate it," she said, handing it to him, ten small yellow sticky papers clinging to it. "I'm so nervous!" she said to Mark. "Aren't you nervous?"

"No," he lied and smiled. "I do this kind of thing every day. How are the horses doing?" he asked, knowing it was one of her favorite subjects. "Any winners?"

"We have a colt in training right now, and he looks hot," she said, taking hold of the lifeline. "You should visit the farm sometime."

"I'd like that," he said. "You know, I'm not sure I ever told you, but Dan Marshall is a friend of mine."

"Dan Marshall, the one who owns *Nahgua*?" she asked, referring to the famous Arabian racing stallion.

Mark nodded. "We met at the Quentin Riding Club," he said, "during one of their shows. He was giving a talk."

"What about?" she asked. "Did he have Nahgua with him?"

Again, Mark nodded. "Beautiful animal."

"I've seen pictures of him," she said, relaxing now. "We bought a daughter of his and she was a great runner."

"Actually, his talk was very interesting," Mark said. "I understood everything he was trying to say about balance."

"I didn't know you're a rider."

"I'm not." He smiled. "Not that I couldn't be," he added. "But it wasn't just about riding. He equated horsemanship with how we balance our own lives. It was fascinating."

"So is your speech, Wanda," Claude said, handing it back to her. "Honest, friendly and hopeful."

"Think so?"

"Know so," he winked, finishing his cup and allowing the server to pour another. "Mark and I have already covered how he started in the business, how the public perceives the industry, that kind of thing. But how did all of you come up with the idea of fighting back under the North American Free Trade Agreement?"

"That? It was Mark's idea," she said.

"Actually it was a professor I know who collects antiques," Mark corrected.

"A professor." Claude commented, making a note.

"He gets around," Mark said. "He says it's all about checks and balances. For all the destruction on one side of life, there is an equal and opposite amount of creation on the other. Things might not happen the way you want them to, but if you let them grow in their own way, sooner or later, Nature finds a way to make things right. But, Nature, for him, isn't separate and apart from mankind. For him, all our cities, our culture, our wars—all of that is Nature in its biggest and most comprehensive form. So, he told me about a fascinating case where a chemical company from Canada got a law in California overruled by the NAFTA and collected millions."

"Nature's balance?" Claude observed. "What was the case?"

Filling him in, Mark added, "It was a stunning victory. And the most sobering thing was, right or wrong, good or bad—harmful, poisonous, pollutant, it doesn' matter—if the NAFTA invokes their rules, it super cedes everything that went before."

"It doesn't seem possible," Claude said. "How could our lawmakers ever pass such a thing?"*

"You'd have to ask forces greater than me," Mark said.

"My research assistant says the whole trade agreement was really set up for manufacturers," Claude said.

"Doing business in more than one North American country, crossing borders, yes," Wanda finished. "But, if you look at it more closely, you'll see it's really for the people holding stock in those companies."

"Investors," Claude said, making a note. "OK, let me get this straight. You went out and found a company in the Greyhound business making, what? Dog food? Muzzles? Those little jackets they wear in the races?"

"Better than that," Mark said.

"How much better?" Claude asked. "Don't you have to prove loss of income because of another country's legislation?"

"That wasn't a problem," Mark said. "But we wanted to represent the whole sport. And that was much broader than any one company's income sheet."

"You guys were going for the jugular," Claude said.

"They call us a blood sport, don't they?" Mark grinned.

"I guess so," Claude acquiesced.

---

*Remarkably, many of NAFTA's most passionate boosters in Congress and among economists never read the 900-plus page agreement. According to critics of the agreement, legislative supporters made pie-n-the-sky promises of NAFTA benefits based on theory and ideological prejudice for anything carrying the term "free trade."

"Maybe that bothers some people," Wanda said. "But if you get right down to it and cut through all the bull, isn't any sport with live players a blood sport? I mean, think about it."

"I don't know what the exact definition would be," Claude said. "But you could probably make a case for that."

"We don't have to make a case," Mark said. "We just have to *be*."

Claude smiled slowly. "Meaning—"

"Meaning it isn't a matter of morals or ethics or personal prejudice," Mark said. "As far as the NAFTA is concerned, we're already here. Doing business in every country that signed its name to their agreement."*

"Pretty firm ground," Claude said.

"Rock solid," Mark said.

"So what company did you go with?" Claude asked. "Our sources don't show a company. All we see is The Greyhound Racing Coalition. Which is . . .?"

"A membership organization," Mark said.

"And you're its national spokesman?" Claude asked. "Just clarifying," he added.

"Yes," Mark said.

"Are you salaried?"

"No."

"What's your compensation, may I ask?"

"Satisfaction." Mark smiled.

"Interesting answer."

---

*According to research into the aftermath of the NAFTA's enactment countries signing the Agreement were actually compelled to change domestic laws—and in at least one case, a national Constitution—in order to bring them in line with the NAFTA's terms.

"Thank you," Mark said.

Claude paused for a moment, took out a cigarette, and looked around the table as if to ask, Does anyone mind?

"Not at all," Mark answered, for himself. "It's a stress reliever."

Tilting his head slightly, catching the full drift of the remark, Claude lay the cigarette aside and reached for coffee instead. Being under stress was a sign of weakness, he told himself. He was in control here, not them. "I'm still missing the angle you guys made your move on," he said. "My information is, this whole NAFTA thing was set up for companies exporting products into other countries in North America."

"Set up for investors," Wanda corrected him. "There's a whole section of the Agreement specifically defending investment and financial services."

"International bankers," Claude said. "A far cry from Greyhound racing."

"You think so?" Mark asked, prodding their collective intellect. "I don't see the difference."

"You don't?" Claude asked. "You don't see the difference between banking and Greyhound racing?"

"I see all kinds of similarity," Mark continued. "Have you ever been to the track and stood in line to place your bet or collect your money?"

"Sure. I've been to the horse races."

"Isn't that the same as standing in line at a bank? And doesn't a bank take your money, saying they'll make you interest?"

"They're supposed to," Wanda said, laughing.

"But they don't always," Mark interjected. "As a matter of fact, if your account is bigger than the amount of insurance they carry, you can lose your money. If you don't think so, do your homework and check out the Great Depression."

"Go on," Claude encouraged him.

"All I'm saying is, I see very little difference between pari-mutuel gambling and the stock market the bank puts your money into."

"Could be," Claude agreed. "But I think you're driving home a bigger point."

"In both cases, you're an investor," Mark concluded.

"And the NAFTA is for investors . . . " Claude said, making a note for later, "but what about the specific company through which you initiated the dispute? Are you saying you did it through a racetrack?"

"No." Tearing open a packet of sugar and stirring it into his cup, Mark said, "We created the entity."

"Created," Claude repeated, scratching his beard.

"The racing industry has several membership organizations," Mark explained. "As it turned out, the attorney who registered The Greyhound Racing Coalition did it under a special charter. He was looking ahead to possible times when we might want to become involved in a member's legal issues."

"Run that by me again," Claude said.

"I'm saying there exists, used by only a very few organizations, a special charter through which an organization can step in to defend any one of its members," Mark explained.

"I've never heard of that."

"I'm not surprised. As it turns out, our attorney realized that if other racing organizations joined The Greyhound Racing Coalition, the collective membership would encompass almost every Greyhound investor living in—and doing business between—the U.S., Canada and Mexico. After that, it was just a matter of connecting the dots to NAFTA."

"But under the NAFTA, you have to prove your product's country of origin, right?"

"You're talking about the Certificate of Origin," Wanda said. "That was interesting." She smiled, remembering the first time it was brought up to the Coalition.

"It turns out we had more than one product that met the NAFTA criterion," Mark said. "So, we decided to keep it simple."

"How simple?" Claude asked.

"Well, first, it had to contain all North American parts," Wanda explained. "It had to be produced entirely in Canada, Mexico or the United States."

"Like a TV show," Claude said. "I'm catching on."

"Exactly," Wanda stressed. "Broadcasting across the borders would be the ticket, though. Now, think about that show being the broadcast of a dog race that people are betting on."

Eyes narrowing, Claude finally set down his coffee cup. "You didn't . . . " he said.

"You're thinking about simulcast signals and gambling over the Internet," Wanda finished, shaking her head with a clever grin. "But that wasn't what we decided to go with."

"But it's perfect," Claude said. "What could be any better?"

"The dogs," Mark said, simply. "And we have tens of thousands of them. "

"What!" Claude exclaimed.

"All made in the United States, Canada and Mexico; bought, sold or traded between all three countries; income of our members affected by anti-racing legislation in the state of Pennsylvania," Mark said, with finality.

"And everywhere else that ever passed the same kind of laws," Wanda added.

"Incredible," Claude said softly, as the full impact of the concept washed over him. *"Incredible!"*

"Ready?" Mark asked, checking his watch.

"As we'll ever be," Wanda smiled.

10:05 AM EST
Executive Office, SportsAnimated, Inc.
New York City . . .

"There's a call for you on line one, Ms. von Havenburg," the secretary announced.

"I'm still going over the cover," Esmeralda said, with a glance at the anxious young man from graphics.

"It's the State Department."

"We'll pick up on this later." Esmeralda smiled at the artist, pushing aside his sketches.

"Do you want to make the changes we talked about?" he asked.

"No, just hold everything until you hear from me." She swiveled her chair around, turning her back to him as he left.

"Esmeralda here."

Signing in, they entered a large room set up for an official news conference. Among the hundred or so people seated at tables spread from wall to wall, they recognized some of the most powerful decision-makers in the sport of Greyhound racing. Up front at the podium, the great-grandson of the founder of the sport, Owen P. Smith, was narrating a slide presentation spiced with colorful anecdotes about the people and dogs filling the screen.

"Here is my great-grandmother. . . . Here's a newspaper article calling her the first woman to head an international sport. See that dog? The story is, the dog had endurance, but it wasn't fast enough to win a race. So, Owen just kept making the races longer and longer until the other dogs tired out."

You mean that's how our 5/16 mile races started? Mark thought to himself. Nothing more scientific than that?

"We have seats for you over here," an attendant said, pointing to a table near the front of the room.

Joining the panel of guest speakers, Wanda and Mark found their places while Claude and his crew took their stations, careful not to block anyone's view.

Nothing more scientific than that, Mark repeated to himself, catching up again with the presentation of Owen Smith's grandson. The raw ingredients of a sport born of anything a few dog lovers could slap together, he thought, imagining how exciting it must have been, how much fun, when the world was open to the newest game in town.

Of course, he knew it was all based on more than that. International sports didn't grow to that level without serious effort and planning. Particularly something noted by the independence of spirit so identified with Greyhound racing. Strong individuals with backgrounds in agriculture had a natural sense of how to let things grow in their own way. And here he was now, at a first-class resort hotel, with some of the finest and most forward-thinking minds in the business.

10:08 AM EST
Executive Office, SportsAnimated, Inc.
New York City . . .

"He isn't answering his cell phone," the secretary said. "Do you want me to leave a message?"

"No," Esmeralda said, impatiently tapping her fingers on the arm of her wheelchair. "Call the Front Desk of the hotel—we'll have him paged."

"Yes, Ms. von Havenburg."

"Front Desk," the pleasant young voice answered. "What's his room number? Oh, he's not a guest here? He's with the Greyhound conference? Well, I might be able to check what room they're in. Can you hold?"

"That won't help me," Esmeralda said, hanging up.

Brought abruptly back to the present by the searing pain of fingernails digging into his forearm, Mark heard the master of ceremonies.

"Ladies and gentlemen, I'm pleased to introduce the queen of international Greyhound news, Wanda Wharton!"

"I'm gonna throw up!" Wanda whispered, her voice cracking.

"Under the podium—not on the microphone!" Mark laughed, pushing her toward the stage.

"Oh, *God*!" she mouthed, looking back at him as he, still grinning, gave her a wink and a thumbs-up.

"Hello. My name is Wanda Wharton, and a lot of you probably know me from WWG.com."

10:18 AM EST
Hutchin's Greyhound Farm
Durbin, West Virginia . . .

Edna Rae Hutchin paused halfway between blue eye shadow and a splash of Moonlit Nile perfume. Studying her face in the mirrored, art deco dressing room table Cecil had bought from a local theater, she wondered if he would remember to pick up the palm tree plants from the florist. She had studied the scene carefully, planning every detail. The low, flat lounge with ornate legs like cobras twisting upward, the long, round pillows on each end . . . the sheer curtains draped ceiling to floor . . . their linen robes and gold-colored waistbands . . . their shoulder-length black wigs trimmed in bangs. It was perfect. Even the Blue Nile wine. Is that you calling, Cecil?

"Hello," she answered, in her grandest Nefertiti impersonation.

A few minutes later, Cecil tucked potted palm plants under each arm, took a can of gold spray paint off the shelf and walked to the front door. Flipping the sign as he always did, he turned around to face the display window showcasing a manikin in coveralls and painter's cap balanced on a stepladder. Setting down the plants, he popped open the can of paint and wrote across the glass in great, swooping letters. Snapping the cap back in place, he set the paint can beside the door, picked up his palm tree plants and walked away from it all. "CLOSED FOR GOOD."

". . . Since we started WWG.com, there have been a lot of changes in the industry." Wanda smiled. This wasn't so bad, she decided, warming up. Maybe she'd do more of this kind of thing. "We've seen our membership grow from a few hundred to thousands of Greyhound breeders, owners, trainers and fans from all over the world. We don't always agree on things— what family does? But, usually, we manage to deal with things and work them out to everybody's satisfaction.

"One of the best things to happen is that, suddenly, members of the sport from different countries could communicate with each other and share information. They could also share bloodlines and discuss pedigrees and performance more than ever before.

"It wasn't surprising that importing and exporting dogs from one country to another, and blending their bloodlines that were, until now, isolated from each other, is something more breeders started doing.

"As we did business together, we became stronger. We could see for ourselves how the sport is perceived in other countries and how they deal with some of the criticisms that have nagged our industry for so long.

"As in anything, the public perception of an industry is the result of the people who make up that industry. That's very true for Greyhound racing. And, as more and more new people are coming to the sport, people from all kinds of professional backgrounds, we are seeing some real changes in the demographics of Greyhound owners and their expectations.

"As for news related to the Greyhound business, we're constantly monitoring the press for anything related to the industry." Wanda smiled again, clearly at ease with herself now. "And I believe our online advertisements and auctions have gone a long way to supplementing the national auctions held by the NGA. For a long time, the industry needed a stronger presence, an easier way for people to get into the sport. Adoption has been just about the only way most people could even get a Greyhound for a long time. But, if they want a puppy, where could they go?

"Since WWG.com, they have a place to find a Greyhound, plus all of our topics are archived, so what we really have is the largest source of Greyhound information on health, pedigrees, politics, economics, racetracks and lots of other things that anybody can find, anywhere. Any questions?" she asked, to a show of hands.

"How did you get into racing?"

"One of my favorite topics," she said, smiling, thinking back. "I first saw Greyhound racing in my home country, Ireland, as a child. My family has been racing their dogs for as long as anybody can remember. We also have horses, and we race them, too. We're lucky enough to race them here in the States, and my husband and I always go to the dog races whenever we travel. I've had a lot of fun reading the adventures of Maddog McDermutt in the *Greyhound Review*, I might add," she chuckled. "He and Elsie certainly get around, don't they?" she asked, to general laughter and applause.

"What gave you the idea for WWG.com, and did you start it alone?"

"Well, that's another good question. No, I didn't start it alone. In fact, it was started in Ireland by a friend of mine, and when I saw what the industry was up against here, how it had everything going for it, but it had almost disappeared from the sporting press, I felt a need to do something about that. Besides, as breeders and owners, don't we want our Greyhound businesses to be around for our kids? What's the point of building something and spending all those years and giving it all that attention unless it's going to be there for your family?" she asked, to a round of approval.

"Well," she said, scanning the room, "if there are no more questions, then I guess that about wraps it up."

"Thank you, Wanda," the master of ceremonies said warmly.

10:31 AM EST
Bastinelli & Taggart, Ltd.
Wheeling, West Virginia . . .

"You have a call, Mr. Taggart," the tinny voice of a secretary reported through the intercom.

"Just a minute!" Brad called out, not taking his eye off the golf ball at his feet as he lined up the putt at the end of the carpet.

"Ping," went the putter.

"Clunk" went the ball as it sank into the little metal cup.

"Brad here," he said, answering the phone and listening for a moment. "Thanks," he said a few minutes later as he hung up and looked to his wife.

"Our next speaker comes to us from the political side of the industry. Please join me in welcoming Mark Whittier from The Greyhound Coalition."

"You're on," Wanda whispered to him. "How did I do?"

"They loved you," he said, taking a last sip of water as he stood and made his way to the podium.

Facing his peers, much as one would face the stockholders of a giant corporation, Mark grinned and pretended to fuss with his shirt collar. "Is my tie on straight?" he asked the audience, poking fun at the importance of the occasion.

Their laughter putting him at ease, he assessed the power of those assembled there and knew the future of Greyhound racing was secured. He knew, on some level, maybe like a Greyhound letting him know what it needs without a spoken word, that there are times when more than what we actually say is conveyed.

Touching the creased and coffee-stained pages of his scribbled notes, he imagined all the people of this very special industry working every day to raise and care for the dogs that inspired them, risking personal criticism and, many times, hardship. These were the unsung heroes, he thought, enabling a domesticated animal to run as free as it possibly could in a society becoming more and more controlled and limited every day, where fewer and fewer animals could live out their instinctive nature. And fewer people as well.

Starting with one Greyhound, he had become part of the last free and independent sport in America. Would his ever be a truly successful racing kennel? There was every chance that it could be. Was owning a top racing kennel the most important thing for him to do? Was that why his life had taken such a turn? Scanning his notes, he didn't know. But, surrounded in Las Vegas by the creativity of world-class entertainers, architects, city planners and service people of every kind, he did know the stewards of this industry were gathered right here, before him. Never before, had a group of people had such an opportunity to guide and inspire an industry to greatness. Never again, might he have the chance facing him now. There was so much to say—so much to be shared, planned for, considered.

Reminding himself that what we say isn't always condensed into a few moments or delivered from a stage, he considered the importance of this moment. How we presented ourselves, how we lived out our lives, together with all the bits and pieces that others knew, or thought they knew, about us—those were the elements of an enduring message. A statement here, a comment there—put them together and you had an impression.

8:19 AM Mountain Time
Syncopation Labs
Denver, Colorado . . .

Rushing to catch the ringing phone, Jack Halstead tossed his new Stetson on the Remington sculpture behind his desk, pushed aside a stack of customer files and made room for a plastic cup of hot coffee.

Checking his caller ID, he started right in. "Saved me a dime." He smiled. "I was gonna call you later about your order. What's that?" He paused, listening intently. "How'd you find out?" he asked. "Whooooo-ee!" he whistled, running a hand through his hair.

"Thank you for inviting me here," Mark began. "Unlike Wanda," he said, "I didn't grow up in this sport. I've always had dogs, yes, and I've always bred and raised them. But I came to Greyhound racing because of a stray dog I found running wild on a mountain. By now, most of you know the dog I'm talking about, Hidden Clue. Did he win more races in his career than any other dog? No. Was he an All-American? Nope. I won't be going out to the Hall of Fame to collect any honors for Clue. He's not in that league. As a matter of fact, he's not all-anything because he's part Irish, part American and part Australian, too," he added, to friendly laughter.

"But I'll tell you what that dog *does* have," he said. "Heart. And *heart*," he repeated, holding up a copy of *SportsAnimated* magazine and waving it high in the air for everybody to see as he introduced Claude Emerson and the crew, "is what's bringing us back to the sporting pages of America!"

"Claude's following our case against the state of Pennsylvania. If some of you still think I'm too new to the game, well, Claude, here, is not even close to making up his mind. That's OK, Claude. You haven't seen your first race yet."

"Looking forward to it!" Claude asserted, for all to hear.

"Well, I hope your dogs always win," Mark said to him. "And when you decide to start raising a few, there're some breeders here who can set you up." He grinned, to general laughter.

"I won't even go there!" Claude laughed, surprised at the lightheartedness of the man he had pegged as stuffy.

"That's OK," an unruffled Mark fired back to more laughter. "We know the media loves us."

"Speech!" someone hollered.

"OK, OK," Mark said, holding up his hands in mock surrender. "Well . . . I guess you want to know how things are turning out for The Greyhound Racing Coalition," he said to scattered applause.

"If you've been following our press releases to the breed clubs and throughout the industry for the last few years, you know we've met with heavy pressure almost from the minute the anti-racing forces found out about us.

"It might sound naïve, but we were completely surprised by their bitter and mean-spirited reaction. Didn't they want the industry to address and take care of what they criticized? Didn't they want us to eliminate the *inherent cruelty* they have blamed us for at every turn? Didn't they want us to take charge of our own affairs and straighten things out?

"Were we ever mistaken!

"News of The Greyhound Coalition hit the anti-racing and adoption chat lines and we were bashed unmercifully. I can hardly imagine an industry or its leaders being treated more rudely. Clearly, we threatened their reason for being," Mark said, smiling.

10:22 AM
Jason Greathouse
Abilene, Kansas . . .

"Howdy, partner! What can I do you out of?"
Jason Greathouse asked, feet propped up on his desk and admiring his spit-shined, pointy-toed, alligator boots.

"No shit!" he hooted, slamming his feet to the ground.

"Hot, hot, hot damn! We gotta make a statement! Call the networks!"

"Although the idea for the Greyhound Racing Coaltion started with members of WWG.com, it didn't take long for it to develop into a consortium, or combined effort, if you will, of every official organization serving the industry.

"Together, and out of respect for racing fans, we began taking on issues concerning the sport and anything relating to it. Along the way, we launched a national newspaper for fans of the sport. We began paying for ads in publications that no longer gave us good press, forcing them to deal with us. We issued regular press releases by the tens of thousands every month, and editors began to question the spin of anti-racing groups that slandered us at every turn.

"It was only a matter of time before we realized that a major lawsuit would be the kind of thing the press could not ignore. We looked into our rights in that direction and went straight to the NAFTA." Mark smiled, to a round of applause.

"There is not a piece of legislation anywhere that will bring an end to the actions of the A.R.M. faster than an affirmative decision from NAFTA. It's been two years since we appealed to NAFTA, and we're still hopeful."

"Like Wanda said, a lot of it comes down to why you're in the business. Well, having a farm and loving dogs, I'm lucky enough to meet a lot of people who animals are important to. People from all walks of life. When it comes to dogs, today they have a greater affect on how we see the world around us than ever before. They're in the news, in movies, books, and they're in all kinds of advertisements. What's their appeal? Those of us in Greyhounds know the answer to that. Dogs appeal to every sense we have. They appeal to our emotions—and it's magic!"

Forget about the evolutionary history of dogs and worrying about where they came from, is what he wanted to say next, but didn't.

"Forget about television documentaries exploring which breed was the *original dog* and traveling to exotic places to find the last remaining members of that breed on earth. That's pretty grand in a *National Geographic* kind of way," he said. "But the truth is lost in so many forgotten memories that it probably doesn't matter much to the dog in your life right now. What *matters* is the diversity of this interesting species, and the possibility that there was no single original breed. So, where our Greyhounds originally came from isn't as important as the simple fact that . . . they're here.

"Do I believe in spontaneous genetics and things like that?" he asked, for those fascinated by pedigrees. "Yes, as a breeder who has seen some fascinating mutations, yes, I do," Mark said, mentioning some of the great champions that had thrilled the public over the years. "I believe in that rare biological spark very much so. I also believe the emotional make-up of a living creature, and its mentality, are affected by its physical appearance. But that could be from my years of dog shows, raising just about every breed of dog there is at one time or another, or even the artist in me speaking," he said, smiling.

"We all know our personalities can rub off on our dogs," he said. "How many of you know a dog that acts just like its owner?"

To embarrassed laughter, a few hands went up.

"I thought so," he said. "Well, all of us know dogs are different from cats or birds or horses and other animals in their basic nature. But we also know there are lots of differences between the individuals in a litter. Customers ask, Which puppy in a litter is the Alpha? Which is the most loving? or Which is the most playful? Sometimes, when looking at a puppy by itself and searching for an emotional connection with this prospective fur-child, people ask me if I think the pup will turn out this way or that. When I say it depends on how they raise their dog more than anything else, some are quite surprised. "The dog is going to learn from you," I say. "Because y*ou* are the greatest teacher."

10:22 AM
Seaside Greyhound Racetrack
Connecticut . . .

Poppy Schwartz finished pushing a stubborn white and red dog into his crate.

"You're never gonna be adopted, you ugly son of a bitch," she fussed. "Why the hell do you keep pissin' your crate like that! Huh?"

Ring! . . . Ring! . . . Ring!

"Lucky, you damn loser, get in your crate! I don't know why I even bother with you guys," she said, hur-

*rying to reach the phone before it stopped ringing.
"Shut up, everybody! Shut up!" she hollered, grabbing the phone on the last ring.*

*" . . . Poppy and her loving Greyhounds here," she
cooed sweetly.*

"The greatest teacher. Each and every one of us,
representing every aspect of our industry, is a teacher.
At Hidden Farms, we raise whole litters together in a
graduation system, like a school. Littermates start out
together, but as they become more dominant, and
their growth and any special feeding they require
changes along the way, they move up the ladder into
the next run. They graduate. It doesn't mean they've
lost sight of their littermates, because they can still
see them running and playing in the next kennel
run beside them. And the new kennel mates aren't
strangers either because they've been housed next to
each other for a while. But, the result is, our litters
don't have just one dominant pup with a bunch of followers. Instead, we end up with a bunch of confident,
independent thinkers! Exactly what you want for the
track.

"When I say, 'you are the greatest teacher,' I'm not
speaking about the rigid discipline one endures in
obedience classes for dogs or riding classes for good
horsemanship. Maybe *rigid* isn't the right word for
them, but I think it illustrates the difference between
fundamental training and the invisible *something*
between you and your dog traveling the same path in
life. I have a favorite novel, *Fate of the Stallion*. It's
about a man who finds an Arabian stallion at a horse
sale and brings him back to his former glory. The neat

thing about the story is how the man's own life mirrors the horse's.

"Before he even knows the horse, there's a scene where Dan Marshall senses his presence, running along the river. The horse seems to be calling him, saying 'Find me! I am yours!' The novel shows the parallels of their lives, how both the man and the stallion share the same fate.

"Likewise, in *The Blue Ribbon,* a novel set in the competitive world of dog shows, there is a scene called 'Miles To Go.'

"In this scene, Robert Sheffield, a dog show judge loved by two different women who own rival kennels, is hiking in the Canadian woods with his Collie, reflecting on love. The path in the woods symbolizes Robert's own path in life, and his dog is right there beside him.

"As many of us do, including myself, Robert has mental conversations with his dog. He's wondering if he made the right decision by letting the woman he loves slip through his fingers. A tragic and life-altering mistake.

"Suddenly, among the trees, the dog sees a deer and runs after it; but, of course, the deer gets away.

"'She got away?' Robert asks. 'It's OK, fella. We've got miles to go.'

"In those miles, we know there will be other people, other animals, and other challenges. New experiences. New loves. Robert is saying there is no time for us to mourn the lures, so to speak, that get away.

"Greyhounds know that about us. They have a way of taking us through life, like guardian spirits. They keep our sense of love and adventure alive in times that are very troubling.

"A very special woman I know—some of you know her, too—Felicia McCrory, says I've been around the block. Well, just between you and me, I've been around the block a *few* times. And all over the neighborhood." He looked over the crowd and smiled to their chuckles. "I've met a lot of people in that neighborhood, and I've come to believe our ability to love is based on what happens to us. It's eroded by the rotten stuff and nurtured by anything that makes us feel good and important. Our dogs have a way of making us feel important," he said as he smiled.

"Some of you know I have an antique restoration business. We fix broken things and make them better. That's what we do. Well, our sport was broken. And it needed repaired."

10:24 A.M.
Wheeling Downs Kennel Compound
Wheeling, West Virginia . . .

Kenita walked up and down the rows of crates, making sure all the racing muzzles had been pulled and set out for dogs heading for the track later that morning. Reaching the end of the last row, she paused and unlatched a crate.

"How's Dee-Dee," she crooned, to the thump-thump of a tail as Dee-Dee nestled deeper into her plush blue velvet, wall-to-wall carpeting.

"That's a good girl," Kenita sang, reaching to caress the dog's silky head, careful not to disturb the halo she knew must be there.

Ignoring the phone, she showered Dee-Dee with praise, just like Carl would have.

"You're a star," she said. "Your picture's in The Review! *My Carl's little girl, a winner," she said, knowing she'd never tell anybody it was her own money Dee-Dee had won in "The Oldest Maiden Stakes." Not even Barry.*

Closing the crate, she hurried down the hallway, through the office door to the ringing phone on the wall.

"Today, we are facing a crumbling economy," Mark said. "Let me rephrase that. We're not just facing a crumbling economy, we're caught up in it. Just about everywhere we turn, things are falling apart.

"All of us know people who have lost their jobs. All of us see businesses closing. We see odd legislation being passed—things we never would have considered before the day in September that changed it all.

"There's an uneasiness around us. And it's growing. As we deal with serious issues more and more, as our families fracture and our natures become more hardened, our pets remain a steady comfort to us and are sometimes the only way to keep our hearts open.

"Recently, I was asked to speak at a high school on behalf of the Greyhound racing industry. As part of my presentation, I mentioned some of the interesting people who race their Greyhounds. Writers, record producers and singers, television and movie actors. I talked about horse racing, dog shows, horse shows, the art world . . . but I might as well have been talking to myself. Because I saw no spark of interest or imagination coming from the kids in that auditorium.

"Oh, they were interested in other things. If I had slipped in a few stories about stabbing the teacher or shooting their classmates, they'd have listened. Both things had happened recently to them. Taking your baby to school with you, how to get money for the latest high, how to live off welfare, these things might have perked up their interest.

"What kind of society wants people like that?

"Was it an *inner city* school? Yes. It's classified as inner city.

"Was it in New York or Chicago or Philadelphia?

"The answer to that is an emphatic *No*. Surprising as it may seem, that school was in Lancaster, Pennsylvania, a place made famous for its industrious Pennsylvania Dutch."

10:27 AM
Wheeling Downs Kennel Compound
Wheeling, West Virginia . . .

Kenita hung up the receiver, then lifted it again waiting for a dial tone. Quickly, she dialed the farm.

Both arms elbow deep in soapy water, Felicia scrambled for a towel. It was about time for him to call. "Mark?"

"Shut up! It's your mother!"

"The hopelessness of those students reflects the hopelessness of their homes," Mark continued. "But they haven't given up. How do I know? I know, because they have pets at home. When I go to schools, I always ask how many students have horses, dogs, cats, fish and other pets. It's usually the first thing they respond to. Sometimes, as I've found out, the only thing.

"In a world where so much is out of their control, these kids don't seem to believe they can reach some of the lofty things I talk about, and maybe they can't. But they *are* in charge of their pets at home, and that's a start.

"Today, right now, the sport of Greyhound racing is more important than ever. It's important because Greyhounds symbolize achievement and attainable victory. You don't have to be a millionaire to get started in Greyhound racing. Let's take care of that symbol. Let's protect one of the last remaining examples of the legendary American Dream, where anyone—no matter what their background, no matter who they are—can start from scratch and end up in the winner's circle.

"That school of the zombies? It took me a while, but I finally figured it out.

"It wasn't a spokesman for the Greyhound industry they wanted that day. What they wanted—what they needed—was a ray of hope.

"Next time, I'm bringing along a puppy and a trophy from The Great American Greyhound Futurity with me!" Mark nodded, with finality, to strong applause.

"These are new days for us!" he said, again waving *SportsAnimated* high in the air for all to see.

"We're raising our heads and fighting back!" he said to mounting applause.

"We took on the state of Pennsylvania!" he hollered. "They made their insulting laws and we said *No Way*!"

"We saw what the legislators in Harrisburg did. We saw who they were afraid of—and we saw who they listened to. We went *beyond* Harrisburg! We went beyond timid lawmakers who don't have the courtesy or common sense to *ask us* to be part of the laws they pass about our industry!

"I ask you—*is that respect?* Is that respect for a sport that has inspired countless people to better themselves, that makes jobs, that creates heroes no cheap supermarket tabloid can tear down?

"When's the last time you heard of a Greyhound athlete being taken to jail for rape?

"When's the last time you heard of a Greyhound athlete taking bribes?

"When's the last time you heard of a Greyhound athlete murdering anyone?

"I can tell you. *Never!*

"And you never will. Because Greyhounds are what they are, and that's all there is to it!

"If they don't want to support Greyhound racing, they don't want to support heroes. If they don't want heroes, they're responsible for what's happening in our schools, our churches, our towns all across this country—and we're not going to stand for it!

"This is a great industry!

"This is a proud industry!

"The pageantry, the heritage of our sport, these things mean something. They mean standards. They mean codes of conduct without Big Brother making laws telling us what to do. Ladies and gentlemen, those kids I told you about aren't lost—they're a living protest!

"With their bodies, every breath, every thought, every fiber of their being, they're saying, Look what you're doing! You're robbing us of self-esteem. You're robbing us of inspiration!

"Well, I believe in inspiration. I believe it behooves us to do everything in our power to inspire people to greatness, and, sometimes, that means seeing a dog run all out—reaching for that lure in front of him, that impossible dream he might not ever get, but he's gonna keep on trying!

"I'm a grown man. I'm out of high school and, frankly, I'm not going back. Not under this government, I'm not. Not under a government that insults our intelligence and makes it a crime for grown people to say my dog is faster than yours, and I believe in my dog so much, here's a few bucks I earned myself that says so!

"We looked at Pennsylvania. We looked at Pennsylvania deciding what we can and can't do with our lives. If people don't want to go to a dog race, that's their choice, isn't it? And if they want to go to a dog race, who does it hurt?

"We looked at Pennsylvania and said, 'You think we're not big enough, mature enough, adult enough to be in charge of our own lives? What gives you that right? *You* work for *us*! *Remember* that!'"

As thunderous applause filled the room, Mark stood firm and sure of himself. "Thank you," he said, beaming. "Thank you for standing your ground. Thank you for showing people what it takes to stick up for what you believe and for holding together what I believe symbolizes the basic, simple process of starting from here," he said, stepping over to the blackboard, drawing a large oval, "and getting to there. Finishing the job," he added, drawing a finish line, "whatever your dream may be!"

To the encouragement of enthusiastic applause and whistles, Mark returned to his seat. Sensing the pulse of his cell phone signal, and recognizing Felicia's number, he braced himself for the call they agreed would only come in case of an emergency.

"Hello."

"Mark! Mark!" came her voice filled with tears.

"I'm here, Felicia," he said, concern overwhelming him as he hunched over to shield his voice from intruding on the president of the dog hauler's association, who was about to speak.

"Mark, I can't believe it. Who would have *believed* it."

"What is it, Felicia? What's wrong? What happened?"

"We just heard from the NAFTA Secretariat," she said, her voice shaking.

Tapping Wanda on the shoulder, Mark locked eyes with Claude across the room.

"Tell me," he said, pointing to the phone and letting Claude know it was important.

"The ruling," she said, phone static cutting her voice into unrecognizable fragments.

"I can't hear you, Felicia!" Holding his breath as she spoke, his mind rushing back and forth over all that had happened since his lonely hike on the mountain that fateful day, he felt a force wash over him.

"Hooooooly shit," he whispered, oblivious to anyone who heard. An uncontrollable smile slashing across his face, stage lights sparkling off his pearly whites, laughter bursting forth, he slammed his fist on the table and jumped to his feet. *"HOT DAMN!"*

Running back to the podium, grabbing the microphone, jamming it against his cell phone, he cried, "Tell them, Felicia! *Tell them!*"

"We WON!" she screamed. "Five hundred million dollars!" she cried, almost unable to believe it. "Half a *BILLION*!"

Claude reached into his pocket for his cell phone and cursed himself for shutting it off. Stunned officials of the racing industry took in the moment they would remember forever: the greatest settlement ever awarded to a national sport. "Lawyers are calling from all over the place!" Felicia told them. "They want to try the case in Vermont, New York, California—every state that passed legislation against the industry," she said, filling the room with heart. "They want to hit every network, every commentator, every organization that tried to ruin us. They want to sweep the country, Mark! They're calling it high stakes—the biggest stakes race ever—and we crossed the finish line first. We won, everybody! We gave it everything we've got . . . and . . . we . . . *won*!"

Epilogue . . .

The Commonwealth of Pennsylvania didn't drop off and fall into the Chesapeake Bay. But, fiscally, they've had a hard time raising enough money to pay the fines and interest NAFTA levied against them. Forced to raise its sales tax to a whopping 11.5 percent, doubling cigarette, gasoline, school and property taxes, it would no longer be the haven of retirees from previously more expensive states like New York. Sixty thousand slot machines currently being installed statewide are hoped to defray the costs. . . .

Edna Rae and Cecil Hutchin sold all their worldly possessions, wrote goodbye letters on papyrus and were last seen in Cairo walking a promenade of five regal Greyhounds. . . .

Poppy Schwartz bought new crates, painted the walls and carpeted her headquarters. After installing a new computer system, starting boxes, electronic lure and enclosing the grandstand with glass for racing in all kinds of weather for the comfort of the patrons, the new owner of Seaside Greyhound Park congratulated herself and said, "Who woulda thunk it?". . .

Former model Barbara Bastinelli caught faithful husband Brad Taggert in a tryst with the company's biggest semen buyer. Vowing to return to her former profession, Bastinelli appeared on TV with Dr. Hollywood for an extreme makeover and got a ten-year contract with Lingering Looks face cream. Brad got a contract to supply 10,000 straws of bull semen to Spain. . . .

Jason Greathouse, former Wall Street whiz, traded in his cowboy hat and Remington bronze for a pent-house apartment on Park Avenue. With Barbara's husband out of the way, Jason saw his chance and had Tiffany's deliver a huge, four-carat diamond to the object of his desire . . . several orders later, he decided to buy direct, and bought a whole diamond mine in West Africa. . . .

Jack Halstead looked over the mailing list for his vet supply company, serving the Greyhound industry from Ireland to Australia. Picking up the catalog, he thumbed to the page announcing his new vaccine. Finally, thanks to the Coalition, no Greyhounds would be lost—no tracks, trainers or haulers would be put out of business because of the dreaded kennel cough. . . .

Building on the success of WWG.com, Wanda Wharton expanded her Internet empire to include a sister site for horse racing and went on to publish a series of how-to books for the care and raising of animal athletes. Husband Clyde is suddenly taking a strong interest. . . .

Kenita McCrory added a small wing to her house to accommodate Carl's beloved Dee-Dee. Complete with scaled-down furniture, central heating, plush carpet and built-in feed bowls—nothing was too good for his girl. As for her, Barry's proposal wasn't as romantic as she had hoped for, but she said yes. . . .

Mark Whittier and his staff decided to stick it out in Pennsylvania, telling his dogs the day will come when they earn bonus checks for being Pennsylvania bred. . . . When last seen, Felicia McCrory Whittier was sporting her 1930s art deco emerald ring on the way to church with little Johnny and Mary. . . .

Recruited by a task force operating under authority of *The Patriot Act*, Barry Dunmoyer accepted a position as a government informant in order to redeem himself in the eyes of the Greyhound community. Barry was assigned to infiltrate top levels of well-known terrorist groups like PETA, HSUS, ALF (and other organizations with suspicious initials).

A mere three months later, returning from a strategy meeting, Dunmoyer's car was found at a rest stop along Route 66. Dunmoyer, himself, however, was never seen again.

Kenita McCrory has a closet shrine in his name. . . .

At least once a week, a beer in hand, Claude Emerson leaned back on his overstuffed, white-velvet couch. Admiring the wall of awards and trophies above his fake fireplace, his attention was drawn to his newest and most prestigious acquisition: *The Walter Cronkite Award for Journalism*. Staring back at him was a golden likeness of the great newsman himself posed as Rodin's *The Thinker*, as if saying, "And that's the way it was."

No, he didn't get a Pulitzer. But hope springs eternal whenever he receives a call from a whip-cracking gambler named Esmeralda.

Just as she had speculated, Esmeralda von Havenburg's exclusive about a national sport standing up for itself hit mainstream news and shot *SportsAnimated*'s circulation through the roof. Neilson ratings ranked her TV show in the top ten for six months in a row.

Prideful of her success, seventy-something Esmeralda bought herself the world's largest collection of knives and printed her smiling visage on all the company credit cards. Sending one to Claude, she enclosed a round-trip airline ticket and a sharp note: "Spend all you like, darling, and trust me. It's for your own good."

As for Hidden Clue, the Greyhound that started it all, the stakes were never higher. As they had done for centuries immemorial, from the sands of ancient Egypt to cheering crowds the world over, Greyhounds would inspire commoners and royalty alike, giving their all in the race to victory.

Watching over his sons and daughters, the wisdom in his silvery face was beautiful, and his eyes—dark, glistening with a force of their own to the end of his days—missed nothing.

APPENDIX

To Whom It May Concern:

The sobering information on the following pages is provided by the dedicated people of the National Animal Interest Alliance. To the knowledge of this publisher, it is the only such documentation of its kind for legislators, educators and reporters taking a responsible look into the broad range of crimes and violence committed in the name of animal rights. For entries posted since publication of this novel, readers may refer to naia@naiaonline.org.

Animal Rights and Environmental Extremists Use Intimidation and Violence to Achieve Their Ends

Animal rights and environmental extremists no longer limit themselves to demonstrations, publicity stunts and radical legislative proposals. Today they embrace physical assaults, vandalism, harassment, theft, property destruction, and terrorism to achieve their ends. Over the past two decades these attacks have mushroomed into the following events:

January 20, 2005 San Luis, CA: ALF activists cut through a 500' segment of 8' high fence at the GNK ranch and released a heard of European fallow deer. The owner, who sells venison at farmer's markets, was able to collect and corral most of the herd. The claim posted on an activist website read "Freedom for these creatures—for whom death is a certainty—was a simple and unskilled operation. We encourage compassionate people everywhere to locate farms in their area and tear down their walls. For the liberation of the helpless we will strike, A.L.F."

January 12, 2005 Auburn, CA: Five incendiary devices were found in an office building under construction. Devices of the same type were discovered in an upscale subdivision in near-by Lincoln on December 27. Official stated the firebombs were capable of extensive damage. Graffiti found on the Lincoln homes included "U will pay" and "Enjoy the world as it is—as long as you can." In a letter sent to the Auburn Journal on January 18, ELF claimed responsibility, and warned of more terrorist attempts to come—"We are setting a new precedent, where there will be at least one or more actions every few weeks," it read. The Joint Terrorism Task Force is investigating.

January 1, 2005 Hever, Kent, England: Seven incendiary devices believed to be display-strength rockets were found on the ground where the Old Surrey Bristow and West Kent Hunt was meeting. Members of the hunt smelled burning and uncovered the set, time-delay fuses. West Kent police extinguished the fuses and are investigating. Over ninety horses were taking part in the hunt, including children on ponies, and there were many people on foot in the area, along with cars and horse-boxes. Graeme Worsley, joint master of the hunt, said: "If you have a firework going off under a horse and its rider you are talking about a potential fatality. These people have a blatant disregard for the safety of anyone, horses or people. It is terrorism, it is nothing to do with animal welfare." The group has been attacked before by hunt saboteurs throwing fireworks and harassing the hunt and hunt followers.

December 30, 2005 Seaquest, FL: SHAC activists claim on the Animal Liberation Press Office website that they broke into the offices of Seaboard

Securities and emptied a file cabinet and smashed computer monitors and a TV. On the website they stated "Here's a message to Kevin, Dennis, Cristian, Adam, Guy and the rest of the Seaboard Securities staff: we now know where you live; we will not hesitate to take this fight to your doorstep if you continue to do business with Huntingdon Life Sciences." The activists further claim that the break-in has caused Seaboard to stop marketing HLS stock.

December 26, 2004 Sylmar, CA: The home of the public information officer of the Los Angeles city Animal Services Department was spray-painted with slogans, including "ALF has eyes on you" and "Resign (expletive)." Her photo and office location and phone number were posted on a website affiliated with ALF, along with those of other Animal Services employees. They are listed under the heading "Players/Targets" which includes images of a target, bullet holes, and ammunition for rifles. The apartment of another Animal Services employee was also vandalized recently.

December 25, 2004 Los Gatos, CA: Eco-terror is suspected in an arson attack which destroyed eight large vehicles—five trucks, two SUVs, and a van at a Chevrolet dealer. The vehicles were singled out though there were smaller cars which were more accessible. A similar case at a nearby Hummer dealer last year remains unsolved.

December 13, 2004 Iowa City, IA: Seashore Hall was again vandalized, with bulletin boards ripped from walls, papers scattered, and food ground into carpets. Police are withholding more information, but at this time don't know if the vandalism is linked to the earlier attack or is a "copy cat" crime.

November 29, 2004 New Orleans, LA: Animal rights activists attacked a magazine store, etching the windows with acid and causing $6000 worth of damage. That same morning a store selling fur was vandalized, with "fur is ugly" etched on their windows, which will cost $20,000 to replace.

November 28, 2004 Sandal, Wakefield, England: Activists painted the letters "ALF" on the front of a home formerly owned by a man whose company dealt with waste from research labs. The address was posted on an activist list, and the current owners, one newly diagnosed with cancer and who have no links to animal research, have been hounded by protestors since they moved in. They are pleading with animal rights activists to leave them alone.

November 24, 2004 Los Angeles, CA: ALF activists caused three incidents of vandalism in the LA area recently. Two McDonalds were targeted, with windows shattered and ALF slogans "Don't feed your kids McKillers," "Stop McKiller" and "We won't sleep until the slaughter ends" spray-painted on walls. Police believe the same group vandalized the home of an executive linked to animal research. They broke windows, threw a smoke bomb into the garage, and spray-painted ALF on the house.

November 13, 2004 Iowa City, IA: The FBI is investigating extensive damage from vandalism at Spense Laboratories and Seashore Hall at the University of Iowa. The vandalism took place in laboratories on locked floors used by the psychology department for animal research. An unknown number of research rats, mice and pigeons were taken or released, over 30 computers and offices were damaged, and hazardous chemicals were dumped. HAZMAT teams from the National Guard were deployed to determine what chemicals were spilled. Until their work was completed and the buildings rendered safe, investigators couldn't enter. Damage is in the tens of thousands of dollars, and many research projects conducted over months and years have been ruined. In a long e-mail to the media and the Animal Defense League, ALF claimed responsibility for the vandalism and described what they had done to the labs. Seven researchers were listed as targets, and the e-mail concluded with their contact information, including the names of their spouses, home addresses, home and cell phone numbers and personal e-mail accounts. The activists made a video-tape of themselves as they vandalized, and sent the tape to media outlets. Parts of it have aired on national TV.

October 17, 2004 Burton, Staffordshire, England: Animal rights fanatics have threatened to dig up the remains of a second person connected to Darley Oaks guinea pig farm. A letter to an elderly cleaner, who has worked at the farm, contained threats to desecrate the grave of her husband. The letter was intercepted by the police who routinely open the mail to the Hall family and people connected with them. Animal rights extremists have also sent hate mail claiming they are in possession of the remains, stolen earlier this month, of the mother of one of the owners of the farm. They further stated that they will not return the remains of Gladys Hammond until the Hall family stop breeding guinea pigs for medical research.

October 12, 2004 Long Island, NY—Letter of Intimidation.

October 10, 2004 Garrett County, Maryland: A group called "The Institute for Public Safety" sent a mass mailing of postcards to landowners in the county, suggesting that 40 percent of bear hunters are alcoholics, drug addicts or mentally unstable. The chairman of the group admitted they made up the statistic, and that they planned to mail more cards to landowners of the other county in the hunt area. Several animal rights groups have sued to stop Maryland's bear hunt.

October 10, 2004 Philadelphia, PA: A major highway connecting the city to its western suburbs was shut down for several hours during rush hour as police and FBI bomb squads dealt with a metal box, with the letters ELF painted on the front, that was attached to an electricity transmission tower.

October 8, 2004 Yoxall, Staffordshire, England: Police suspect animal rights activists for desecrating and removing most of the remains from the grave of an 82 year old woman, whose family breeds guinea pigs for medical research. The Hall family, who run the breeding farm, local villagers, and others with connections to them have been under attack by animal rights activists for five years. They have been suffered hate mail, malicious phone calls, hoax bombs, a pedophile smear campaign and arson attacks. Local businesses have been forced to stop dealing with the family, cars and homes have been vandalized, and villagers terrorized by night visits from activists. Police are investigating, and state that at least two people were involved in the desecration. The Animal Liberation Front praised it. While denying responsibility, a spokesman said: "This is direct action on an inanimate being. Nobody has been harmed. If this stunt does not get that farm closed, maybe the next one will."

October 3, 2004 Grand Rapids, MI: The Ringling Brothers and Barnum and Bailey circus train was vandalized by animal rights activists. Parking booths and a glass door were damaged, and graffiti painted on the train. Police, working with the FBI, are withholding the name of the animal rights group which is taking credit for the vandalism.

October 3, 2004 Melbourne, Australia: Activists from Animal Liberation Victoria crashed the RSPCA's formal ball, and threw red paint over RSPCA's national president, Hugh Wirth while shouting "The RSPCA has blood on its hands.". One protestor got up on stage and spoke against the RSPCA's business with Pace Farms, Australia's largest egg producer. He was removed by security guards, and the other protestors were escorted out. Dr. Wirth will be pressing assault charges.

September 20, 2004 Penrith, Hale, Altrincham, UK: Residents in these areas have received bogus letters, some purporting to come from "a concerned mother" stating that a named individual was a pedophile, and "assaulted her daughter." In Hale and Altrincham about 180 letters have been mailed over three weeks. In Penrith, the person named has also had extensive damage to his car. The letters are part of a campaign by animal rights activists targeting employees of companies linked to biomedical research.

September 12, 2004 London, England: The

(London) Times obtained a five page "hit list", dated July 2004, that was circulated among animal rights extremists against the use of animals in biomedical research. More than 150 named individuals, including 21 children, are targeted for violent attacks, harassment, and intimidation. The list includes home addresses and phone numbers of 87 employees of Huntington Life Sciences and companies connected to it, 47 employees' wives, and 21 children. The document gives concrete suggestions for many kinds of attacks, and further gives advice on avoiding detection for extremists seeking more violent forms of protest.against the people listed. The document states "Whatever you do, just do it and show them no mercy . . . make these perverts suffer . . . You can be as extreme as you like…the possibilities are endless . . ."

September 9, 2004 Runcorn, England: Poison-pen letters pushed through doors and posted in public, naming neighbors as pedophiles and giving graphic details of a fictional sex act, have been found in the district. The false claims urge the recipient to confront the individual named and "let him know you know," and are being made against individuals known to be targeted by SHAC.

September 8, 2004 Prestbury, Macclesfield, Alderley Edge, England: Nineteen company directors of Emerson Developments Holdings Ltd. have been victims of poison pen letters and attacks of criminal vandalism to their homes and cars. Last week letters were sent to neighbors of one director, calling him a pedophile. The directors have received threatening letters. An Internet posting, purportedly from ALF, said, "We want Emerson to kick out Yamanouchi. We will not let up until our aim is achieved . . . We know where you are but you won't know when we are coming back; we do not let go ever." Emerson has been targeted because it leases property to Yamanouchi Pharmaceuticals, a customer of Huntington Life Sciences.

September 5, 2004: East Peckham, England: Animal Rights activists vowed to launch ten "terror attacks" a night across Britain. An ALF spokesman at a "training camp" for AR activists to learn "direct action" said "Ten attacks a night would be an absolute minimum . . . Think of the number of butcher shops: at least a couple of windows are already being broken every night and then you have people spraying graffiti on cars to those targeting employees of Huntingdon Life Sciences." There have been reports of at least six serious incidents in the last ten days, including attacks on cars and other property of people connection with GlaxoSmithKline, HLS, and a farm raising guinea pigs for research.

July 30, 2004 Austin, TX: Tejas Securities, a US marker maker, has stopped trading shares in Life Science Research, the company that owns Huntington Life Sciences after directors, executives, analysts, and traders were bombarded with abusive e-mails.

July 30, 2004 Charlotte, NC: Activists vandalized a fleet of utility trucks owned by Utiliquest. All the trucks were marked with "ELF" and all had their tires slit.

July 30, 2004 Dorset, England: The "Lobster Liberation Front" claims responsibility for two attacks on a Dorset lobsterman. Activists seriously damaged his boat, set his catch loose, and splashed red paint over his house. Weeks earlier the same boat, boat-house, and lobster pots were vandalized. An anonymous e-mail on an Animal Rights website threatened "war against the industry" and "real damage must begin" if lobster fishing continues. Welsh police are investigating similar attacks in Wales.

July 21, 2004 Chetsey, Surrey, England: Following a firebomb attack by ALF activists, RMC group, the world's biggest concrete company, pulled out of building a biomedical research laboratory at Oxford University. The arson caused ?150,000 worth of damage as incendiary bombs destroyed the control center, three trucks, and a crane. It took firefighters three hours to control the blaze. A message on the ALF website said: "This attack is a warning to RMC that collaboration in animal torture at Oxford or anywhere else will not be tolerated, and a further warning to all involved in building the Oxford laboratory to expect similar ruthless treatment." RMC group said the violence was "putting lives at risk." RMC was sub-contracted to Montpellier, the lead construction contractor that pulled out of the project on July 19, following animal rights actions against its directors and shareholders.

July 19, 2004 Gloucestershire, England: Montpellier construction group has pulled out of a contract to build a biomedical research laboratory at Oxford University. Walter Lily, its subsidiary, is abandoning the project due to a campaign by animal rights activists, which included hoax letters to shareholders urging them to sell their shares or face actions from animal rights activists. Directors have had paint poured on their cars, threatening late-night phone calls, and graffiti painted on their houses. A local businessman, working for another firm in the same group as Walter Lily, received an anonymous, threatening letter, in which activists promised to forge criminal records and post them to hundreds of his neighbours. It said the records would allege "a string of sexual offences committed by yourself throughout your adult life".

July 7, 2004 Provo, UT: The letters "ALF" were found in seven locations at Brigham Young university's agriculture center, near a recycling building where firefighters put out a suspicious fire. Fire damaged a corner of the building, and two small tractors, and is estimated to be at least $30,000. No animals were in the building. This was the third incident at BYU attributed to ALF in the last six weeks. Someone broke into a barn and released animals, and later equipment researchers were using to test the breeding habits of fish was removed from an aquarium.

July 3, 2004 Bournemouth, England: ALF activists vandalized equipment of construction company RMC - targeted because the company supplied concrete for a new research lab being built at Oxford University. Tractors, bulldozers, and a crane were severely damaged in the raid.

June 22, 2004 London, England: Investors in the construction group Montpellier are being attacked because it is the main contractor for a primate research center at Oxford University. Montpillier directors' vehicles have been vandalized, and the staff at a company supplying a small amount of concrete have been targeted with letter bomb hoaxes and late-night phone calls. Investors in Montpellier received letters representing "Stop the Oxford Torture Lab" asking them to sell their holdings, saying that if they didn't sell within a month their details will be published on the Internet. The letter said "This will prompt activity by the animal rights movement to persuade these shareholders to sell." Montpellier share value has fallen by one-fifth.

June 14, 2004 West Jordan, UT: ELF claimed responsibility for an arson fire that consumed the Stock Building Supply lumberyard, with damages estimated at 1.5 million dollars. The three-alarm fire was one of the biggest they ever fought, said the town's firefighters, and it burned dangerously close to businesses in a nearby strip mall. The letters ELF were spray-pained on the main building and a truck at the scene. An ELF-signed fax sent to a local radio station mentioned four future targets, including an SUV dealership and another lumber company. Two years ago the ELF calling-card was found at an vandalized construction site in the town.

June 13, 2004 Rockville, MD: Police believe three arson fires, involving a pick-up truck, SUV, and a Mexican restaurant are connected. The area around the restaurant was also vandalized. Damage is estimated at $48,000.

May 28, 2004 Prairie City, OR: Activists damaged five pieces of logging equipment use in a timber salvage operation. Metal shavings were poured into the engines, fuel and hydraulic systems. Repairs will take weeks, cost $100,000 and cause expensive production delays at lumber mills. FBI has joined the investigation, which bears the hallmarks of eco-terrorism.

May 8, 2004 Oakland PA: Animal activists protesting the use of foie gras toppled an obelisk and smashed a statue of the Venus de Milo that were in front of an Oakland restaurant after the owners refused to take foie gras off the menu.

April 21, 2004, Long Island, NY: The ALF claims to have broken into Forest Laboratories to steal data, documents and blueprints relating to a new facility, as part of their actions for World Week for Animals in Laboratories. Photos said to be samples from the theft were posted online at BiteBack magazine. There has been no confirmation of the break-in and theft in the news media.

April 21, 2004 USA: SHAC America, as part of their involvement in World Week for Animals in Laboratories, has posted reports from "anonymous activists" on their website describing harassing visits to various targeted company offices and at employees' homes. Descriptions of the visits and taunting messages were posted online , but have not been reported in the news media.

April 21, 2004 Snohomish, WA: Two new homes were destroyed and another heavily damaged in an arson attack. At second construction site workers found plastic bottles filled with flammable liquid and a threatening note. An attempted arson was found at a third site, where a fire had started and apparently gone out. Officials said the note, which mentioned ELF, apparently came from an eco-terrorist group and the incendiary devices were similar to ones used by the ELF. Total damage was over a million dollars.

April 21, 2004 Monrovia, CA: Animal rights

activists spray-painted the historic Upton Sinclair house with slogans of "Puppy killers," "Murderers," "ALF," and "you can't hide." Protesters dressed in black, some with skull masks, chanted animal rights slogans over a bullhorn, targeting the homeowner, an executive with Sumitomo Corporation which has ties to HLS. The chants were personal - "(You) are a sick pervert that enjoys animal abuse" and "…we know where you sleep at night." Earlier they had protested at a local Petco, and at another Sumitomo employee's home. A recording at the Animal Defense League office announces many protests this week, which animal rights activists call the "World Week for Animals in Laboratories." Some protests are scheduled at homes of various executives—one called "UCLA monkey killer,"—and at Sumitomo's offices.

April 20, 2004 Elk Creek, Vancouver, CA: Eco-terrorists threatened the lives of loggers by spiking hundreds of trees. Workers found more than 100 spikes in logs going through saw mills there. Demonstrators had stage a major effort in October to try to stop logging in the area.

April 11, 2004 Carral, Spain: Animal extremists bored holes in the wall of a mink farm barn allowing 6,500 mink to escape. Eight hundred are still loose, and five hundred were found dead. Graffiti saying "For a life at liberty" signed ALF, was scrawled on a barn wall.

April 10, 2004 Roxborough, PA: Four beagle puppies and numerous rodents were stolen from the Walter Biddle High School of Agriculture Sciences. The thieves, suspected to be animal rights activists, left a message spray painted on the walls of the new kennel reading "Go experiment on yourselves. We're free - The Animals." The school doesn't conduct animal experiments, and the animals were used to teach animal care and husbandry. **Addendum**: Animal rights activists have have claimed responsibility for the theft. The claim was made, in a long note posted on an anarchist/activist website, as part of the animal rights "World Week for Animals in Laboratories," and accused the school of many abuses. Activists state all the animals will be placed in "loving homes."

March 29, 2004 Lake Oswego, OR: Animal activists vandalized the office building of Sumitomo Corporation, which is affiliated with Huntingdon Life Science (HLS. Red paint was splashed around the building, and graffiti stated " SUMITOMO DUMP HLS." In an anonymous online claim activists warned, "Paint today. Tomorrow- who knows? Hells coming to rip off the doors of your privileged heaven." Sumitomo has been the target of numerous attacks by SHAC.

March 24, 2004 Charlotte, NC: Eco-terrorists are suspected in more than a dozen arsons that have destroyed or heavily damaged expensive homes under construction in suburban neighborhoods. Authorities are asking the public for help in tracking down the arsonists and builders are being encouraged to hire security firms to protect homes under construction.

March 9, 2004 Kitzbuhel, Austria: A protester set fire to a woman's mink coat while she was wearing it. Police suspect lighter fluid was used to ignite the fur. Patrons in a bar realized the back of the coat was burning, and extinguished the fire before the woman was injured. The coat was destroyed in the attack, and the culprit has not been caught.

March 5, 2004 Bloomington, IN: Nine SUVs were vandalized in one twenty-four hour period. Their windshields were ruined by acid that permanently etched the glass causing thousands of dollars worth of damages.. The police suspect ELF activists.

March 5, 2004 York, England: Paul LeBoutillier was sentenced to five years for making harassing phone calls to Huntingdon Life Sciences shareholders and to HLS affiliate Covance Company employees.

March 3, 2004 Staffordshire, England: Staff and managers of Wolverhampton & Dudley Breweries and Green King, two pub companies, have been threatened and harassed by animal rights activists, because the Hall family, owners of Darley Oaks Farm, which breeds guinea pigs for research, frequents these pubs. In response to the threats, as well as thousands of e-mails, and 1300 phone calls, the managers have asked the Hall family to stop using their pubs, to protect both their own safety and that of the pubs' staff and other customers. Steven Oliver, managing director of W $ BD's Union Pub Company said "The threat was of such a serious nature that we felt we had to act." Copies of the letters to the Halls were sent to the activist group, Save the Newchurch Guinea Pigs, whose website targets companies supplying or used by the Hall family. Other pubs in England have been targeted by animal rights activists because the pubs were believed to support hunting.

March 2, 2004 Scotland: A group calling itself "Badgers Unknown" posted the names, homes addresses, and phone numbers of over one hundred UK celebrities on a website under the heading

"Celebrity Bloodsports Scum", urging activists to carry out firebomb attacks. The Countryside Alliance, a group supporting hunting and fishing, whose officers were included in the list, was able to get the website removed from one Internet service provider, only to have it reappear elsewhere.

February 17, 2004 North Lima, OH: Vandals broke windows in a construction trailer, sprayed a fire extinguisher and scratched the initials "ELF" on the side of a piece of construction equipment at the construction site of a new showroom for a fireworks company.

February 13, 2004 United Kingdom: Animal rights activists are targeting mothers and mothers-in-law of judges who have banned the activists from harassing companies linked to biomedical research. Home addresses and phone numbers have been posted on a website, as well as home details of the directors of a company linked to HLS. The website states "They are not immortal. They don't live in fireproof homes."

February 8, 2004 Milford Sound Fjord, New Zealand: An unknown saboteur connected a hose to a boat's diesel tank, pouring fuel into the water at a World Heritage fjord site. The site is home to a rare species of penguin and a major tourist attraction. Officials said that the 3,400 gallon fuel spill was intentional and "eco-terrorism and economic sabotage."

February 7, 2004 Charlottesville, VA: ELF claimed responsibility of an attack on the construction site of a new shopping center. Two trucks and a piece of heavy machinery were torched, and glass and gauges were broken in all the trucks and bulldozers on the site. The owner says it will cost $220,000 to replace the ruined track hoe and doesn't know if the burned trucks can be repaired. A banner left on the site read "Your construction = long term destruction - ELF"

January 22, 2004 Fayettville, AR: Five Hummers were vandalized. The letters ELF were spray-painted on the vehicles, tires were slashed and windows broken.

January 13, 2004 Richmond, VA: Three men claiming to belong to ELF pled guilty to federal charges of "conspiracy to destroy by fire." Adam Blackwell, John Wade, and Aaron Linas vandalized construction equipment, MacDonalds and Burger King restaurants, and tried to destroy a crane. They etched anti-SUV slogans on 25 vehicles at a Ford dealership. They face sentences of up to five years, and must pay restitution of over $200,000.

December, 2003 California: During the holiday season, some Chiron employees and their families received at their homes, through the mail, a box with coal, dog feces and a card that read "May your violence against the animals come back to haunt you in the new year! If you think that gift is bad just wait to see what Elves all across the USA have in store for you in the days to come!"

December 24, 2003 Stockholm, Sweden: A package of lamb and a letter from "Animals Liberation Front" (sic) claiming that meat had been poisoned in nine Stockholm supermarkets was left at the TT news agency. The agency also received a phone call taking credit for the action and stating, " We will not undertake any action that could physically injure people, but economically we will injure them greatly." A similar threat was made against a super-market in Upsala in November. No poisoned meat was found there.

December 23, 2003, Vancouver, Canada: Safeway is warning shoppers to check their turkeys after receiving three threatening letters from an animal rights group. Activists claim to have thawed several frozen turkeys and injected them with arsenic. This is the fourth time in ten years that animal rights activists claim to have tampered with holiday turkeys in British Columbia.

December 19, 2003 Norfolk, UK: Activists from VIVA broke into sheds at several turkey farms owned by Bernard Matthews. They claimed their videos showed dead and injured bird, however, the owner of the farms blamed the activists for causing the birds to panic.

December 12, 2003 Castel di Sangro, Italy: ALF criminals raided a mink farm and opened cages. ALF's e-mail states, "This is the fourth successful mink liberation in 2003."

November 18, 2003 Portland, Australia: Animal rights activists contaminated sheep feed with a "shredded, ham-type material" to make 50,000 sheep unsuitable for shipment to Muslim countries. The activists are protesting Australia's live export trade. The sheep may have to be euthanized, because under Australian law, sheep fed animal products are unfit for human consumption. It's unclear how many of the 50,000 animals were exposed to the tainted feed. Police said they had arrested a 40-year-old man in connection with the incident.

November 14, 2003 Burton-on Trent, England:

Army bomb disposal experts were called out after dozens of fireworks were thrown at a house linked to a guinea pig breeding farm. Police believe the attack, which left unexploded fireworks under cars, is linked to recent animal rights harassment focused on the farm. Last month leaflets were passed out, wrongly accusing a client of the farm of being a convicted pedophile.

November 6, 2003 Asheville, NC: Vandals struck the Little Pigs Bar-B-Que restaurant, spray-painting ALF, "murderer," and other graffiti on two catering vans. Windows were broken in a van and in the main building.

November 1, 2003 New Hyde Park, NY: Sometime over Halloween weekend a resident's home and cars were spray-painted with the slogan ALF and "Stop HLS." The homeowner has no connection with Huntington Life Science (HLS), the long time target of animal rights extremists.

October 27, 2003 Newchurch, England: An arson attack by animal rights terrorists destroyed an unused house at Darley Oaks Farm, where guinea pigs are bred for research. Activists calling themselves "Save the Newchurch Guinea Pigs" have been protesting outside the farm for four years. The protests have escalated into violence and intimidation against the owners of the farm and anyone doing business with them. On its website, the group has published contact information for the farm owner and associates. Dairy businesses buying milk from the farm as well as the firm's solicitors, have withdrawn their services due to the protests. Explosive devices have been found near the homes of employees on four occasions. Electricity to an entire village was cut off and an intensive campaign of hate mail and threatening letters was conducted against the family. The arson attack, along with the partial destruction of a golf course used by family members is believed to be ALF's work. Criminal attacks on the farm have increased to such a degree that the local police had to apply to the Home Office for an extra £250,000 to deal with it.

October 26, 2003 Forest Lake, MN: Authorities in Minnesota are investigating a fire that destroyed a nearly completed $5–6 million lakeside mansion. Following a front page newspaper article describing the home, the owner began receiving harassing phone calls. In addition to the article, the owner, who is an avid hunter, had recently hung hunting trophies in the house. Investigators from the Bureau of Alcohol, Tobacco, Firearms, and Explosives and the state fire marshal are considering the possibility that the fire was set by someone from an environmental group.

October 24, 2003 Sevenoaks, England: Bomb disposal experts were called to detonate a suspect package, a transparent lunchbox in which bubble wrap and wiring were visible. The package had been left near a road where children walked to school, outside the home of a director of Daiichi Pharmaceuticals, which does business with HLS. The executive had been the target of a previous bomb scare, and the windows of his house had been smashed. A controlled explosion was carried out by the bomb squad.

October 24, 2003 Martinsville, IN: ELF activists sabotaged a Wal-Mart construction site. Survey stakes were removed, and walls and machinery spray-painted. Over a dozen pieces of heavy machinery and vehicles were vandalized, with slashed tires, cut fuel hoses, and sand poured in fuel tanks.

October 6, 2003, Los Alamos, NM: US Forest Service officials discovered today that constuction equipment used to improve fish habitat on the Rio Cebolla river had been vandalized. Someone cut electrical wires and broke a window on a backhoe and slashed tires on a water trailer. ELF, the acronym for Earth Liberation Front was scratched onto both vehicles.

October 3, 2003 California: Using the Internet, animal extremists claimed credit for stealing credit card numbers and charging $25,000 to the accounts of two Chiron executives. They claimed possession of credit cards belonging to other Chiron employees and threated to use them too, unless Chiron severs its ties to Huntingdon Life Sciences (HLS).

October 3, 2003 Santa Monica, CA: In the early morning hours, ALF activists vandalized the home of Jerry Greenwalt, the head of Animal Services for Los Angeles. His home and car were splattered with red paint, and the initials "ALF" were scrawled on the property. ALF had recently distributed flyers denouncing Greenwalt and his department throughout his neighborhood. Animal rights activists targeted Greenwalt and his department for its policy of euthanizing animals, even though under his leadership the number of animals euthanized has decreased more than 25 per cent.

September 26, 2003 Pleasanton, CA: FBI and agents of the Bureau of Alcohol, Tobacco, Firearms and Explosives are investigating an early morning explosion at Shaklee Corporation that caused minor glass damage. The action closely resembled an incident last month in which bombs were detonated at Chiron Corporation, which a group calling itself "Revolutionary Cells of the Animal Liberation Brigade" claimed were in protest of Chiron's relationship with Huntingdon Life Sciences. Shaklee is a subsidiary of Yamanouchi Pharmaceuticals, which is also a customer of HLS. Yamanouchi has been the target of vandalism and protests by SHAC activists in the past.

September 24, 2003 Pullman, WA: Early in the morning, two small incendiary devices were ignited on a concrete driveway leading to Wegner Hall at Washington State University's College of Veterinary Medicine. The devices, which were made from plastic and glass containers and an accelerant, resembled Molotov cocktails. The arson caused no injury or damage due to their location and the time of day. The devices had extinguished themselves by the time WSU police arrived. No one has yet taken credit for the arson, but it's interesting to note that only two weeks before, People for the Ethical Treatment of Animals (PeTA) issued a press release alleging that animal researchers at WSU vet school were bashing goats with sledgehammers. PeTA based its charge on information from a whistleblower at the vet school. WSU officials flatly denied the charge.

September 24, 2003, Baton Rouge, LA: The Animal Liberation Front (ALF) a terrorist group that targets people and industries that work with animals has taken credit for vandalism at the Louisiana State University School of Veterinary Medicine. Damages are estimated to reach several hundred thousand dollars according to the LSU Police Captain, Ricky Adams. ALF claimed that it destroyed computers and splashed red paint inside the lab to stop the suffering of research animals. No note was left at the site, but late Wednesday, The Reveille, LSU's student newspaper, received an e-mail signed by the Animal Liberation Front taking credit for the destruction. The FBI is investigating the break-in and the validity of the note.

September 24, 2003 Martiny Township, Michigan: The Earth Liberation Front claimed responsibility for four incendiary devices that were found inside the Ice Mountain Spring Water Company's pumping station today. The Company workers who discovered the devices, plastic bottles filled with flammable liquid, were not hurt. The anarchist group, ELF justified its attempted arson at Ice Mountain Spring Water Company, formerly Perrier Group of America, of stealing well water for profit.

September 19, 2003 Farmington, CA: Animal activists broke into a duck barn at Sonoma Foie Gras and stole four ducks. Last month the restaurant and homes of partners in the foie gras business were vandalized.

September 19, 2003: San Diego, CA: ELF arsonists destroyed four houses under construction, three in one development and the fourth at a site located about three miles away. According to local TV news, a banner at the site of the first fires read, "Development is destruction. Stop raping nature. The ELFs are mad." Damage from the fires is estimated at one million dollars. The FBI, Bureau of Alcohol, Tobacco, Firearms and Explosives, Joint Terrorism Task Force, and the local Metro Arson Strike Team are investigating.

September 5, 2003 Putten, Netherlands: Approximately 120 animal activists, arriving in two buses and other vehicles, broke into a fur farm, damaged farm vehicles and the security system, and released 6000 mink. Most mink were recaptured. Forty-nine of the activists were arrested after a neighbor blocked one of the buses with his tractor. Before the raid, the activists had held an international camp near the German border. The same weekend, 15 activists were arrested in an action against two Japanese companies, and about 7000 mink were released from a farm in Denmark.

September 4, 2003 Santa Fe, NM: A dozen SUVs were vandalized at a Santa Fe car dealership, painted with words such as "sloth" and "greed" and signed off by the Earth Liberation Front's initials, "ELF." Approximately one third of the dealer's inventory was damaged by the yellow paint. The FBI is conducting an investigation.

August 28, 2003 Emeryville, CA: In the predawn hours, 2 explosions rocked Chiron corporation, Emeryville's largest employer. Chiron is a pharmaceutical firm that contracts with Huntingdon Life Sciences (HLS), the international animal testing firm under attack by animal rights terrorists for several years. Although no group has claimed responsibility for the blasts, the radical New Jersey animal rights cell, Stop Huntingdon Animal Cruelty, has a long history of inciting hatred against all who do business with HLS. Operating like anti-abortion terrorists, they maintain a website that demonizes Chiron employees and lists their home addresses along with actions taken against them. These include late night visits to the homes of Chiron executives, awakening family members and planting fake tombstones in their yards. Website messages warn Chiron to stop doing business with HLS and call employees "sick animal-killing scum." The FBI labels such attacks as terrorism because of their intimidating effect. Although no injuries or major property damage were reported, Chiron's 2000 employees were told to stay home Thursday and two of the town's major streets remained closed for several hours.

August 25, 2003 Sultan, WA: ALF activists cut fences at a small mink farm and released 10,000 mink, causing $500,000 in damages and incalculable losses in genetic history. Fifty volunteers worked to round up the mink, capturing about two-thirds of the traumatized animals. Scores died of dehydration or were killed on a nearby highway. Pen-raised mink are not equipped for life in the wild and some of the recaptured ones may die as well. The case is similar to two earlier break-ins at other fur farms in the county. An ALF e-mail said that the group plans to continue such actions.

August 22, 2003 West Covina, CA: ELF took responsibility for firebombing a Chevrolet dealership that destroyed 20 SUV Hummers and damaged 20 more, and, in a separate blaze, collapsed a warehouse roof. People near the dealership were evacuated. SUVs in three nearby cities were also vandalized with similar slogans. "ELF." "Fat, Lazy Americans" and "I (heart) Pollution" were among the graffiti, some profane, spray-painted on the cars. ELF issued an e-mail calling the incidents "ELF actions." The Fire Chief said the noxious smoke produced by the blaze created more pollution than the destroyed SUVs would have generated over their lifetime on the road. Damages exceed one million dollars and the FBI is investigating the vandalism as domestic terrorism.

August 15, 2003 Sonoma, CA: Animal activists broke into a new restaurant, after vandalizing the homes of two of the owners last month and publishing their names, addresses and phone numbers on the Internet. Objecting to the owners' ties to the production of foie gras, the activists broke through a wall of the restaurant, and painted slogans on the walls, electric outlets, and fixtures. They poured dry concrete down the drains, and turned on the water, flooding two adjacent buildings as well as the restaurant. Water seeped into the adobe walls of the historic building, and damage is estimated at $50,000. PETA has a national campaign against the nation's three foie gras producers.

August 6, 2003 Occold, England: According to the Business Review (UK), in mid July the Occold branch of the animal research firm, Huntingdon Life Science (HLS) received a telephone threat warning that the manager's wife and children could be kidnapped. Threats are nothing new to HLS, whose employees have been constant targets of animal rights terror for several years: They've been beaten, had their cars firebombed, tires slashed, had vehicles painted red and received ongoing threats. Their suppliers, investors and shareholders have also been targeted. Because of the escalating harassment, vandalism and violence, a High Court ruled in June that activists can not come within 50 yards of the homes of HLS employees or the two main HLS centers.

August, 4, 2003 Los Angeles, CA: Sherman Austin, a 20 year old anarchist was sentenced Monday to a year in jail. He was arrested for disorderly conduct in February at the World Economic Forum in New York. While there federal charges were being laid in California for distributing information related to explosives on his website. The sentence was more than recommended, but Austin took a plea bargain because he feared that he could be charged with terrorism, adding a possible 20 years to his sentence. Austin, who admitted posting links to bomb sites so that people could build and use them during demonstrations, must also pay a $2,000 fine and refrain from unapproved computer use and from associating with others who advocate physical force as a means of social change for 3 years. Throughout the animal rights and eco-terrorist movements, radical websites have been used to vilify targets and instructed readers on how to build bombs.

August 3, 2003 USA and UK: Websites belonging to Stop Huntingdon Animal Cruelty (SHAC) in the UK and USA are bragging that they firebombed a warehouse in Sussex, England belonging to their target, Huntingdon Life Sciences. Several vehicles stored there were destroyed.

August 3, 2003 Fresno, CA: Kelly Higginbotham, a self-described member of the Animal Liberation Front was arrested on August 3, 2003 on suspicion of making terrorist threats. According to the Fresno County Sheriff's Department, she is accused of calling in bomb threats to the Harris Ranch and beef pro cessing plant saying there were bombs planted at both facilities and warning that "everyone would die." In February, California State University at Fresno hosted a conference on Revolutionary Environmentalism. The speakers panel was a who's who of animal rights terrorists, including convicted felons who publicly advocate arson and other acts of violence as acceptable methods of achieving change.

August 1, 2003 San Diego, CA: A $20–50 million blaze swept through a 5-story apartment complex under construction in the University Town Centre neighborhood of San Diego. No injuries were reported. Although the terrorist group ELF did not immediately take responsibility for the arson, a banner warning, "If you build it, we will burn it—ELF" was left at the apartment site. Rodney Coronado, the ELF backer who did prison time for the Michigan State University fire bombing in 1992 and has received financial support from tax-exempt PeTA, was scheduled to speak at Summer Revolution, "Animal Liberation Weekend August 1st - 3rd", which happened to be in town at the same time. Coronado promotes arson as his preferred method of terrorism to his radical following.

July 2003 Mill Valley and Santa Rosa, CA: For several weeks vandals have been attacking the home of two restauranteurs involved in the production and sale of foie gras. Slogans saying "Murderers" and "Foie gras is animal torture" have been sprayed on their homes and etched onto cars and windows. One of the men, a prominent chef, was mailed a videotape that was shot from his garden showing his family relaxing inside their home, and sent threatening letters saying "Stop or be stopped." PeTA has a campaign against US producers of foie gras.

July 28, 2003 Maalahti, Finland: Five suspected animal activists were arrested after allegedly trying to raid a fur farm. Their vehicle had objects used in similar raids. A year earlier the farm had been broken into, and 1000 mink released. Following this, an alarm system was installed, and the raiders only had time to break two locks before the owner and security guards were alerted.

July 25, 2003 Bjornhult, Sweden: Swedish ALF activists placed incendiary devices at an empty fox farm, protesting the owner's plans to change his operation to mink farming.

July 22, 2003 Amsterdam: Animal rights activists damaged the Arnhem branch of AMN Amro bank. Activists have been painting slogans and damaging the bank's ATM machine around the country for months. They are trying to force the bank to drop the Biomedical Primate Research Centre in Rijswijk as its customer.

July 17, 2003 Southwest France: Activists ransacked a field of GM maize of French biotech firm Biogemma. Attackers also damaged one of Monsanto's CM maize fields in Montech, France.

July 2, 2003 South Windsor, CT: Signs of the Earth Liberation Front, "ELF" and "no sprawl," were spray-painted on a newly completed house in South Windsor, Connecticut. An unidentified man called police and said the graffiti was done by an ELF activist.

June 29, 2003 Bracknell, England: Sixty protesters cut through two wire fences at Jealott's Hill Research Center, intending to destroy a crop of GM wheat. Instead, they destroyed a crop of ordinary wheat that was part of an important project investigating a fungal disease. This was a project that researchers had been working on for years.

June 24, 2003 Los Angles, CA: The Los Angeles chapter of the Animal Defense League placed home addresses, phone numbers and home photos of the Mayor James Hahn and Chief of Animal Services, Jerry Greenwalt, on their website and on flyers placed around the city. The website gives directions to Greenwalt's home and urges activists to "stop by…" The activists want the Mayor to fire Greenwalt, and hire someone to run a "no kill" shelter.

June 24, 2003 Frankfurt, Germany: German PETA activists sprayed fake blood and threw chicken feathers on the chief of YUM! Brands as he opened a KFC restaurant. PETA is offering photos of the incident to the media. PETA Director of Vegan Outreach director Bruce Friedrich is quoted in the PETA news release as saying, "There is so much blood on this chicken-killer's hands, a little more on his business suit won't hurt."

June 23, 2003 Edmund, OK: The home of a stock trader working for a company trading HLS stock was vandalized by ALF activists. They covered the house with red and black paint, cut the phone, DSL, and cable lines to the house, and published his home and business addresses and phone numbers on their website. The DirectAction website stated, "Skip, this is just the beginning of our focus on you and it will continue until you join the laundry list of market makers who caved into the demands of the compassionate public. Charles Schwab, Paragon, Brokerage

America, Merrill Lynch, have all fled from doing business with HLS and soon you will too." His business, Legacy Trading, had been vandalized by SHAC on May 18.

June 22, 2003 Austin, TX: ALF activists vandalized the home of an employee of Abbott Labs, a client of HLS. His house was covered with red paint and the slogans "Abbott Kills" and "ALF." Activists published his home and business addresses, phone numbers, and names of his wife and daughter on ALF's website.

June 22, 2003 Missoula, MT: Forty veteran activists, including the founders of Earth First!, the Ruckus Society, Rainforest Action Network, and the National Forest Protection Alliance are staging a week long "boot camp" the in Bitterroot National Forest to train eighty "novices" in civil disobedience and other tactics of forest protest. The encampment is planned to follow the Western Governors' Association forest summit meeting in Missoula on June 17–19.

June 19, 2003 Lowell, OR: Arson at the Middle Fork Ranger Station of the US Forest Service is being investigate by Alcohol, Tobacco, and Firearms agents. AFT is usually called in when eco-terrorism is suspected. Twenty firefighters responding were able to save to adjacent buildings.

June 14, 2003 Santa Cruz, CA: Environmental activists scratched the slogan ELF into ten new SUVs, causing $15,000 worth of damage.

June 5, 2003 Chico, CA: Another arson attempt was made at a shopping center under construction. Workers found remnants of several small fires, and ELF spray-painted on the door of a work truck at the site. The FBI is exploring connections with arson attempts at two McDonalds in March, and SUVs in May, in Chico.

June 4, 2003 Washington Township, MI: Two nearly completed homes were destroyed in early morning fires. "ELF" and "Stop sprawl" were spray painted on nearby construction equipment. The houses had a combined value of $700,000. The same message was found when arson destroyed two unfinished houses in Superior Township on March 21.

June 3, 2003 Chico, CA: ELF claimed the attempted arson of a new home. The fire burned through a PVC pipe holding water, dousing the flames so the damage was minimal, about $100. "Save our bio-region ELF" was painted on the sidewalk.

June 2, 2003 New York City: Five PETA anti-fur protesters were arrested and changed with disorderly conduct and criminal mischief. Wearing bloody fur coats, with their legs "caught" in traps, they blocked the entrance of the Conde Nast building and dumped red paint on the building entrance. Vogue magazine is published in the building.

May 23, 2003 San Diego: Twenty activists dressed in black, wearing balaclavas, and carrying red candles protested outside the home of an HLS employee. A message to her, posted on the SHAC website read "tonight 250 flyers were distributed in your neighborhood alerting your neighbors that you're a vicious animal abuser. You've already been hit by the ALF, you've already gotten early morning wake-up calls, you have masked activists protesting in front of your home, your censor lights are a joke, the cops are too slow to get there within a reasonable time, and thousands of activists know where you live. What's it going to take for you to quit HLS?"

May 21, 2003 Inverurie, Scotland: Three PETA activists, one dressed in a cow suit, were arrested for breach of the peace for trying to dump two tons of cow manure at the entrance to a Scottish beef event. They were were arrested before dumping the load.

May 20, 2003 Anchorage AK: Five Iditarod sled dogs were released into downtown traffic from their boxes on dog trucks. Four were quickly recovered but a new lead dog was missing all night and found by Animal Control. One dog had injured his pads running on pavement.

May 18, 2003 Edmund, OK: The FBI is investigating a case of "domestic terrorism" at Legacy Trading, which trades HLS stock. Window and door glass was broken, and red paint poured on the walk and in the office, with damages estimated at $4000. This is the third incidence of vandalism at the company. SHAC members have called the business hundreds of times a day, typing up phone lines, and have published personal information - names, phone numbers, addresses and social security numbers, of the owner and his neighbors on the SHAC website. The owner, Skip Boruchin said he would continue to trade the stock. "No person or organization or individual has the right to dictate to me that I cannot do a legal business in this country," he said. "They have no business trying to force me out of my house . . . out of my neighborhood because I run a legal business in Edmond."

May 5, Sacramento, CA: At 3:00 am, SHAC activists with blaring sirens and bullhorns showed up at the home of an executive of a company that supplies software to HLS. SHAC plastered his neighborhood with photos of a mutilated dog, and posted his home and work phone numbers on the Internet, inviting activists to make hundreds of calls. "We'll be back, scumbag" and "...we know where you live, we know where you work, and we'll make your life hell until you pull out of HLS" was posted to SHAC's website. SHAC's website also has a state-by-state point-and-click map listing Huntington Life Science affiliates. SHAC says its home visits to people with tenuous ties to animal research have "broken new ground." Other extremist groups are adopting the same tactics.

May 4, 2003 Chico, CA: The FBI is investigating an attempted firebombing at Wittmeier Auto Center. Plastic milk containers filled with flammable liquid and rigged to ignite were left under two SUVs. While no group claimed responsibility, the method was similar to arson attempts by ALF activists at two Chico McDonalds in March.

April 27, 2003, Hudene and Faglavik, Sweden: Three activists calling themselves "Bye Bye Egg Industry" broke into two hatcheries belonging to Grimarnas, Inc., Sweden's largest producer of laying chickens. Brooding machines and other equipment was destroyed, and 42,000 eggs were cooled, killing the embryos. The loss of machinery and eggs is estimated at $240,000. Two activists were arrested at one factory, and the other the next morning as he was passing out leaflets about the destruction. All three were released pending trial. They left behind a letter and a vegan cake at both factories.

April 22, 2003 London, England: SHAC is targeting thirteen Japanese firms with ties to HLS. A page on the SHAC website says "Japanese companies kill animals at HLS," and urges activists to " really put the pressure on" the firms, saying they are SHAC's main focus. A Daiichi Pharmaceuticals director had his windows smashed and car damaged at his home in Kent. Another director was targeted at his London home by protesters with klaxon horns and megaphones. Protesters told his neighbors, who were awakened by the noise, to expect more late-night disturbances. Sumitomo Corporation, a trading house, was visited by a noisy protest at its city offices. Tony Blair ordered a security review, and concern was expressed by diplomats at the Japanese embassy.

April 22,2003 Suffolk, England: Homes of HLS employees were targeted by SHAC extremists. Car tires were slashed, paint and paint-stripper poured over cars, and letters and phone calls threatening violence were made.

April 22, 2003 England: "Violent scum" and ALF were spray-painted on a car belonging to the master of the Woodland Pytchley Hunt, and the cars tires punctured. The hunt master said that hunt saboteurs have tried to knock him off his horse and sprayed acid at the hunt during the season.

April 20, 2003 Droxford, England: ALF activists broke into a chicken farm and stole 1023 hens, taking them away in horse trailers. Caging systems, conveyor belts, and feeding apparatus were damaged and the building spray-painted with slogans. Robin Webb an ALF spokesman, said the chickens would be given homes as "companion animals."

April 15, 2003 Santa Cruz, CA: ELF activists

attacked 15 SUVs with bright orange paint, and in an ELF press release, complained that the local paper did not cover the story.

April 11, 2003 Santa Cruz, CA: Vandals spray-painted an estimated 65 SUVs and trucks with references to ELF and anti-war slogans. Forty-five new vehicles were marked at a Ford dealership, and 18 to 20 vehicles parked at local residents' homes.

April 5, 2003 Lockport IL: ALF activists claimed responsibility for setting fire to a store belonging to a man convicted of slaughtering and selling endangered tigers and leopards for rugs, trophies, and meat. The e-mail from ALF also contained treats against all convicted in operating the exotic animal ring. Accelerant chemicals were collected at the arson scene, which was confined to a back meat-cutting room. The e-mail was similar to the one sent following vandalism and the cutting of truck brake lines at the Supreme Lobster and Seafood Company in February.

April 4, 2003 East Tennessee State University TN: PETA's national lecturer, Gary Yourofsky in an emotional display of anger, forced the cancellation of a lecture he was to give, opposing the use of animals in scientific and medical research. The director of the University's Division of Laboratory Animal Resources, placed pamphlets in support of animal research, and a placard stating "Opposing Views" on a cart outside the lecture room. Yourofsky became angry when he saw the cart, and was abusive to the organizer of the lecture, even using an analogy comparing her to the KKK. He slung the cart across the hall, scattering pamphlets on the floor. Public safety officers were called, the lecture canceled, and Yourofsky left the building.

April 2, 2003 St. Polten, Austria: ALF claimed responsibility for an arson, which completely destroyed three hunting cabins.

March 30, 2003 Los Angeles, CA: CBC's California branch office, which works with HLS in the Asian market, was vandalized. The front glass window and door were smashed, and messages demanding CBC sever all ties to HLS were spray-painted on the building and parking lot.

March 28, 2003 Montgomery, AL: A federal cargo truck was set on fire and five other vehicles were spray-painted with anti-war slogans and "ELF" at a Navy Recruiting Station.

March 27, 2003 San Diego, California: The Animal Liberation Front posted the following message to an employee of Huntington Life Sciences, an animal testing laboratory, after dumping red paint on her car, puncturing three tires, and scrawling "HLS SCUM" across her garage door: **A message to Claire:** 'You can install all of the motion sensor lights in the world and it won't make a difference. You've been marked. We've been watching you and Kevin following your trip overseas last April 19th. We've been in your house while (you were) in San Francisco. We've "bumped" into you at Costco. You've given us the time while in line at Bank of America. We've been watching your house. We've been watching you and your family. You've provided us with a wealth of information and amusement. But the fun can only last for so long. In consideration of Kevin being out of town so often, think of your family's security as your windows could be put through tomorrow night. We won't forget the animals you've helped murder at Huntingdon. Until you quit or until HLS closes, we're bringing your work home for you." A.L.F.

March 25, 2003 Petaluma, CA: Animal activists struck the Rancho Veal plant, one of the few surviving slaughterhouses in the state, setting a fire that caused about $10,000 damage to the roof. Skylights were smashed, a back door broken, and "Stop the Killing" spray-painted on the back of the building. In January 2000, arsonists set off incendiary devices in three buildings at the plant, causing $250,000 in damage. Other protests in the past saw activists chaining themselves to the gate or to concrete barrels, and obstructing the driveway for eight hours.

March 23, 2003 Yarra Glen, Victoria, Australia: ALF torched a hurdle on a racetrack, and painted a slogan on the track, in retaliation for the death of one horse and injury to another at the Classic Steeple steeplechase race.

March 23, 2003 Los Angeles, CA: ALF activists smashed windows at the home of a businessman who works in a corporation connected to the CEO of HLS.

March 23, 2003 Beverley Hills, CA: ALF shot out the glass front door of the offices of E-Trade, which trades HLS shares.

March 23, 2003 West Hollywood, CA: ALF activists cracked the front display window of a store selling furs.

March 21, 2003 Superior Township, MI: Two homes under construction were burned to the ground in a new subdivision. Damages were estimated at $400,000. "ELF" and "no sprawl" were spray-painted on the garage of a nearby house. These were the third and fourth fires set in the subdivision in the last seven months.

March 21, 2003 London, England: Animal rights activist Sonia Hayword was jailed for 15 months, for causing rocks to be thrown through the windows of a person she mistakenly believed to be connected with HLS.

March 18, 2003 Tyrone, NY: Susan E. Coston, shelter manager for Farm Sanctuary, pled guilty to criminal trespass for taking a lamb from a Tyrone farm in November. She was sentenced to 100 hours of community service and ordered to pay $200 in restitution to the farm owner.

March 17, 2003 Chicago, IL: Kayla Werdon, A PETA activist, was arrested and charged with disorderly conduct, after disrupting traffic by being "improperly clothed." She was wearing shoes, shorts, a St. Patrick's Day hat, and stickers covering her nipples, and refused to cover up and stop handling out leaflets on veganism.

March 10, 2003 Vichte, Belgium: ALF militants targeted a fur farm, opening all the cages and releasing 1500 mink. Most were recaptured.

March 10, 2003 Dublin, Ireland: The Citywest Hotel in Dublin canceled an annual conference organized by the Institute of Animal Technicians, a professional organization whose members are in charge of animals used in research laboratories. Most members are from academia, and a few are HLS employees. SHAC activists invaded the hotel, let off stink bombs and jammed the hotel switchboard with protest calls. SHAC spokesperson Natasha Avery said the hotel had been put under "relentless" pressure and the cancellation of the conference that SHAC forced was a "real slap in the face for the industry."

March 9, 2003 Nissedal and Hamar, Norway: ALF claimed responsibility for arsons at two fur farm feed suppliers, which caused damages of millions of kroner. The fires were ignited by incendiary devices put under trucks and in buildings. ALF said the arsons were because "these factories play a big part in the Norwegian fur trade assault on animals…and are a strategic goal in the struggle against the Norwegian fur trade."

March 7, 2003 Galicia, Spain: ALF terrorists attacked a fur farm, releasing over 300 mink.

March 4 & 11, 2003 Chico, CA: An ALF activist attempted to torch a McDonalds early March 4th. A restaurant worker found two one-gallon containers filled with a flammable liquid near doors behind the restaurant. "Meat is Murder," "Species Equality," and "ALF" were spray-painted on the building. Notes claiming ALF responsibility were found in a phone booth and at the office of the local weekly newspaper. Instructions for similar incendiary devices are available on the ALF website. A week later a small fire was set by vandals at a second McDonalds. "Liberation" and "ALF" were spray-painted on the walls.

March 3, 2003 Berlin, Maryland: ALF activists cut through windows at the Merial Select Laboratory and stole 115 baby chickens. ALF stated in an Internet release that Merial was targeted because they are a client of HLS. The release stated "Any friend of HLS is an enemy of the ALF. We know who their clients are. We are out there and you are next."

March 2003, Melbourne, Australia: ALF activists vandalized three Ford dealerships, spraying cars with corrosive fluids. Notes were left saying the vandalism was because Ford sponsored rodeo events.

March 2003 Melbourne, Australia: ALF targeted the Jenny Hoo boutique shop twice in one month. Locks were superglued, "Fur is murder" painted on the walls, and red paint splattered on the shop.

February 27, 2003 Berlin, MD: ALF activists stole 115 baby chicks from Merial Select Laboratory, cutting through windows and wire mesh to avoid alarmed doors. Merial, which makes multiple animal vaccines and wormers, was targeted because they are a client of HLS. Activists said, "Any friend of HLS is an enemy of the ALF. We know who their clients are. We are out there and you're next."

February 27, 2003 Scotland: TV cook Clarissa Dickson Wright revealed that she gets up to 12 death threats a week from animal rights activists. She is targeted because of her pro-hunt views. Wright has been accosted at book signing, and her bookshop has been attacked. A detective is assigned to her, who she can call for advice about threats or for security if she is going to make a public appearance.

February 25, 2003 Temple Hill, England: After Peter Day shot a fox that had bitten his baby, he received threats of window smashing and car fire-bombing in a letter signed "Peter Hunt Saboteur." The local police warned Day and his neighbors to be vigilant.

February 23, Gothenburg, Sweden: ALF activists super-glued several gas pumps and credit card machines at a Shell gas station. Anti-HLS slogans were spray-painted on the building, stating the action would continue until Shell stopped using HLS.

February 23, 2003 Lidkoping, Sweden: Wolds fur shop was attacked and had its windows smashed six times by ALF activists.

February 21, 2003 USA: PETA launched "Holocaust on your Plate" - a campaign using a display of eight panels showing photos of farms and slaughterhouses side by side with photos of emaciated adults and children looking out through bars at Nazi death camps, comparing the slaughter of chickens to the murder of six million Jews.

February 19, 2003 Ballymanus, Ireland: ALF activists claimed to have removed sections of fence at a mink farm and released 1000 mink. However, the farm owner stated that though they did open cages containing 1000 animals, most were rounded up, and only 50 were missing.

February 18, 2003–March 3, 2003 Cambridge, England: A mole at the Deloitte and Touche accounting firm, auditor to Huntington Life Sciences, stole landline and mobile phone numbers, and e-mail and home addresses of senior managers and their secretaries for SHAC (Stop Huntington Animal Cruelty). SHAC then announced plans to use the information to block phones with jamming software, occupy offices, and stage protest demonstrations at private homes against the firm. Natasha Avery, Co-leader with Gregory Avery, of SHAC, said "The company will be a global target. We will be hitting them all over the world." With SHAC activists using the information, D&T managers and their employees were the victims of criminal damage—acid and spray-painting attacks on cars and homes—and noisy protests outside homes late at night, intimidating spouses and children. Offensive slogans were painted on homes, and neighbors were leafleted with material stating they were living next to "murderers." After two weeks of continual harassment, D&T severed its relationship with HLS, following Marsh, Inc. which had insured the company and left after spending millions for round-the-clock protective measures for its employees. As a result of SHAC's intimidation campaigns, the British government is now supplying banking and insurance to HLS, and it has moved its headquarters to the US. Following the announcement of D&T's withdrawal of services to HLS, SHAC said it would cease its campaign and begin targeting HLS customers. Natasha Avery stated, "We'll see who has taken on the audit when the first quarter figures come out and that firm will have to deal with us. . . . Our message to any company has always been very simple. If you deal with Huntington you deal with SHAC, and we will target whoever we want to achieve our aim of closing the place down. No company will stand in our way, be it insurer, bank, accountant or whatever. And passing laws against us is laughable because we will always find a way around them. In any case, going to prison is a small price to pay if it means closing HLS down."

February 1, 2003 Pyramid Hill, Victoria, Australia: ALF activists broke into a pig farm and removed 70 sow stall gates and gate pins, causing about $4000 in damages.

February, 2003, Virginia: PETA President Ingrid Newkirk sent a letter to Palestinian leader Yasser Arafat, after a donkey laden with explosives was used in a bomb attack on the West Bank. Newkirk asked Arafat to "appeal to all who listen to you to leave animals out of this conflict." Newkirk showed no corresponding concern over suicide bombings that kill people. "It's not my business to inject myself in human wars," she told the Washington Post.

January 26, 2003 Washington, DC: At a conference at American University called the National conference on Organized Resistance, Rodney Coronado showed the audience how to build a cheap incendiary device. "Here's a little model I'm going to show you here. I didn't have any incense, but—this is a crude incendiary device. It is a simple plastic jug, which you fill with gasoline and oil. You put in a sponge, which is soaked also in flammable liquid—I couldn't find an incense stick, but this represents that. You put the incense stick in here, light it, place it—underneath the 'weapon of mass destruction,' light the incense stick—sandalwood works nice—and you destroy the profits that are brought about through animal and earth abuse. That's about—two dollars. "Coronado further stated, "You know, those people—I think they should appreciate that we're only targeting their property. Because frankly I think it's time to start targeting them."

January 23, 2003 Klamath Falls, Oregon: An employee of a Japanese company planning to build a hog farm received written death threats, and had car tires slashed.

January 21, 2003 South Australia: Animal activists broke into a pig farm, and welded together a number of sow stalls.

Jan 16, 2003 New York: State Susan Coston, a

Farm Sanctuary employee, illegally entered a sheep producer's barn and stole a lamb, which she took to FS property. The crippled lamb was then taken to the Cornell veterinary school, with FS listed as the owner. Charges were filed against Coston, and FS now claims she acted on her own and not on their behalf.

January 4, 2003 Poole, England: ALF activists broken into an egg farm barn, expecting to find hens in cages. Instead, they caused a stampede of over 7000 free-range hens, and about 150 were crushed or suffocated. The farm had been targeted 15 years ago, when scores of hens were turned loose, only to be killed by foxes.

January 1, 2003 Newton, MA: Working over several nights an activist spray-painted environmentalist and peacnik slogans on 16 SUVs.

January 1, 2003 Erie County, Pennsylvania: ELF activists ignited jugs full of gasoline under vehicles in a Ford dealer's lot. The fires damaged or destroyed two Ford trucks and two SUVs.

December 29, 2002 Milford, Utah: Activists from the United Animal Rights Coalition (UARC) broke into a hog farm and stole two pigs. Such break-ins are a matter of concern since activists don't follow biosecurity protocols designed to protect the animals from disease.

December 28, 2002 Philadelphia, Pennsylvania: ELF activists attacked a housing development, severely damaging construction vehicles and the model home on the property.

December 28, 2002 Doebein, Germany: ALF activists smashed windows of several vehicles belonging to a meat packing company, and painted slogans on the walls of the plant building.

December 19, 2002 Emst, Netherlands: A member of the Dutch ALF stole 33 chickens from an egg farm. This is the second time the farm was broken into and birds were stolen.

December 18, 2002 London, England: The UK government has agreed to provide insurance services to Huntington Life Sciences, following an intimidation campaign by SHAC against Marsh, Inc, its former insurers. The Royal Bank of Scotland, Citibank, CSFB, HSBC, and Barclays all withdrew support from HLS after staff and shareholders were subject to harassment and intimidation by SHAC, and the UK government was forced last year to provide banking services to the company.

December 1, 2002 The Hague, Netherlands: Activists attacked the building housing Marsh, Inc. with paint, glue and acid, and vowed to return until Marsh broke its connection with HLS.

November 23, 2002 San Polo D'Enza, Italy: Animal rights activists broke into a dog breeding farm and stole 128 beagles being raised for research. The activists spray-painted "murderers" and "ALF will free all" on the buildings and walls. November 11, 2002 Thionville, France Animal rights activists broke into a mink farm in eastern France and released 1000 animals from their cages. Firefighters and volunteers searched for the animals with little success. The farm owner estimates his loss at $30,000.

November 11, 2002 Shreveport, LA & Vancouver, Canada: PETA unveiled two new advertising ventures. A PETA ad, which the Vancouver Province refused to run, compares the murder of women on a British Columbia pig farm to the treatment of animals slaughtered for food. The ad features headlines describing the mutilated bodies of the women, and ends by saying "If this leaves a bad taste in your mouth, become a vegetarian." A billboard, which was rejected by all four New Orleans outdoor advertising firms, depicts former Ku Klux Klan member David Duke with a milk mustache. The ad says "Got (lactose) Intolerance? The White Stuff Ain't the Right Stuff. MilkSucks.com."

November 1, 2002 Richmond, Virginia: Vandals who left messages crediting ELF damaged SUVs in several incidents recently. Twenty-five SUVs on the lot of a Ford dealer were permanently defaced with a glass-etching cream. The cream was also used to write ELF on the windows of a Burger King and two MacDonalds. A week later, SUVs parked near homes were severely damaged with an ax or hatchet. Vandalism and attempted arson have also been reported recently at highway and home construction sites in the area. The FBI is investigating.

November 1, 2002 Washington, DC: PETA has issued an alert against contributing to the American Lung Association as well as a call for a boycott of the Bank of America because it sends corporate contributions to the March of Dimes - both organizations which fund animal-based biomedical research. The anti-charity campaign by PETA and PCRM, through PRCM's new "Council of Humane Giving" uses misinformation on the use of animals in research.

October 31, 2002 California: SHAC activists went "trick or treating" to the homes of three people who work for businesses connected Kirby Cramer, a investor in HLS. If the door was opened, the activists responded by throwing leaflets and blood-covered stuffed animals, while screaming their message through megaphones. One couple was told their home address and personal details were on the Internet. At one home, where the door wasn't opened, the activists left photos and stink bombs, along with their leaflets and bloodied stuff animals.

October 25, 2002 Boston, MA: Twelve animal rights activists linked to SHAC were indicted for stalking an employee of Marsh Inc., which SHAC accuses of doing business with Huntington Life Sciences. The dozen activists allegedly harassed the Marsh executive for five months, calling him "puppy killer" and standing outside his home at all hours with a megaphone screaming threats, including threatening to burn down his house. Prosecutors said SHAC's goal is to intimidate Marsh into refusing insurance brokerage business with HLS.

October 25, 2002 Beijing, China: Two PETA activists, Yvonne Taylor and Kayla Worden, stripped naked and displayed a banner protesting a Beijing fur fashion show in a busy Beijing shopping district. Police confiscated their passports, and Chinese officials subsequently deported the women.

October 25, 2002 Boston, MA: Twelve animal rights activists linked to SHAC were indicted for stalking an employee of Marsh Inc., which SHAC accuses of doing business with Huntington Life Sciences. The dozen activists allegedly harassed the Marsh executive for five months, calling him "puppy killer" and standing outside his home at all hours with a megaphone screaming threats, including threatening to burn down his house. Prosecutors said SHAC's goal is to intimidate Marsh into refusing insurance brokerage business with HLS. 43 indictments were handed down, including among other charges criminal harassment, attempted extortion, and conspiracy.

October 24, 2002 Washington, DC: The Florida Election Commission has charged Farm Sanctuary with 210 counts of breaking campaign finance laws in their campaign to get Amendment 10, dealing with the use of gestation crates at hog farms, on the Florida ballot. Farm Sanctuary co-founder Gene Bauston was personally named. The Commission charged that Farm Sanctuary illegally and willfully acted as the ballot committee's cashier and unlawfully promised donors a federal tax deduction.

October 18, 2002 Winter Park, Colorado: The town's water supply has been threatened in a letter by a group claiming to be ELF. The Denver Water Board also received a letter from ELF on October 2. ELF's press office said, in an e-mail to the Associated Press, that while they don't say the threat isn't real, they usually get notice after an action has been taken. Security in the area has been stepped up since 9/11.

September, 22, 2002: Animal activists are urging action against Shell, BP, GlaxoSmithKline, Merck and 59 other companies which have links with the Huntington Life Sciences. SHAC (Stop Huntington Life Cruelty) has posted contact information for the companies on their website, urging activists to lobby the companies and organize demonstrations against them to force them to drop dealings with HLS. "The only way we are going to stop HLS is if every single one of us opposed to what they are doing stands up and takes action against them with determination and force" reads the SHAC website.

September 2, 2002, Edmund, OK: The FBI is "actively investigating" SHAC to see if any federal laws have been broken. SHAC had posted on its website personal information (names, addresses, and social security numbers) of nineteen neighbors of Skip Boruchin, a market maker for stock of Huntington Life Sciences. SHAC has been harassing Boruchin with pickets and hundreds of phone calls daily to force him to stop marketing HLS. Boruchin has stood firm, so SHAC has focused on his neighbors. An except from the website stated "Skip Boruchin is a man who can not be moved by reason or sympathy . . . So we regretfully announce that since Skip can not be figuratively moved, he must be literally moved . . . Below is a small sample of information currently available on his neighbors. We have other information for some of them—e-mail accounts . . . credit card information, birthdates, etc. This information will be periodically leaked to the public and to animal liberation groups to do with as they will."

August 22, 2002, Lohja, Finland: Animals rights activists representing Justice for Animals targeted a fur store owner. During their protest at the owner's home, they told her children that their mother was "a murderer," that they should be ashamed of her, and that "your mother will kill that {family} dog." The store owner said her children had become fearful, having nightmares, and being afraid the protesters would return.

August 20, 2002 London, England: Robert Moaby, linked to SHAC, was jailed for four and half years for sending e-mail death threats to senior corporate figures and financial backers of HLS living in New York and Toronto. In sentencing him, the judge said "These were not idle threats. They must be seen in the context of a violent campaign against HLS and its associated companies."

August 18, 2002 Eugene, Oregon: FBI and the Oregon State Police are investigating instances of sabotage to Bonneville Power Administration transmission lines. Environmental activists have been shooting at and damaging the insulators of the power lines in several different areas. The sabotage has caused brush fires, and repairs and power outages have cost BPA and other suppliers $40,000.

August 11, 2002: Arson by the ELF caused $700,000 worth of damage at a Forest Service lab in Irvine, PA, and destroyed 70 years of research focused on maintaining a healthy forest ecosystem. An e-mail from Elf's office said "While innocent life will never be harmed in any action we undertake, where it is necessary, we will no longer hesitate to pick up the gun to implement justice, and provide the needed protection for our planet that decades of legal battles, pleading protest, and economic sabotage have failed so drastically to achieve." It further stated that all Forest Service stations were targeted, and, if rebuilt, the Pennsylvania station would be targeted for complete destruction.

July 10, 2002 Seattle, WA: The FBI is searching for the activists who set off smoke bombs in two downtown buildings where Marsh, Inc., which insures HLS, has offices. The buildings were completely evacuated with no injuries. The Fire Department reports that the bombs are an incendiary type that, if they had come in contact with combustible materials, would have caused high-rise fires. SHAC did not take credit, but "applauded" the animal rights activists who set the bombs and left notes.

July 9, 2002 San Francisco, CA: A SHAC activist deliberately vomited over the HLS display at the World Congress of Pharmacology Conference. The next day more activists overturned the company's literature table, yelling and calling the HLS personnel "puppy killers."

June 22, 2002 Seattle, WA: An activist protesting the round-up and culling of geese tried to interfere with wildlife officials by repeatedly driving his car in front of their trucks and slamming on the brakes. He hit a truck driven by a federal wildlife official, sending the man to the hospital where he was treated with back and neck injuries.

May 3, 2002 Blomington, IN: A series of explosions was planned at the Sims Poultry Company. Company trucks were connected by gasoline trails to a refrigerator truck that was rigged to explode. The refrigerator truck burned, but the others failed to catch fire. Sims Poultry had been targeted in the past. ALF took credit for the arson in a press release May 15.

March 15, 2002 Traveler's Rest, Ontario, CA: A group calling itself Activists Working for Animal Rights broke into a fox farm and released 40 foxes. The activists cut through a chain link fence and carved a note on a door threatening to "burn" next time. Most of the foxes were recaptured, but three died after being struck by vehicles on a nearby highway.

February 14, 2002 Trenton, NJ: Two PETA

activists filed a lawsuit against the state of New Jersey following a collision of their car with a deer. PETA charged that New Jersey's wildlife management programs were planned to increase the deer population "despite the known dangers an increased deer population poses to motorists," and thus the state violated the obligations of the government to provide for public safety.

Feb 12, 2002, Washington DC: FBI testimony before the House Ecoterror Hearing. "Domestic terrorism is the unlawful use, or threatened use, of violence by a group or individual based and operating entirely within the United States (or its territories) without foreign direction, committed against persons or property to intimidate or coerce a government, the civilian population, or any segment thereof, in furtherance of political or social objectives...During the past several years, special interest extremism, as characterized by the Animal Liberation Front (ALF) and the Earth Liberation Front (ELF), has emerged as a serious terrorist threat . . . The FBI estimates that the ALF/ELF have committed more than 600 criminal acts in the United States since 1996, resulting in damages in excess of 43 million dollars."

November 11, 2001 San Diego, CA: ALF broke into the contract animal research lab of Sierra Biomedical, smashing equipment and destroying research files as well as the company's transport van. The damage was estimated at $50,000. An ALF communique stated "No high-price contract is worth murder nor is it worth what the ALF will do to stop these murders. We were thorough and determined, they will not soon recover from our visit."

October 19, 2001 Portland, Oregon: Two anti-logging activists were indicted in the first federal prosecution in Oregon of alleged eco-terrorism by ELF. Jacob Sherman and Michael Scarpetti, aka "Tre Arrow," were charged with four felonies in connection with a fire that destroyed cement trucks in April, 2001, causing damage estimated at $210,000. They also face another federal indictment for fire-bombing three logging trucks in June, 2001, during the protest of the Eagle Creek Lumber Sale. Investigators found similarities in the two arson attacks.

October 18, 2001 Glenwood, Iowa: ALF cut wire mesh pen fencing and released approximately 162 pigeons, ducks, and geese. They emptied nesting boxes, removed breeder tags, and damaged or destroyed sheds on the property. This was their second action against this farm.

October 17 and 24, 2001 In Ellsworth, Iowa: Animal Rights terrorists attacked a small fur farm twice in six days, releasing 1700 mink to be hit by cars or fall victim to dogs, starvation, stress and cold. ALF claimed credit for the raids.

October 16, 2001 Jewell, Iowa: ALF released an estimated 200 mink from Isebrand Fur Farm, which had been previously targeted by ALF in 1999 when 3000 mink were released. This is the 70 time animals have been released from fur farms in North America.

October 12, 2001, East Lansing, MI: A letter containing an unknown white powder caused the evacuation of a mailroom, and the subsequent decontamination of 17 people, at Michigan State University. The substance was later found to be harmless. Evidence in the letter indicated it came from an animal rights group. The school had previously been targeted by activists in December, 1999 when arson, claimed by ELF, caused $900,000 worth of damage at a Michigan State animal research facility.

September 26, 2001 OR: In testimony before Portland City Council members considering the continuation of a joint terrorism task force, the associate director of the Oregon Regional Primate Research Center recounted his trip from Oregon Health Sciences University to a Florida university for a job interview. Animal rights activists posted the details of his trip on the Internet before his departure. Animal rights activists greeted him at the airport, accompanied him to most of his meetings (open to the public under Florida's "open meeting" laws), knocked on his hotel door at night and made threatening phone calls to him at his hotel. The university assigned a state police escort for him; he was surrounded by extremists at the airport upon his departure, and did not get the job, as he was considered a political liability.

September 24, 2001 UT: A card left at a gas and oil exploration site near Moab claimed ELF credit for vandalizing seismic equipment used in the operation.

September 21, 2001 UK: Ashley Broadley Glynn Harding, the mail bomber who sent 15 letter bombs to animal-related businesses and individuals over a three-month period last winter, was sentenced to indefinite detention in mental hospital. Additional court ordered restrictions mean that Harding will not be released until the Home Secretary is satisfied that he poses no risk to the public. The bomber's mail terror campaign injured two adults and one child, one woman lost her left eye, the child scarred for life. A trial, evidence indicated that he had intended to mail as many as 100 letter bombs.

September 20, 2001 Washington, DC: The Fund for Animals and Animal Legal Defense Fund filed suit against the Bureau of Land Management to block the removal of 21,000 wild horses from federal lands across the west. The suit argues that BLM never fully studied the potential impact of culling the wild herds.

September 20, 2001 NM: ALF claimed responsibility for the 4:15 a.m. arson at the White Sands Research Center, Coulston Foundation Labs in Alamogordo. The facility, holding the world's largest collection of domesticated chimpanzees, sustained estimated losses of $1 million in tools, equipment and records. Researchers at the lab study cures for aids, hepatitis and other illnesses. In the attack, bombs were placed at two locations, one went off and one failed to ignite.

September 20, 2001 UT: Activists targeted Tucson's Ronald McDonald statue in front of the Ronald McDonald House, a home for families of seriously ill children. The "ALF", "ELF", swastikas and vulgarities left on statue were the same as those found on the walls of a McDonald's restaurant destroyed in Tucson on September 8, 2001.

September 19, 2001 UK: Scotland's parliament passed a bill outlawing hunting with dogs, which would also end foxhunting by the end of next year.

September 19, 2001 NY: ELF activist Connor Cash, previously charged with arson and arson conspiracy for torching five Long Island homes under construction last winter, was indicted by a federal grand jury on a charge of providing material support to terrorists. Cash's transportation and procurement of materials used in ELF arson and vandalism raids were the basis for the added charge.

September 18, 2001 UK: Eleven people suspected of being key players in animal rights extremism are arrested on fraud charges, stemming from misusing tens of thousands of pounds obtained from the government's Department for Education and Skills. Detectives believe the five men and six women arrested at eight different locations diverted the money to fund animal rights activities.

September 16, 2001 UK: Investors doing business with Huntingdon Life Sciences won tentative approval from the Financial Services Authority to conduct business anonymously. A draft agreement is now before the Association of Private Client Investment Managers and Stock-Brokers to complete the procedures necessary to shield participants from animal rights activist protests and assaults.

September 14, 2001 IN: Charges against Frank Ambrose for tree spiking were dropped in Bloomington by the prosecution today, with reservation for pursuing the same or other charges in the future. Citing their conclusion after investigation that a larger conspiracy was involved in the tree spiking, authorities dismissed the case. Ambrose had been charged in January with spiking trees in June, 2000, at a logging site in the Monroe State forest, after being connected with visits to the timber sale and hardware used in tree spiking.

September 11, 2001 CA: Lindsay Parme, Geoff Dervishian and Lisa Lakeman, arrested at a July 21 2001 fur protest against Nieman Marcus in San Fran cisco are convicted on five charges, including conspiracy, obstruction of business and passively resisting arrest; sentencing to follow.

September 10, 2001 Germany: Animal rights slogans were left at a site where approximately 10,000 mink were released from a farm in Neuenkirchen, Osnabruk.

September 9, 2001 IA: Double T farms in Glenwood lost all of its 215 Carneaux pigeons, bred for research, in a night time break-in. ALF claims credit for the release. Damages estimated by Double T are $10,000. Farm offials reported that 24 birds were recovered.

September 8, 2001 AZ: ALF claimed an estimated half million in damage at a McDonald's arson in Tucson. "ALF," "ELF," obscenities and swastikas were spray-painted on the buildings in the attack.

September 7, 2001 IA: 14,000 Mink were released and abandoned in a night time raid on Earl Drewelow & Sons Mink Farm at Boyd. Fences were knocked down and much of the operation's facilities were destroyed. ALF claimed credit for the action, which caused estimated losses of over $100,000. About one-third of the mink found their way back, but most did not survive, hundreds were killed by passing cars after swarming on the nearby highway and others have been subsequently spotted at half-size, starving and hostile in the surrounding area.

September 7, 2001 SD: Vandals bypassed an electric fence during daylight hours and released 100 o 200 mink from a farm in Arlington. The owner was eeding mink in nearby sheds when the release ccurred, all mink were recovered.

September 6, 2001 UK: Protesters chained themselves to drums at a Shell oil refinery near Ellesmere Port, Cheshire in a demonstration against Shell product testing connections with Huntingdon Life Sciences. Police arrested 27 protesters after the road to the plant had to be closed, disrupting rush hour traffic.

September 5, 2001 IA: 200 head of cattle were released from a sale barn at Decorah, and were later recovered.

September 3, 2001 IL: ALF claimed responsibility for breaking, entering and releasing more than 750 ducks and ducklings from the Whistling Wings duck breeding facility in Hanover.

August 29, 2001 New Zealand: The 34th International Congress of Physiological Sciences in Christchurch, attended by over 3,000 scientists, received a death threat aimed at California Michael Stryker, a sleep deprivation research scientist. Animal rights protesters amassed to protest the conference and police responded with sufficient force to keep a lid on violence throughout the conference. An anonymous letter received by government officials and the press stated that a "good California doctor" was targeted and that before leaving New Zealand, ". . . he may be dead."

August 28, 2001 WI: In the continuation of a battle which included overwhelming support and approval last April for the first mourning dove hunt in Wisconsin, animal rights forces obtained an eleventh hour injunction against the hunt, scheduled for Saturday, September 1, 2001. Relying on ambiguity in regulation and contesting the authority of the Wisconsin Department of Natural Resources to allow the hunt, animal rights attorneys succeeded in putting enough evidence before Dane County Circuit Court Judge Daniel Moeser to put a hold on the hunt. Hunt officials are trying to notify the expected 30,000 hunters that the hunt is called off.

August 27, 2001 Canada: Hunt of a Lifetime announced plans to provide a deer hunting trip for a child with a life-threatening illness. The trip fills in the gap left when the Make a Wish Foundation two years ago succumbed to animal rights pressure to deny hunting trips for children similarly afflicted. The parents of the child asked the media to not reveal their location as they've been receiving disturbing calls from animal rights activists.

August 26, 2001 India: Eddie Bauer, L.L. Bean, Timberland and Casual Corner announced that leather from India will not be purchased. Travel 2000, German-based Bader, Gap, Inc., Liz Claiborne, J. Crew, Marks & Spencer and others have declared similar policies. The announcements follow animal rights publicity surrounding slaughter and leather processing practices in India.

August 23, 2001 Netherlands: In the second major mink farm attack in Europe this summer, hundreds of mink were destroyed on roads and in the surrounding area of a mink farm in Valkensward, near Eindhoven, when approximately 17,000 mink were released.

August 21, 2001 Norway: An ALF press release claimed credit for releasing about 1,200 mink from a farm in Telemarken, Norway, southeast of Oslo. Almost all of the animals were recovered.

August 21, 2001 NY: ELF claimed credit for damage in a misguided attempt to vandalize a site they believed to be carrying on genetic research. The Cold Spring Harbor Laboratory, involved in cancer research, sustained an estimated $15,000 in destruction.

August 20, 2001 Scotland: A box and note claiming the contents to be anthrax arrived at St. Andrews University, where William of Wales, future King of England, is enrolled. Analysis proved the substance to be curry powder, police suspected the anti-royalist Scottish National Liberation Army and also the animal rights' movement, which condemns William's love of fox hunting.

August 16, 2001 UK: One of the three men who assaulted Brian Cass, managing director of Huntingdon Life Sciences, at his home, received a sentence of three years in jail for his part in the attack. David Blenkinsop and two others donned ski masks and ambushed Cass as he arrived home, bludgeoning him with wooden staves and pickaxe handles. DNA on the handles and Blenkinsop's clothing helped convict him of the offense. Police are still searching for the other two attackers.

August 14, 2001 UK: A Brighton retail shop suffered 4 smashed windows after animal rights protesters complained about sales of products made from rabbit fur. Damages to the Southern Handicrafts shop were estimated at "hundreds" of pounds.

August 11, 2001 UK: An animal rights march in Oxford resulted in injury to two police officers involved in a scuffle with some of the 500 protesters. The marchers protested research at Huntingdon Life Sciences.

August 5, 2001 OR: PETA targeted Oregon for protests against the March of Dimes because of its support of research performed at the Oregon Primate Research Center. Billboards were scheduled for Salem and Portland, and protests planned at March of Dimes offices in Portland and Eugene. March of Dimes officials noted that OPRC research benefits drug addicted babies and the blind.

August 3, 2001 MD: Montgomery County authorities attribute dognappings by animal rights activists who appear to be dissatisfied with police response to dog abuse calls. Police are looking for Patricia L. Tereskiewicz, on information that she had taken two dogs from the back yard of an owner who had been the subject of animal abuse complaints.

August 2, 2001 UK: The Bank of New York found the names of account holders posted on the Internet by animal rights protesters. The bank, which does business with Huntingdon Life Sciences laboratories, had to change hundreds of internal passwords and seek the source of internal leaks. A protest group stormed the 49th floor bank offices at Canary Wharf in London a day earlier, but guards prevented them from getting past the reception area.

July 31, 2001 Spain: 13,000 mink were released from a farm in la Puebla de Valverde, near Madrid. 270 feet of fences were torn down and 1,150 cages were opened. The local citizenry recovered about 6,000 mink.

July 28, 2001 UK: Glynn Harding, a 26-year-old schizophrenic, admitted three charges of causing bodily injury by explosives and 12 counts of sending an explosive with intent. He also admitted to possessing bomb making materials. His participation in a highly publicized letter bomb campaign last winter and this spring blinded one woman in one eye and left a six-year-old girl scarred.

July 27, 2001 WA: A anonymous group using ELF communiqué-releasing services announced the spiking of "hundreds" of trees in units 5,6 and 7 of the Upper Greenhorn timber sale in the Cowlitz Valley Ranger District in the Gifford Pinchot National Forest. They claimed that 60-penny nails were inserted high and low in the 99-acre timber sale area.

July 25, 2001 NY: Via communiqué, a group calling itself Pirates for Animal Rights claimed credit for sinking a yacht owned by a Bank of New York executive. The scuttling and moorage damage were claimed to be in reaction to BNY financial services that could be interpreted as benefiting Huntingdon Life Sciences. Subsequent inspection by authorities revealed that the vandals had drilled several holes above the water line and cut a fuel hose on a 21' boat and had not sunk it.

July 23, 2001 St. Lucia: The coast guard escorted the Sea Shepherd out of St. Lucia's waters in the Caribbean after complaints of harassment against fishermen.

July 21, 2001 KY: ELF vandals slashed tires on 15 vehicles, spray-painted slogans and broke windows at the Dynergy power plant. An ELF communiqué claimed credit for the action.

July 19, 2001 UK: A nude Bruce Friedrich, campaign manager for PETA, charged President George W. Bush as he arrived at Buckingham Palace. Friedrich had a web address painted on his back, was clad in only shoes and eyeglasses. Police hauled him away, he was not charged, and later claimed that PETA had sent out 40,000 start-up packs from internet requests resulting from the publicity

July 17, 2001 CA: Authorities were called to investigate Heavenly Valley Ski Resort's new gondola in South Lake Tahoe after a 2x16-inch stick was found wired to a steel cable, safety sensors had been wired to the gondola cable and broken, and the letters ELF had been formed with wire at the base of one of the support towers.

July 17, 2001 NE: In the fourth golf course vandalism incident in the Omaha area since late June, greens and fairways were dug up and buildings were spray painted. ELF was spray painted in one sand trap, damages were estimated at $5-7,000 at the most recent golf course vandalism. Three teens were arrested on July 19th and indicated association with the ELF.

July 13, 2001 NJ: Eight protesters were arrested in Brunswick at the Bank of New York following a demonstration against Huntingdon Life Sciences. Two juveniles were released, but the remaining 6 adults were held in lieu of $25,000 bail on charges ranging from trespass to criminal mischief to endangerment of persons.

July 5, 2001 OR: Federal law enforcement officials met with US Senator Ron Wyden (D-OR) to discuss threats posed by domestic terrorist organizations such as ALF and ELF and laws that require law enforcement to follow ethical standards in seeking warrants for wiretaps and other investigative work. The laws have been interpreted by the Oregon

Supreme Court as applying to covert police actions, and thus prohibiting the use of deception in such efforts. Law enforcement officials note that this ruling seriously hampers their efforts to gather information and admissible evidence in the course of their work.

July 4, 2001 MI: An ELF act of arson gutted a Weyerhaeuser office in protest over support for the genetic engineering work on poplar and cottonwood trees conducted by Oregon State University and the University of Washington. An communiqué claimed credit for the attack, along with responsibility for the destruction of eight Ford Expeditions by arson at Roy O'Brien Ford in June, and the destruction of two plate glass windows and a drive-through at a newly-built McDonald's, also in June.

June 22, 2001 UK: Marks & Spencer stopped selling Indian leather products in response to PETA's two-year campaign against leather imports from India.

June 17, 2001 WI: An early morning fire substantially damaged the Redgranite feed facility, formerly known as a Mink Farm. Two firefighters were hurt in fighting the blaze, one was treated and released, one held in intensive care for smoke inhalation.

June 15, 2001 NY: Twelve activists were arrested while demonstrating against Huntingdon Life Sciences at the Greenlawn Branch of the Bank of New York. Police reported that the demonstrators stormed the bank building and disrupted business. They were arrested, charged with riot in the second degree, and held in lieu of $500 bail.

June 14, 2001 AZ: Mark Warren Sands was

arrested and indicted on 22 counts for setting fires to eight homes in Phoenix and Scottsdale between April 9, 2000 and January 18, 2001. Some of the luxury homes, under construction when torched, were valued at over a $million each. Sands claimed at his initial hearing that "God's work has to be done."

June 14, 2001 AZ: Mark Warren Sands was arrested and charged with arson and extortion in the fires of recently built and under construction luxury homes in Phoenix and suburban Scottsdale. A 22-count federal indictment charges Warren with setting 8 fires. He was arrested earlier this year after being caught tagging a home under construction with the acronym "CSP," said to stand for Coalition to Save the Preserves.

June 13, 2001 NJ: At least fifteen demonstrators were taken into custody after violating a restraining order requiring them to stay away from the home of an executive of Huntingdon Life Sciences. The protesters gathered at the home in the evening after a day of protests at a Bank of New York in Brunswick and also at the HLS laboratory in East Brunswick.

June 13, 2001 NY: Five Long Island branches of the Bank of New York were attacked by ALF and ELF protesters claiming that BNY was doing business with Huntingdon Life Sciences. Protesters painted ALF, ELF and graffiti and smashed at least 13 windows, glued ATM keypads and jammed card slots with plastic. A joint press release by ALF and ELF, issued from British Columbia, claimed responsibility for the effort (and also claimed 25 windows smashed). The protest was aimed at breaking ties with US businesses that provide a means for investment in

Huntingdon Life Sciences. The communiqué also announced a schedule for harassment and protests aimed at the bank and included names, phone numbers and addresses of targets, using both business locations and personal residence locations.

June 12, 2001 AZ: Four luxury homes burned overnight in a construction project inside an upscale gated community. Authorities are looking for ties to previous arson fires of luxury homes by eco-terrorists. The initials CSP, standing for "Coalition to Save the Preserves," were sprayed on at least one home. Two of the homes had been sold and two were still on the market. None were occupied yet, and damage was estimated at $2 million. The four homes in total were valued at $5 million.

June 12, 2001 OR: Jeffrey Michael Luers, age 22, was sentenced to 22 years, 8 months in prison for his part in arson attacks in Eugene last year. Another activist apprehended in the same arson, Craig Marshall, entered into a plea bargain agreement last November and is now serving a 5-year sentence. Luers's defense that he took pains not to injure people and was frustrated about the growing ecological destruction of the planet did not mitigate the measure 11 mandatory sentencing guidelines or otherwise soften his sentencing. The same auto dealership that Luers was convicted of torching went up in flames again on March 30, 2001, damaging 35 SUV's and producing over a $1 million in damage.

June 12, 2001 MO: A 30-year-old animal rights activist attacked a "Survivor" series cast member at a workplace safety promotion, pepper spraying him in the face and hitting several onlookers, including chil dren, as well. Police arrested the attacker. Michael Skupin, who lasted six weeks on "Survivor," attributed the attack to his killing of a pig for food on the series.

June 11, 2001 UT: A Bed, Bath & Beyond store became the latest target for animal rights protesters attacking supporters of Huntingdon Life Sciences. The ALF claimed that the smashing of 45 windows and spray painting of slogans was in retaliation for Bed, Bath & Beyond financial dealings with Stephens, Inc., a New Jersey investment company connected with Huntingdon Life Sciences, a British drug testing laboratory.

June 10, 2001 ID: In a second attack on the biotechnology building at the University of Idaho, ELF members removed survey stakes and painted anti-bioengineering slogans on the outside of the building. An ELF communique published on June 18, 2001 claimed credit for the activity.

June 10, 2001 ID: Anti-bioengineering activists destroyed pea patches at the Siminis research center in Filer. A communique release claimed credit for removing pea plants from about 20 patches, suspected of being genetically altered, and detailed information on how the facility had been identified through use of the internet and USDA public information on research projects.

June 6, 2001 OR: Jeffrey Luers, charged and convicted of 5 counts of arson for attacks on the Joe Romania truck lot and the Tyee Oil Company last year, faces a possible sentence of 7 ? years in prison. The Romania lot was the target of a second arson by others still at large this past March, with damages estimated at $1 million.

June 6, 2001 UK: About a dozen animal rights activists chained themselves by their throats to the doors of Morgan Stanley's offices in east London. The demonstration attempted to block entry to the building and was conducted because of Morgan Stanley's association with Huntingdon Life Sciences.

June 5, Washington, DC: At a joint-university news conference MSU's director of the Agricultural Biotechnology Support Project estimated that the university would spend more than $1 million in security improvement and repairs as a result of the arson that destroyed her office in January, 2000.

June 5, 2001 MI: The director of Agricultural Biotechnology at Michigan State University estimated that nearly $1 million had been spent to improve security and rebuild the fourth floor of the agriculture hall after arson destroyed her office in January, 2000.

June 5, 2001 OH: PETA launched its campaign against Burger King by passing out leaflets to school children in Dayton, Ohio. Students leaving Wilbur Wright Middle School were met by Mercy for Animals members handing out paper crowns with golden points impaling pigs and cows and details of how animals are treated in factory farms.

June 4, 2001 WI: Lawmakers are drafting legislation to make intentionally infecting animals with diseases illegal in an effort to head off agri-terrorism.

June 2, 2001 WA: After assessing the extent of wreckage from an ELF arson attack at the Center for Urban Horticulture on May 21, 2001, University of Washington requests $5.4 million from the state legislature for program and building repairs.

June 2, 2001 UK: About a dozen protesters demonstrated for approximately an hour in front of Iams offices in Leicestershire. Asking passing motorists to stop supporting the pet food company, protesters objected to animal experimentation in the manufacturing of pet food.

June 1, 2001 OR: The Oregon legislature unanimously approved the third and final part of a package intended to combat eco-terrorism. Last month, HB2344 and HB2385 were signed into law, expanding Oregon's racketeering statutes to include crimes against research, livestock and agricultural facilities and make "interference with agricultural research" a new crime. HB2947 includes technical clarifications of the crimes of research and animal interference and interference with livestock production.

June 1, 2001 OR: Incendiary devices were placed under 6 log trucks in Estacada. One went off, three trucks were burned, one destroyed. The trucks were to be used in Eagle Creek watershed logging operations, which have been protested for about two years to date. Damage was estimated at $50,000 for the destroyed truck.

June 2001, Detroit, MI: ELF vandalized a McDonalds.

May 31, 2001 Canada: In a raid late this month, Toronto police arrested two men and put out an appeal for apprehension of a third in connection with animal cruelty charges stemming from the videotaped skinning of live animals. The video showed a cat being tortured and killed allegedly by a self-styled artist and vegan protesting animal cruelty. Anthony Ryan Wenneker, 24, and Jessie Champlain Powers, 21 were arrested. The raid turned up a headless, skinned cat in the refrigerator, along with other animal skeletons, including a dog, some mice and rats, and the videos. Police are searching for the third person seen in the videos.

May 23, 2001 UK: Three men, ages 34, 31 and 34, were arrested for the attack on Brian Cass, Director of Huntingdon Life Sciences. The baseball bat brandishing attackers split Cass' scalp and bruised him and sprayed a would-be rescuer with CS gas on February 22, 2001. One of the men was arrested at an animal sanctuary run by TV script writer Carla Lane.

May 23, 2001 UK: Three activists climbed atop the roof of Japanese pharmaceutical company Yamanouchi in West Byfleet, Surrey. Yamanouchi has ties to Huntingdon Life Sciences.

May 23, 2001 UT: Animal rights activist Eric Ward was sentenced to two days in jail and ordered to pay a $1,850 fine, $375 restitution for damage to property and $715 to the fire department. The sentencing stemmed from a protest at the L'Ours Blanc fur store in Salt Lake City.

May 22, 2001 CA: The combination of the 1998 ban on certain kinds of traps and the ban on cougar hunting in California has been accompanied by a rise in alarming statistics. USDA recently released figures showing that the 5,600 animal kills by predators in 1995 had jumped to 14,900 last year. The loss to ranchers was estimated at $5 million in the year 2000. Mountain lions killed 3,300 cattle and calves last year, compared to 1,500 animal kills five years ago.

May 21, 2001 OR/WA: Two sites in Oregon and Washington were the subjects of ELF arson attacks

The Oregon attack at Clatskanie destroyed an equipment building and a maintenance building; about a half dozen pickups, all-terrain vehicles and a semi-trailer at Jefferson Poplar Farms tree nursery. The Washington blaze gutted laboratories and offices at the University of Washington's Center for Urban Horticulture in Seattle. ELF anti-genetic engineering graffiti was left in Oregon, no clues in Washington, however ELF claimed credit for both arsons in subsequent communications later in the month. The Oregon damage was estimated at $500,000. No genetically engineered trees were grown on the 7,300 acre facility. Washington's toll came to the loss of 20+ years of research, destroyed irreplaceable books, data, research specimens and laboratory samples, displacement of 28 staff members and students from Merrill Hall and $5.4 million in damage.

May 16, 2001 CA: Anti-biotech activists destroyed an undetermined amount of strawberry, tomato and onion plants at an ELM-owned research facility in Brentwood.

May 14, 2001 PA: ALF claims responsibility for hacking into Primate Products, a company that supplies primates for Huntingdon Life Sciences animal testing work. The web site was changed in content and graphics.

May 14, 2001 CA: Seven more activists were arrested for blocking a Pacific Lumber Co. logging crew's access to the Mattole River watershed in Humboldt County near Scotia.

May 13, 2001 MS: Since the beaver trapping ban of 1996, the Massachusetts beaver population, which has no natural predator to control its expansion, has tripled. The population is conservatively estimated at 61,000 today, and without controls, it's possible to grow to 100,000. Tree damage and waterway interference are causing significant property owner problems. The state enacted legislation last summer that gave local health departments the authority to trap and kill beavers when public health and safety is threatened, but did not fund the measure, leaving the cost for containment and correction up to the towns or private citizens.

May 11, 2001 CA: In connection with protests over Pacific Lumber Co. logging of 3,000 acres of old growth timber at the Mattole River watershed near Scotia, a 19-year-old AmeriCorps volunteer took a group of high school students to the protest site under the auspices of the Urban Pioneer Program offered by McAteer High School. The Program allows students to explore everything from rock climbing to auto mechanics, so when permission slips were requested for a trip to Humboldt County, parents apparently provided them. The students were supposed to be studying organic farming and efforts to revive salmon, however, the volunteer leader, a member of the Earth First! Environmental protest group took the group to the protest site where the students, aged 15 to 17, were arrested by police and taken to the Eureka juvenile hall (more than 20 protesters have been arrested at the site in the past few weeks). The volunteer leader, David Wehrer of San Francisco, was in trouble with school authorities and was also charged by the Humboldt County District Attorney with 16 criminal charges: 8 counts of felony child endangerment and 8 counts of contributing to the delinquency of a minor, a misdemeanor. The charges of trespass were dropped against the high school students.

May 10, 2001 UK: Thirteen Huntingdon Life Sciences protesters entered the Bank of New York's first floor reception area dressed as office workers, and eight of them chained themselves together. One month ago, SHAC protesters occupied the bank's offices on the 49th floor for 11 hours. Security personnel hauled the thirteen involved in this incident out to the street, none were arrested.

May 10, 2000 Canada: Loggers in the forests of the West Kootenays found trees spiked with concrete plugs. The concrete spikes, set in plastic piping and slipped into holes bored into the trees, had bark glued to the exposed ends, making visual detection nearly impossible and rendering magnetic detection useless. No one has claimed credit for the potentially lethal act.

May 10, 2001 CO: In a bizarre scenario, a non-profit horse rescue group, setting up shop on their 50-acre farm was ordered by land use authorities to "move" a colony of prairie dogs and to revegetate the property while it attempted to rescue horses. Because zoning regulations don't distinguish between moving and extermination, and because it's legal to kill prairie dogs on private property, and because revegetation is difficult to impossible over a colony of prairie dogs, the rescue group hired workers to stuff the prairie dog holes with newspapers soaked with poison. A zoning official stopped the rescue group from the activity, claiming that the poison would make the prairie dogs bleed internally and burst open, and members of the animal rights group Rocky Mountain Animal Defense came out and spent 4 hours removing the newspapers before being stopped and ordered to leave by the sheriff's department. In addition, the horse rescue group had asked the state Division of Wildlife for help in moving the prairie dogs, and the Division had spent $2,385 plus labor and equipment to create a new habitat on 35 acres of the rescue group's land and the Division is now contemplating charging the group for the work, if the extermination is completed and there are no prairie dogs to relocate.

May 9, 2001 Israel: Shraga Segal, an immunologist and former dean of the Ben-Gurion University medical school, resigned his post as chairman of the government body that supervises research involving animals. Segal received a faxed death threat and threats of violence against his family.

May 5, 2001 TX: Protesters acting against housing development in 37 acres of thick cedar woods in West Lake Hills, torched a backhoe and left graffiti on a portable toilet, causing $82,000 in damage.

May 4, 2001 UT: US District Court Judge Bruce Jenkins ruled that language in Utah's new commercial terrorism law may be unconstitutional. The statute prohibits light or sound waves from disrupting a business. That, for the judge, was too vague for enforcement without violating first amendment protections.

May 3, 2001 WA: Washington's voter-approved anti-trapping measure appears to prohibit the Washington Dept. of Fish and Wildlife from trapping river otters, one of the major predators of salmon and trout in state fish hatcheries. The Department is wrestling with ways to interpret the language or methods to gain an exemption that would permit trapping to protect the fish.

May 2, 2001 UK: 92 people were arrested in London during May Day violence. Protesters included environmentalists, animal rights groups and campaigners against arms trade. Police were organized and prevented the massive disruptions that occurred last year, and characterized this year's crowd as "largely peaceful." However, Westminster City Council estimated the damage in the violence-hit areas to stores, shops and other businesses to be $29 million and lost business. The cost for police protection was not included in the tally.

April 29, 2001 NY: More than 250 ducks were removed from the Cornell University Duck Laboratory and Farm in Eastport, Long Island. Workers Sunday morning found graffiti and dead animals and forcibly entered barns. Police believe ALF activists are behind the theft and damage. According to researchers, the ducks were being used in duck virus research and were on a special diet and probably would not survive in the wild or outside the laboratory.

April 28, 2001 CA: ALF activists entered the ICRC Company in Castroville and stole 28 rabbits. An ALF communiqué released after the theft revealed that the thieves did now know exactly what kind of research was being conducted at the facility.

April 27, 2001 WA: Governor Gary Locke signed into law this week a measure that would make it a misdemeanor to knowingly interfere with or recklessly injure a guide dog, or to allow one's dog to obstruct or intimidate a guide dog. Repeat offenses could net up to one year in jail and a $5,000 fine. The measure sailed through the legislature in record time after reports of blind people being harassed by animal rights fanatics, both verbally and by looking for opportunities to separate the guide dogs from their owners.

April 27, 2001 IL: Two SHAC activists attempted to occupy the Chicago Branch of Stephens Inc. Investment Company. Two activists caused a disruption in the NY Stephens Building.

April 26, 2001 MS: 30 activists from the Boston Coalition for Animal Liberation tried to take over the local offices of the Stephens Incorporated Investment Company. They were protesting the Stephens link with Huntingdon Life Sciences. No activists made it into the building, but three chained themselves outside, using pipe and bicycle chains. Twelve activists attempted to occupy the Stephens office in San Francisco. Three ADL activists attempted to storm the Stephens office in Atlanta.

April 26, 2001 OR: On the heels of cougar complaints rising from 151 in 1992 to 645 in 2000, an Oregon Senate panel approved a bill to allow shooting cougar and bear without hunting tags or licenses if the animals pose a threat to humans. Oregon voters passed a ban on cougar/bear hunting with dogs in 1994, causing a rural uproar over the inherent dangers in such protection. Despite animal rights proponents' assurances of relative safety, researchers say that there were more cougar attacks - and resulting deaths - in the 1990s than in any decade in the past century. Under the bill, animals that exhibit aggressive behavior or break into a home, attack pets, or are repeatedly spotted during the day near structures used by humans could be killed.

April 25, 2001 NJ: The State Commission of Investigation released a report on SPCA chapters throughout New Jersey, citing poor conditions, deplorable conditions, absence of financial controls, wanton spending and duplicitous activity. The investigation concluded in December, 2000, and recommended stripping the SPCAs of their power to enforce animal cruelty laws. It also recommended that municipalities should be mandated to place the enforcement function with their animal control officers. The report concluded that the welfare of animals in the state was not being served.

April 22, 2001 Germany: In one of the biggest arson attacks in Germany, a farm near Dresden that had been the target of animal rights activists on the internet was burned to the ground. Living quarters, feed houses and 8 large buildings that were used to house mink were destroyed. The farm was unoccupied and no animals were present, as it was being converted to crop farming for the upcoming year. The arsonists placed road spikes on the route to the farm, which prevented fire personnel from stopping the blaze.

April 20, 2001 WA: Over 300 mink were released from a farm in Snohomish County. All were female, with most due to give birth within the next few weeks. Over 200 of them were rounded up and returned to the farm through help from local farm families. Estimated losses due to the release are $35,000.

April 19, 2001 WA: Animal rights activists entered a Snohomish mink farm property from the back property line, walked through heavy woods, jumped two fences and barriers to get to the coop area, and released about 200 animals, causing an estimated loss of $35,000. The vandals released animals going from cage to cage and tore up ID cards on the cages that tracked breeding information. Some mink were recovered, many of the lost ones were pregnant. This is the fourth time Brainard's fur farm has been hit in the past five year.

April 19, 2001 UK: In the US District Court for the District of New Jersey, the US subsidiary of Huntingdon Life Sciences joined in the filing of an amended complaint against SHAC, Voices for Animals, Animal Defense League, In Defense of Animals, and certain individuals. The amended filing asserts claims under the Civil Racketeer Influenced and Corrupt Organization Statute (RICO) and cited physical attacks on individual employees, death threats, bomb threats, destruction of property, burglary, harassment and intimidation; and also asserts claims for interference with contractual relations and economic advantage. The original plaintiffs in the action were the Stephens Group and its wholly owned investment-banking subsidiary, Stephens, Inc.

April 18, 2001 WA: State officials determined that IBP Inc., the Northwest's biggest meat packing plant, would not face charges of inhumane slaughter after a prosecutor and state investigators concluded that a clandestine video of slaughterhouse scenes was heavily edited and misleading. A viewing of the full video footage, provided by the Humane Farming Association and other animal rights groups showed corrections of the edited excerpts by workers.

April 16, 2000 Finland: On April 16th, two men

and two women were arrested for animal liberation incidents dating back to August, 2000. On April 19th, another man was arrested. Arrested were Brandon David Elder, Mia Liisa Muhonen, Vesa Hyttinen (spokesperson for an animal rights group "Oikeutta elaimille," or "Justice to Animals"), Hannele (Hanna) Kauppinen, and Kristo Muurimaa.

April 15, 2001 OR: ELF arsonists struck at Ross Island Sand & Gravel in Portland, burning 3 cement trucks and causing $210,000 in damage. A company spokesman said that the incident also put three truck drivers out of work until the trucks could be repaired.

April 12, 2001 UK: Reports on the Stop Huntingdon Animal Cruelty web site indicated that a director of a bank holding HLS shares and a drugs company director were the targets of residential protests and vandalism, with the targets' car windows broken, "calling cards" left, and "garden furniture" rearranged. The report was later edited to remove references to the vandalism after a spokesperson for SHAC disclaimed responsibility for entries on the web site and stated support only for peaceful demonstrations.

April 12, 2001 Washington DC: According to "Animal People" (April 2001), IRS authorities are investigating claims of undocumented and unaccounted excess benefit transactions, lodged by a former legal executive secretary/office manager in the office of the General Counsel for the Humane Society of the United States.

April 10, 2001 UK: In what has become standard "house call" harassment, a director of the British arm of the Bank of New York was greeted at his home in

Southern England after work by about 50 animal rights protesters with air horns and whistles, some chanting at the tops of their lungs, and accompanied by a PA system recording of a dog howling. The noise lasted about an hour, attracted police and neighbors. The director's bank provides American depository receipts, which permit investors in the US to own shares in Huntingdon Life Sciences.

April 10, 2001 UK: The chief executive of Charles Schwab Europe described employees as being personally threatened, harassed and intimidated by animal rights protesters as the brokerage announced pulling out of trading in Huntingdon Life Sciences shares. Claiming that it was impossible to trade the stock through normal channels, the brokerage response was in reaction to pressure from a concentrated animal rights campaign against customers, investors, creditors and staff of Europe's largest research company.

April 8, 2001 UK: Roche, a pharmaceutical manufacturer with product testing links to Huntingdon Life Sciences, filed an injunction against the internet listing of names, telephone numbers and addresses of the company's scientists and directors. Roche claimed that after publication, employees had been harassed at home by demonstrations and at least one assault, and over the telephone with abusive calls, including death threats. Roche also filed a 50,000-pound suit for breach of copyright for the unauthorized publication of the company's building plans. Animal rights activists Heather James, John Smith and Gamal Gamal were named in the lawsuits.

April 8, 2001 Canada: The Calgary Herald carried an article by Grady Semmens which reported on reactions to the hoof and mouth disaster in Britain. The article cited Ingrid Newkirk of PETA, as saying in reaction to the disease outbreak, "If that hideousness came here, it wouldn't be any more hideous for the animals - they are all bound for a ghastly death anyway...I openly hope that it comes here. It will bring economic harm only for those who profit from giving people heart attacks and giving animals a concentration camp-like existence." The Edmonton Sun carried an article the day before citing an interview in which Newkirk reportedly said that introduction of foot and mouth to North America "would be a wake-up call."

April 5, 2001 OR: In early morning hours the FBI, BATF and Oregon State Police served warrants and conducted a search of the business site, personal residence and vehicles of ELF spokesman Craig Rosebraugh. Two others living at his residence were also named in the search. The FBI indicated that it was looking for information relating to the March 30, 2001 auto dealership fire in Eugene, Oregon. Rosebraugh was served with a subpoena to testify before a federal grand jury in Eugene on April 18, 2001.

April 5, 2001 CA: Activists trespassing on Humboldt County land owned by Pacific Lumber Co. were arrested for blocking the company's access road to the area. Two Earth First! Protesters were arrested after an elaborate blockade had been set up for 128 days. The company claimed that the protesters had threatened their wildlife biologists in their efforts to prevent logging on 3,000 acres in the Mattole River watershed.

April 3, 2001 MN: An outlet mall in Albertville closed temporarily when several milk jugs filled with gasoline were discovered on the roof. In one report, ALF claimed credit for the attempted arson, indicating that Nike had been the intended target. Nike shoes and clothing were sold at the outlet mall. Later reports indicated that ELF claimed credit for the attempt as a protest against Nike's role in globalization.

April 2, 2001 UT: The Utah Animal Rights Coalition and two of its members, Summer Adams and Bill French, filed suit to strike down a law passed by the 2001 legislature protecting animal enterprises. Language in the law included prohibitions of anyone from interfering with a business by physically entering the building or emitting a sound wave or light ray that enters the building (people targeted by protests have complained that laser beams have been directed into their homes at night, with the implication that they could be coming from rifles). The lawsuit claimed violation of constitutionally protected free speech.

April 2, 2001 NJ: Three adults and a 17-year old girl were arrested at a noisy protest outside the Huntingdon Life Sciences lab in East Millstone. Police sprayed about a dozen protesters with pepper spray. Arrested were Adam Weissman; Nichola Hensey; Justin Kelley and the teenager.

April 2, 2001 Germany: Wolfgang Ullruch, former head of a German animal rights foundation, went on trial for allegedly pocketing more than $31 million in donations and membership fees. He and two former assistants of the German and European Animal Relief Organization are accused of taking more than $45 million through a network of firms from 1994 to 1999.

April 1, 2001 NJ: The Animal Defense League relayed a message claiming ALF credit for stealing 14 beagles from a Huntingdon Life Sciences lab in East Millstone. The theft took place the day before a major protest planned for the facility and the day after protests at the residences of Huntingdon employees.

March 30, 2001 VA: An environmental radical group claiming to be a part of ELF spiked trees in a 300-acre tract in Westmoreland County on the Northern Neck timber tract. Rock Hill Lumber spokesmen said the company would have to invest an additional $30–40,000 to use metal detectors and take other safety measures when it harvests the timber next month.

MARCH 30, 2001 0R: The Joe Romania Chevrolet auto dealership in Eugene lost more than 30 new vehicles, gutting several Suburban and Tahoe model cars and causing $1 million in damage. This same dealership was torched last year and one accused arsonist from that fire, Jeffery Michael Luers, is scheduled to go on trial on April 3, 2001. A communiqué released by ELF spokesman Craig Rosebraugh described the incident and claimed credit for the destruction on behalf of ELF principles without specifically naming a group or individuals.

March 29, 2001 MD: Two animal rights activists were arrested after climbing on a Burger King counter and attempting to close the restaurant. Nicholas

Jonathan Patch and Sarah Anne Clifton were charged with unlawful entry.

March 28, 2001 UK: Dresdner Kleinwort Wasserstein removed themselves as the last remaining broker in Huntingdon Life Sciences, withdrawing after an incident involving one of their senior members and animal rights protesters over the weekend.

March 27, 2001 UK: Winterflood Securities deregistered as a market maker for Huntingdon Life Sciences amid mounting protests outside its offices and the homes of directors. Unless a second broker can be found shortly, HLS will be forced to move from the SEAQ trading platform to SEATS Plus, which is primarily used by groups with only one broker. Winterflood officials reported that the protests had moved from their business site to the homes of at least 6 employees, with up to 60 protesters outside a personal residence, threatening and abusive phone calls and terrified families.

March 27, 2001 NC: A state court dismissed two lawsuits against Virginia-based Smithfield Foods. The action had been filed by the Water Keeper Alliance in an attempt to force the hog producer to abide by environmental regulations without going through DEQ to seek enforcement of federal regulations. The coalition filed a similar suit last month in Florida and filed notice of intent to sue in Missouri. Last August, the company and attorney general of North Carolina agreed to conduct research on new waste management technologies. Smithfield committed $15 million to help fund research and $50 million for environmental enhancement programs.

March 27, 2001 Australia: Environmental rad

cals hold trees hostage in attempt to prevent a bat slaughter. In what officials term the most difficult and serious threat to the Melbourne Botanic Gardens in its 155-year history, a colony of 20,000 fox bats has been slated for culling. They have been destroying plants, some of which are rare exhibits from around the world. Frightening the bats had not worked, so culling by lethal injection and sharpshooting is slated. Activists vowed to cut down a tree for every animal that is killed, and have marked trees that they say are the first to go. According to Garden officials, vandalism has already occurred in reaction to their plans.

March 26, 2001 TX: Three unnamed ranchers and the Texas Farm Bureau and the American Farm Bureau Federation obtained a July 9, 2001 trial date in a lawsuit that seeks a permanent injunction against disclosure by the USDA of names and addresses of farmers using government-provided predator defense livestock collars, designed for use with goats and sheep. The collars are charged with lethal doses of fluoroacetate, which are discharged if bitten by a predator. Activist groups claim a right to the information in order to monitor taxpayer-sponsored federal programs.

March 26, 2001 Washington, DC: The Florsheim Group reportedly ended its leather contract with India, citing documentation provided by PeTA that showed unacceptable treatment of animals. Gap, J Crew, Clarks and Liz Claiborne are also reported to have ended leather contracts with India under similar scenaraios.

MARCH 25, NETHERLANDS: A slaughterouse burned, causing more than $4 million damage near Eindhoven. ALF admitted responsibility for the arson. The facility was closed for a few days prior to the fire due to hoof and mouth disease restrictions.

March 25, 2001 UK: An animal rights protester at a drug firm in Welwyn Garden City, Hertfordshire, was arrested after refusing to remove her hood and show her face fully.

March 24, 2001 OR: A group calling itself "GenetiX Alert" claimed responsibility for destroying over 800 young poplars used in research in two locations in the Corvallis area. Some trees were genetically engineered and others were produced with normal hybrid breeding practices. They were being used in studies on flowering, fertility and cross-pollination.

March 23, 2001 IL: Signs depicting farm animal slaughter in graphic and profane terms were discovered on L trains in Chicago. 28 were removed from the Orange Line and 15 were taken from the Blue Line. The situation was unusual because of the number of signs and the care taken in their format, designed to fit in with other rail car ads.

March 21, 2001 NV: At least seven protesters were arrested at a banking seminar hosted by Stephens Inc., financial supporter of Huntingdon Life Sciences. Las Vegas police were in complete control of the Desert Inn Golf Course and the Monte Carlo Hotel, both focal points of the conference.

March 17, 2001 CA: An ALF communique claimed credit for a raid on Sunny-Cal Eggs in Beaumont, that cited removal of 468 chickens from the premises and reminded readers of the last raid at this site, which occurred in June, 2000. Contact with the company revealed no knowledge or evidence of any break-in or any fowl removal.

March 16, 2001 GA: 5 Animal rights activists were arrested at a demonstration outside the Augusta Golf Club during a coordinated telephone blockade and public protests. The subject of the demonstration was Warren Stephens' recent membership into the exclusive, low-profile club. Those jailed were Chris Edward Freeman, Randall Reid Smith, Lauren Teresa Ornflas, Caitlin Petrakis Childs, and Joseph William Bateman. Instructions on the internet bearing the intro "from lauren@idausa.org" gave specific directions on clogging up the club's telephone system, both locally and through long distance calls. Lauren@idausa also offered to pay for long distance charges if calls were made.

March 12, 2001 UK: Llin golding, a Member of Parliament for Newcastle-under-Lyme in Staffordshire and opponent of a hunting ban bill, was warned that she is on an activist hit list because of her support of hunting. She was told to look for explosives under her car and suspicious parcels or envelopes in the mail. Golding has already found a coffin with a skull on it in her garden, along with an effigy of a dead huntsman and tombstones and anti-hunting banners scattered around.

March 8, 2001 OH: Student protesters demonstrated in front of Bricker Hall at Ohio State University. A group calling itself "Protect Our Earth's Treasures" criticized university funding and support of AIDS-related research that uses cats and methamphetamines to investigate the link between the drug and HIV replication rates.

March 8, 2001 UK: 62-year old disabled Peter

Rainbow was fishing alone near Harston, Cambs, when a mob of about 20 balaclava-wearing animal rights protesters terrorized him with shouting, pick-axe handles, baseball bats, drums and bullhorns. The intimidation continued until Rainbow called the police.

March 5, 2001 Long Island, NY: At least eight 10X10 plate glass windows and one neon sign were smashed at the Old Navy Outlet Center in Huntington. ELF claimed credit for the attack, which was aimed at the owners, the Fisher family, for their involvement in and support of the timber industry.

March 5, 2001 OH: On Sunday night/Monday morning, anti-research activists coated four sides of Ohio State University's Bricker Hall and University President William Kirwan's home with red letter protest graffiti. They also glued locks shut at Bricker Hall, which houses the university's administrative offices. Protests were aimed at AIDS-related research that used cats.

March 2, 2001 UK: On the heels of Huntingdon Life Sciences Managing Director Brian Cass' beating by hooded activist thugs, the British Parliament approved legislation to allow company directors threatened with violence to keep their home address-es secret.

March 2, 2001 OR: A communique from ELF claims that units 6 and 8 of the Judie Timber Sale in the Umpqua National Forest has been spiked with 60-penny nails and 8- and 10-inch spikes placed high and low. Survey stakes were pulled and destroyed. The Seneca Jones Corporation purchased the timber on the US Forest Service Sale.

March 2, 2001 NY: Two Schaller and Weber Meat Packing Plant trucks were burned by incendiary devices planted underneath them in an early morning raid by ALF activists.

February 27, 2001 CT: Connecticut State University bans circus animal acts at O'neill Center after protests by student animal rights activists.

February 27, 2001 AR: Animal rights activists from around the world staged a "sit-in" to shut down web site services of Stephen, Inc. of Little Rock, Arkansas. Stephens was targeted as the biggest shareholder and chief financier of Huntingdon Life Sciences. An anonymous group calling itself the Animal Liberation-Tactical Internet Response Network unleashed a "floodnet" program, used world wide by more than a thousand activists' computers, which slowed down and clogged Stephens' system.

February 26, 2001 Galt, CA: Ringling Bros. And Barnum & Bailey settled a lawsuit filed by an animal rights group by agreeing to turn over some retired elephants to the group and pay for their care. The amount of money and number of elephants were not disclosed in the settlement agreement.

February 26, 2001 UK: Animal rights activists target homes and property of Countryside Alliance members who have registered for a march in London next month. The Surrey Anti-Hunt Campaign internet site urges making the most of the absence of owners who may join the march.

February 26, 2001 UK: In the wake of the foot and mouth disease disaster, in which at least 7,000 UK cattle and sheep have already been scheduled for destruction to prevent spreading, BBC 2's Newsnight reported that it had been told by high-level sources at the Ministry of Agriculture that its search for the source of the outbreak was considering the possibility that animal rights activists might have deliberately brought the virus into the UK.

February 24, 2001 Nantes, France: About 10,000 hunters in Nantes protested passage of a law restricting hunting practices in France, while hundreds of hunters blocked roads for nearly two miles in a protest north of Bordeaux. At issue is the exclusion of hunters from the lawmaking process by Green party member and Environment Minister Dominique Voynet, and the new law, which restricts hunting seasons.

February 24, 2001 UK: Glynn Harding, a 26-year old man and one of three arrested last Saturday for sending letter bombs to agricultural interests, was charged with 15 counts of sending explosive devices from Dec. 15, 2000, through February 21, 2001. The other two arrested individuals were released without charge.

February 24, 2001 UK: Ben Gunn, Chief Constable of Cambridgeshire, reported that he had obtained an additional 1 million pounds from the Government to offset the 1.8 million pound cost of additional work caused by activist assaults on Huntingdon Life Sciences.

February 23, 2001 VA: Virginia enacted legislation making malicious damage or destruction of any farm product grown for testing or research for product development at private research facilities or universities or federal, state or local governmental agencies a Class 1 misdemeanor or Class 6 felony, depending on the value of the product. Courts in determining the market value of the damaged or destroyed products are to consider the cost of production, research, testing, replacement, and product development directly related to the product damaged or destroyed.

February 23, 2001 Washington, DC: Research by the Guest Choice Network turns up allegations that the communications director for the Animal Farm Reform Movement has been sending letters to the editor to daily newspapers across the country under different names. The latest was a warning opinion piece about mad cow disease, appearing word for word in at least 11 dailies.

February 23, 2001 CO: The Rocky Mountain Animal Defense threatens to sue over the extermination of 300 prairie dogs near core buildings at the 670-acre Denver Federal Center, which houses 25 federal agencies. February 20, 2001 CA: In an early morning raid, ELF arsonists broke into a warehouse, set incendiary devices and torched a research cotton gin at Delta & Pine Land Co. in Visalia. Damages were estimated at $700,000.

February 23, 2001 UK: In a major public escalation of animal rights terrorist violence, the managing director of Huntingdon Life Sciences was attacked as he arrived home by three masked goons wielding baseball bats or ax handles. Brian Cass, 53, bludgeoned with head and body wounds and bruises, including a 3-inch scalp gash, was saved from further injury by his girl friend's screams and the aid of two passersby. One of the Good Samaritans chased the attackers, but was debilitated by CS gas from one of the attackers. Cass, stitched up and back at work the next day, vowed to continue the work of HLS, which includes government mandated tests seeking cures for dementia, diabetes, AIDS, asthma and other diseases. In reaction to the attack, Ronnie Lee, ALF founder who is no longer with the group, condoned the attack and expressed surprise that it didn't happen more often, declaring that Cass got off "lightly." Other animal rights groups publicly backed off condoning the act, but expressed "understanding" of how it could occur. In calendar year 2000, 11 Huntingdon employees' cars were firebombed.

February 21, 2001 UK: Two men ages 26 and 36, and one 31 year-old woman were arrested in connection with letter bombing attacks against at least eleven agricultural businesses. Since December 10, 2000, three bombs were intercepted, but 5 of 10 others exploded, causing serious eye and facial injury to two adults, and leg wounds to a 6-year old daughter of one of the intended victims. Authorities considered all of the bombs potentially lethal. The businesses included pet supply, pest control, farming, agricultural supply, and a livestock auction agency.

February 17, 2001 UK: Rock Star Bryan Ferry is targeted by animal rights activists for declaring his support of foxhunting. Ferry's reunion tour of Roxy Music is threatened with protests; he cancels plans for attending a March pro-hunting demonstration in London.

February 13, 2001 Scotland: A letter bomb was sent to an agricultural entity in the Borders. Army experts were called out to defuse the bomb.

February 12-16, 2001 Long Island, NY: Suffolk County arsonist suspects are arrested. Four teenagers were charged with burning trucks and 9 homes under construction; and with plotting to burn a duck farm and a McDonald's. The group is linked to ELF and ALF. Arrested were Connor Cash, 19; and Jared McIntyre, Matthew Rammelkamp and George Mashkow III, all aged 17. Each could face 5 to 20 years in jail, $500,000 in fines and $358,000 in restitution.

February 12, 2001 UK: An agricultural firm in North Yorkshire received a letter bomb which was defused without incident by army experts.

February 11, 2001 UK: Nearly 1,000 animal rights protesters in Southern England attacked facilities of GlaxoSmithKline, Eli Lilly, Novartis, Roche, Bayer and Pharmacia. They also targeted homes belonging to company executives. Organized by Stop Huntingdon Animal Cruelty, the rally met at a central location and split to 9 locations where they smashed facility windows, broke and entered, destroyed machinery and upended cabinets. 87 were arrested with more arrests expected, pending individual identification from videotapes of the protests.

February 10, 2001 Finland: Karri Konsti's fur farm suffered destruction of all cages and the release of 40 foxes on this date, in the fourth raid on his facility. The foxes were dyed and released inside the farm property to confuse breeding efforts.

February 7, 2001 Washington DC: A McDonald's franchise was vandalized, with damage attributed to the Animal Liberation Front.

February 7, 2001 UK: Barclays Stockbrokers, a subsidiary of Barclays bank, announced that it will cease to hold Huntingdon Life Sciences shares in Barclays nominee accounts on behalf of its clients. In aking this move, a Barclays spokesman explained that "our first responsibility is to the safety and welfare of our staff and their families. Unfortunately we cannot currently guarantee the safety of our people because of the actions of a very small group of animal rights extremists. Until the actions of this group have been stopped—and we welcome the Government's recent comments on this matter—we feel the only responsible course of action is to stop holding Huntingdon Life Sciences shares for clients in our nominee company. We deeply regret this decision."

February 6, 2001 NY: Credit for smashing a Corlina Furs front window was claimed in an ALF communique.

February 5, 2001 UK: One of the 47 beagles stolen from the hunt kennel in Kent a month ago was returned to the kennel, recovered near Bristol by police on a tip. The dog had been castrated and an attempt had been made to remove its ear tattoo. Julian Greensides was arrested and charged with handling stolen goods. The hunt has put up a 5,000 pound reward for the recovery of the hounds and the capture of those responsible.

February 5, 2001 Buffalo, NY: ALF claims credit for a night time raid on a University of Buffalo campus Burger King, smashing 4 display windows and a glass door, and spray-painting the restaurant sign.

Feburary 4, 2001 Charlotte, NC: Ringling Brothers and Barnum and Bailey Circus train cars were vandalized with spray paint slogans, credit claimed by an ALF communique.

February 4, 2001 UK: In an attack near Nantwich Cheshire Beagles master George Murray, his wife and five other hunt members were assaulted by maske animal rights activists. At least five hunt members were injured by the stick- and whip-wielding attackers. Murray was beaten, kicked in the head and face and his wife was punched in the face. They were threatened with death as retribution for the death 10 years ago of hunt saboteur Michael Hill.

February 1, 2001 UK: Huntingdon Life Sciences reported more than 400 attempts by protest hackers to infiltrate its web site in the 4th quarter of 2000.

January 31, 2001 UK: Animal activist Charlotte Lewis was sentenced to six months in jail after pleading guilty to sending hate mail to staff members of Huntingdon Life Sciences. Her letters included the warning "If you don't quit HLS then your life will not be worth living. You will always have to be looking over your shoulder." Another letter read "This is a warning. Your life is in grave danger if you don't stop working at HLS. You will find yourself having a gun aimed at your stupid ugly head." Evidence against Lewis included DNA tests matching her saliva on the backs of postage stamps.

January 31, 2001 UK: Pershing, a division of the Credit Suisse First Boston investment bank, severs its links to Huntingdon Life Sciences, a drug-testing group. Investors holding shares in nominee accounts, which enabled anonymity, were asked to take their shares back in their own names and told that Pershing would stop buying HLS shares on their behalf. The move, according to Pershing's managing director, was aimed at protecting Pershing's own staff—who could not remain anonymous in normal operations—from harassment, intimidation and assault by animal rights activists. This move by Pershing follows withdrawals from HLS support already undertaken by the fund manager Phillips & Drew; broker WestLB Panmure; the bank HSBC; and broker TD Waterhouse.

January 31, 2001 UK: A letter bomb exploded in Cumbria in a charity shop owned by the British Heart Foundation. The woman who opened the package was not injured.

January 30, 2001 UK: Two nail bombs, sent to an agricultural supplier in Sheffield and a cancer research campaign shop in Lancashire, were detected and defused by authorities before being opened by the recipients. Both bomb attacks were linked to letter bomb mailings that started in mid-December.

January 27, 2001, Philadelphia, PA: The Pride of the Sea, a fish distributor struck by ALF activists earlier in the month again sustained night time truck tire slashings.

January 26, 2001 AZ: The tally has reached 11 for torched Expensive homes under construction in the Phoenix area. No one has claimed credit for the arson attacks, but circumstances suggest opposition to urban sprawl and ecosystem disturbance.

January 26, 2001 Netherlands: The Dutch government became the second European country to ban the breeding of animals for fur production. The 200 mink farms currently operating in the Netherlands were given 10 years to scale back production to closure. Current Dutch fur production yields 2.8 million furs annually, mainly for the Italian market.

January 25, 2001 VT: In response to a decision to remove "Got Milk?" posters from Burlington school premises, Governor Howard Dean told dairy industry officials that the state would be willing to help pay the costs of any lawsuits filed by a group that objected to the portrayal of milk as a healthy food. Superintendent Donna Jemillo's removal of the posters two weeks ago, after PETA objections, considered "equal space" for anti-milk ads an unworkable alternative.

January 25, 2001 MN: Frank B. Ambrose was arrested in Bloomington on charges of timber spiking, a charge punishable by up to 18 months in prison and a $10,000 fine. Ambrose is the Midwest organizer for the American Lands Alliance. At least 26 trees in an 80-acre stand of oak and other hardwoods were found to have been spiked, after which the Earth Liberation Front claimed responsibility for the act through an internet posting. Officials claimed that the distinctive 10-inch nails driven into trees were traced to Ambrose.

January 24, 2001 UK: Animal rights activist Matthew Holborrow, 26, was convicted of harassment and put under a restraining order prohibiting any approach closer than a half mile from Ponteland mink farmer Peter Harrison's land. Hexham magistrates noted three occasions of harassment stemming from pointing a video camera into a house occupied by Harrison's parents. The farm has been the target of more than 400 protests in the last three years, with Holborrow present at about 20. Harrison claimed stress, family distress and a heart attack stemming from the harassment.

January 23, 2001 France: The French fashion house Chanel suffered a web site hacker smear protesting fur fashion only hours before presenting its latest haute couture collection. Chanel's site was altered by the insertion of gory pictures and charges of "murderers." The hacking is under investigation.

January 23, 2001 UK: The Stop Huntingdon Animal Cruelty group (SHAC) claimed to have information on the identity of the anonymous US financial backer who rescued Huntingdon Life Sciences from dissolution recently. SHAC Spokesman Greg Avery said, "We will destroy them. They will come to rue the day they had anything to do with Huntingdon Life Sciences... They must be mad if they think they can keep it a secret." Protesters have established a track record of intimidating and backing off businesses and investors that could provide financial support for HLS. Tactics include publishing the names and addresses of shareholders, with web site invitations to "...get a list of shareholders in your area..."

HLS is the biggest contract research firm in the UK, with most of the work on new medicines for dementia, asthma, AIDS and diabetes. In the last 10 years nearly every new drug has had some of its research done there. Over the course of animal rights protests, HLS stock has gone from a 1990 level of 335 pence to one penny in the week of January 15–19, 2001. The value of HLS also fell from 350 million pounds to 5 million pounds.

Cambridge police received an extra one million pounds to help with the added costs of policing the protests at HLS.

January 22, 2001 Canada: The Crown Isle golf resort in the retirement community of Courtenay broke its silence, disclosing vandal attacks over the past few months. Damage included spray paint graffiti, destroyed course fixtures and slogans against "the rich" painted on greens with turpentine. A communique to the Comox Valley Record protested the development of green space and warned against building high end housing around the golf course.

January 22, 2001 UK: A pet shop supplier in Newcastle received a letter bomb. The device failed to explode.

January 21, 2001 France: Nearly 400 mink were released from a fur farm near Fecamp in northwestern France, according to police. ALF slogans were left at the farm, the value of the lost mink is not immediately known.

January 19, 2001 OR: Elaine Close joined Craig Rosebraugh on the witness list of people subpoenaed to testify at Josh Harper's criminal contempt trial scheduled for February 6, 2001 in Portland, Oregon. Harper is charged with refusing to cooperate with a federal grand jury investigating the work of ALF and ELF.

January 18, 2001 Washington DC: London Mayor Ken Livingstone, appearing at a luncheon in his honor during the US Conference of Mayors meeting, took a glass of water in the face from a PETA spokesperson who was upset over the plan to rid Trafalgar Square of pigeons. Bruce Friedrich, attending the luncheon under a faked press affiliation, asked the mayor about the plan, pronounced it "all wet," tossed the water at Livingstone and was hustled out of the room by security.

January 17, 2001 UK: A bill to ban fox hunting passed the House of Commons, setting up a battle in the House of Lords and pitting urban dwellers vs. rural traditionalists over the issues of liberty, democracy and a rural way of life.

January 14, 2001 NY: Radicals struck on Long Island, torching equipment shortly after 5 a.m. at a North Shore construction company. ELF claimed credit for the attack, which caused about $8,000 damage, destroying a pickup truck and burning a 14-ton payloader.

January 13, 2001 OR: The Oregon Regional Primate Research Center was cleared of allegations of animal abuse after inspection by 6 officials of the US Dept. of Agriculture. An investigation by USDA followed allegations by former employee Matt Rossell, who filed a formal complaint and released secretly shot videotape purporting to document animal abuse at the facility. USDA reported no abuse, but recommended improving monkey housing, providing more frequent fresh produce regularly, exploring new ways of collecting semen samples, and gathering monkeys in less stressful fashion.

January 12, 2001 UK: A letter bomb was sent to a pet shop in Coventry, it did not explode.

January 11, 2001 CO: Chairman Bernard Black of the Colorado State Wildlife Commission, who is black, reports that Stephanie Tidwell, a part-time staff member for an animal rights organization, called for a lynch mob after a heated meeting about allowing the aerial shooting of coyotes as a way to protect mule deer. Tidwell, according to Black's wife, said after the meeting, "what we need now is a lynch mob." When Dorothy Black told Tidwell to watch her language, the Chairman said three animal rights activists verbally assaulted and intimidated him and his wife. Tidwell later admitted to making an unfortunate statement, the Rocky Mountain Animal Defense organization sent

Black a letter communicating regret over the incident. Nicole Rosmarino, the official member of RMAD in attendance at the hearing, denied that she was involved and Bettina Rosmarino says she is no longer actively involved with the group.

January 11, 2001 UK: A letter bomb sent to a fish and chips shop in Flintshire exploded without injury to anyone. Letter bombings since December 15th using the same materials and targeting animal- and research-related enterprises are linked for investigation by authorities. MI5 is called in by the to assist police from several jurisdictions in the investigation.

January 11, 2001 TX: Houston billboard companies joined Cheyenne and Tucson companies in rejecting PETA backed billboards picking on the rodeo and meat-eating. The rodeo board pictures a buxom blond in a black cowboy hat with the words, "No one likes an eight-second ride," and "Buck the rodeo." The anti-meat ad pictures a bikini-clad model holding several large sausages with the words, "I threw a party, but the cattlemen couldn't come." Both boards were rejected for various reasons, including impropriety, offensiveness, sexual explicitness and promoting a political cause rather than goods and services.

January 10, 2001 UK: Animal rights activists were suspected of placing an incendiary device under the car of a prominent fox hunt supporter in Surrey. It ignited, destroying two cars and damaging another. Members of three hunt organizations were told to be on the lookout for attacks after their names and addresses were discovered on an internet "hit list."

January 10, 2001 UK: Cambridgeshire police chief Ben Gunn disclosed that the extra expense for policing the protests at Huntingdon Life Sciences have cost 2.6 million pounds over the past 14 months. He added that the tone of the protests was becoming increasingly bitter.

January 10, 2001 MT: Three protesters were arrested after hindering Department of Livestock efforts to manage bison. Wandering bison are slated for hazing back into Yellowstone or trapping and testing for brucellosis or if elusive, shot. About 20 bison are outside the park. Three organizations also filed 60-day notices of intent to sue Montana and the Federal government for failure to complete a bald eagle survey before building the buffalo trap.

January 9, 2001 Washington DC: PETA publicizes its intent to announce a negative publicity campaign against Burger King tomorrow. It wants Burger King to follow the practices McDonald's moved to after the PETA campaign against them.

January 6, 2001 UK: Attendees at Uttoxeter racecourse evacuated during the fifth race after receipt of a bomb threat at the facility. It was the third time a day of racing had been curtailed because of a bomb threat since cancellation of the Grand National in 1997.

January 6, 2001 UK: 47 beagles were stolen from a hunt kennel in Kent by animal activists. All of the stolen beagles had ID tattoos on their right ears, only 4 remained at the kennel, apparently missed by the activists. (See continuation at February 5, 2001.) As to professed plans of ALF to place the hounds in "safe, loving homes," Dan Murphy, the joint master of the Wye Beagles Hunt, said the hounds would wreak havoc in a domestic environment: "People who think that they are getting a gentle Labrador or collie that will fall asleep in front of the fire are in for a big shock. They are naïve if they think that these hunting animals will become cuddly pets."

January 5, 2001 NY: Animal rights activist Andy Stepanian received a 90-day sentence for breaking a Long Island fur store window. Judge A. Corso had indicated the possibility of a community service sentence earlier, but gave Stepanian 90 days and refused a stay of sentence pending appeal.

January 5, 2001 Philadelphia, PA: The Pride of the Sea, a fish distributor, sustained vandalism damage including slashed truck tires, a punctured radiator, moth balls in the gas tank and glued building locks. Credit for the damage was subsequently claimed by an ALF communique. See January 27th report for additional damage to the same facility.

January 5, 2001 UK: Livestock auction estate agents in East Yorkshire are attacked by letter bomb. One female staff member sustained serious eye injuries from the explosion.

January 5, 2001 UK: A farmer in North Yorkshire was injured by nails from an exploding letter bomb.

January 2, 2001 OR: An ELF arson attack against the Superior Lumber Co. administrative offices in Glendale caused $400,000 damage. This is the third holiday arson against an Oregon timber business in as many years.

December 30, 2000 UK: A mail bomb sent to a pest control company in Cheshire exploded, injuring the owner's 6-year old daughter who was helping her father with the mail. The girl was cut on her legs and feet by shrapnel from the envelope. Authorities suspect animal rights activists in the bombing.

December 30, 2000 NY: ELF arsonists torch three luxury homes under construction and spray graffiti on a fourth in Mt. Sinai on Long Island. Damages amount to $160,000.

December 29, 2000 NY: ALF vandals smashed windows and spray-painted anti-fur slogans on the front of Tres Chic, a Hewlitt, Long Island furrier shop. 10 coats inside the store were doused with with red paint.

December 28, 2000 UK: The ban on fur farming, effective June 2003 will cause closure of a mink farm in north Devon at a cost estimated at more than 6 million pounds. The farm now breeds 30,000 mink a year from a stock of 6,500 adult animals that have been built up over an 80-year selective breeding program. The farm employs 10 full-time and 40 part-time workers, and is one of 13 farms slated for closure by the ban deadline. Part of the farm will be sent to a satellite operation in Denmark, but 6,500 of the mink will have to be killed in the shutdown.

December 26, 2000 UK: Traditional Boxing Day hunting meets, 300 of them, produced clashes between hunting advocates and animal rights protesters. An estimated 325,000 turned out to support the Countryside Alliance in favor of continued hunting activities, while protesters from the Hunt Saboteurs' Association and the League Against Cruel Sports showed up at 120 meets in combined numbers under 500. Much verbal conflict, one arrest, and some hurled eggs and potatoes were the only reported incidents to mar the event.

December 25, 2000 Canada: An ALF communique claimed credit for placing 7 incendiary devices beneath seven trucks at a Burnaby, BC meat distribution company.

December 19, 2000 NY: A house under construction at Miller Place. Long Island, is torched and credit is claimed by ELF, with damages of $50,000.

December 17, 2000 KS: The Kansas City Star discovered a propaganda scheme in its letters to the editor. An animal rights response to an earlier letter concerning fast food chicken matched letters sent under different names to newspapers across the country and in Canada. Each letter had a different local author name attached to it and what appeared to be a local address.

December 16, 2000 CA: Approximately 30 anti-fur activists were arrested in front of Neiman Marcus in Union Square, San Francisco. They locked themselves into metal sleeves in front of the department store in one of their weekly demonstrations against Neiman Marcus participation in fur fashion.

December 15, 2000 UK: Agricultural suppliers in North Yorkshire received a letter bomb that did not explode.

December 12, 2000 UK: HSBC, the world's second-largest bank, "reviewed" its position over Huntingdon Life Sciences shares and opted to sever its ties with HLS. The move followed intense pressure from animal rights protesters.

December 11, 2000 UK: A subcontractor on his way to work for AstraZeneca. a major UK drug company, found cannisters attached to wires inside his van and a black bin liner propped up next to his vehicle. While phoning police inside his home, the van exploded, shaking neighbors in their beds. Due to the type of bomb and the employment connection to the drug company, Police suspect animal rights activists in the blast.

December 11, 2000 Canada: ALF claims credit for the arson destruction of a truck belonging to the Ferry Market warehouse, a meat distributor in Vancouver, BC.

December 9, 2000 NY: A fire causes $200,000 damage in a condo under construction at Middle Island. ELF claims credit, opening "an unbounded war on urban sprawl"

December 7, 2000, Haupauge, Long Island, NY: ELF and ALF activists smashed windows and spray-painted anti-meat slogans at McDonalds corporate offices.

December 6, 2000 NV: Dawn Carr, the animal rights activist who put a tofu pie in the face of newly crowned Miss Rodeo America 2000 last year has been sentenced to one year of probation and ordered to pay $1,700 restitution for damages done to the dress of 21 year-old Brandy DeJongh.

December 6, 2000 MN: The University of Minnesota's Student Organization for Animal Rights, with California-based In Defense of Animals, is offering a $10,000 reward for anyone who can provide information that a researcher is in violation of animal abuse laws. The announcement preceded a presentation by Matt Rossell, a former employee of the Oregon Primate Research Center who surreptitiously videotaped activities while working at the center and, after quitting, filed a formal USDA complaint jointly with the Animal Legal Defense Fund alleging animal abuse. The university views the act as outrageous.

akin to putting a bounty on the head of researchers and other people who are working to find cures for diseases.

December 6, 2000 Washington, DC: A coalition of environmentalists, farm groups and animal activists, spearheaded by fifteen law firms contributing $50,000 each, announced an all-out assault on factory hog farms. They plan to scrutinize Illinois hog operations for possible lawsuits.

December 3, 2000 UK: Police warn Huntingdon Life Sciences personnel and anyone connected to HLS support activities, contracted or financial, that they may become targets of animal rights protesters. The animal rights group has already gone after HLS staff with harassment, intimidation and car bombings, and has also published names and addresses of shareholders on the internet, urging readers to "adopt a director" to harass and intimidate.

One unnamed victim, a retired salesman from Surrey, reported that "They call at all hours, sometimes after midnight and up to eight times a day. This is a form of terrorism and it's very frightening . . ." He gave police a dossier of hate male and documentation of goods sent to his home by mail order firms. Other shareholders have been mail-ordered collect three-piece suits, garden sheds, sex toys and pornography. The activists are also writing to shareholders' neighbors, sending pictures of mutilated animals and informing them of their neighbor's support for animal experimentation. HLS said the mutilation photograph was not taken on its premises.

December 1, 2000 CA: San Deigo-based Jack In The Box received a letter targeting the fast food franchise chain with a publicity campaign and boycott if it doesn't certify animal usage suitable to PETA's demands. On the heels of its public battle with McDonalds over this same issue, PETA also mailed similar letters to Wendy's, KFC and other fast food companies.

November 30, 2000 VA: The beaver population has exploded, partly because of a program that imported them to restore their numbers, and the results are becoming expensive. USDA calls it an epidemic of destruction of private property, roads and crops. A proposed beaver management plan to rid the area of nuisance rodents is projected to cost as much as $272,000, or $135 per beaver. Ironically, trapping controlled them in the past, when pelts fetched about $30 apiece on the fur market. Today, the price for beaver pelts is around $8 and no one is trapping them.

November 28, 2000 UT: Jeremy Lee Parkin of Salt Lake City was arraigned on multiple felony counts for the release of 30 mink from a fur farm last year and the break-in and destruction of breeding records. Parkin faces up to 30 years in prison if convicted as charged.

November 28, 2000 NC: Three stores in Cary suffered leather and fur merchandise vandalism in the post-Thanksgiving shopping rush. Wilson's Leathers, the Limited and the Gap each discovered slashings and dark marker damage to leather and fur on three consecutive days, amounting to over $5,000 in losses.

November 27, 2000 CO: ELF claims credit for torching one of the first luxury homes under construction in a new Boulder County subdivision, damages $500,000. Activists blame the failure of the vot ers to defeat a ballot measure controlling growth.

November 22, 2000 UK: The fur farming (prohibition) bill to outlaw in England and Wales the farming of animals for the value of their fur was set for approval today. Effective January 1, 2003, it makes UK the first country to introduce a national ban.

November 21, 2000 OH: PETA is ready to premier advertising against clothing retailer Express for selling leather garments. A 30-second spot produced to curtail the desire for leather urges buyers to "steer clear of Express." Express has been the target of on site protest pressure from PETA since October

November 20, 2000 Germany: A German animal protection charity is being charged with the diversion of more than DM 100 million to secret bank accounts in Switzerland. Reports in the press indicate suspicion that "Deutsches Tierhilfswerk" collected DM 356 million in 1998, but only DM 2 million was actually applied to animal protection projects.

October 28, 2000 OR: Animal rights activists demonstrated outside the Portland home of Oregon Health Sciences University president Peter Kohler, publicizing alleged abuse at OHSU. Former OHSU employee Matt Rossell held a news conference, showing a video intended to portray abuse, and the Animal Legal Defense Fund filed a formal complaint with USDA to address the claims of abuse at the University Primate Center.

October 27, 2000 UK: Animal activists throwing rocks at the home and kennels of a major hunt last month caused the erection of a perimeter 10-foot barbed wire steel fence. Last week, more than 100 posters of chief huntsman Mike Brycroft, his wife and their 17-month old child, captioned "Meet the Brycrofts - they kill for fun" were put up in the local area. The Brycrofts are now under police guard as they prepare for the first meet of the season.

October 26, 2000 CT: Animal rights activists bidding on rights to trap on state land hope to deny trapping activity. On the heels of a court challenge that threw out state regulations requiring proof of trapping activity by successful bidders, the activists are ready to spend $36,000 again this year. In 1998, they won bids for 35 parcels amounting to 47,000 acres. In 1999, the court challenge effectively canceled the auction. This year, 160,000 acres is up for grabs on 122 parcels.

October 25, 2000 WI: Tina Kaske, animal rights activist and former public relations director for Alliance for Animals, filed a complaint with police in Madison based on claims that she had been called "trash" and a "terrorist" by talk show host John "Sly" Sylvester. Kaske claimed that Sylvester threatened to give out her home address over the air, that he asked callers to shoot off firearms as a tribute to her, and that an unknnown and ininvited 2 a.m. visitor at her apartment was somehow connected to Sylvester. Kaske left her position as Alliance for Animals spokeswoman because of the negative publicity. Police filed the complaint and never contacted Sylvester "because of his First Amendment rights."

October 23, 2000 UK: Two hunt members received death threats and car bombs. Both were on a publicized list of seven huntsmen considered to be "legitimate targets" by the Hunt Retribution Squad." All seven had received threatening letters or

September 4, 2000. Amateur whip David Pitfield's van was destroyed by one bomb in South Nutfield, Surrey. The bomb under a woman hunt member's vehicle in East Sussex, discovered five hours later, did not detonate and was removed by army bomb experts. Both bombs were considered lethal.

October 22, 2000 UT: Animal rights groups are filing a lawsuit challenging Utah's passage of Proposition 5 in 1998, which established a constitutional requirement that citizen-driven initiatives to change the state's wildlife regulations must win 67 percent of the vote in 20 of Utah's 29 counties in order to pass. Plaintiffs in the suit include the Initiative & Referendum Institute of Washington, HSUS, Fund for Animals and Rep. David Jones, D-Salt Lake City.

October 21, 2000 NY: A Moriches, Long Island duck farm lost at least 19 ducks in an ALF activist raid. Some birds were taken, fences were cut to allow the escape of others, and ALF graffiti was spray-painted on buildings.

October 20, 2000 Finland: An estimated 1500 foxes were dyed with henna and breeding cards were removed from a fox farm near Iisalmi. An ALF communique claimed credit for the raid.

October 18, 2000 IN: ELF graffiti accompanied damage to heavy logging equipment in the Martin State Forest. Destruction included cut hoses, smashed gauges and sand poured into fuel tanks and radiators. Damages amounted to $55,000. ELF later claimed credit for the incident.

October 17, 2000 VA: HSUS, Fund for Animals, a coalition of Virginia voters and Philip Hirschkop joined others in filing a lawsuit contending that

Virginia Dept. of Game and Inland Fisheries fact sheets are partisan leaflets supporting a proposed amendment to the state's constitution and that the agency's action amounts to taking a position on the amendment. Plaintiffs seek removal of the fact sheet from distribution around the state and deletion of the same information on the agency's web site.

October 16, 2000 Netherlands: The Dutch ALF claimed responsibility for building damage and torching three meat delivery vans in Rotterdam.

October 16, 2000 Australia: The RSPCA is caught disseminating misinformation about electronic training collars. A look at the campaign also leads to speculation as to the foundation for criminalizing the use of electronic collars in several Australian states, and the source for the Department of Customs definition of electronic collars as an illegal import, along with hand grenades and rocket launchers. During a court proceeding which led to an injunction against the RSPCA, a picture of a dog claimed to have an electronic collar-generated neck burn was found to have been a picture of a dog with an infection, not a burn. A photo of an RSPCA officer's arm showed three "burn" marks corresponding to the three probes of a No-Bark collar while the middle probe is actually plastic and conducts no electricity. Innotek Australia also introduced evidence of university research showing a collar's output to be 3000 times less than an electric fence, 50 times below the human threshold of pain and 6 times less than static electricity.

October 14, 2000 South Africa: Animal wildlife expert Ron Thomson, former head of Zimbabwe's Hwange National Park, sounded an elephant overpop ulation alarm, noting that with elephant numbers doubling every ten years, huge swaths of Zimbabwe, South Africa, Namibia and Botswana would be reduced to an uninhabitable desert. Thomson, calling for a lifting of the ivory trade ban, accused animal rights groups of hijacking the conservation debate by putting the sanctity of elephants above all else. "This is a fundamental error. It will lead to the destruction of the soil and plants which sustains them along with countless other species." Thomson estimated that half of the current 200,000 elephant population would have to be culled in order to avoid massive desertification problems.

October 14, 2000 MA: A security system warning apparently headed off a mink release in Hinsdale. At least two trespassers had cut 25 feet of fencing and entered sheds but were unsuccessful in releasing mink.

October 9, 2000 Norway: Animal rights activists released more than 1500 mink at a farm in southern Norway. About half were captured, but many of them were at risk of dying from exposure suffered during the release.

October 7, 2000 PA: Fund for Animals and others joined as plaintiffs in a lawsuit aimed at preventing a state-controlled bobcat hunt designed to reduce the bobcat population in the state by 5%. Bobcats are not endangered or threatened in the state.

October 6, 2000 WA: 29 animal rights activists are suing the city for civil rights violations connected with their arrest and detention at an anti-fur demonstration during the Democratic National Convention in Seattle. Claims include being forced to sit handcuffed or stand with their hands behind their heads in the sun for hours without water, vegetarian food, or medical attention, being strip searched and having been prohibited from calling lawyers. Charges against 41 of the 42 people arrested in the demonstration were eventually dismissed.

October 3, 2000 Washington DC: USDA agreed in an out of court settlement to expand its regulation of research animals to include rats, mice and birds. The agreement is the result of a lawsuit instituted by the American Anti-Vivisection Society, an animal rights group. The cost to biomedical laboratories is estimated to be $80–90 million if implemented. The agreement has yet to be approved by a federal judge.

September 26, 2000 Denmark: ALF vandals released more than 4000 mink from two Danish farms overnight, one near Soeroe and the other near Frederikssund.

September 25, 2000 Denmark: ALF vandals released 8000 mink in a night time raid at a fur farm near Frederikssund.

September 26, 2000 CA: Protesters at Bouvray Furs, a Los Angeles jewelry store, were arrested after an incident caught on videotape where two demonstrators kicked the locked security screen to the store. 42 animal rights activists were arrested, two were charged. One wound up going before a judge. The convicted protester, when finally identified by the court, was wanted in Illinois for contributing to the delinquency of a minor and had a prior conviction for aggravated sexual assault.

September 24, 2000 CA: Four protesters locked themselves together at the neck in an anti-fur demonstration at Bloomingdale's, Sherman Oaks. Store per sonnel surrounded the protesters with curtains and turned on music to drown out the chanting until police arrived. Two adults were held in jail in lieu of $10,000 bail and two juveniles were released to their parents.

September 17, 2000 OR: ALF activists struck Sunshine Dairy Foods, the smallest dairy in Portland, causing $3000 damage to vans, refrigerated trucks and a building.

September 28, 2000 NY: Andrew Stepanian, president of the Animal Defense League, was convicted of criminal mischief for throwing wooden logs through the window of a Huntington, Long Island fur store. Stepanian's cohort in the night time attack pled guilty to one count of fourth-degree criminal mischief on May 19th and was sentenced to 45 days in jail and given three months probation. Stepanian faces two and one-third to seven years in prison, with sentencing to be pronounced on November 17, 2000.

September 20, 2000 VA: In a night time raid, vandals painted golden arches on the front of PETA's Norfolk headquarters and threw raw ground meat at the building.

September 17, 2000 Finland: ALF raiders returned to the Christer Ronlunds mink farm which was raided three days earlier and this time released 2000 to 2500 mink.

September 14, 2000 Finland: The Finnish ALF raided the Christer Ronlunds mink farm near Voyri, releasing 600 mink.

September 13, 2000 NC: ALF forces claim credit for the release of 20 cats from the Gaston County Animal Shelter. Subsequent damage assessment by the County revealed destroyed fencing enclosures, a broken door and the absence of 58 cats which had been rounded up as part of an anti-rabies initiative to protect staff and students at nearby Belmont Abbey College.

September 12, 2000 Faroe Islands: A Faroese court fined Paul Watson $37,000 (US) or 60 days in prison in the case of nonpayment. The penalty was based on Watson's violation of Faroe Island immigration laws when he entered Faroese waters with the vessel "Ocean Warrior" to protest a Faroese pilot whale hunt this past summer. Watson, unwelcome in Faroese waters and persona non grata in all the Nordic countries, chose to be judged in absentia.

September 11, 2000 IL: The National Dairy Council and the National Fluid Milk Processor Promotion Board went on the offensive, noting that the Physicians Committee for Responsible Medicine and PETA are trying, with their current anti-milk campaign, to generate media coverage on an animal rights agenda based on little fact and no actual news. Both dairy organizations point out that PCRM's milk-cancer connection views have been repeatedly denounced by the American Medical Association, National Osteoporosis Foundation and the American Council on Science and Health. In fact, the researchers who conducted the health study used by PCRM to support their publicity campaign disagree with PCRM's position on the issue.

September 9, 2000 IN: A fire at the Republican Party Committee Headquarters in Bloomington caused $1,500 damage to the exterior of the building A communique from ELF claimed credit, blaming plans to extend an interstate highway, stating that th arson was "a reminder to politicians…that we are watching and that we will not sit idly by as they push for plans like I-69."

September 5, 2000 UK: In a partial summary of protest and intimidation, Huntingdon Life Sciences reports that their 750-employee facility receives about 500 abusive telephone calls per day, 200 at the switchboard and 300 directly to extensions within the system. All calls are recorded. Examples include, "You torturer, I hope you get cancer." "If I saw you on the street, I would stab you in the face." "You f** animal torturer, you animal abuser, you f** bitch." "I hope you get cancer, I hope you get murdered on the way home from work today." Employees of HLS also receive similarly intimidating mail at their homes.

September 5, 2000 Taiwan: A campaign started last June by the British Union for the Abolition of Vivisection and the Animal Protection Institute produced results when China Airlines announced that effective September 5th, it would no longer accept live primates destined for experimentation as cargo. China Airlines was the second largest carrier of primates to the US in 1999. Delta instituted an embargo in June and joined TWA, United and Continental in refusing to transport monkeys to the US. Other carriers have repeatedly rejected the urging of animal rights forces to end such shipments.

September 5, 2000 UK: After the recent rash of car firebombings outside the personal residences of employees at the beleaguered Huntingdon Life Sciences research facility employees have been told to register their cars at the company address, rather than their homes. One researcher, speaking out on the pressure, indicated that she is now on medication and having firebombing nightmares and struggling to put in 1 ? workdays a week. She has been harassed going to and coming from work, firebombed at home with damages of 5,000 pounds, and assailed even on her new mobile phone number.

September 2, 2000 WA: A Seattle woman who demonstrated in opposition to the Makah whale hunt by racing her personal watercraft too close to a Makah Indian Canoe was ordered to perform 120 hours of community service and to stay away from the Makah Indian reservation. Erin Abbott, age 24, sustained a broken shoulder in the incident when a Coast Guard 21-foot inflatable boat collided with her. Abbott's attorney has announced an intent to sue the Coast Guard over the matter.

September 2, 2000 Italy: PETA activists dumped manure outside the venue for the fashion week catwalk shows in Milan. Torrential rains happened to beat clean-up service personnel to the punch, washing away the entire mess shortly after the incident.

September 2, 2000 UK: Animal rights protestors rampaged through Surrey and Burstow Fox Hound Kennels at Felbridge, Surrey, hurling bricks and stones and spraying CS gas. One police officer needed hospital treatment after the raid. Animal rights spokesperson Dawn Preston said the incident had been provoked the day before, when a hunt saboteur had been "deliberately run-over" at Horsted Keynes.

August 30, 2000 Wellington, CO: ALF activists ripped wire from two bird coops, broke a lock on a ra cage and drilled through a corrugated metal wal before tripping a motion sensor alarm and fleein from Genesis Laboratories. Activists claimed that the predawn raid scattered 168 bobwhites and 11 ducks, all of which were native wildlife from eastern Colorado and Wyoming and which were undergoing animal experimentation. Genesis Labs corrected the information by explaining that the birds were quail and mallards, most of which had been bred in captivity. The ducks had clipped wings, could not fly and did not return, so were assumed eaten by other wildlife in the area. Some quail were found dead at the coop, apparently killed from stress and mishandling during the raid. Some of the quail were to be used in an EPA study to determine whether poisons used to kill rodents would harm birds, and others were simply aviary residents. The raid caused about $500 in physical damage, inestimable costs for bird losses, and resulted in the hiring of armed security to protect the property.

August 28, 2000 UK: "Urban terrorists" are blamed for planting fire bombs under cars outside the homes of Huntingdon Life Sciences workers. Five of six went off, destroying two cars and badly damaging three others. No people were injured, but one family had to be rescued from their home through a back door and a 7-month pregnant woman had to be treated for shock. Since becoming a target for animal rights protests, the cost for Cambridgeshire police involvement alone in the Huntingdon Labs controversy has run up to one million pounds.

August 23, 2000 Washington, DC: McDonald's Corp., which has long been targeted by animal rights protests, adverse publicity campaigns and the bombing and vandalizing of its franchise establishments world wide by animal rights forces, announced recently that they have adopted new standards for the treatment of animals by their suppliers. These standards were the work of their own panel of scientific advisers and are to be "a natural evolution from our animal welfare program," according to Robert Langert, senior director of public and community affairs for McDonalds. Langert asserted that "This is our pathway to be a leader on this issue." (See related news item dated June 27, 2000.)

August 15, 2000 Los Angeles, CA: 25 protesters were arrested after banging on the windows of Edward Borovay Furs during the second day of the Democratic National Convention.

August 12, 2000 Los Angeles, CA: An activist dressed in a pink pig costume dumped four tons of animal manure in front of a hotel housing Democratic National Convention guests. The activist was arrested and the truck impounded.

August 6, 2000 Holland: An ALF communiqué claimed responsibility for the torching of two storage buildings and the subsequent release of mink from a mink farm in Barchem. The farm had been "visited" by ALF twice previously, with the claimed release of more than 10,000 mink.

July 31, 2000 Dusty, WA: Anti-biotech activists used machetes and scythes to destroy five acres of genetically engineered canola at Monsanto facilities.

July 31, 2000 Norfolk, VA: Reports from Richmond, Virginia indicate that PETA took in 2,103 companion animals last year, found homes for 386 and euthanized 1,325.

July 27, 2000 Minneapolis, MN: Preliminar

estimates for security at the International Society for Animal Genetics conference indicate that it was the most expensive police action in state history, approaching $1 million. According to the Hennepin County Sheriff's department, riot gear, preparations, food, logistics, trooper availability, buses and drivers and additional deputy availability tallied more than $770 thousand, with figures yet to be determined for overtime for about 100 deputies; overtime for between 400 and 500 officers; and costs for sending 50 officers to Minneapolis.

July 27, 2000 New Orleans: "Survivor" producer Mark Burnett obtained a restraining order against an irate viewer who sent a threatening message to him after viewing the episode that included survivors eating rats. According to court papers, the message read: "Thankfully, there are people out there who have no qualms about (vengeance) against those who profit and glorify from the deaths of animals." The order prohibits following, contacting, or distributing information about how to contact Burnett.

July 22, 2000 Milo, ME: Activists destroyed 1500–2000 genetically engineered trees at MEAD Corporation facilities.

July 21, 2000 Anchorage, AK: The Sierra Club, Greenpeace USA, and the American Oceans Campaign won a federal US District Court ruling in Seattle that bans trawling for pollock, cod and other fish in Alaska waters. The ban, citing a "reasonably certain threat of imminent harm" to Stellar sea lions, covers waters deemed to be critical habitat for the animals. Estimates of losses by the fishing industry if the ban affects the last half of this year and the first half of next year amount to more than $275 million.

July 20, 2000 Rheinlander, WI: ELF claimed credit for a July 19, 2000 attack defacing US Forest Service trucks and destroying 500 research pine and broadleaf trees and saplings. A guard at the North Central Research Station Forest Biotechnology Laboratory in Rheinlander, Wisconsin discovered the vandalism in progress and prevented further damage.

July 15, 2000 Ann Arbor, MI: Activists cut through fencing and locks at the Humane Society of Huron Valley over the weekend and removed a dog on death row. The animal had been the subject of court battles for two years after biting a newspaper carrier delivering a paper to the home of the owner. The dog was held at a shelter until it attacked another dog and an evaluator, after which it was transferred to Huron Valley.

July 20, 2000 Cold Spring Harbor, NY: Activists destroyed a research cornfield, leaving graffiti denouncing genetic engineering. The field was where Dr. Barbara McClintock's studies of Indian corn genetics in the 1940's led to a Nobel prize for her work. The corn plants that were destroyed also happened to be the result of natural plant breeding.

July 11, 2000 Copenhagen, Denmark: Activists released 1800 mink from a farm north of Copenhagen in a night raid. 1700 were recovered. This farm was also attacked in the spring of 1998. July 11, 2000 Washington, DC The Performing Animal Welfare Society, the American Society for the Prevention of Cruelty to Animals, the Fund for Animals and the Animal Welfare Institute pooled their resources to file suit against Ringling Brothers and Barnum and Baile

Circus, charging Ringling Brothers and its parent company with violating the Endangered Species Act and other animal protection laws.

July 10, 2000 Surrey, UK: A rabbit farmer of 22 years handed over 600 of his 1000 rabbits to animal rights activists for placement, with the remainder to be given up next week. Activists targeted the farm as a lab animal production facility and forced the concession by laying siege to the farmer's home for 12 days, smashing windows and threatening his staff and family.

July 9, 2000 Long Island, NY: ALF activists claimed credit for smashing 20 large plate glass windows in the early morning hours at Macy's in Garden City, and painting anti-fur slogans on the side of the building.

July 10, 2000 Corpus Christi, TX: Three men were arrested from a crowd of approximately 70 protesting a proposed dolphin exhibit at the Texas State Aquarium. Construction of the 400,000 gallon habitat exhibit is awaiting the raising of $1.5 million in funds. One protester, lashed to one of two 15-foot steel tripods that were placed in a roadway, was detained and found to be carrying what police described as crack cocaine. Another was arrested for disorderly conduct and a third was arrested for inciting a riot.

July 3, 2000 Austria: The ALF is credited with an early morning fire that destroyed two generators, a tractor and a part of a circus tent and a truck belonging to the Circus Knie, an Austrian National Circus.

July 2, 2000 North Vernon, IN: A fire destroyed truck and caused an estimated $100,000 damage at the Rose Acre chicken farm. At the feed mill, the words "Polluter, animal exploiter, your turn to pay" were spray-painted on a concrete wall, along with the letters "ALF." The incident also disrupted the feeding routine at the 1.8 million chicken ranch.

June 29, 2000 Bloomington, IN: The Earth Liberation Front (ELF) claimed credit for spiking trees in two counties in southern Indiana. "Hundreds" of spikes were claimed to have been set both high and low in trees on timber sales that were prepared for cutting. Officials have found about 20 such spikes to date.

June 27, 2000 Chicago, IL: PETA bargained with McDonald's, offering to abandon its "Unhappy Meal" campaign against the chain if McDonald's would agree to stop buying eggs and pork from US suppliers who confine animals in cages or stalls considered by PETA to be too small. PETA also sought McDonald's non-buying agreements from producers who remove beaks from hens to prevent pecking injuries. The "Unhappy Meals" are mock-ups of McDonald's children's hamburger meal box, but with Ronald McDonald brandishing a bloody knife on the side of the box, and toy animals with missing heads and limbs found inside. PETA said it would call for regular demonstrations around the world and would pass out Unhappy Meals in Great Britain. (See related news item dated August 23, 2000.)

June 24, 2000 Honolulu, HI: A federal cour order protecting endangered and threatened sea tur tles called for 100% of longline ships to have a feder al observer on board on every fishing trip within 3 days or face suspension until compliance is achieve The National Marine Fisheries Service has tw trained observers stationed in Honolulu, and the long-line fishery includes 115 boats and 600 crew members. The order was written to remain in effect until the NMFS completes an environmental impact statement on how the fishery affects sea turtle populations. NMFS was given until April 1, 2001 to complete the task.

June 24, 2000 Eugene, Oregon: Anarchists with past actions linked to timber sale disruption and rain forest demonstrations were indicted on arson charges for allegedly trying to set fire to a 12,000 gallon gasoline tanker truck. On May 27, a driver for Tyree Oil found a section of cloth stuck in the fuel tank of his double-trailer fuel truck. The cloth was draped over a gallon milk jug filled with fuel and soap. Two devices were set, but crude ignition delay mechanisms failed to ignite the jugs. Jeffrey Michael Luers, 21, and Craig Andrew Marshall, 27 were arrested for this incident while being investigated for (and subsequently charged with) another arson that had caused $40,000 damage at a car dealership.

June 19, 2000 UK: Animal rights activists have been sending death threats to scientists conducting "badger culling trials," experiments designed as part of a five-year trial to establish if there is a link between badgers and TB in cattle. The harassment has been going on for two years, but the increased gravity of threats warranted increased police protection. A spokesman for scientists noted the irony that the trials might lead to fewer badgers being killed, as there is no clear evidence that badgers are to blame for bovine TB to date.

June 16, 2000 Paris, France: Brigitte Bardot was

found guilty of inciting "hatred or racial violence" by a French court and fined $3,000. Her offense consisted of including criticizism in her book of a Muslim festival in which sheep are slaughtered.

June 15, 2000 Lyndeborough, NH: Activists tore down a fence and released approximately 500 mink from Richard Gauthier's farm. He recovered about 200 by the afternoon of the incident, but many were nursing mothers that required matching back up with their offspring. About 100 litters remained without mothers. Gauthier's farm was vandalized in 1998 and he has received a threatening letter filled with razor blades.

June 14, 2000 Sacramento, CA: Activists have filed a million-dollar civil rights violation lawsuit against the University of California, the chief of a primate research lab, the UC Davis chancellor and police. The suit alleges beating and falsely arresting animal rights demonstrators, and is the second such suit in two years to be lodged against UC. The plaintiffs were arrested on June 12, 1999 at a primate lab protest and all had their charges dismissed. They have charged violations of US and California civil rights laws, false arrest, false imprisonment, malicious prosecution and excessive force.

May 22, 2000 Washington, DC: US Fish & Wildlife Service records dating from October 1997 through January 1998 were ordered destroyed, according to a USF&W employee. The 8-year employee, Bonnie Kline, testified at House Resources Subcommittee hearings that she was instructed to destroy the computer files, which apparently contained information on spending that was sought by th

House Resources Subcommittee. She refused the order. She then lost her security clearance, the combination to her safe was changed, and she now says the files are missing. No terrorist group has claimed responsibility for the disappearing files.

May 21, 2000 UK: A meat processing plant in Oxfordshire had ten bombs planted, one exploded and nine defused by bomb disposal officers. No injuries occurred in the attack, no one claimed responsibility for it. It was the second incident in as many hours as Regal Rabbits was attacked, with a 7-rabbit release by ALF in Great Bookham, Surrey.

May 18, 2000 Philadelphia, PA: An animal rights group based in Helsinki, Finland, is reported as attempting to dismantle barriers against US import of human body parts—to enable the sale stateside of PetCloaks fashions. These articles are reported to be animal clothing created from the skins of cadavers in the Far East and distributed by "Animal Mights," a fringe group in Helsinki. Spokesperson Maija Kiiski maintains that "turnabout is fair play."

May 16, 2000 UK: After picketing at least two homes earlier in the month, arsonists attacked the animal testing staff of Huntingdon Life Sciences research laboratory. Cars belonging to four members of the animal lab's staff were set on fire; two of the fires spread to houses where children were sleeping. No one was injured. The fires were set simultaneously, apparently to make local fire suppression response more difficult.

May 16, 2000 Burlington, WA: ALF burglars steal more than 200 chickens from an egg farm. Activists cut wire on about 60 cages and took approximately $1,500 worth of chickens.

May 9, 2000 Kauai, Hawaii: Hawaiian "elves" destroyed corn crop research at the Novartis center on Kauai. A group calling themselves the "Menehune" claimed credit for the raid, which described complete destruction of one test plot and enough pollen mixing throughout other test plots to invalidate the experiments.

May 1, 2000 UK: May Day demonstrators rampaging through central London hurled bricks and bottles at police, smashed store and car windows, and trashed a McDonald's restaurant, breaking windows, tearing down the large "M" sign and distributing food. Three police officers and nine civilians were hospitalized and nine other policemen suffered minor injuries. 42 were arrested.

May, 2000 UK/NY: Huntingdon Life Sciences pressure tactics against stockholders are proposed for US colleagues at a New York annual meeting of Huntingdon Life Sciences.

April 26, 2000 UK: The Association of the British Pharmaceuticals Industry warned that Britain's drug companies could be forced to shift their research activities abroad to avoid an outbreak of terrorist attacks by animal rights groups. Association president Bill Fullagar noted the recent rise in biophobia and animal extremism, stating, "It cannot fail to have an effect on considerations about how and where we do research." See May 16, 2000 for related information.

April 25, 2000 UK: AMP news reports that blackmail charges were filed against the leader of a group that had targeted stockholders of Huntingdon Life Sciences. Niels Hansen was questioned regarding 1,700 counts of alleged blackmail, which correspond ed to the number of letters sent to stockholders warning of protests outside their homes unless they sold their stock in the company. See May 16, 2000 for related information.

April 24, 2000 San Diego, CA: 17 windows were broken at Neiman Marcus department store, ALF graffiti reported to have been apparent at the scene.

April 19, 2000 Dinan, France: A bomb explosion at a McDonald's restaurant killed an employee—a 28-year old relative of the owner. The bomb shattered windows and blew off a part of the restaurant's roof. No one has stepped up to claim credit for the bombing, but the Breton Revolutionary Army, which is seeking greater autonomy for Brittany's Breton-speaking population, is at least one suspect group. However, the mayor of Dinan, Rene Benoit, said that Dinan "is a very calm town. It has no link to the Breton independence movement, which some people say is linked to the attack."

April 8, 2000 Salt Lake City, UT: ALF graffiti was left at a burglarized leather shop, at a Burger King and two Arby's restaurants. Vandals smashed windows, scattered glass and spray-painted the buildings.

April 7, 2000 Sonoma County, CA: An anti-biotech group calling itself the "Petaluma Pruners" destroyed grape plant root stock grown by the biotechnology corporation Vinifera.

April 1, 2000 University of Minnesota: A group calling itself the "Genetic Jokers" trashed 6 vehicles belonging to the US Forest Service, sprayed graffiti, jammed locks and coated windows with etching cream at the offices of the USFS North Central Forest Experiment Station research building.

April, 2000 San Diego, CA: Physicians Committee for Responsible Medicine puts up a billboard in opposition to the March of Dimes.

March 29, 2000 British Columbia: A group calling itself the "Ministry of Forest Defense" destroyed 1,600 test trees at a provincial seed orchard.

March 28, 2000 UK: A radical animal rights organization threatens doorstep protests against stockholders of Huntingdon Life Sciences unless they sell their holdings. Share prices fell heavily on the London Exchange immediately after the threat. See April 25, 2000 report for further action on this item.

March 27, 2000 Boston, Mass: Four protesters were arrested and charged with disorderly conduct outside the nation's largest biotechnology conference.

March 25, 2000 Minnesota: ELF claimed credit for sabotaging construction equipment and materials being used in a highway rerouting that was claimed to endanger water resources. They smashed parts, cut hoses and dumped dirt and sand into the gas tanks and oil tubes of four vehicles, and destroyed a half mile of survey stakes.

March 25, 2000 Chandler, AZ: Revlon manager Richard D. Simer's finger was blown off and his legs and chest were peppered with shrapnel when he opened a package bomb addressed to him and delivered to his driveway. No suspects have been named and no person or group has claimed credit for the bombing.

March 17, 2000 San Francisco Bay Area: The College of Notre Dame in Belmont, CA, experienced the unplanned end of a 72-year old research project when thieves broke into a university professor's ani mal trailer and stole all 250 test mice from their cages. Biology professor Elizabeth Center's work with the mice utilized generational observations of colony development that started in 1928 in seeking causes of genetic birth defects and osteoporosis. No animal rights groups have claimed credit for the rodent theft.

March 13, 2000 Viroqua, Wisconsin: ALF claimed responsibility for attempting to torch a former mink feed supply house. The warehouse once served as Kickapoo Fur Foods, but now houses gourmet dog food. The incendiary devices failed to ignite and caused minimal damage.

March 10, 2000 New York: Chrissy Hynde, lead singer of The Pretenders, along with PETA president Ingrid Newkirk, Paul Haje and Paul Chetirkin were charged with criminal mischief and trespassing after they tore leather and suede garments inside a display window at a Gap store in midtown Manhattan.

March 3, 2000 Holland: ALF releases 2–3,000 mink in conjunction with raid noted above on February 27, 2000/

March, 2000 UK: In the first week of March, 2000, while the head of a lab monkey production center slept in her home, along with her husband and 12-year old son, arsonists broke into their garage and torched their two cars. The woman, a former veterinarian, has been the subject of continuing attacks. Last year 25 men and women hid behind balaclavas and used bricks to smash the front and side windows of her house and the family cars. She has driven into her remote-controlled entry garage to find four thugs waiting with sledge hammers to smash the front, side and back windows of her car while she was trapped inside. A hearse was sent to her house after a local undertaker had been told that she was dead. The staff at her place of employment has received threatening letters with razors inside, and they have also had similar visits at their homes from terrorists. Local authorities are investigating the current incident as an arson, seeking ALF suspects.

February 27, 2000 San Francisco Bay Area: An ALF tag was left on the building after smashing 29 windows at Neiman Marcus causing $100,000 in damages. Two activists attending a fur protest at the same location the following day were arrested and charged with trespassing and felony vandalism in connection with the damage. ALF's Bay area damage claims from December 20, 1999 through this incident amount to an estimated $500,000.

February 27, 2000 Holland: ALF claimed credit for releasing two to three thousand mink in combination with a raid on March 3, 2000, at mink farms in the villages of Putten and Barchem. The release was timed to preempt the breeding season. The group also took breeding cards and destroyed them off site and left ALF graffiti and the reminder "While you sleep, ALF destroys your world."

February 25, 2000 San Francisco Bay Area: ALF used incendiary devices to burn down four trucks at B&K Universal in Fremont.

February 15, 2000 Vancouver, BC: A group calling itself "The Lorax" claimed credit for inserting 5- and 10-inch spikes into hundreds of trees in the Elaho Valley, about 3 hours north of Vancouver, BC Reasons for the action were claimed as tree cutting prevention and preservation of grizzly bear habitat.

February 9, 2000 University of Minnesota: ELF claimed credit for overturning 800 genetically engineered oat plants that were the subject of a disease resistance experiment. They also sabotaged construction vehicles and sifted salt into concrete destined for a controversial highway project in Minneapolis.

February 6, 2000 Bellingham, WA: Psychology labs in Miller hall at Western Washington University were spray painted. Suspects were the same ALF activists who released rats and rabbits in October, 1999.

January 29, 2000 Monroe, WA: Activists broke in and released 60 mink from Brainard's Fur Farm in Monroe, Washington.

February 23, 2000 San Francisco Bay Area: The Sonoma County Farm Bureau announced a $50,000 reward for information leading to the arrest and conviction of ALF-claimed raids in the Bay area. Later, on March 16, 2000, the Farm Bureau's office was broken into, trashed, files strewn, desk contents scattered, but nothing of value was taken. No one yet has claimed responsibility for the vandalism.

January 24, 2000 Bloomington, IN: ELF claimed credit for torching a house in a development that was criticized as endangering the water supply for the Bloomington area. The $200,000 in damage destroyed the start of a $700,000 finished product.

January 23, 2000 San Francisco Bay Area: ALF attempted arson by inserting flammable material through the mail slot at Primate Products in Redwood City.

January 20, 2000 Long Island, NY: ALF launched multiple attacks on 7 fur stores across Nassau and Suffolk counties in early morning hours. Damage included broken windows, damaged vehicles, locks glued shut, graffiti, lighting destruction, billboard damage and utility vandalism.

January 16, 2000 Plymouth, Wisconsin: Two vanloads of masked terrorists descended on the farm of Gene Meyer and proceeded to harass and terrorize him. His neighbor copied down the visitors' license plate numbers and called the police, who then found the vans and the occupants and arrested 14 suspects, ranging in age from 17 to 26. Meyer's farm had been the target of a mink raid on August 9, 1999, when 3,000 animals were released. On that date also, the United Feed mill, just 10 minutes away, was torched, causing $1.2 million in damage. Both actions were claimed for credit by the ALF. Among those charged with disorderly conduct while masked were Kim Berardi, 22, director of the Animal Defense League of Chicago; and Matthew Bullard, 25, of the Student Organization for Animal Rights in Minnesota.

January 15, 2000 San Francisco Bay Area: ALF planted five incendiary devices in offices and trucks at Petaluma Farms. All ignited. Two trucks were destroyed.

January 11, 2000 San Francisco Bay Area: The "Reclaim the Seeds" group broke into the Western Regional Research Center of the USDA's Agricultural Research Service at the U of Cal's Plant Gene Expression Center in Albany, CA. Their communique claimed to have destroyed over half the crop and to have "ruined the experiment."

January 10, 2000 Stanwood, WA: ALF was credited for a raid on the R&R Research and Rabbitry facility in Stanwood, which took 23 rabbits.

January 3, 2000 San Francisco Bay Area: ALF planted five incendiary devices in offices, storage facilities and trucks at Rancho Veal Corp. in Petaluma. Rancho Veal was hit in 1997 by ALF, too. The current arson created $250,000 in damages.

January 3, 2000 UK: In a second mink raid on Crowhill Farm in Ringwood in less than 18 months, ALF released 300 of the 1,400 animals at the facility. The prior raid released up to 3,000 into the surrounding countryside.

January 1, 2000 Belgium: ALF attacked a store of the Belgian fur company Pelsland by pouring benzine through a ventilation duct and lighting it. The fire went out for lack of oxygen without damaging the building severely. An ALF spray-painted tag was left at the scene.

December 31, 1999 Michigan State University: ELF claimed responsibility for torching the Agriculture Hall, destroying property and years of research on genetically engineered crops. Damages have been estimated at more than $1 million. Catherine Ives, a target in the raid, lost academic records, lecture notes, slide presentations, books, and her passport in the fire, describing it as seeing her entire career go up in smoke. Her $18 million program was targeted by ELF for accepting funding from Monsanto. Ives acknowledged that Monsanto once did contribute $2,000 to her program to train African farmers in modern agricultural methods.

December 25, 1999 Monmouth, Oregon: Forest industry Boise Cascade's regional headquarters were destroyed in a fire. Credit claimed by Earth Liberation Front (ELF). Damages were estimated at $1 million.

December 20, 1999 San Francisco Bay Area: ALF attempted major destruction but failed in an arson attempt at Fulton Poultry Processors. One of four incendiary devices went off, causing minor damage.

November 20, 1999 Washington State University: ALF raid on poultry research facility, destruction and trashing in several labs and offices.

October 26, 1999 UK: Graham Hall, award-winning TV filmmaker was tortured by animal rights extremists in a sadistic revenge ritual. Earlier this year Hall won the highest award British TV can bestow for his expose on the fanatics behind the Animal Liberation Front. Eleven months following airing of his expose he was kidnapped at gun point, blindfolded and driven to an unidentified house where he was bound and told he would be killed. After several hours his assailants surrounded him, forced his head between his legs and burned ALF into his bare back in 4″ high letters using a branding iron. According to Hall, as they ended their branding ritual one of them made a comment about justice being done and another chuckled something about the justice department, which is the name given to the part of ALF that takes credit for criminal actions against people, as opposed to property. Before the ordeal ended animal extremists threatened to harm Hall's family, to torch his house and to kill him if he went to the police. Hall's back is permanently mutilated from the branding. Surveillance equipment picked up an intruder attempting to climb into his yard carrying something that looked like a pickaxe handle. Once spotted, the intruder quickly retreated.

While denying any knowledge of the attack, Robin

Webb, ALF's official spokesperson issued a chilling warning to Hall and any others who might try to get in the way of the Animal Liberation Front's crusade saying, "people who make a living in this way have to expect from time to time to take the consequences of their actions."

October 25, 1999 USA: Following a communique by an animal rights group calling itself the Justice Department warning that it mailed over eighty razor blade,booby-trapped packages to primate research scientists, seven such envelopes were received by primate research facilities in various parts of the country.In September similar envelopes with razor blades, some dipped in rat poison,were mailed to fur farmers.

October 24, 1999 Bellingham, WA: Animal rightists broke into Western Washington University stealing several laboratory animals.Campus police said that the vandalismassociated with the break in points to the Animal LiberationFront. October 22, 1999 Warwick, Rhode Island:In the early morning hours a fur store's delivery van was destroyed by fire.Local police believe the fire was set by a radical animal-rights group.The Animal Liberation Front's acronym "ALF" was spray painted on the building along with slogans against killing animals.

October 24, 1999 Western Washington University: ALF raid, 37 rats and 4 rabbits released.

October 16, 1999 Nassau, Long Island, NY: The Animal Liberation Front attacked four McDonalds outlets in Nassau, Long Island, NY. Total damage costs from the broken windows and spray paint exceeded $23,000.

September 4, 1999 USA: The Justice Department,

an animal rights terrorism organization, claimed responsibility for booby-trapped razor blade packages sent through the mail to dozens of mink farmers, fur farm suppliers, and fur industry officials. The Frontline Information Service of the Animal Liberation Front reported that the envelopes included the following message: "You have been targetted (sic). You have until autumn of ther (sic) year 2000 to release all of your animal captives and get out of the bloody fur trade. If you do not heed our warning your violence will be turned back upon you." Some of the razor blades had been dipped in rat poison.

August, 1999 USA: Biotech crop killers calling themselves the "Seeds of Resistance" hacked down a half-acre plot of experimental corn at the University of Maine-owned Rogers Farm. Plant gene-splicing in this experiment was aimed at reducing the need for herbicide use.

August 31, 1999, Fulton County, GA: ALF torches a McDonalds restaurant. 1998, Belgium: The ALF claimed responsibility for nine attacks against McDonalds and another fast food restaurant.

August 29, 1999 Orange, California: The Animal Liberation Front stole 46 dogs from Bio-Devices Inc., a research facility. ALF spray-painted "Vivisection is Fraud" and "Animal Liberation" on the walls.

August 28, 1999 West Islip, Long Island, New York: The Animal Liberation Front took credit for stealing a stump-tailed macaque from a pet store on August 27.

August 23, 1999 Westboro, Massachusetts: Eight animal-rights activists face charges they threatened to kill a man they believed was an anima researcher, police said. The suspects, some dressed in military fatigues and wearing black bandannas over their faces, allegedly confronted the man at his Northboro home late Saturday night and yelled, "Animals live and he's going to die." Police said the suspects damaged the man's mailbox and threw a rock through the car window of someone who was visiting him. No one was injured.

August 14, 1999 Salisbury, Maryland: Vandals broke into Frank Parson's Mink Ranch at about 5 a.m. and released about 20 animals.

August 12, 1999 Antwerp, Belgium: A McDonald's fast food restaurant was burnt to the ground today, and police believe the fire was the work of a militant animal rights group that has claimed responsibility for similar attacks in the past. The letters "ALF" were painted at the scene.

August 11, 1999 USA: Farmers from several US states received dangerous mail today. The envelope size varied from standard size 10 business envelopes in gray to 9 x 11 or business-size envelopes in white or manila. Inside were 3 x 5 inch index cards with razor blades attached with a written threat to get out of the fur trade and a drawing of a bomb. All were postmarked in New York.

August 9, 1999 Plymouth, Wisconsin: During the early morning hours, United Feeds' mill in Plymouth, Wisconsin was burned to the ground. The Animal Liberation Front claimed credit for the $1.5 million blaze in a report that said they "strategically placed four incendiary devices in the mill."

August 9, 1999 Plymouth, Wisconsin: Between 2–3 a. m., vandals released 3000 mink from Gene

Myer's Fur Farm. A neighbor videotaped a low-flying aircraft without numbers in the area the previous evening.

August 9, 1999 Orkelljunga, Sweden: Five Beagles were stolen from a facility that breeds dogs for research.

August 7, 1999 Escanaba, Michigan: The Earth Liberation Front claimed credit for torching two fishing boats in the driveway of a veterinarian at 3:20 a. m. Neighbors spotted the flames and awoke the doctor. ELF left behind its signature in 18-inch letters on the garage door. Police and federal law enforcement agencies are investigating.

August 3, 1999 Bristol, Wisconsin: Animal rights terrorists released more than 3000 mink from the Krieger Farm before dawn. Neighbors helped the Kriegers retrieve most of the animals. In claiming credit for the raid, ALF said that the Kriegers are "a known supplier of mink fur to Neiman Marcus, the well-known national chain currently under attack by animal activists across the US for its fur sales."

July 10, 1999 USA: Jersey Cuts, a meatpacking facility in Howell, New Jersey has closed. They had been struck twice by the Animal Liberation Front, the second attack being a firebombing that completely destroyed three trucks at a cost of $180,000.

June 25, 1999 USA: The Animal Liberation Front takes responsibility for the firebombing of a truck at Worldwide Primates, Inc. in Miami, Florida, the business of a primate dealer and his family. The action was claimed to be "in support of the 1999 Primate Freedom Tour."

June 10, 1999 England: Animal rights activists

chained a 62-year-old woman to a fence and demanded that she and her husband close their farm, Britain's
only licensed cattery supplying cats for research. She
was terrorized but unhurt; she managed to free herself
after a few minutes.

May 9, 1999 USA: ALF claimed responsibility for
the Mother's Day arson at Childer's Meat Company in
Eugene, Oregon "In honor of Mother Earth and all the
cows who have their babies stolen from them to help
furnish the meat and dairy industries." Raiders used
20 gallons of diesel fuel/unleaded gasoline mixture in
four buckets to ignite the fire that caused $150,000
damage.

April 24, 1999 USA: Animal rights protesters
broke into three research labs at the University of California at San Francisco, shattering glass, overturning
refrigerators, and destroying medical research.

April 5, 1999 USA: A dozen laboratories at the
University of Minnesota were vandalized and dozens
of research animals were stolen in a raid by the ALF.
Damages estimated at $1,000,000. Research into
Alzheimers disease and cancer was destroyed or
stolen and cages and equipment were damaged.

March 27, 1999 USA: Six vehicles belonging to
Big Apple Circus were destroyed by firebombs in
Franklin, New Jersey. ALF claimed credit.

October 22, 1998 Sweden: 5700 mink released
from fur farm near Vaenersborg.

October 18, 1998 USA: ELF, Earth Liberation
Front, claimed responsibility for $12 million Vail Ski
Resort fire.

October 6, 1998 Germany: Fur farm release of
2500 mink ($150,000) near Fladderlohausen.

September 16, 1998 World: the Internet Division of the Animal Liberation Front announced a cyberspace campaign against people who use the internet to conduct animal-related businesses. ALF threatened denial of service attacks, e-mail bombardments, virus attacks, and web server hacking to destroy data.

August 28, 1998 USA: ALF and ELF claimed responsibility for release of 2800 mink in Rochester, Minnesota.

August 27, 1998 USA: Release of 3000 mink at fur farm in Beloit, Wisconsin.

August 20, 1998 USA: Release of 2500 mink at fur farm in Jewell, Iowa.

August 20, 1998 USA: Release of 350 domestically raised foxes in Guttenberg, Iowa.

August 18, 1998 USA: Attack on Pearl Lake, Minnesota fur farm ended with 2500 mink released.

August 9, 1998 UK: 6000 mink released in Hampshire, England; 1000 more released days later. Many died on roads or were killed by fearful residents. Some escape and damage native wildlife population.

July 4, 1998 USA: Middleton, Wisconsin-based United Vaccines Research Facility was attacked with 150 mink and ferrets released. ALF and ELF claimed responsibility.

June, 1998 USA: Arson at US Department of Agriculture Wildlife Services facility near Olympia, Washington, destroys $1.5 million research projects and causes $400,000 damage to facility.

May, 1998 USA: Arson at a veal slaughterhouse in Florida caused $500,000 damage.

November 23, 1997 USA: Animal rights group

that calls itself the justice department sent letters to media warning of poisoned turkeys in supermarkets in the east.

September 12, 1997 USA: Animal rightists smashed windows and doors with sledgehammer at Boys Town research center and damaged van parked nearby. Boys Town staff received death threats.

August 16, 1997, West Jordan, UT: ALF burned a McDonalds to the ground, causing $400,000 in damages.

July 21, 1997 USA: Cavel West Horse Slaughter Plant was torched in Redmond, Oregon causing $1,000,000 in damage with blaze threatening nearby propane storage tank. Entire water supply of Redmond was used fighting the fire and residents had to give up using city water. ALF claimed responsibility.

June 29, 1997, Crystal City, VA: 200 Animal Rights activists harassed customers and employees at a McDonalds, blocking the restaurant's driveway for two hours. Police in riot gear used pepper spray to disburse the crowd. Eighteen people were arrested on criminal trespass charges, and three face additional charges of vandalism for throwing food.

May 30, 1997 USA: More than 9000 mink were released at Oregon fur farm causing $750,000 damage.

April 19, 1997 USA: Activists smashed windows and sprayed paint walls of soon-to-open family enterprise, Golden Coral Restaurant in Maryland, causing $65,000 in damage.

March 19, 1997 USA: A trapping supply store in Ogden, Utah, was torched with the night watchman inside. He confronted the arsonists and they fled.

March 11, 1997 USA: Five pipe bombs exploded at the Fur Breeders Agricultural Coop in Utah causing nearly $1,000,000 in damage. Bombs were spiked with screws and metal and were ignited using gasoline and a five minute fuse. Federal authorities arrested and convicted Josh Ellerman, a 19-year-old follower of ALF and the Straight Edge movement, which is another offshoot of the animal rights movement.

February 15, 1997, Troy MI: The ALF attacked a McDonalds with a foul-smelling chemical, and spraypainted "McS---, McMurder, McDeath" on the bathroom walls.

January 9, 1997 USA: Outdoor Hunter/Outfitter Shop was firebombed. No group takes credit but federal authorities suspect ALF

January 4, 1997 USA: More than 20 stores and restaurants in Salt Lake City had their windows shot or smashed out. Sabotaged enterprises included McDonalds, Arby's, Kentucky Fried Chicken, a trapping outfitter, a leather shop, milk trucks and others.

Nov 12, 1996 USA: A firebomb was lobbed through window of Bloomington, Minnesota, fur store causing $2,000,000 damage. Firefighters disputed claims by Coalition to Abolish the Fur Trade (CAFT) that no lives were put at risk.

October 14, 1996, Eugene, OR: The ELF spraypainted graffiti and glued locks at a McDonalds.

11/10/92 Minneapolis, Minnesota: Swanson Meats* Arson $100,000+

10/24/92 Logan, Utah: Utah State University Break-in/Arson $110,000

2/28/92 Lansing, Michigan: Michigan State University East Break-in/Arson $125,000

6/10/91 Corvallis, Oregon: Oregon State University Break-in/Arson Vandalism 75,000

7/1/89 Lubbock, Texas: Texas Tech University Break-in $50,000–70,000

4/2/89 Tucson, Arizona: University of Arizona Break-in /Arson/ Theft $250,000

1/29/89 Dixon, California: Dixon Livestock Building* Arson/Vandalism $250,000

8/15/88 Loma Linda, California: Loma Linda University: Break-in/Theft $10,000

6/5/88 San Jose, California: Sun Valley Meat Packing Company* Arson/Vandalism $300,000

11/28/87 Santa Clara, California: V. Melani Poultry* Arson/Vandalism $230,000

11/25/87 San Jose, California: Ferrara Meat Company* Arson $420,000

9/1/87 Santa Clara, California: San Jose Valley Veal & Beef Co., Arson $35,000

4/16/87 Davis, California: University of California, Davis Arson/Vandalism $4,500,000

12/6/86 Bethesda, Maryland: SEMA Corporation* and National Institutes of Health, Theft $100,000

11/24/86 Wilton, California: Omega and HMS Turkey Ranches* Theft/Vandalism, 12,000

10/26/86 Eugene, Oregon: University Of Oregon Break-in/Theft $50,000

5/1/86 Gilroy, California: Simonsen Laboratories* Vandalism $165,000

4/20/85 Riverside, California: University of California-Riverside Break-in/Theft $600,000

12/9/84 Duarte, California: City of Hope Research Inst.* and Medical Center, Break-in Theft $400,000–$500,000

5/29/84 Philadelphia, Pennsylvania: University of Pennsylvania Break-in/Theft $20,000

12/25/83 Torrance, California: Harbor-UCLA Medical Center Break-in/Theft $58,000

Quotes from the Leaders of the Animal Rights Movement

Pets and Pet Ownership versus Guardianship

"In a perfect world, animals would be free to live their lives to the fullest: raising their young, enjoying their native environments, and following their natural instincts. However, domesticated dogs and cats cannot survive "free" in our concrete jungles, so we must take as good care of them as possible. People with the time, money, love, and patience to make a lifetime commitment to an animal can make an enormous difference by adopting from shelters or rescuing animals from a perilous life on the street. But it is also important to stop manufacturing "pets," thereby perpetuating a class of animals forced to rely on humans to survive."

　　—PETA pamphlet, Companion Animals:
　　　　Pets or Prisoners?

"In a perfect world, we would not keep animals for our benefit, including pets,"

　　—Tom Regan, emeritus professor of philosophy at
　　　　North Carolina State University and author of
　　　　"Empty Cages"—speaking at University of
　　　　Wisconsin-Madison campus, March 3, 2004

"Our goal: to convince people to rescue and adopt instead of buying or selling animals, to disavow the language and concept of animal ownership."

—Eliot Katz, President In Defense of Animals,
     In Defense of Animals website, 2001

"I don't use the word "pet." I think it's speciesist language. I prefer "companion animal." For one thing, we would no longer allow breeding. People could not create different breeds. There would be no pet shops. If people had companion animals in their homes, those animals would have to be refugees from the animal shelters and the streets. You would have a protective relationship with them just as you would with an orphaned child. But as the surplus of cats and dogs (artificially engineered by centuries of forced breeding) declined, eventually companion animals would be phased out, and we would return to a more symbiotic relationship—enjoyment at a distance."

—Ingrid Newkirk, PETA vice-president, quoted
     in The Harper's Forum Book, Jack Hitt, ed.,
     1989, p.223.

"It is time we demand an end to the misguided and abusive concept of animal ownership. The first step on this long, but just, road would be ending the concept of pet ownership."

—Eliot Katz, President "In Defense of Animals,"
     Spring 1997

"Pet ownership is an absolutely abysmal situation brought about by human manipulation."

  —Ingrid Newkirk, national director, People for the
    Ethical Treatment of Animals (PeTA), Just Like Us?
    Harper's, August 1988, p. 50.

"Liberating our language by eliminating the word 'pet' is the first step . . . In an ideal society where all exploitation and oppression has been eliminated, it will be NJARA's policy to oppose the keeping of animals as 'pets.'"

  —New Jersey Animal Rights Alliance, "Should Dogs
    Be Kept As Pets? NO!" Good Dog! February 1991,
    p. 20.

"Let us allow the dog to disappear from our brick and concrete jungles—from our firesides, from the leather nooses and chains by which we enslave it." John Bryant, Fettered Kingdoms:

  —An Examination of A Changing Ethic
    Washington, DC: People for the Ethical
    Treatment of Animals, (PeTA), 1982, p. 15.

"The cat, like the dog, must disappear... We should cut the domestic cat free from our dominance by neutering, neutering, and more neutering, until our pathetic version of the cat ceases to exist."

  —John Bryant, Fettered Kingdoms: An Examination
    of A Changing Ethic (Washington, DC: People for
    the Ethical Treatment of Animals (PeTA), 1982, p. 15.

"As John Bryant has written in his book Fettered Kingdoms, they [pets] are like slaves, even if well-kept slaves."

—PeTA's Statement on Companion Animals.

"In a perfect world, all other than human animals would be free of human interference, and dogs and cats would be part of the ecological scheme."

—PeTA's Statement on Companion Animals.

"You don't have to own squirrels and starlings to get enjoyment from them . . . One day, we would like an end to pet shops and the breeding of animals. [Dogs] would pursue their natural lives in the wild . . . they would have full lives, not wasting at home for someone to come home in the evening and pet them and then sit there and watch TV,"

—Ingrid Newkirk, national director, People for the Ethical Treatment of Animals (PeTA), Chicago Daily Herald, March 1, 1990.

Animal Agriculture and Breeding Purebred Dogs and Pedigreed Cats

"We have no ethical obligation to preserve the different breeds of livestock produced through selective breeding. . . . One generation and out. We have no problem with the extinction of domestic animals They are creations of human selective breeding."

—Wayne Pacelle, Senior VP of Humane Society of the US, formerly of Friends of Animals and Fund for Animals, Animal People, May, 1993

"[A]s the surplus of cats and dogs {artificially engineered by centuries of forced breeding) declined, eventually companion animals would be phased out, and we would return to a more symbiotic relationship—enjoyment at a distance."
—Ingrid Newkirk, "Just Like Us? Toward a Notion of Animal Rights", Harper's, August 1988, p. 50.

"[Animal] Fancies provide an escape from the real world, a sense of purpose in a lot of purposeless lives, a chance to play God by breeding animals, and a chance to play celebrity by showing them."
—Phil Maggitti, The Animals' Agenda, December 1991.

"Breeders must be eliminated! As long as there is a surplus of companion animals in the concentration camps referred to as "shelters", and they are killing them because they are homeless, one should not be allowed to produce more for their own amusement and profit. If you know of a breeder in the Los Angeles area, whether commercial or private, legal or illegal, let us know and we will post their name, location, phone number so people can write them letters telling them 'Don't Breed or Buy, While Others DIE.'"
—"Breeders! Let's get rid of them too!" Campaign on Animal Defense League's website, September 2, 2003.

"I'm not only uninterested in having children. I am opposed to having children. Having a purebred human baby is like having a purebred dog; it is nothing but vanity, human vanity."
—Ingrid Newkirk, PeTA's founder and president,

New Yorker magazine, April 23, 2003

"Our goal is to make [the public think of] breeding [dogs and cats] like drunk driving and smoking."

—Kim Sturla, former director of the Peninsula Humane Society and Western Director of Fund for Animals, stated during Kill the Crisis, not the Animals campaign and workshops, 1991

"The bottom line is that people don't have the right to manipulate or to breed dogs and cats ... If people want toys, they should buy inanimate objects. If they want companionship, they should seek it with their own kind."

—Ingrid Newkirk, founder, president and former national director, People for the Ethical Treatment of Animals (PeTA), Animals, May/June 1993

"My goal is the abolition of all animal agriculture."

—JP Goodwin, employed at the Humane Society of the US, formerly at Coalition to Abolish the Fur Trade, as quoted on AR-Views, an animal rights Internet discussion group in 1996.

Animal Equality and Anti-Humanity

"Surely there will be some nonhuman animals whose lives, by any standards, are more valuable than the lives of some humans."

—Peter Singer, Animal Liberation: A New Ethic for Our Treatment of Animals, 2nd ed. (New York: New York Review of Books, 1990), p. 19.

"Six million people died in concentration camps, but six billion broiler chickens will die this year in slaughterhouses."

—Ingrid Newkirk, founder, president and former national director, People for the Ethical Treatment of Animals, as quoted in Chip Brown, "She's A Portrait of Zealotry in Plastic Shoes," Washington Post, November 13, 1983, p. B10.

"Humans are exploiters and destroyers, self-appointed world autocrats around whom the universe seems to revolve."

—Sydney Singer, director, the Good Shepherd Foundation, "The Neediest of All Animals," The Animals Agenda, Vol. 10, No. 5 (June 1990), p. 50.

"If you haven't given voluntary human extinction much thought before, the idea of a world with no people in it may seem strange. But, if you give it a chance, I think you might agree that the extinction of Homo Sapiens would mean survival for millions, if not billions, of Earth-dwelling species ... Phasing out the human race will solve every problem on earth, social and environmental."

—"Les U. Knight" (pseudonym), "Voluntary Human Extinction," Wild Earth, Vol. 1, No. 2, (Summer 1991), p. 72.

"We feel that animals have the same rights as a retarded human child because they are equal mentally in terms of dependence on others."

—Alex Pacheco, Director, PETA, New York Times, January 14, 1989.

"If enough people are determined to stand up to an issue, you know what? It's gonna get solved. Saying that human concerns outweigh animal concerns is just more bullshit."

—Chris DeRose, Last Chance for Animals: SHAC rally, Edison, New Jersey, November 30, 2002

"Man is the most dangerous, destructive, selfish, and unethical animal on earth."

—Michael W. Fox, Scientific Director and former Vice President, Humane Society of the United States, as quoted in Robert James Bidinotto"

"Torturing a human being is almost always wrong, but it is not absolutely wrong."

—Peter Singer, as quoted in Josephine Donovan "Animal Rights and Feminist Theory," Signs: Journal of Women in Culture and Society, Winter 1990, p. 357.

"The life of an ant and that of my child should be granted equal consideration."

—Michael W. Fox, Scientific Director and former Vice President, The Humane Society of the United States, The Inhumane Society, New York, 1990

"Back to the Pleistocene!"

—Earth First! slogan, as quoted by Virginia I. Postrel, "The Green Road to Serfdom," Reason, April 1990, p. 24.

"I am not a morose person, but I would rather not be here. I don't have any reverence for life, only for the entities themselves. I would rather see a blank space where I am. This will sound like fruitcake stuff again but at least I wouldn't be harming anything."

—Ingrid Newkirk, founder, president and former national director, People for the Ethical Treatment of Animals (PeTA), as quoted in Chip Brown, "She's a Portrait of Zealotry in Plastic Shoes," Washington Post, November 13, 1983, p. B10.

"What could be the basis of our having more inherent value than animals? Their lack of reason, or autonomy, or intellect? Only if we are willing to make the same judgment in the case of humans who are similarly deficient."

—Tom Regan, "The Case for Animal Rights," In Defense of Animals, Peter Singer, ed. (Oxford: Blackwell, 1985), p. 23.

Audience member: "If you were aboard a lifeboat with a baby and a dog, and the boat capsized, would you rescue the baby or the dog?" Regan, "If it were a retarded baby and a bright dog, I'd save the dog."

—Tom Regan, "Animal Rights, Human Wrongs," speech given at University of Wisconsin, Madison, October 27, 1989.

"A rat is a pig is a dog is a boy."

—Ingrid Newkirk, PeTA's founder and president, Washingtonian Magazine, August 1986

"If it were a child and a dog I wouldn't know for sure . . . I might choose the human baby or I might choose the dog."

—Susan Rich, outreach coordinator, People for the Ethical Treatment of Animals (PeTA), on the Steve Kane Show, WIOD-AM radio, Miami, Florida, February 23, 1989.

"If an animal researcher said, 'It's a dog or a child,' a liberator will defend the dog every time."

—"Screaming Wolf" (pseudonym), A Declaration of War: Killing People to Save Animals and the Environment (Grass Valley, California: Patrick Henry Press, 1991), p. 14.

"What we must do is start viewing every cow, pig, chicken, monkey, rabbit, mouse, and pigeon as our family members."

—Gary Yourofsky, Humane Education Director, PETA, The Toledo Blade, June 24, 2001

[Expressing opposition to use of bug sprays] "Only a few of the million you kill would have bitten you."

—Dr. Michael Fox, Scientific Director and former Vice President of Humane Society of the US (HSUS), Returning to Eden, Fox publication

"Humans have grown like a cancer. We're the biggest blight on the face of the earth."

—Ingrid Newkirk, PeTA's founder, president and former national director, Readers Digest, June 1990

Biomedical Research

"To those people who say, `My father is alive because of animal experimentation,' I say `Yeah, well, good for you. This dog died so your father could live.' Sorry, but I am just not behind that kind of trade off."
—Bill Maher, PETA celebrity spokesman

"If the death of one rat cured all diseases, it wouldn't make any difference to me." Chris DeRose, director,
—Last Chance for Animals, as quoted in Elizabeth Venant and David Treadwell, "Biting Back," Los Angeles Times, April 12, 1990, p. E12.

"I don't approve of the use of animals for any purpose that involves touching them – caging them."
—Dr. Neal Barnard, president, Physician's Committee for Responsible Medicine(PCRM), The Daily Californian (February 9, 1989) quoting Bernard's address to an audience at International House (Berkeley).

"An [animal] experiment cannot be justifiable unless the experiment is so important that the use of a brain-damaged human would be justifiable."
—Peter Singer, Animal Liberation: A New Ethic for Our Treatment of Animals, 2nd ed. (New York Review of Books, 1990), p. 85.

" Medical research is immoral even it it's essential."
—Ingrid Newkirk, PeTA's founder and president, Washington Post, May 30, 1989

"Even if animal tests produced a cure [for AIDS], 'we'd be against it.'"

—Ingrid Newkirk, national director, People for the Ethical Treatment of Animals (PeTA), as quoted in Fred Barnes, "Politics," Vogue, September 1989, p. 542.

"I do not believe that it could never be justifiable to experiment on a brain-damaged human."

—Peter Singer, Animal Liberation: A New Ethic for Our Treatment of Animals, 2nd ed. (New York: New York Review of Books, 1990), p. 85.

"There could conceivably be circumstances in which an experiment on an animal stands to reduce suffering so much that it would be permissible to carry it out even if it involved harm to the animal . . . [even if] the animal were a human being."

—Peter Singer, Animal Liberation: A New Ethic for Our Treatment of Animals, 2nd ed. (New York: New York Review of Books, 1990), p. 85

"I would not knowingly have an animal hurt for me, or my children, or anything else."

—Cleveland Armory, founder, Fund for Animals (Larry King Show, October 29, 1987).

"In appropriate circumstances we are justified in using humans to achieve goals (or the goal of assisting animals)."

—Peter Singer, in Behavioral and Brain Sciences (1990, Volume 3,), p. 46.

"If it [abolition of animal research] means there are some things we cannot learn, then so be it. We have no basic right not to be harmed by those natural diseases we are heir to."

—Tom Regan, as quoted in David T. Hardy,
"America's New Extremists: What You Need to
Know About the Animal Rights Movement."
(Washington, DC: Washington Legal Foundation,
1990), p. 8.

"If natural healing is not possible, given the energy of the environment, it may be right for that being to change form. Some people call this death."

—Sydney Singer, director, Good Shepherd
Foundation, The Earth Religion (Grass Valley,
California: ABACE Publications, 1991), p. 52.

"Animal experiments occupy a central place in the material and spiritual edifice of our whole civilization. We are speaking here of one of those foundation stones whose removal could cause the whole house to collapse."

—Rudolph Bahro, Building the Green Movement,
trans. Mary Tyler (London: GMP, 1986) p. 203.

"If my father had a heart attack, it would give me no solace at all to know his treatment was first tried on a dog,"

—Ingrid Newkirk, founder, president and former
national director for People for the Ethical
Treatment of Animals, (PeTA), Washington Post,
Nov. 13, 1983.

"Even granting that we [humans] face greater harm than laboratory animals presently endure if . . . re-search on these animals is stopped, the animal rights view will not be satisfied with anything less than total abolition."

—Tom Regan, The Case for Animal Rights, 1983

"Even painless research is fascism, supremacism."

—Ingrid Newkirk, PeTA's founder and president,
Washington Magazine, August 1986

Opposition to Hunting

"The entire animal rights movement in the United States reacted with unfettered glee at the Ban in England . . . We view this act of parliament as one of the most important actions in the history of the animal rights movement. This will energize our efforts to stop hunting with hounds."

—Wayne Pacelle, CEO, Humane Society of the US
(HSUS), London Times, December 26, 2004

"If we could shut down all sport hunting in a moment, we would."

—Wayne Pacelle, Senior VP Humane Society of the
US (HSUS), formerly of Friends of Animals and
Fund for Animals, Associated Press, Dec 30, 1991

"Our goal is to get sport hunting in the same category as cock fighting and dog fighting."

—Wayne Pacelle, Senior VP Humane Society of the US (HSUS), formerly of Friends of Animals and Fund for Animals, (Bozeman (MT) Daily Chronicle (October 8, 1991)

"We are going to use the ballot box and the democratic process to stop all hunting in the United States . . . We will take it species by species until all hunting is stopped in California. Then we will take it state by state.

—Wayne Pacelle, Senior VP Humane Society of the US (HSUS), formerly of Friends of Animals and Fund for Animals, Full Cry Magazine, October 1, 1990.

On Free Press

"We are complete press sluts."

—Ingrid Newkirk, PeTA's president and founder, The New Yorker, April 14, 2003

"Probably everything we do is a publicity stunt . . . we are not here to gather members, to please, to placate, to make friends. We're here to hold the radical line."

—Ingrid Newkirk, PeTA's president and founder, USA Today, September 3, 1991

Animal Welfare vs. Animal Rights

"The theory of animal rights simply is not consistent with the theory of animal welfare . . . Animal rights means dramatic social changes for humans and non-humans alike; if our bourgeois values prevent us from accepting those changes, then we have no right to call ourselves advocates of animal rights."
—Gary Francione, The Animals' Voice, Vol. 4, No. 2 (undated), pp. 54–55.

"I find that as I get older I seem to become more of a Luddite . . . And hearing animal experimenters describe me as a Luddite—which used to think I was not. And now I think Ned Lud had the right idea and we should have stopped all the machinery way back when, and learned to live simple lives."
—Ingrid Newkirk, national director, People for the Ethical Treatment of Animals (PeTA), speech at Loyola University, October 24, 1988.

"Not only are the philosophies of animal rights and animal welfare separated by irreconcilable differences . . . the enactment of animal welfare measures actually impedes the achievement of animal rights . . . Welfare reforms, by their very nature, can only serve to retard the pace at which animal rights goals are achieved."
—Gary Francione and Tom Regan, "A Movement's Means Create Its Ends," The Animals' Agenda, January/February 1992, pp. 40–42.

"Humane care (of animals) is simply sentimental, sympathetic patronage."

> —Dr. Michael W. Fox, Humane Society of the US, in 1988 Newsweek interview

"I despise 'animal welfare.' That's like saying, 'Let's beat the slaves three times a week instead of five times a week'."

> —Gary Yourofsky, founder, Animals Deserve Adequate Protection Today and Tomorrow (ADAPTT), PeTA's national lecturer, quoted in "As Threats of Violence Escalate, Primate Researchers stand Firm", Chronicle of Higher Education, Washington, DC, November 12, 1999

"The major success of this decade [the 1980s] has been the reapplication of the concept of rights in the human population to nonhuman species."

> —John Kullberg, president, American Society for the Prevention of Cruelty to Animals, as quoted in Charles Oliver, "Liberation Zoology," Reason, 22, No. 2 (June 1990), p. 24.

"As long as humans have rights and non-humans do not, as is the case in the welfarist framework, then non-humans will virtually always lose when their interests conflict with human interests. Thus welfare reforms, by their very nature, can only serve to retard the pace at which animal rights goals are achieved."

> —Francione & Regan, "A Movement's Means Create Its Ends," Animals' Agenda, Jan.–Feb., 1992

578

". . . the animal rights movement is not concerned about species extinction. An elephant is no more or less important than a cow, just as a dolphin is no more important than a tuna . . . In fact, many animal rights advocates would argue that it is better for the chimpanzee to become extinct than to be exploited continually in laboratories, zoos and circuses."
—Barbara Biel, The Animals' Agenda, Vol 15 #3.

"It's not about loving animals. It's about fighting injustice. My whole goal is for humans to have as little contact as possible with animals."
—Gary Yourofsky, founder of Animals Deserve Adequate Protection Today and Tomorrow (ADAPTT), now employed as PeTA's national lecturer

"We're looking for good lawsuits that will establish the interests of animals as a legitimate area of concern in law."
—Ingrid Newkirk, PeTA's founder and president, Insight on the News. July 17, 2000

"We are not especially 'interested in' animals. Neither of us had ever been inordinately fond of dogs, cats, or horses in the way that many people are. We didn't 'love' animals."
—Peter Singer, Animal Liberation: A New Ethic for Our Treatment of Animals, 2nd ed. (New York Review of Books, 1990), Preface, p. ii.

On Forming Political Alliances

"We would be foolish and silly not to unite with people in the public health sector, the environmental community, [and] unions, to try to challenge corporate agriculture."

—Wayne Pacelle, Senior VP Humane Society of the US, formerly of Friends of Animals and Fund for Animals, at the Animal Rights 2002" Convention, July 1, 2002.

"Once we get three more directors elected, the Sierra Club will no longer be pro-hunting and pro-trapping and we can use the resources of the $95-million-a-year budget to address some of these issues."

—Paul Watson, Founder, Sea Shepherd Conservation Society, NY Times, March 16, 2004

"If we are not able to bring the churches, the synagogues, [and] the mosques around to the animal rights view, we will never make large-scale progress for animal rights in the United States."

—Norm Phelps, Program Director, Fund for Animals: "Animal Rights 2002" convention, July 2, 2002.

Criminal Acts and Terrorism

"Here's a little model I'm going to show you here. I didn't have any incense, but—this is a crude incendiary device. It is a simple plastic jug, which you fill with gasoline and oil. You put in a sponge, which is soaked also in flammable liquid—I couldn't find an incense stick, but this represents that. You put the incense stick in here, light it, place it—underneath the 'weapon of mass destruction,' light the incense stick—sandalwood works nice—and you destroy the profits that are brought about through animal and earth abuse. That's about—two dollars. "

—Rodney Coronado, animal rights felon for the 1992 Michigan State University fireboming, and recipient of PeTA funds, speaking at "National conference on Organized Resistance, American University, Washington DC, January 26, 2003.
Note: Coronado pled guilty to the charges stemming from the 1992 MSU arson case but even so, PeTA donated $45,200 to the Coronado Support Committee in 1995. During the previous year, while Coronado was still on the loose and living underground, PeTA granted a loan (not yet repaid) to Coronado's father for $25,000.

"If someone is killing, on a regular basis, thousands of animals, and if that person can only be stopped in one way by the use of violence, then it is certainly a morally justifiable solution."

—Jerry Vlasak, spokesman for Animal Defense League, Penn & Teller Bullsh*t, April 1, 2004

"It is dangerous to engage in even the most innocuous-seeming discourse with the FBI/ Homeland Security/ a local detective . . ."
—Ingrid Newkirk, PeTA's founder and president,
Letter to activists posted on Yahoo, March 17, 2003

"So-called activists who talk to the police disgust me, and I think one of the major reasons the animal liberation movement has not made more significant gains is because many activists do not understand the evolutionary nature of this movement. We're fighting a major war, defending animals and our very planet from human greed and destruction. There is no room for collaborators."
—David Barbarash, Spokesperson for the Animal Liberation Front (ALF) No Compromise, the journal of the Animal Liberation Front

"There are about 2,000 people prepared at any one time to take action for us . . . The children [of targeted scientists and executives] are enjoying a lifestyle built on the blood and abuse of innocent animals. Why should they be allowed to close the door on that and sit down and watch TV and enjoy themselves when animals are suffering and dying because of the actions of the family breadwinner? They are a justifiable target for protest."
—Robin Webb, ALF leader, Sunday Herald (Scotland) Sept. 19, 2004

"KFC has no excuse for refusing to adopt these basic, minimal animal-welfare standards . . . After two years of fruitless negotiations with the company, we're trying a more personal approach."

—Bruce Friedrich, PETA Director quoted in August 19, 2003 PeTA press release announcing PeTA's intent to dispatch activists to Louisville, KFC's headquarters, to interact with the community, churches, institutions, neighbors of KFC's president, and CEO, etc., in order to get KFC to submit to PeTA's demands.

"When you're a 20-something grassroots activist, and you're deciding how to spend your time and money to make a difference, it makes a lot of sense to cause a million in damage with just $100 of investment. That's a better return than any other form of activism I've been involved in."

—Rodney Coronado, LA Weekly, August 29, 2003.

"Getting arrested is fun."

—Dan Mathews, PeTA's director of international campaigns quoted in Orange County Weekly (CA), July 25–31, 2003.

"Every time a police agency pepper-sprays or uses pain-compliance holds against our people, their cars should burn."

—Rodney Coronado, convicted felon in the 1992 Michigan State University firebombing and beneficiary of PeTA funds, "Conference on Organized Resistance," American University, January 26, 2003

"In England we do have some problems with legislation that prevents us from buying certain products, but over here you don't have the same excuse. You've heard [Black Panther leader] Mr. [Bobby] Seale: you're allowed to bear arms. Why are you here now listening to me? You can go out and get animal liberation!

—Robin Webb, British Animal Rights Terrorist, speaking at a Stop Huntingdon Animal Cruelty (SHAC) rally, Edison, New Jersey, November 30, 2002

"Whether or not the public regards . . . direct action as fringe or as extremist or terroristic or whatever label they want to put on it, doesn't really matter to us because the public at large is apathetic and is going to sit on its ass regardless of whether it agrees with us or not,"

—Kevin Kjonaas, National Director, Stop Huntingdon Animal Cruelty USA (SHAC USA); spokesperson, Animal Defense League; New York organizer, Viva! USA; quoted in Animal rights advocates clash with U. Minnesota researchers. Dylan Thomas, Minnesota Daily, University of Minnesota, November 11, 2002.

"I am convinced that we can shut down a lot of these animal abuse industries whether the public agrees with it or not. And whether these industries are shut down by violent or non-violent acts in the end, to me, doesn't really matter.

—David Barbarash, Spokesperson for the Animal Liberation Front (ALF) No Compromise, BBC Documentary, "Beastly Business" (October 1, 2000)

"Hit them in their personal lives, visit their homes . . . Actively target U.S. military establishments within the United States . . . strike hard and fast and retreat in anonymity. Select another location, strike again hard and fast and quickly retreat in anonymity . . . Do not get caught. DO NOT GET CAUGHT. Do not get sent to jail. Stay alert, keep active, and keep fighting."

—Craig Rosenbraugh, radical animal rights spokesperson for terrorism and a recipient of PeTA funds, in Open letter to activists, published on the Independent Media Center website, March 17, 2003

"Today's terrorist is tomorrow's freedom fighter."

—Kevin Kjonaas, National Director and spokesperson, Stop Huntingdon Animal Cruelty USA (SHAC USA) Animal Rights 2002 Convention, June 30, 2002

"[Grocers who sell veal] have no idea what's coming . . . If they have me arrested, that's good for me, [and] bad for them. We have 75,000 members of our club who aren't going to like it".

—Dee Crenshaw, Organizer. Farm Sanctuary, Alexandria (LA) Daily Town Talk, March 18, 2001

"Sometimes breaking the law, and sometimes pushing the boundaries of what's told to us is . . . what is right and wrong, doesn't matter. And it comes down to questioning what is effective and what is not effective."

—Kevin Kjonaas, Spokesperson and National Director for Stop Huntingdon Animal Cruelty USA (SHAC USA), speaking at "Animal Rights 2002" convention, June 30, 2002

"I will be the last person to condemn ALF [the Animal Liberation Front]."
—Ingrid Newkirk, PeTA's president and founder, The New York Daily News, December 7, 1997

"If an 'animal abuser' were killed in a research lab firebombing, I would unequivocally support that, too."
—Gary Yourofsky, founder of Animals Deserve Adequate Protection Today and Tomorrow (ADAPTT), now employed as PeTA's national lecturer

"Bank executives have had their yachts sunk behind their houses. Cars have been blown up; windows have been smashed; offices have been stormed. We're tired of yelling at buildings—no one cares. We're tired of yelling at executives while they're in those buildings, and allowing them to go home and forget about us who are out there that afternoon— we're going to their homes. We're doing what's effective. We're shutting this company down."
—Lauren James, Organizer, "Conference on Organized Resistance," American University, January 26, 2003

"The employees . . . are not good people, and do not deserve to enjoy the Holiday season. Let's make this one so stressful, they won't be able to balance their hot cider between shaking hands."
—E-mail message dated December 15, 2002 from (SHAC) Stop Huntingdon Animal Cruelty

"We encourage others to find a local Earth raper and make them pay for the damages they are inflicting on our communities . . . Furriers, meat packers, bosses, developers, rich industry leaders are all Earth rapers . . . We must inflict economic sabotage on all Earth rapers."

—Craig Rosenbraugh, recipient of PETA funds,
Spokesperson for Earth Liberation Front (ELF)
statement, August 1, 1999

"A burning building doesn't help melt people's hearts, but times change and tactics, I'm sure, have to change with them . . . If you choose to carry out ALF-style actions, I ask you to please not say more than you need to, to think carefully who you trust, to learn all you can about how to behave if arrested, and so to try to live to fight another day."

—Ingrid Newkirk, PeTA's founder and president,
Interview in ALF quarterly Bite Back, February,
2003

"In light of the events on September 11, my country has told me that I should not cooperate with terrorists. I therefore am refusing to cooperate with members of Congress who are some of the most extreme terrorists in history."

—Craig Rosebraugh, animal rights radical, spokesperson for animal and earth related crimes and recipient of PETA funds, statement following Rosebraugh's subpoena to testify before a Congressional subcommittee on eco-terrorism, November 1, 2001

"Why should any one of us feel that 'it shouldn't be me taking that brick and chucking it through that window? Why shouldn't I be going to that fur farm down the road and opening up those cages?' It's not hard; it doesn't take a rocket scientist. You don't need a 4-year degree to call in a bomb hoax. These are easy things, and they're things that save animals: And so I want all of you in this room to, A) Question not just what is right and wrong, but what is effective, And B) why can't all of us be doing it? I think the animal rights movement is strong—that's my opinion. [But] it's time to start flexing our muscles."

—Kevin Kjonaas, Spokesperson and National
Director, Stop Huntingdon Animal Cruelty USA
(SHAC USA) "Animal Rights 2002" convention,
June 30, 2002

"If we really believe that animals have the same right to be free from pain and suffering at our hands, then, of course we're going to be, as a movement, blowing things up and smashing windows . . . I think it's a great way to bring about animal liberation . . . I think it would be great if all of the fast-food outlets, slaughterhouses, these laboratories, and the banks that fund them exploded tomorrow. I think it's perfectly appropriate for people to take bricks and toss them through the windows . . . Hallelujah to the people who are willing to do it."

—Bruce Friedrich, PeTA's director of Vegan Outreach,
Animal Rights Conference, 2001

"Huntingdon Life Sciences is going to close. You can't close it with those evil riot police there, but they're not always here! It's not always daylight ... Come here when it's dark, when there's no moon, with people you can trust! There are individuals in there who need you to do that! But when you get them out, don't leave the equipment or the building standing either! Smash it! Smash it! Smash it once and for all!"

—Robin Webb, British Animal Rights Terrorist, speaking at a Stop Huntingdon Animal Cruelty (SHAC) rally, East Millstone, New Jersey, outside a medical research facility, December 1, 2002

"Although fish and chip shops haven't been targeted before so far as I can remember, they would be considered legitimate targets."

—Robin Webb, UK Spokesperson for animal rights terrorism, The UK Guardian December 12, 2001

"Believe me, you don't have to worry about prison. I've been there—it's a doggle. You can put your feet up and recharge your batteries, and go back out there when you're released and start all over again. You can go to education to read up. I mean someone, someone actually read up on electronics while they were in prison, and went out and started doing electronic incendiary devices. Use your time inside to teach yourself!"

—Robin Webb, British Spokesperson for Animal Rights Terrorism, speaking at SHAC rally, Edison, New Jersey, November 30, 2002

"We're a new breed of activism. We're not your parents' Humane Society. We're not Friends of Animals. We're not EarthSave. We're not Greenpeace. We come with a new philosophy. We hold the radical line. We will not compromise! We will not apologize, and we will not relent! . . . Vivisection is not an abstract concept. It's a deed, done by individuals, who have weaknesses, who have breaking points, and who have home addresses!"

—Kevin Kjonaas, animal extremist and National
  Leader-spokesperson for Stop Huntingdon Animal
  Cruelty USA, (SHAC-USA) rally, East Millstone,
  New Jersey, outside a medical research facility,
  December 1, 2002

"I think [food producers] should appreciate that we're only targeting their property. Because frankly I think it's time to start targeting them."

—Rodney Coronado, convicted felon for the 1992
  firebombing of Michigan State University research
  facility (57 months in federal prison, 3 years probation), speaking at the "Conference on Organized
  Resistance," American University, January 26, 2003.

"As a direct-action warrior, it made a lot of sense to me to attack institutions in the fur trade . . . we need to destroy them by any means necessary."

—Rodney Coronado, convicted felon of 1992
  Michigan State University firebombing and benefi-
  ciary of PeTA funds, "Conference on Organized
  Resistance," American University, January 26, 2003

"Our philosophy is to go for one company at a time, and go for its finances. If we had gone down and protested outside HLS every day for the last five years we would have got nowhere,"

—Greg Avery, SHAC, BBC Online, October 5, 2004

If a car being blown up in a driveway or animals being liberated from a lab scares them, then I would say that fear pales by comparison to the fear that the animals have every day. The kind of true violence that these animals endure at the hands of people at Huntingdon leaves me with little sympathy.

—Kevin Kjonaas, National Director and spokesperson, Stop Huntingdon Animal Cruelty USA, (SHAC USA); spokesperson, Animal Defense League; New York organizer, Viva! USA; as quoted in A harsh animal-rights campaign targets NJ firm, workers. Chris Mondics, The Philadelphia Inquirer, July 14, 2002.

"Throughout the late '80s, me and a handful of friends just like you people here, we started to break windows, we started to slash tires, we started to rescue animals from factory farms and vivisection breeders, and we graduated to breaking into laboratories . . . As long as we emptied the labs of animals, they were still easily replaced. So that's when the ALF in this country, and my cell, started engaging in arson."

—Rodney Coronado, convicted felon for 1992 Michigan State University firebombing and PeTA funds beneficiary, speaking at SHAC rally, Edison, New Jersey, November 30, 2002

"Arson, property destruction, burglary and theft are 'acceptable crimes' when used for the animal cause."

—Alex Pacheco, Director, PETA

"Last night in San Diego a bunch of townhouses were burned down, and reporters from two corporate TV stations just asked me, 'What good does that do your movement?' . . . If that hadn't happened, you wouldn't be here tonight. People willing to risk their lives to protect the environment by destroying buildings built on the habitat of endangered species make people take notice . . . Fire is a very sacred power, one of the key elements of our planet . . . We use fire to cleanse ourselves, and when we address buildings and institutions that have no other purpose but to destroy life, fire is the only way to stop them. When people ask if someday someone might get hurt by one of our actions, I ask them why they don't get so concerned about the people who are killing animals for a living. That is what the terrorism in this society is. Destroying property to protect life is the most sacred thing we can do."

—Rod Coronado, Earth Liberationist, convicted arsonist in 1992 Michigan State University firebombing and beneficiary of PeTA funds, speaking "Revolution Summer" in Hillcrest, CA (a suburb of San Diego), August 1, 2003, the day a $50 million fire credited to the Earth Liberation Front torched an apartment construction project, Zenger's Newsmagazine, 2003.

"The $10,000 microscope was destroyed in about 10 seconds with a steel wrecking bar we purchased ... for less than $5. We consider that a pretty good return on our investment."
—ALF memo about destruction of lab at U. of Oregon Oct. 1986

"[behind every corporation] there are people who have homes and liability and privacy issues."
—Kevin Kjonaas, (SHAC) Stop Huntingdon Animal Cruelty leader and spokesperson, quoted in the Mercury News, San Jose, California, May 10, 2003

"We have a 100 per cent success rate. Whoever we choose to target is finished."
—Heather James, SHAC co-leader , London Evening Standard, March 29, 2004

"It doesn't matter if there are people in there. They're irrelevant! It doesn't matter about the police. They're irrelevant! It doesn't matter about the high fences. They're irrelevant! It doesn't matter about the doors. They're irrelevant! It doesn't matter about the locks. They're irrelevant! What matters is our brothers and sisters in there. Smash everything when the cops aren't here! Get them out!" . . . "We'll sweep th police aside. We'll sweep the government aside. We'll sweep Huntingdon Life Sciences aside, and we'll raz this evil place right to the ground!"
—Robin Webb, British Animal Rights Terrorist, Speaking at Stop Huntingdon Animal Cruelty, (SHAC) rally, East Millstone, New Jersey, outside medical research facility, December 1, 2002

"I wish we all would get up and go into the labs and take the animals out or burn them down."

— Ingrid Newkirk, President, PETA, National Animal Rights Convention June 27, 1997

"It's time for the animal rights movement to take this [fur] industry and drive the final nail into the coffin by whatever means it takes. If that means being outside the executives houses, if that means blockading their doors, whatever it takes."

— John 'J.P.' Goodwin, Humane Society of the US Campaign Director, former executive director of the Coalition to Abolish the Fur Trade, in speech at the World Congress for Animals, June 20, 1996

"Physically shut down financial centers . . . Using any means necessary, shut down the national networks of NBC, ABC, CBS, CNN, etc. Not just occupations but actually engage in strategies and tactics which knock the networks off the air . . . Spread the battle to the . . . very heads of government and U.S. corporations . . . "When you see the loss of 9 billion [animal] lives each year, it's inappropriate to hold a sign or pass out a petition. It's appropriate to go out and burn down the factory farm."

— Joshua Harper, recipient of PETA funds, The Seattle Post-Intelligencer, June 18, 2001

"Damaging the enemy financially is fair game."

— Alex Pacheco, animal rights radical, PeTA co-founder and one of its original 3 board members, Washington City Paper, December 18, 1987

"Animal liberation, of which the anti-vivisection movement is a part, animal liberation is not a campaign. It is not a struggle. It is a war! It is an all-out bloody war, in which the countless hundreds of millions of casualties have, so far, all been on one side. How can we allow that to continue?"

—Robin Webb, British spokesperson for animal rights terrorism, speaking at SHAC rally, Edison, New Jersey, November 30, 2002

"Would I rather the research lab that tests animals is reduced to a bunch of cinders? Yes."

—Ingrid Newkirk, PeTA's president and founder, New York Daily News, December 7, 1997

"A lot of people think that—Oh my god, that's going too far, you know. People can support bringing animals out of labs, but they can't support arson. Well, I'm sorry. I'm not here to, to please people. I'm not here to win the support of people. I'm here to represent my animal relations who are suffering this very second. And I don't care what anybody says about what I do to achieve their freedom."

—Rodney Coronado, convicted felon for 1992 Michigan State University firebombing and PeTA beneficiary, speaking at SHAC rally, Edison, New Jersey, November 30, 2002

"[I see] a spark of hope in every broken window every torched police car."

—Joshua Harper, recipient of PeTA funds, The Seattle Post-Intelligencer, June 18, 2001

"Property destruction is a legitimate political tool called economic sabotage, and it's meant to attack businesses and corporations."

— David Barbarash, Spokesperson for the Animal Liberation Front (ALF), NPR radio show, "The Connection" January 7, 2002

"Get arrested. Destroy the property of those who torture animals. Liberate those animals interned in the hellholes our society tolerates."

— Jerry Vlasak, Animal Defense League, Internet post to AR Views list, June 21, 1996

"Perhaps the mere idea of receiving a nasty missive will allow animal researchers to empathize with their victims for the first time in their lousy careers. I find it small wonder that the laboratories aren't all burning to the ground. If I had more guts, I'd light a match."

— Ingrid Newkirk, PeTA founder and president, The Chronicle of Higher Education November 12, 1999

"I would be overjoyed when the first scientist is killed by a liberation activist."

— Vivien Smith, Former ALF Spokesperson, USA Today, September 3, 1991

'Our nonviolent tactics are not as effective. We ask nicely for years and get nothing. Someone makes a threat, and it works."

— Ingrid Newkirk, PeTA's founder and president, US News and World Report, April 8, 2002

"Setting fire to the feed truck falls within the work they [the ALF] do. It was most likely done in an effort to cause the most damage possible to the farm without hurting anyone or any animals. What these farmers do to chickens is terrorism—what we do is not."

—David Barbarash, Associated Press story filed after the arson of a poultry truck in Indiana caused $100,000 in damage, July 3, 2000

"Getting together three or four friends of mine, we came back a week later to that farm, we broke into the main laboratory, we trashed every single piece of equipment, we stole documents and lists of fur farms across the nation. And we started a fire in an experimental fur farm, an experimental feed building, where they manufactured the experimental diets which were the focus of research at this farm. And that fire destroyed all the equipment, and in the ensuing raid, the raid that happened caused enough damage that six months later that lab was forced to shut down. That was five people, folks—once again maybe like twelve hundred dollars, a couple weeks of planning, five people. But that wasn't the end. I knew I had to continue, and for the next—oh gosh, a little over a year— we took out, one by one, every recipient of what's called the Mink Farmers Research Foundation. It's a foundation whose sole purpose is to aid research to benefit the fur farm industry."

—Rodney Coronado, convicted felon for 1992 Michigan State University firebombing and PeTA funds beneficiary, speaking at SHAC rally, Edison, New Jersey, November 30, 2002